W9-BYZ-671

PRAISE FOR THE CLASSIC *LENSMEN* SERIES AND E. E. SMITH

FINALIST FOR SPECIAL 1966 HUGO FOR ALL-TIME BEST SERIES

"The *Lensmen* books represent that rarest of all qualities in SF: the sense of wonder, given form and texture and epic scale. These are the books I cut my teeth on as a fan, and together they comprise one of the true milestones in science fiction literature.
Let me be plainer: BUY THESE BOOKS.
You won't regret it."

J. Michael Straczynski,
creator of the hit television show: *Babylon 5*

"The most towering figure in science fiction, thanks to the enormous scope of his novels."

Isaac Asimov

"...within the burgeoning field Smith was the greatest. And for one reason only: His stories struck the sense of wonder like lightning. His huge, galactic, cosmic adventures were electrifyingly new. After reading Smith, you could look up at the night sky as never before, and be filled with a whole new range of awesome posibilities."

David Hartwell,
Age of Wonders

"George Lucas's Star Wars films are directly descended from Smith's space sagas."

Edward James,
Science Fiction in the 20th Century

"The *Lensmen* saga is a 2001 monolith from the dawn of science fiction. It's all here—a secret destiny for Mankind that prefigures David Brin's *Uplift* series; a universe-spanning saga that dwarfs the worlds of *Star Trek*, *Babylon 5*, and *Star Wars*; a dream of a giant future that will take you further than you thought possible. You are Kim Kinnison . . . You have it in your blood to save the universe . . ."

Stephen Baxter

"It was E.E. Smith who started science fiction off on the trillion year spree which is now an integral part of its image."

Brian Aldiss,
Billion Year Spree

"Heroes and strong women. Galaxy-spanning drug rings and incorruptible peace-keepers. Wise, kind aliens and evil conspiracies. Spaceships and superweapons. Honour, glory–even naked babes. All packed together in one rollicking rollercoaster ride. I've been reading and re-reading *Children of the Lens* for decades. This book has *everything*!"

Nicola Griffth

"The space opera to end all space operas . . . which even George Lucas would be hard put to top. "

Neil Barron (editor),
Anatomy of Wonder

"'Doc' Smith was a big influence. A series of reprints came out in England in the early '70s, which was when I read them. I was just mesmerized."

Peter F. Hamilton

GRAY
LENSMAN

THE WORKS OF EDWARD E. SMITH

The Skylark Series
    The Skylark of Space
    Skylark Three
    Skylark of Valeron
    Skylark Duquesne

The Lensmen Series
    Triplanetary
    First Lensman
    Galactic Patrol
    Gray Lensman
    Second Stage Lensmen
    Children of the Lens
And the associational Lensmen novel:
    Vortex Blaster

The Subspace Series
    Subspace Explorers
    Subspace Encounter

Other Novels
    The Galaxy Primes
    Masters of Space (with E. Everett Evans)
    Spacehounds of IPC

Collections
    The Best of E. E. "Doc" Smith

The Gray Lensman sent his sense of perception out beyond the confining walls and let it roam the void. (P. 47)

GRAY
LENSMAN

By
EDWARD E. SMITH, Ph.D.

Illustrated by
Ric Binkley

OLD EARTH BOOKS
BALTIMORE, MARYLAND   1998

SF
S6H6lgr

This edition of *Gray Lensman* is a facsimile of the original 1951 Fantasy Press edition (copyright E. E. Smith). An earlier version of this novel was published serially in *Astounding Science Fiction*, October 1939–January 1940.

1 2 3 4 5 6 7 8 9 / 00 99 98

Old Earth Books
Post Office Box 19951
Baltimore, Maryland 21211-0951

Library of Congress Catologing-in-Publication Data

Smith, E. E. (Edward Elmer), 1890-1965.
    Gray Lensman / by Edward E. Smith ; illustrated by Ric Binkley.
    p. cm. (The history of civilization ; v. 4)
ISBN: 1-882968-12-3 (pbk.: alk. paper)
    I. Title   II: Series: Smith, E. E. (Edward Elmer), 1890–1965. History of civilization ; v. 4.
PS3537.M349G73   1997
813.54—dc20   96–32944
                                                    CIP

To
LLOYD

CONTENTS

FOREWORD

by
John Clute

S O HERE WE ARE. THE STORY HAS
started, and it does not stop. After the pleasures and miseries
of *Triplanetary* and *First Lensman*, after two tumultuous
volumes of prelude and back story and dark hint and deck
clearance, we are ready to begin at the beginning. We open the
first page, and we plunge headfirst into the heartwood and
arterial surge of the vast edifice of the *Lensmen* sequence as
E.E. Smith first conceived it, in the 1920s, long before he began
parcelling his tale out in serial form over a 12-year period
(1937–1949) through the increasingly dignified pages of
Astounding Science Fiction.

The first of them, *Galactic Patrol*, appeared in 1937–1938,
before John W. Campbell, Jr. became editor of *ASF* and—fully
conscious that he was attempting to do so—created the first
and best Golden Age of Science Fiction, which lasted from
1939 until World War Two took most of his writers away (they
never came back, not really, not in their hearts, but that is
another story). *Galactic Patrol* was soon followed by *Gray
Lensman* (1939–1940) and by *Second Stage Lensmen* (1941–
1942) and, several years later, by the final volume, *Children
of the Lens* (1947–1948). The gap between the first three
volumes and that last installment may be variously explained:
Doc Smith was involved in non-combatant war work, which
may have kept him from concentrating fully on his History of

Civilization; the series reaches a penultimate climax with *Second Stage Lensmen*, 20 years of internal chronology now having to pass before the Kinnison children—the Children of the Lens themselves—are old enough to take their places at the very tiptop of the great hierarchical ladder of Civilization; and John W. Campbell himself may have had some practical reservations about the nature of the future promulgated by Smith (and by *ASF's* other great wartime writer, A.E. Van Vogt).

These reservations—if he indeed felt or expressed them—were entirely justified, of course. Campbell's Golden Age of Science Fiction heralded not only a maturation in the style and subject matter of American pulp sf, conveyed primarily through the explosive irruption into the field of writers such as Isaac Asimov, L. Sprague de Camp, Robert A. Heinlein, Theodore Sturgeon, but also a *domestication* not simply of the future as such but, more importantly, of the profound oddness of the futures typically envisaged by pulp writers of the preceding generation, such as E.E. Smith. (One of the reasons Van Vogt is best understood as a pulp writer—a pulp writer who photosynthesizes cut helium for breakfast—is the profound weirdness of his future worlds.) This oddness of American pulp sf cannot be conceptually soothed away by references to (or fondish memories of) the stylistic crudeness of so much of what appeared in the magazines between 1925 and approximately 1940, nor is it enough to say that a Technic Age writer such as E.E. Smith is a kind of Grandma Moses, an Outsider Artist from the earliest days of pulp, an author of cartoon edisonades we can enjoy for their rural innocence, of space operas that perfectly (though crudely) limn the American Dream *circa* 1930, the way Heinlein and Asimov clearly limn something like the American Dream a few significant years later.

All of that may be true, or sort of. But it's not enough.

Because there's a secret here.

This is the secret. Doc Smith and his peers—and A.E. Van Vogt, who walked alone—may all have loved the task of conceiving futures, but, at the same time, each one of these sf writers manifestly displayed a very deep distrust and fear of anything that hinted at any of the unfolding "real" futures that have refilled the water holes of our infancy with mutagens. The *Lensmen* series is escapist, as much good fiction is, and we love it for that, but it does not escape 1930: it escapes the future.

Certainly both writers invoke superscience and super Technics, in terms only marginally more magical than those used by Golden Age writers, but they do so to transport us out of reach of anything that might actually happen. If it can be said that, in 1998, sf is best defined as an historical body of story concerning the real nature of the 20th century, then it must be said that neither E.E. Smith nor A.E. Van Vogt could remotely be described as contributing to that body of story. Hence the extraordinary cultural fixity of our home planet in Doc Smith's vision of Tellus: it is a world in which nothing dangerous (i.e., nothing that might resemble 1998 or, for that matter, 1938) has been allowed to happen. Women are gals, nuclear families are tender-trap monads, "culture" is a froth of vaguely indecent curds and whey, there is no democracy to take away the toys of the game, because the World Government (which seems to have been run for hundreds of years by successive Kinnisons) has solved every political problem in the entire world. There are no computers (not even in the last-written volumes of the series), no punk, no genetic engineering, no Marlon Brando, no perestroika, no Bob Dylan, no cities, no Hillary Clinton Wife Spoof, no Unabomber, no ghettos, no suburbs, no planetary crises of any sort (atomic, ecological, ethnic, whatever), nothing. This may sound as though Smith is trying to describe Paradise, but, of course, he's not, because Eden is not best described by what it is not. Tellus in the *Lensmen* is a spinster's bedroom, a mantra of denials limned through a sleight-of-hand of side-of-the-mouth descriptive passages designed precisely *not* to describe the penis swamp of the world to come.

Hence—finally—we see the basic structure of Civilization as it is defended by the Arisians. For once the world and human nature have been stripped from a definition of Civilization, it is no hard task to describe it. Civilization consists in not being tempted by the world or by human nature—two regions of discourse occupied solely by Boskone. Civilization is everything the 20th century is not, except maybe Nancy Reagan. Civilization is Just Say No. Civilization is pesticide. Civilization is easy.

Lensmen Civilization is, of course, instant death for you and me.

So how can we love E.E. Smith so deeply? (I myself am a Boskonian bug any Kinnison would spray, but I reread the *Lensmen* as often as I reread Tolkien or Freddy the Pig.) I can think of two reasons. First, it is a deep relief to escape from the live world, to pretend for a nonce that the real world is a spinster's bedroom with a secret portal starward. Second, the *Lensmen* is one of the greatest stories ever told. That may be all we need. (I think it may be all I need.)

And so here we are. The story has started, and it does not stop. It is a tale that expands remorselessly in space and time. We begin with the graduation of Kim Kinnison at the top of his class from the top of the (surely unconsciously) phallic Wentworth Hall, a 90-story prong "dominating twice a hundred square miles of campus, parade-ground, airport, and space-port." He then gets his Lens, the Arisian device that authenticates his physical and moral right to act, to own the world of action to come. Licensed by this opening sequence as a paladin, as an arrowhead of the self-ruling chivalry of Lensmen, Kinnison is immediately plunged into the galaxy-wide war between Arisia and Eddore, goes through a maelstrom of adventures in *Galactic Patrol*, by virtue of which he meets new races, discovers new weapons, infiltrates Boskone, defeats vast space armadas, and, in a superbly violent final cataclysm, personally defeats Helmuth, who speaks for Boskone:

> First Kinnison; the bullets whining, shrieking off the armor of his personal battleship and crashing through or smashing ringingly against whatever happened to be in the ever-changing line of ricochet. Then Helmuth; and as the fierce-driven metal slugs tore in their multitudes through his armor and through and through his body, riddling his every vital organ, that was THE END

It is, of course, not the end. The first paragraph of *Gray Lensman* makes that clear:

> Among the world-girdling fortifications of a planet distant indeed from star cluster AC 257-4736 there squatted sullenly a fortress quite similar to Helmuth's own. Indeed, in some respects it was even superior to the base of him who spoke for Boskone. It was larger and stronger. Instead of one dome, it had many. It was dark and cold withal, for its occupants had practically nothing in common with humanity save the possession of high intelligence.

For readers of *ASF* in 1939, this first paragraph must have had an astonishing impact, one we can never quite replicate in our own imaginations. But it's worth saying a couple of things. First, in 1939, sequels were still uncommon in the sf world, and nothing would have prepared readers for the explosive vista of this opening, which swallows its predecessor whole. Second, readers in 1939 did not quite share Kinnison's limited knowledge of the unfolding situation, as this first paragraph creates a powerful dramatic irony—and hence, in the context of space opera, a powerful sense of wonder—that will deeply "tease" readers' understanding of the story. But neither they, nor anyone else in 1939, could know that there would be two more volumes—Smith would not retrofit the back story of the History of Civilization into the full series for another 15 years—and that each succeeding volume would also eat its predecessor whole. So, the readers of 1939 plunged wide eyed into wonder.

This is what they found, as the years passed.

Each volume of the *Lensmen* main sequence ends in a defeat of Boskone, and each new volume (except, of course, the last) begins with the discovery that the Boskone so resoundingly eliminated is nothing but a young and subordinate version of what must surely be the true and final Boskone, that the "true" Boskone is older, more malevolent, more powerful, and more insidious than could have been dreamed. But E.E. Smith's genius does not lie in the notion of an hierarchy of evil (and few contemporary readers are likely to pay much attention to the phobic response to this century that

underlies Smith's description of Boskonian evil); his genius
lies in his construction of a story that, like peeling an onion
outward, narrates hierarchy.

It is absolutely brilliant, and it works each time. No wonder
we come back, again and again, to the heart of the onion that
is the heart of Story and await there, eyes peeled, for the peeling
to begin.

T WO THOUSAND MILLION OR SO YEARS AGO, AT THE time of the Coalescence, when the First and Second Galaxies were passing through each other and when myriads of planets were coming into existence where only a handful had existed before, two races of beings were already old; so old that each had behind it many millions of years of recorded history. Both were so old that each had perforce become independent of the chance formation of planets upon which to live. Each had, in its own way, gained a measure of control over its environment; the Arisians by power of mind alone, the Eddorians by employing both mind and mechanism.

The Arisians were indigenous to this, our normal space-time continuum; they had lived in it since the unthinkably remote time of their origin; and the original Arisia was very Earth-like in mass, composition, size, atmosphere, and climate. Thus all normal space was permeated by Arisian life-spores, and thus upon all Earth-like or Tellurian planets there came into being races of creatures more or less resembling Arisians in the days of their racial youth. None except Tellurians are Homo Sapiens, of course; few can actually be placed in Genus Homo; but many millions of planets are peopled by races distantly recognizable or belonging to the great class of MAN.

The Eddorians, on the other hand, were interlopers— intruders. They were not native to our normal space-time system, but came to it from some other, some alien and horribly different other, plenum. For eons, in fact, they had been exploring the macrocosmic All; moving their planets from continuum to continuum; seeking that which at last they found—a space and a time in which there were enough planets, soon to be inhabited by intelligent life, to sate even the Eddorian lust for dominance. Here, in our own space-time, they would stay; and here supreme they would rule.

The Elders of Arisia, however, the ablest thinkers of the race, had known and had studied the Eddorians for many cycles of time. Their integrated Visualization of the Cosmic All showed what was to happen. No more than the Arisians themselves could the Eddorians be slain by any physical means, however applied; nor could the Arisians, unaided, kill all of the invaders by mental force. Eddore's All-Highest and his Innermost Circle, in their ultra-shielded citadel, could be destroyed only by a mental bolt of such nature and magnitude that its generator, which was to become known throughout two galaxies as the Galactic Patrol, would require several long Arisian lifetimes for its building.

Nor would that building be easy. The Eddorians must be kept in ignorance, both of Arisia and of the proposed generator, until too late to take effective counter-measures. Also, no entity below the third level of intelligence, even— or especially?—of the Patrol, could ever learn the truth; for that knowledge would set up an inferiority complex and thus rob the generator of all ability to do the work for which it was designed.

Nevertheless the Arisians began building. On the four most promising planets of the First Galaxy—our Earth or Sol Three, Velantia, Rigel Four, and Palain Seven—breeding programs, aiming toward the highest mentality of which each race was capable, were begun as soon as intelligent life developed.

On our Earth there were only two blood lines, since humanity has only two sexes. One was a straight male line of descent, and was always named Kinnison or its equivalent. Civilizations rose and fell; Arisia surreptitiously and unobtrusively lifting them up, Eddore callously knocking them down as soon as it became evident that they were not what Eddore wanted. Pestilences raged, and wars, and famines, and holocausts and disasters that decimated entire populations again and again, but the direct male line of descent of the Kinnisons was never broken.

The other line, sometimes male and sometimes female, which was to culminate in the female penultimate of the Arisian program, was equally persistent and was characterized throughout its prodigious length by a peculiarly spectacular shade of red-bronze-auburn hair and equally striking gold-flecked, tawny eyes. Atlantis fell, but the red-headed, yellow-eyed child of Captain Phryges had been sent to North Maya, and lived. Patroclus, the red-headed gladiator, begot a red-headed daughter before he was cut down. And so it went.

World Wars One, Two, and Three, occupying as they did only a few moments of Arisian-Eddorian time, formed merely one incident in the eons-long game. That incident was important, however, because immediately after it Gharlane of Eddore made what proved to be an error. Knowing nothing of the Arisians, or of what they had done to raise the level of intelligence of mankind, he assumed that the then completely ruined Earth would not require his personal attention again for many hundreds of Tellurian years, and went elsewhere: to Rigel Four, to Palain Seven, and to Velantia Two, or Delgon, where he found that his creatures, the Overlords, were not progressing satisfactorily. He spent quite a little time there; time during which the men of Earth, aided almost openly by the Arisians, made a phenomenally rapid recovery from the ravages of atomic warfare and fantastically rapid advances in both sociology and technology.

Virgil Samms, the auburn-haired, tawny-eyed Crusader who was to become the first wearer of Arisia's Lens, took advantage of the general demoralization to institute a really effective planetary police force. Then, with the advent of inter-planetary flight, he was instrumental in forming the

Interplanetary League. As head of the Triplanetary Service, he took a leading part in the brief war with the Nevians, a race of highly intelligent amphibians who used allotropic iron as a source of atomic power.*

Gharlane of Eddore came back to the Solarian System as Gray Roger, the enigmatic and practically immortal scourge of space, only to find his every move blocked—blocked so savagely and so completely that he could not even kill two ordinary human beings, Conway Costigan and Clio Marsden. Nor were these two, in spite of some belief to the contrary, anything but what they seemed. Neither of them ever knew that they were being protected; but Gharlane's blocker was in fact an Arisian fusion—the four-ply mentality which was to become known to every Lensman of the Galactic Patrol as Mentor of Arisia.

The inertialess drive, which made an interstellar trip a matter of minutes instead of lifetimes, brought with it such an increase in crime, and made detection of criminals so difficult, that law enforcement broke down almost completely. As Samms himself expressed it:

"How can legal processes work efficiently—work at all, for that matter—when a man can commit a murder or a pirate can loot a space-ship and be a hundred parsecs away before the crime is even discovered? How can a Tellurian John Law find a criminal on a strange world that knows nothing whatever of our Patrol, with a completely alien language—maybe no language at all—when it takes months even to find out who and where—if any—the native police officers are?"

Also, there was the apparently insuperable difficulty of the identification of authorized personnel. Triplanetary's best scientists had done their best in the way of a non-counterfeitable badge—the historic Golden Meteor, which upon touch impressed upon the toucher's consciousness an

---

* For a complete treatment of matters up to this point, including the discovery of the inertialess—"free"—space-drive, the Nevian War, and the mind-to-mind meeting of Mentor of Arisia and Gharlane of Eddore, see *Triplanetary*, Fantasy Press, Reading, Pa.

unpronounceable, unspellable symbol—but that best was not enough. What physical science could devise and synthesize, physical science could analyze and duplicate; and that analysis and duplication had caused trouble indeed.

Triplanetary needed something vastly better than its meteor. In fact, without a better, its expansion into an intersystemic organization would be impossible. It needed something to identify a Patrolman, anytime and anywhere. It must be impossible of duplication or imitation. In fact, it should kill, painfully, any entity attempting imposture. It should operate as a telepath, or endow its wearer with telepathic power—how else could a Tellurian converse with peoples such as the Rigellians, who could not talk, see, or hear?

Both Solarian Councillor Virgil Samms and his friend of old, Commissioner of Public Safety Roderick Kinnison, knew these things; but they also knew how utterly preposterous their thoughts were; how utterly and self-evidently impossible such a device was.

But Arisia again came to the rescue. The scientist who had been assigned the meteor problem, one Dr. Nels Bergenholm—who, all unknown to even his closest associates, was a form of flesh energized at various times by various Arisians—reported to Samms and Kinnison that:

1) Physical science could not then produce what was needed, and probably never could do so. 2) Although it could not be explained in any symbology or language known to man, there was—there *must* be—a science of the mind; a science whose tangible products physical science could neither analyze nor imitate. 3) Virgil Samms, by going in person to Arisia, could obtain *exactly* what was needed.

"Arisia! Of all the hells in space, why Arisia?" Kinnison demanded. "How? Don't you know that nobody can get anywhere near that damn planet?"

"I *know* that the Arisians are very well versed in that science. I *know* that if Councillor Samms goes to Arisia he will obtain the symbol he needs. I *know* that he will

never obtain it otherwise. As to *how* I know these things—
I can't—I just—I *know* them. I tell you!"

And, since Bergenholm was already as well known for
uncannily accurate "hunches" as for a height of genius
bordering perilously closely on insanity, the two leaders of
Civilization did not press him further, but went immediately
to the hitherto forbidden planet. They were—apparently—
received hospitably enough, and were given Lenses by
Mentor of Arisia. Lenses which, it developed, were all that
Bergenholm had indicated, and more.

The Lens is a lenticular structure of hundreds of
thousands of tiny crystalloids, built and tuned to match the
individual life force—the ego, the personality—of one individual entity. While not, strictly speaking, alive, it is
endowed with a sort of pseudo-life by virtue of which
it gives off a strong, characteristically-changing, polychromatic light as long as it is in circuit with the living mentality
with which it is in synchronization. Conversely, when worn
by anyone except its owner, it not only remains dark but
it kills—so strongly does its pseudo-life interfere with any
life to which it is not attuned. It is also a telepathic communicator of astounding power and range—and other
things.

Back on Earth, Samms set out to find people of Lensman caliber to send to Arisia. Kinnison's son Jack, and his
friend Mason Northrop, Conway Costigan, and Samm's
daughter Virgilia—who had inherited her father's hair and
eyes, and who was the most accomplished muscle-reader
of her time—went first. The boys got Lenses, but Jill did
not. Mentor, who was to her senses a woman seven feet
tall, told her that she did not then and never would need a
Lens—and it should be mentioned here in passing that no
two entities who ever saw Mentor ever saw the same thing.

Frederick Rodebush, Lyman Cleveland, young Bergenholm, and a couple of commodores of the Patrol—Clayton
of North America and Schweikert of Europe—just about
exhausted Earth's resources. Nor were the other Solarian
planets very helpful, yielding only three Lensmen—Knobos

of Mars, DalNalten of Venus, and Rularion of Jove. Lensman material was extremely scarce stuff.

Knowing that his proposed Galactic Council would have to be made up exclusively of Lensmen, and that it should represent as many solar systems as possible, Samms visited the various systems which had been colonized by humanity, then went on: to Rigel Four, where he found Dronvire the Explorer, who was of Lensman grade; and next to Pluto, where he found Pilinixi the Dexitroboper, who very definitely was not; and finally to Palain Seven, an ultra-frigid world where he found Tallick, who might—or might not—go to Arisia some day. And Virgil Samms, being physically tough and mentally a real Crusader, survived these various ordeals.

For some time the existence of the newly-formed Galactic Patrol was precarious indeed. Archibald Isaacson, head of Interstellar Spaceways, wanting a monopoly of interstellar trade, first tried bribery; then, joining forces with the machine of Senator Morgan and Boss Towne, assassination. The other Lensmen and Jill Samms saved her father's life, after which Kinnison took Samms to the safest place on Earth—deep underground beneath The Hill: the tremendously fortified, superlatively armed fortress which had been built to be the headquarters of the Tri-planetary Service.

But even there the First Lensman was attacked, this time by a fleet of space-ships in full battle array. By that time, however, the Galactic Patrol had a fleet of its own, and again the Lensmen won.

Knowing that the final and decisive struggle would of necessity be a political one, the Patrol took over the Cosmocrat party and set out to gather detailed and documented evidence of corrupt and criminal activities of the Nationalists, the party then in power. Roderick ("Rod the Rock") Kinnison ran for President of North America against the incumbent Witherspoon; and, after a knock-down-and-dragout political battle with Senator Morgan, the voice of the Morgan-Towne-Isaacson machine, he was elected.

And Morgan was murdered—supposedly by dis-
gruntled gangsters; actually by his Kalonian boss, who was
in turn a minion of the Eddorians—simply and merely
because he had failed.*

North America was the most powerful continent of
Earth; Earth was the Mother Planet, the Leader, the Boss.
Hence, under the sponsorship of the Cosmocratic Government of North America, the Galactic Council and its arm,
the Galactic Patrol, came into their own. At the end of
R. K. Kinnison's term of office, at which time he resumed
his interrupted duties as Port Admiral of the Patrol, there
were a hundred planets adherent to Civilization. In ten
years there were a thousand; in a hundred years a million:
and it is sufficient characterization of the light but effective
rule of the Galactic Council to say that in all the long history
of Civilization no planet whose peoples have ever voted to
adhere to Civilization has ever withdrawn from it.

Time went on; the prodigiously long blood-lines, so
carefully manipulated by Mentor of Arisia, neared culmina-
tion. Lensman Kimball Kinnison was graduated Number
One of his class—as a matter of fact, although he did not
know it, he was Number One of his time. And his female
counterpart and complement, Clarrissa MacDougall of the
red-bronze-auburn hair and the gold-flecked tawny eyes,
was a nurse in the Patrol's immense hospital at Prime Base.

Shortly after graduation Kinnison was called to Prime
Base by Port Admiral Haynes. Space piracy had become
an organized force; and, under the leadership of someone
or something known as "Boskone", had risen to such
heights of power as to threaten seriously the Galactic
Patrol itself. In one respect Boskonia was ahead of the
Patrol, its scientists having developed a source of power
vastly greater than any known to Galactic Civilization. It
had fighting ships of a new and extraordinary type, from
which even convoyed shipping was no longer safe. Being
faster than the Patrol's fastest cruisers and yet more heavily

---

* *First Lensman,* Fantasy Press, Reading, Pa.

armed than its heaviest battleships, they had been doing practically as they pleased throughout space.

For one particular purpose, the engineers of the Patrol had designed and built one ship—the *Britannia*. She was the fastest thing in space, but for offensive armament she had only one weapon, the "Q-gun". Kinnison was put in command of this vessel, with orders to: 1) Capture a Boskonian war-vessel of late model; 2) Learn her secrets of power; and 3) Transmit the information to Prime Base.

He found and took such a warship. Sergeant Peter vanBuskirk led the storming party of Valerians—men of human ancestry, but of extraordinary size, strength, and agility because of the enormous gravitation of the planet Valeria—in wiping out those of the pirate crew not killed in the battle between the two vessels.

The *Brittania's* scientists secured the desired data. It could not be transmitted to Prime Base, however, as the pirates were blanketing all channels of communication. Boskonian warships were gathering for the kill, and the crippled Patrol ship could neither run nor fight. Therefore each man was given a spool of tape bearing a complete record of everything that had occurred; and, after setting up a director-by-chance to make the empty ship pursue an unpredictable course in space, and after rigging bombs to destroy her at the first touch of a ray, the Patrolmen paired off by lot and took to the lifeboats.

The erratic course of the cruiser brought her near the lifeboat manned by Kinnison and vanBuskirk, and there the pirates tried to stop her. The ensuing explosion was so violent that flying wreckage disabled practically the entire personnel of one of the attacking ships, which did not have time to go free before the crash. The two Patrolmen boarded the pirate vessel and drove her toward Earth, reaching the solar system of Velantia before the Boskonians headed them off. Again taking to their lifeboat, they landed upon the planet Delgon, where they were rescued from a horde of Catlats by one Worsel—later to become Lensman Worsel of Velantia—a highly intelligent winged reptile.

By means of improvements upon Velantian thought-screens the three destroyed a group of the Overlords of Delgon, a sadistic race of monsters who had been preying upon the other peoples of the system by sheer power of mind. Worsel then accompanied the two Patrolmen to Velantia, where all the resources of the planet were devoted to the preparation of defenses against the expected attack of the Boskonians. Several other lifeboats reached Velantia, guided by Worsel's mind working through Kinnison's ego and Lens.

Kinnison intercepted a message from Helmuth, who "spoke for Boskone", and traced his communicator beam, thus getting his first line upon Boskone's Grand Base. The pirates attacked Velantia, and six of their warships were captured. In these six ships, manned by Velantian crews, the Patrolmen again set out for Earth and Prime Base.

Then Kinnison's Bergenholm, the generator of the force which makes inertialess flight possible, broke down, so that he had to land upon Trenco for repairs. Trenco, the tempestuous, billiard-ball-smooth planet where it rains forty-seven feet and five inches every night and where the wind blows at eight hundred miles an hour—Trenco, the source of thionite, the deadliest of all deadly drugs—Trenco, whose weirdly-charged ether and atmosphere so distort beams and vision that it can be policed only by such beings as the Rigellians, who possess the sense of perception instead of those of sight and hearing!

Lensman Tregonsee, of Rigel Four, then in command of the Patrol's wandering base upon Trenco, supplied Kinnison with a new Bergenholm and he again set out for Tellus.

Meanwhile Helmuth had deduced that some one particular Lensman was the cause of all his set-backs; and that the Lens, a complete enigma to all Boskonians, was in some way connected with Arisia. That planet had always been dreaded and shunned by all spacemen. No Boskonian who had ever approached that planet could be compelled, even by the certainty of death, to go near it again.

Thinking himself secure by virtue of thought-screens given him by a being from a higher-echelon planet named Ploor, Helmuth went alone to Arisia, determined to learn all about the Lens. There he was punished to the verge of insanity, but was permitted to return to his Grand Base alive and sane: "Not for your own good, but for the good of that struggling young Civilization which you oppose."

Kinnison reached Prime Base with the all-important data. By building super-powerful battleships, called "maulers", the Patrol gained a temporary advantage over Boskonia, but a stalemate soon ensued. Kinnison developed a plan of action whereby he hoped to locate Helmuth's Grand Base; and asked Port Admiral Haynes for permission to follow it. In lieu of that, however, Haynes told him that he had been given his Release; that he was an Unattached Lensman— a "Gray" Lensman, popularly so called, from the color of the plain leather uniforms they wear. Thus he earned the highest honor which the Patrol can give, for the Gray Lensman works under no supervision or direction whatever. He is as absolutely a free agent as it is possible to be. He is responsible to no one; to nothing save his own conscience. He is no longer of Tellus, nor of the Solarian System, but of Civilization as a whole. He is no longer a cog in the immense machine of the Patrol: wherever he may go he *is* the Patrol!

In quest of a second line upon Grand Base, Kinnison scouted a pirate stronghold upon Aldebaran I. Its personnel, however, were not even near-human, but were wheelmen, possessed of the sense of perception; hence Kinnison was discovered before he could accomplish anything and was very seriously wounded. He managed to get back to his speedster and to send a thought to Port Admiral Haynes, who rushed ships to his aid. In Base Hospital Surgeon-Marshal Lacy put him back together; and, during a long and quarrelsome convalescence, Nurse Clarissa MacDougall held him together. And Lacy and Haynes connived to promote a romance between nurse and Lensman.

As soon as he could leave the hospital he went to Arisia

in the hope that he might be given advanced training—a theretofore unthought-of idea. Much to his surprise he learned that he had been expected to return for exactly such training. Getting it almost killed him, but he emerged from the ordeal infinitely stronger of mind than any man had ever been before; and possessed of a new sense as well—the sense of perception, a sense somewhat analogous to sight, but of vastly greater power, depth, and scope, and not dependent upon light.

After trying out his new mental equipment by solving a murder mystery upon Radelix, he succeeded in entering an enemy base upon Boyssia II. There he took over the mind of a communications officer and waited for the opportunity of getting the second, all-important line to Boskonia's Grand Base. An enemy ship captured a hospital ship of the Patrol and brought it in to Boyssia Base. Nurse MacDougall, head nurse of the captured vessel, working under Kinnison's instructions, stirred up trouble which soon became mutiny. Helmuth, from Grand Base, took a hand; thus enabling Kinnison to get his second line.

The hospital ship, undetectable by virtue of the Lensman's nullifier, escaped from Boyssia II and headed for Earth at full blast. Kinnison, convinced that Helmuth was really Boskone himself, found that the intersection of his two lines—and therefore the pirates' Grand Base—lay in star cluster AC 257-4736, well outside the galaxy. Pausing only long enough to destroy the Wheelmen of Aldebaran I, the project in which his first attempt had failed so dismally, he set out to investigate Helmuth's headquarters. He found a stronghold impregnable to any massed attack the Patrol could throw against it, manned by beings each wearing a thought-screen. His sense of perception was suddenly cut off—the pirates had thrown a thought-screen around the entire planet. He then returned to Prime Base, deciding en route that boring from within was the only possible way in which that stupendous fortress could be taken.

In consultation with Port Admiral Haynes, the zero hour was set, at which time the massed Grand Fleet of the

Patrol was to attack Helmuth's base with every projector that could be brought to bear.

Pursuant to his plan, Kinnison again visited Trenco, where the Patrol forces extracted for him fifty kilograms of thionite, the noxious drug which, in microgram inhalations, makes the addict experience all the sensations of doing whatever it is that he wishes most ardently to do. The larger the dose, the more intense the sensations; the slightest overdose resulting in an ecstatic death. Thence to Helmuth's planet; where, working through the unshielded brain of a dog, he let himself into the central dome. Here, just before the zero minute, he released his thionite into the air-stream, thus wiping out all the pirate personnel except Helmuth, who, in his inner sanctum, could not be affected.

The Grand Fleet of the Patrol attacked, but Helmuth would not leave his retreat, even to try to save his Base. Therefore Kinnison had to go in after him. Poised in the air of Helmuth's inner sphere there was an enigmatic, sparkling ball of force which the Lensman could not understand, and of which he was in consequence extremely suspicious.

But the storming of that quadruply-defended inner stronghold was precisely the task for which Kinnison's new and ultra-cumbersome armor had been designed; and in the Gray Lensman went.*

---

* *Galactic Patrol*, Fantasy Press, Reading, Pa.

AMONG THE WORLD-GIRDLING
fortifications of a planet distant indeed from star cluster
AC 257-4736 there squatted sullenly a fortress quite
similar to Helmuth's own. Indeed, in some respects it was
even superior to the base of him who spoke for Boskone.
It was larger and stronger. Instead of one dome, it had
many. It was dark and cold withal, for its occupants had
practically nothing in common with humanity save the
possession of high intelligence.

In the central sphere of one of the domes there
sparkled several of the peculiarly radiant globes whose
counterpart had given Kinnison so seriously to think, and
near them there crouched or huddled or lay at ease a many-
tentacled creature indescribable to man. It was not like an
octopus. Though spiny, it did not resemble at all closely a
sea-cucumber. Nor, although it was scaly and toothy and
wingy, was it, save in the vaguest possible way, similar to
a lizard, a sea-serpent, or a vulture. Such a description by
negatives is, of course, pitifully inadequate; but, unfortunately, it is the best that can be done.

The entire attention of this being was focused within
one of the globes, the obscure mechanism of which was
relaying to his sense of perception from Helmuth's globe

and mind a clear picture of everything which was happening within Grand Base. The corpse-littered dome was clear to his sight; he knew that the Patrol was attacking from without; knew that that ubiquitous Lensman, who had already unmanned the citadel, was about to attack from within.

"You have erred seriously," the entity was thinking coldly, emotionlessly, into the globe, "in not deducing until after it was too late to save your base that the Lensman had perfected a nullifier of sub-ethereal detection. Your contention that I am equally culpable is, I think, untenable. It was your problem, not mine; I had, and still have, other things to concern me. Your base is of course lost; whether or not you yourself survive will depend entirely upon the adequacy of your protective devices."

"But, Eichlan, you yourself pronounced them adequate!"

"Pardon me—I said that they *seemed* adequate."

"If I survive—or, rather, after I have destroyed this Lensman—what are your orders?"

"Go to the nearest communicator and concentrate our forces; half of them to engage this Patrol fleet, the remainder to wipe out all the life of Sol III. I have not tried to give those orders direct, since all the beams are keyed to your board and, even if I could reach them, no commander in that galaxy knows that I speak for Boskone. After you have done that, report to me here."

"Instructions received and understood. Helmuth, ending message."

"Set your controls as instructed. I will observe and record. Prepare yourself, the Lensman comes. Eichlan, speaking for Boskone, ending message."

The Lensman rushed. Even before he crashed the pirate's screens his own defensive zones flamed white in the beam of semi-portable projectors and through that blaze came tearing the metallic slugs of a high-calibre machine rifle. But the Lensman's screens were almost those of a battleship, his armor relatively as strong; he had at his command projectors scarcely inferior to those opposing his advance. Therefore, with every faculty of his newly-enlarged mind concentrated upon that thought-screened, armored head behind the bellowing gun and the flaring projectors, Kinnison held his line and forged ahead.

Attentive as he was to Helmuth's thought-screen, the Patrolman was ready when it weakened slightly and a thought began to seep through, directed at that peculiar ball of force. He blanketed it savagely, before it could even begin to take form, and attacked the screen so viciously that the Boskonian had either to restore full coverage instantly or else die there and then.

Kinnison feared that force-ball no longer. He still did not know what it was; but he had learned that, whatever its nature might be, it was operated or controlled by thought. Therefore it was and would remain harmless; for if the pirate chief softened his screen enough to emit a thought he would never think again.

Doggedly the Lensman drove in, closer and closer. Magnetic clamps locked and held. Two steel-clad, warring figures rolled into the line of fire of the ravening automatic rifle. Kinnison's armor, designed and tested to withstand even heavier stuff, held; wherefore he came through that storm of metal unscathed. Helmuth's, however, even though stronger far than the ordinary personal armor of space, failed; and thus the Boskonian died.

Blasting himself upright, the Patrolman shot across the inner dome to the control panel and paused, momentarily baffled. He could not throw the switches controlling the defensive screens of the gigantic outer dome! His armor, designed for the ultimate of defensive strength, could not and did not bear any of the small and delicate external mechanisms so characteristic of the ordinary space-suit. To leave his personal tank at that time and in that environment was unthinkable; yet he was fast running out of time. A scant fifteen seconds was all that remained before zero, the moment at which the hellish output of every watt generable by the massed fleet of the Galactic Patrol would be hurled against those screens in their furiously, ragingly destructive might. To release the screens after that zero moment would mean his own death, instantaneous and inevitable.

Nevertheless he could open those circuits—the conservation of Boskonian property meant nothing to him. He flipped on his own projector and flashed its beam briefly across the banked panels in front of him. Insulation burst into flame, fairly exploding in its haste to disintegrate; copper and silver ran in brilliant streams or puffed away in clouds of sparkling vapor: high-tension arcs ripped, crashed, and crackled among the writhing, dripping, flaring bus-bars. The shorts burned themselves clear or blew their fuses, every circuit opened, every Boskonian defense came down; and then, and only then, could Kinnison get into communication with his friends.

"Haynes!" he thought crisply into his Lens. "Kinnison calling!"

"Haynes acknowledging!" a thought instantly snapped back. "Congrat . . ."

"Hold it! We're not done yet! Have every ship in the Fleet go free at once. Have them all, except yours, put out full-coverage screens, so that they can't look at this base—that's to keep 'em from thinking into it."

A moment passed. "Done!"

"Don't come in any closer—I'm on my way out to you. Now as to you personally—I don't like to seem to be giving orders to the Port Admiral, but it may be quite essential that you concentrate on me, and think of nothing else, for the next few minutes."

"Right! I don't mind taking orders from *you*."

"QX—now we can take things a bit easier." Kinnison had so arranged matters that no one except himself could think into that stronghold, and he himself would not. He would not think into that tantalizing enigma, nor toward it, nor even *of* it, until he was completely ready to do so. And how many persons, I wonder, really realize just how much of a feat that was? Realize the sort of mental training required for its successful performance?

"How many gamma-zeta tracers can you put out, chief?" Kinnison asked then, more conversationally.

A brief consultation, then "Ten in regular use. By tuning in all our spares we can put out sixty."

"At two diameters' distance forty-eight fields will surround this planet at one hundred percent overlap. Please have that many set that way. Of the other twelve, set three to go well outside the first sphere—say at four diameters out—covering the line from this planet to Lundmark's Nebula. Set the last nine to be thrown out about half a detet—as far as you can read them accurately to one decimal—centering on the same line. Not much overlap is necessary on these backing fields—just contact. Release nothing, of course, until I get there. And while the boys are setting things up, you might go inert—it's safe enough now—so I can match your intrinsic velocity and come aboard."

There followed the maneuvering necessary for one inert body to approach another in space, then Kinnison's incredible housing of steel was hauled into the airlock by means of space-lines attached to magnetic clamps. The outer door of the lock closed behind him, the inner one opened, and the Lensman entered the flagship.

First to the armory, where he clambered stiffly out of his small battleship and gave orders concerning its storage. Then to the control room, stretching and bending hugely as he went, in vast relief at his freedom from the narrow and irksome confinement which he had endured so long. He wanted a shower badly—in fact, he needed one—but business came first.

Of all the men in that control room, only two knew Kinnison personally. All knew of him, however, and as the tall, gray-clad figure entered there was a loud, quick cheer.

"Hi, fellows—thanks." Kinnison waved a salute to the room as a whole. "Hi, Port Admiral! Hi, Commandant!" He saluted Haynes and von Hohendorff as perfunctorily, and greeted them as casually, as though he had last seen them an hour, instead of ten weeks, before; as though the inter-

vening time had been spent in the veriest idleness, instead
of in the fashion in which it actually had been spent.

Old von Hohendorff greeted his erstwhile pupil cordially enough, but:

"Out with it!" Haynes demanded. "What did you do?
How did you do it? What does all this confounded rig-
marole mean? Tell us all about it—all you can, I mean,"
he added, hastily.

"There's no need for secrecy now, I don't think," and
in flashing thoughts the Gray Lensman went on to describe
everything that had happened.

"So you see," he concluded, "I don't really *know* anything. It's all surmise, suspicion, and deduction. Maybe
nothing at all will happen; in which case these precautions,
while they will have been wasted effort, will have done us
no harm. In case something *does* happen, however—and
something will, for all the tea in China—we'll be ready for it."

"But if what you are beginning to suspect is really
true, it means that Boskonia is inter-galactic in scope—
wider-spread even than the Patrol!"

"Probably, but not necessarily—it may mean only that
they have bases farther outside. And remember I'm arguing
on a mighty slim thread of evidence. That screen was hard
and tight, and I couldn't touch the external beam—if there
was one—at all. I got just part of a thought, here and there.
However, the thought was 'that' galaxy; not just 'galaxy',
or 'this' or 'the' galaxy—and why think that way if the guy
was already in this galaxy?"

"But nobody has ever . . . but skip it for now—the
boys are ready for you. Take over!"

"QX. First we'll go free again. Don't think much, if
any, of the stuff can come out here, but no use taking
chances. Cut your screens. Now, all you gamma-zeta men,
throw out your fields, and if any of you get a puncture, or
even a flash, measure its position. You recording observers,
step your scanners up to fifty thousand. QX?"

"QX!" the observers and recorders reported, almost as
one, and the Gray Lensman sat down at a plate.

His mind, free at last to make the investigation from which it had been so long and so sternly barred, flew down into and through the dome, to and into that cryptic globe so tantalizingly poised in the air of the Center.

The reaction was practically instantaneous; so rapid that any ordinary mind could have perceived nothing at all; so rapid that even Kinnison's consciousness recorded only a confusedly blurred impression. But he did see something: in that fleeting millionth of a second he sensed a powerful, malignant mental force; a force backing multiplex scanners and sub-ethereal stress-fields interlocked in peculiarly un-identifiable patterns.

For that ball was, as Kinnison had more than sus-pected, a potent agency indeed. It was, as he had thought, a communicator; but it was far more than that. Ordinarily harmless enough, it could be so set as to become an infernal machine at the vibrations of any thought not in a certain coded sequence; and Helmuth had so set it.

Therefore at the touch of the Patrolman's thoughts it exploded: liberating instantaneously the unimaginable forces with which it was charged. More, it sent out waves which, attuned to detonating receivers, touched off strategically-placed stores of duodecaplylatomate. "Duodec", the con-centrated quintessence of atomic violence!

"Hell's . . . Jingling . . . Bells!" Port Admiral Haynes grunted in stunned amazement, then subsided into silence, eyes riveted upon his plate; for to the human eye dome, fortress, and planet had disappeared in one cataclysmically incandescent sphere of flame.

But the observers of the Galactic Patrol did not depend upon eyesight alone. Their scanners had been working at ultra-fast speed; and, as soon as it became clear that none of the ships of the Fleet had been endangered, Kinnison asked that certain of the spools be run into a visitank at normal tempo.

There, slowed to a speed at which the eye could clearly discern sequences of events, the two old Lensmen and the young one studied with care the three-dimensional pictures of what had happened; pictures taken from points of projection close to and even within the doomed structure itself.

Deliberately the ball of force opened up, followed an inappreciable instant later by the secondary centers of detonation; all expanding magically into spherical volumes of blindingly brilliant annihilation. There were as yet no flying fragments: no inert fragment *can* fly from duodec in the first few instants of its detonation. For the detonation of duodec is propagated at the velocity of light, so that the entire mass disintegrates in a period of time to be measured only in fractional trillionths of a second. Its detonation pressure and temperature have never been measured save indirectly, since nothing will hold it except a Q-type helix of pure force. And even those helices, which must be practically open at both ends, have to be designed and powered to withstand pressures and temperatures obtaining only in the cores of suns.

Imagine, if you can, what would happen if some fifty thousand metric tons of material from the innermost core of Sirius B were to be taken to Grand Base, separated into twenty-five packages, each package placed at a strategic point, and all restraint instantaneously removed. What would have happened then, was what actually *was* happening!

As has been said, for moments nothing moved except the ever-expanding spheres of destruction. Nothing *could* move—the inertia of matter itself held it in place until it was too late—everything close to those centers of action simply flared into turgid incandescence and added its contribution to the already hellish whole.

As the spheres expanded their temperatures and pressures decreased and the action became somewhat less violent. Matter no longer simply disappeared. Instead, plates and girders, even gigantic structural members, bent, buckled, and crumbled. Walls blew outward and upward. Huge chunks of metal and of masonry, many with fused and dripping edges, began to fly in all directions.

And not only, or principally, upward was directed the force of those inconceivable explosions. Downward the effect was, if possible, even more catastrophic, since conditions there approximated closely the oft-argued meeting between the irresistible force and the immovable object. The planet was to all intents and purposes immovable, the duodec to the same degree irresistible. The result was that the entire planet was momentarily blown apart. A vast chasm was blasted deep into its interior, and, gravity temporarily overcome, stupendous cracks and fissures began to yawn. Then, as the pressure decreased, the core-stuff of the planet became molten and began to wreak its volcanic havoc. Gravity, once more master of the situation, took hold. The cracks and chasms closed, extruding uncounted cubic miles of fiery lava and metal. The entire world shivered and shuddered in a Gargantuan cosmic ague.

The explosion blew itself out. The hot gases and vapors cooled. The steam condensed. The volcanic dust disappeared. There lay the planet; but changed—hideously and awfully changed. Where Grand Base had been there remained nothing whatever to indicate that anything wrought by man had ever been there. Mountains were leveled, valleys were filled. Continents and oceans had shifted, and were still shifting; visibly. Earthquakes, volcanoes, and other seismic disturbances, instead of decreasing, were increasing in violence, minute by minute.

Helmuth's planet was and would for years remain a barren and uninhabitable world.

"Well!" Haynes, who had been holding his breath unconsciously, released it in an almost explosive sigh. "That is inescapably and incontrovertibly *that*. I was going to use that base, but it looks as though we'll have to get along without it."

Without comment Kinnison turned to the gamma-zeta observers. "Any traces?" he asked.

It developed that three of the fields had shown activity. Not merely traces or flashes, but solid punctures showing the presence of a hard, tight beam. And those three punctures were in the same line; a line running straight out into inter-galactic space.

Kinnison took careful readings on the line, then stood motionless. Feet wide apart, hands jammed into pockets, head slightly bent, eyes distant, he stood there unmoving; thinking with all the power of his brain.

"I want to ask three questions," the old Commandant of Cadets interrupted his cogitations finally. "Was Helmuth Boskone, or not? Have we got them licked, or not? What do we do next, besides mopping up those eighteen super-maulers?"

"To all three the answer is 'I don't know.'" Kinnison's face was stern and hard. "You know as much about the whole thing as I do—I haven't held back anything I even suspect. I didn't tell you that Helmuth was Boskone; I said that everyone in any position to judge, including myself, was as sure of it as one could be about anything that couldn't be proved. The presence of this communicator line, and the other stuff I've told you about, makes me think he wasn't. However, we don't actually *know* any more than we did before. It is no more certain now that Helmuth was *not* Boskone than it was before that he *was*. The second question ties in with the first, and so does the third—but I see they've started to mop up."

While von Hohendorff and Kinnison had been talking, Haynes had issued orders and the Grand Fleet, divided roughly and with difficulty into eighteen parts, went raggedly outward to surround the eighteen outlying fortresses. But, and surprisingly enough to the Patrol forces, the reduction of those hulking monsters was to prove no easy task.

The Boskonians had witnessed the destruction of Helmuth's Grand Base. Their master plates were dead. Try as they would, they could get in touch with no one with authority to give them orders, with no one to whom they could report their present plight. Nor could they escape: the slowest mauler in the Patrol Fleet could have caught any one of them in five minutes.

To surrender was not even thought of—better far to die a clean death in the blazing holocaust of space-battle than to be thrown ignominiously into the lethal chambers of the Patrol. There was not, there could not be, any question of pardon or of sentence to any mere imprisonment, for the strife between Civilization and Boskonia in no respect resembled the wars between two fundamentally similar and friendly nations which small, green Terra knew so frequently of old. It was a galaxy-wide struggle for survival between two diametrically opposed, mutually exclusive, and absolutely incompatible cultures; a duel to the death in which quarter was neither asked nor given; a conflict which, except for the single instance which Kinnison himself had engineered, was and of stern necessity had to be one of ruthless, complete, and utter extinction.

Die, then, the pirates must; and, although adherents to a scheme of existence monstrous indeed to our way of thinking, they were in no sense cowards. Not like cornered rats did they conduct themselves, but fought like what they were; courageous beings hopelessly outnumbered and outpowered, unable either to escape or to choose the field of operations, grimly resolved that in their passing they would take full toll of the minions of that detested and despised Galactic Civilization. Therefore, in suidical glee, Boskonian engineers rigged up a fantastically potent weapon of offense, tuned in their defensive screens, and hung poised in space, awaiting calmly the massed attack so sure to come.

Up flashed the heavy cruisers of the Patrol, serenely confident. Although of little offensive strength, these vessels mounted tractors and pressors of prodigious power, as well as defensive screens which—theoretically—no projector-driven beam of force could puncture. They had engaged mauler after mauler of Boskonia's mightiest, and never yet had one of those screens gone down. Theirs the task of immobilizing the opponent; since, as is of course well known, it is under any ordinary conditions impossible to wreak any hurt upon an object which is both inertialess and at liberty to move in space. It simply darts away from the touch of the harmful agent, whether it be immaterial beam or material substance.

Formerly the attachment of two or three tractors was

all that was necessary to insure immobility, and thus vulnerability; but with the Velantian development of a shear-plane to cut tractor beams, a new technique became necessary. This was englobement, in which a dozen or more vessels surrounded the proposed victim in space and held it motionless at the center of a sphere by means of pressors, which could not be cut or evaded. Serene, then, and confident, the heavy cruisers rushed out to englobe the Boskonian fortress.

Flash! Flash! Flash! Three points of light, as unbearably brilliant as atomic vortices, sprang into being upon the fortress' side. Three needle-rays of inconceivable energy lashed out, hurtling through the cruisers' outer screens as though they had been so much inactive webbing. Through the second and through the first. Through the wall-shield, even that ultra-powerful field scarcely flashing as it went down. Through the armor, violating the prime tenet then held and which has just been referred to, that no object free in space can be damaged—in this case, so unthinkably vehement was the thrust, the few atoms of substance in the space surrounding the doomed cruisers afforded resistance enough. Through the ship itself, a ravening cylinder of annihilation.

For perhaps a second—certainly no longer—those incredible, those undreamed-of beams persisted before winking out into blackness; but that second had been long enough. Three riddled hulks lay dead in space, and as the three original projectors went black three more flared out. Then three more. Nine of the mightiest of Civilization's ships of war were riddled before the others could hurl themselves backward out of range!

Most of the officers of the flagship were stunned into temporary inactivity by that shocking development, but two reacted almost instantly.

"Thorndyke!" the admiral snapped. "What did they do, and how?"

And Kinnison, not speaking at all, leaped to a certain panel, to read for himself the analysis of those incredible beams of force.

"They made super-needle-rays out of their main pro-jectors," Master Technician LaVerne Thorndyke reported, crisply. "They must have shorted everything they've got onto them to burn them out that fast."

"Those beams were hot—plenty hot," Kinnison cor-roborated the findings. "These recorders go to five billion and have a factor of safety of ten. Even that wasn't any-where nearly enough—everything in the recorder circuits blew."

"But how could they handle them . . ." von Hohendorff began to ask.

"They didn't—they pointed them and died," Thorn-dyke explained, grimly. "They traded one projector and its crew for one cruiser and *its* crew—a good trade from their viewpoint."

"There will be no more such trades," Haynes declared.

Nor were there. The Patrol had maulers enough to englobe the enemy craft at a distance greater even than the effective range of those suicidal beams, and it did so.

Shielding screens cut off the Boskonians' intake of cosmic power and the relentless beaming of the bull-dog maulers began. For hour after hour it continued, the cordon ever tightening as the victims' power lessened. And finally even the gigantic accumulators of the immense fortresses were drained. Their screens went down under the hellish fury of the maulers' incessant attack, and in a space of minutes thereafter the structures and their contents ceased to exist save as cosmically atomic detritus.

The Grand Fleet of the Galactic Patrol remade its formation after a fashion and set off toward the galaxy at touring blast.

And in the control room of the flagship three Lensmen brought a very serious conference to a close.

"You saw what happened to Helmuth's planet," Kinni-son's voice was oddly hard, "and I gave you all I could get of the thought about the destruction of all life on Sol III. A big enough duodec bomb in the bottom of an ocean would do it. I don't really *know* anything except that we hadn't better let them catch us asleep at the switch again—we've got to be on our toes every second."

And the Gray Lensman, face set and stern, strode off to his quarters.

Wide-Open Two-Way

DURING PRACTICALLY ALL OF the long trip back to Earth Kinnison kept pretty much to his cabin, thinking deeply, blackly, and, he admitted ruefully to himself, to very little purpose. And at Prime Base, through week after week of its feverish activity, he continued to think. Finally, however, he was snatched out of his dark abstraction by no less a personage than Surgeon-Marshal Lacy.

"Snap out of it, lad," that worthy advised, smilingly. "When you concentrate on one thing too long, you know, the vortices of thought occupy narrower and narrower loci, until finally the effective volume becomes infinitesimal. Or, mathematically, the then range of cogitation, integrated between the limits of plus and minus infinity, approaches zero as a limit . . ."

"Huh? What are you talking about?" the Lensman demanded.

"Poor mathematics, perhaps, but sound psychology," Lacy grinned. "It got your undivided attention, didn't it? That was what I was after. In plain English, if you keep on thinking around in circles you'll soon be biting yourself in the small of the back. Come on, you and I are going places."

"Where?"

"To the Grand Ball in honor of the Grand Fleet, my boy—old Doctor Lacy prescribes it for you as a complete and radical change of atmosphere. Let's go!"

The city's largest ball-room was a blaze of light and color. A thousand polychromatic lamps flooded their radiance downward through draped bunting upon an even more colorful throng. Two thousand items of feminine loveliness were there, in raiment whose fabrics were the boasts of hundreds of planets, whose hues and shades put the spectrum itself to shame. There were over two thousand men, clad in plain or beribboned or bemedaled full civilian dress, or in the variously panoplied dress uniforms of the many Services.

"You're dancing with Miss Forrester first, Kinnison," the surgeon introduced them informally, and the Lensman found himself gliding away with a stunning blonde, ravishingly and revealingly dressed in a dazzlingly blue wisp of Manarkan glamorette—fashion's *dernier cri*.

To the uninformed, Kinnison's garb of plain gray leather might have seemed incongruous indeed in that brilliantly and fastidiously dressed assemblage. But to those people, as to us of today, the drab, starkly utilitarian uniform of the Unattached Lensman transcended far any other, however resplendent, worn by man: and literally hundreds of eyes followed the strikingly handsome couple as they slid rhythmically out upon the polished floor. But a measure of the tall beauty's customary poise had deserted her. She was slimly taut in the circle of the Lensman's arm, her eyes were downcast, and suddenly she missed a step.

" 'Scuse me for stepping on your feet," he apologized. "A fellow gets out of practice, flitting around in a speedster so much."

"Thanks for taking the blame, but it's my fault entirely—I know it as well as you do," she replied, flushing uncomfortably. "I *do* know how to dance, too, but . . . well, you're a Gray Lensman, you know."

"Huh?" he ejaculated, in honest surprise, and she

looked up at him for the first time. "What has that fact got to do with the price of Venerian orchids in Chicago—or with my clumsy walking all over your slippers?"

"Everything in the world," she assured him. Nevertheless, her stiff young body relaxed and she fell into the graceful, accurate dancing which she really knew so well how to do. "You see, I don't suppose that any of us has ever seen a Gray Lensman before, except in pictures, and actually to be dancing with one is . . . well, it's really a kind of shock. I have to get used to it gradually. Why, I don't even know how to talk to you! One couldn't possibly call you plain Mister, as one would any ord . . ."

"It'll be QX if you just call me 'say'," he informed her. "Maybe you'd rather not dance with a dub? What say we go get us a sandwich and a bottle of fayalin or something?"

"No—never!" she exclaimed. "I didn't mean it that way at all. I'm going to have this full dance with you, and enjoy every second of it. And later I'm going to pack this dance card—which I hope you will sign for me—away in lavender, so it will go down in history that in my youth I really did dance with Gray Lensman Kinnison. Perhaps I've recovered enough now to talk and dance at the same time. Do you mind if I ask you some silly questions about space?"

"Go ahead. They won't be silly, if I'm any judge. Elementary, perhaps, but not silly."

"I hope so, but I think you're being charitable again. Like most of the girls here, I suppose, I've never been out in deep space at all. Besides a few hops to the moon. I've taken only two flits, and they were both only interplanetary—one to Mars and one to Venus. I never could see how you deep-space men can really understand what you're doing—either the frightful speeds at which you travel, the distances you cover, or the way your communicators work. In fact, according to the professors, no human mind can understand figures of those magnitudes at all. But you must understand them, I should think . . . or, perhaps . . ."

"Or maybe the guy isn't human?" Kinnison laughed deeply, infectiously. "No, the professors are right. We can't understand the figures, but we don't have to—all we have to do is to work with 'em. And, now that it has just percolated through my skull who you really are, that you are *Gladys* Forrester, it's quite clear that you and I are in the same boat."

"Me? How?" she exclaimed.

"The human mind cannot really understand a million of anything. Yet your father, an immensely wealthy man, gave you clear title to a million credits in cash, to train you in finance in the only way that really produces results—the hard way of actual experience. You lost a lot of it at first, of course; but at last accounts you had got it all back, and some besides, in spite of all the smart guys trying to take it away from you. The fact that your brain can't envisage a million credits hasn't interferred with your manipulation of that amount, has it?"

"No, but that's entirely different!" she protested.

"Not in any essential feature," he countered. "I can explain it best, perhaps, by analogy. You can't visualize, mentally, the size of North America, either, yet that fact doesn't bother you in the least while you're driving around on it in an automobile. What do you drive? On the ground, I mean, not in the air?"

"A DeKhotinsky sporter."

"Um. Top speed a hundred and forty miles an hour, and I suppose you cruise between ninety and a hundred. We'll have to pretend that you drive a Crownover sedan, or some other big, slow jalopy, so that you tour at about sixty and have an absolute top of ninety. Also, you have a radio. On the broadcast bands you can hear a program from three or four thousand miles away; or, on short wave, from anywhere on Tellus . . ."

"I can get tight-beam short-wave programs from the moon," the girl broke in. "I've heard them lots of times."

"Yes," Kinnison assented dryly, "at such times as there didn't happen to be any interference."

"Static *is* pretty bad, lots of times," the heiress agreed.

"Well, change 'miles' to 'parsecs' and you've got the picture of deep-space speeds and operations," Kinnison informed her. "Our speed varies, of course, with the density of matter in space; but on the average—say one atom of substance per ten cubic centimeters of space—we tour at about sixty parsecs an hour, and full blast is about ninety. And our ultra-wave communicators, working below the level of the ether, in the sub-ether . . ."

"Whatever that is," she interrupted.

"That's as good a definition of it as any," he grinned at her. "We don't know what even the ether is, or whether or not it exists as an objective reality; to say nothing of what we so nonchalantly call the sub-ether. We can't understand gravity, even though we make it to order. Nobody yet has been able to say how it is propagated, or even whether or not it *is* propagated—no one has been able to devise any kind of an apparatus or meter or method by which its nature, period, or velocity can be determined. Neither do we know anything about time or space. In fact, fundamentally, we don't really *know* much of anything at all," he concluded.

"Says you . . . but that makes me feel better, anyway," she confided, snuggling a little closer. "Go on about the communicators."

"Ultra-waves are faster than ordinary radio waves, which of course travel through the ether with the velocity of light, in just about the same ratio as that of the speed of our ships to the speed of slow automobiles—that is, the ratio of a parsec to a mile. Roughly nineteen billion to one. Range, of course, is proportional to the square of the speed."

"Nineteen billion!" she exclaimed. "And you just said that nobody could understand even a million!"

"That's the point exactly," he went on, undisturbed. "You don't have to understand or visualize it. All you have to know is that deep-space vessels and communicators cover distances in parcecs at practically the same rate that Tellurian automobiles and radios cover miles. So, when some space-flea talks to you about parsecs, just think of miles in terms of an automobile and a teleset and you'll know as much as he does—maybe more."

"I never heard it explained that way before—it does make it ever so much simpler. Will you sign this, please?"

"Just one more point." The music had ceased and he was signing her card, preparatory to escorting her back to her place. "Like your supposedly tight-beam Luna-Tellus hookups, our long-range, equally tight-beam communicators are very sensitive to interference, either natural or artificial. So, while under perfect conditions we can communicate clear across the galaxy, there are times—particularly when the pirates are scrambling the channels—that we can't drive a beam from here to Alpha Centauri. . . . Thanks a lot for the dance."

The other girls did not quite come to blows as to which of them was to get him next; and shortly—he never did know exactly how it came about—he found himself dancing with a luscious, cuddly little brunette, clad—partially clad, at least—in a high-slitted, flame-colored sheath of some new fabric which the Lensman had never seen before. It looked like solidified, tightly-woven electricity!

"Oh, Mr. Kinnison!" his new partner cooed, ecstatically, "I think all spacemen, and you Lensmen particularly, are just too perfectly darn *heroic* for anything! Why, I think space is just *terrible!* I simply can't *cope* with it at *all!*"

"Ever been out, Miss?" he grinned. He had never known many social butterflies, and temporarily he had forgotten that such girls as this one really existed.

"Why, of *course!*" The young woman kept on being exclamatory.

"Clear out to the moon, perhaps?" he hazarded.

"Don't be ridic—*ever* so much farther than that— why, I went clear to *Mars!* And it gave me the screaming *meamies,* no less—I thought I would *collapse!*"

That dance ended ultimately, and other dances with other girls followed; but Kinnison could not throw himself into the gayety surrounding him. During his cadet days he had enjoyed such revels to the full, but now the whole thing left him cold. His mind insisted upon reverting to its problem. Finally, in the throng of young people on the floor, he saw a girl with a mass of red-bronze hair and a supple, superbly molded figure. He did not need to await her turning to recognize his erstwhile nurse and later assistant, whom he had last seen just this side of far-distant Boyssia II.

"Mac!" To her mind alone he sent out a thought. "For the love of Klono, lend a hand—rescue me! How many dances have you got ahead?"

"None at all—I'm not dating ahead." She jumped as though someone had jabbed her with a needle, then paused in panic; eyes wide, breath coming fast, heart pounding. She had felt Lensed thoughts before, but this was something else, something entirely different. Every cell of his brain was open to her—and what *was* she seeing! She could read his mind as fully and as easily as . . . as . . . as Lensmen were supposed to be able to read anybody's! She blanketed her thoughts desperately, tried with all her might not to think at all!

"QX, Mac," the thought went quietly on within her mind, quite as though nothing unusual were occurring. "No intrusion meant—you didn't think it; I already knew that if you started dating ahead you'd be tied up until day after tomorrow. Can I have the next one?"

"Surely, Kim."

"Thanks—the Lens is off for the rest of the evening." She sighed in relief as he snapped the telepathic line as though he were hanging up the receiver of a telephone.

"I'd like to dance with you all, kids," he addressed at large the group of buds surrounding him and eyeing him hungrily, "but I've got this next one. See you later, perhaps," and he was gone.

"Sorry, fellows," he remarked casually, as he made his way through the circle of men around the gorgeous red-head. "Sorry, but this dance is mine, isn't it, Miss MacDougall?"

She nodded, flashing the radiant smile which had so

aroused his ire during his hospitalization. "I heard you invoke your spaceman's god, but I was beginning to be afraid that you had forgotten this dance."

"And she said she wasn't dating ahead—the diplomat!" murmured an ambassador, aside.

"Don't be a dope," a captain of Marines muttered in reply. "She meant with *us—that's* a Gray Lensman!"

Although the nurse, as has been said, was anything but small, she appeared almost petite against the Lensman's mighty frame as they took off. Silently the two circled the great hall once; lustrous, goldenly green gown—of Earthly silk, this one, and less revealing than most—swishing in perfect cadence against deftly and softly stepping high-zippered gray boots.

"This is better, Mac," Kinnison sighed, finally, "but I lack just seven thousand kilocycles of being in tune with this. Don't know what's the matter, but its clogging my jets. I must be getting to be a space-louse."

"A space-louse—you? Uh-uh!" She shook her head. "You know very well what the matter is—you're just too much of a man to mention it."

"Huh?" he demanded.

"Uh-huh," she asserted, positively if obliquely. "Of course you're not in tune with this crowd—how could you be? I don't fit into it any more myself, and what I'm doing isn't even a baffled flare compared to your job. Not one in ten of these fluffs here tonight has ever been beyond the stratosphere; not one in a hundred has ever been out as far as Jupiter, or has ever had a serious thought in her head except about clothes or men; not one of them all has any more idea of what a Lensman really is than I have of hyper-space or of non-Euclidean geometry!"

"Kitty, kitty!" he laughed. "Sheathe the little claws, before you scratch somebody!"

"That isn't cattishness, it's the barefaced truth. Or perhaps," she amended, honestly, "it's both true and cattish, but it's certainly true. And that isn't half of it. No one in the Universe except yourself really *knows* what you are doing, and I'm pretty sure that only two others even suspect. And Doctor Lacy is *not* one of them," she concluded, surprisingly.

Though shocked, Kinnison did not miss a step. "You *don't* fit into this matrix, any more than I do," he agreed, quietly. "S'pose you and I could do a little flit somewhere?"

"Surely, Kim," and, breaking out of the crowd, they strolled out into the grounds. Not a word was said until they were seated upon a broad, low bench beneath the spreading foliage of a tree.

Then: "What did you come here for tonight, Mac—the *real* reason?" he demanded, abruptly.

"I . . . we . . . you . . . I mean—oh, skip it!" the girl stammered, a wave of scarlet flooding her face and down even to her superb, bare shoulders. Then she steadied herself and went on: "You see, I agree with you—as you say, I check you to nineteen decimals. Even Doctor Lacy, with all his knowledge, can be slightly screwy at times, I think."

"Oh, so that's it!" It was not, it was only a very minor part of her reason; but the nurse would have bitten her tongue off rather than admit that she had come to that dance solely and only because Kimball Kinnison was to be there. "You knew, then, that this was old Lacy's idea?"

"Of course. You would never have come, else. He thinks that you may begin wobbling on the beam pretty soon unless you put out a few braking jots."

"And you?"

"Not in a million, Kim. Lacy's as cockeyed as Trenco's ether, and I as good as told him so. He may wobble a bit, but *you* won't. You've got a job to do, and you're doing it. You'll finish it, too, in spite of all the vermin infesting all the galaxies of the macro-cosmic Universe!" she finished, passionately.

"Klono's brazen whiskers, Mac!" he turned suddenly and stared intently down into her wide, gold-flecked, tawny eyes. She stared back for a moment, then looked away.

"Don't look at me like that!" she almost screamed. "I can't stand it—you make me feel stark naked! I know your

Lens is off—I'd simply die if it wasn't—but you're a mind-reader, even without it!"

She did know that that powerful telepath was off and would remain off, and she was glad indeed of the fact; for her mind was seething with thoughts which that Lensman must not know, then or ever. And for his part, the Lensman knew much better than she did that had he chosen to exert the powers at his command she would have been naked, mentally and physically, to his perception; but he did not exert those powers—then. The amenities of human relationship demanded that some fastnesses of reserve remain inviolate, but he had to know what this woman knew. If necessary, he would take the knowledge away from her by force, so completely that she would never know that she had ever known it. Therefore:

"Just what do you know, Mac, and how did you find it out?" he demanded; quietly, but with a stern finality of inflection that made a quick chill run up and down the nurse's back.

"I know a lot, Kim." The girl shivered slightly, even though the evening was warm and balmy. "I learned it from your own mind. When you called me, back there on the floor, I didn't get just a single, sharp thought, as though you were speaking to me, as I always did before. Instead, it seemed as though I was actually inside your own mind—the whole of it. I've heard Lensmen speak of a wide-open two-way, but I never had even the faintest inkling of what such a thing would be like—no one could who has never experienced it. Of course I didn't—I couldn't—understand a millionth of what I saw, or seemed to see. It was too vast, too incredibly immense. I never dreamed any mortal *could* have a mind like that, Kim! But it was ghastly, too—it gave me the shrieking jitters and just about sent me down out of control. And you didn't even know it—I know you didn't! I didn't want to look, really, but I couldn't help seeing, and I'm glad I did—I wouldn't have missed it for the world!" she finished, almost incoherently.

"Hm . . . m. That changes the picture entirely." Much

to her surprise, the man's voice was calm and thoughtful; not at all incensed. Not even disturbed. "So I spilled the beans myself, on a wide-open two-way, and didn't even realize it* . . . I knew you were backfiring about something, but thought it was because I might think you guilty of petty vanity. And I called *you* a dumbbell once!" he marveled.

"Twice," she corrected him, "and the second time I was never so glad to be called names in my whole life."

"Now I *know* I was getting to be a space-louse."

"Uh-uh, Kim," she denied again, gently. "And you aren't a brat or a lug or a clunker, either, even though I *have* called you such. But, now that I've actually got all this stuff, what can you—what can we—do about it?"

"Perhaps . . . probably . . . I think, since I gave it to you myself, I'll let you keep it," Kinnison decided, slowly.

"Keep it!" she exclaimed. "Of course I'll keep it! Why, it's in my mind—I'll *have* to keep it—nobody can take *knowledge* away from anyone!"

"Oh, sure—of course," he murmured, absently. There were a lot of thing that Mac didn't know, and no good end would be served by enlightening her farther. "You see, there's a lot of stuff in my mind that I don't know much about myself, yet. Since I gave you an open channel, there must have been a good reason for it, even though, consciously, I don't know myself what it was." He thought intensely for moments, then went on: "Undoubtedly the subconscious. Probably it recognized the necessity of discussing the whole situation with someone having a fresh viewpoint, someone whose ideas can help me develop a fresh angle of attack. Haynes and I think too much alike for him to be of much help."

"You trust *me* that much?" the girl asked, dumbfounded.

"Certainly," he replied without hesitation. "I know

* Of course this was not the true explanation; but at that time only Mentor of Arisia had any idea of the real power of Clarissa Mac-Dougall's mind. E.E.S.

enough about you to know that you can keep your mouth shut."

Thus unromantically did Kimball Kinnison, Gray Lensman, acknowledge the first glimmerings of the dawning perception of a vast fact—that this nurse and he were two between whom there never would nor could exist any iota of doubt or of question.

Then they sat and talked. Not idly, as is the fashion of lovers, of the minutiæ of their own romantic affairs, did these two converse, but cosmically, of the entire Universe and of the already existent conflict between the cultures of Civilization and Boskonia.

They sat there, romantically enough to all outward seeming; their privacy assured by Kinnison's Lens and by his ever-watchful sense of perception. Time after time, completely unconsciously, that sense reached out to other couples who approached; to touch and to affect their minds so insidiously that they did not know that they were being steered away from the tree in whose black moon-shadow sat the Lensman and the nurse.

Finally the long conversation came to an end and Kinnison assisted his companion to her feet. His frame was straighter, his eyes held a new and brighter light.

"By the way, Kim," she asked idly as they strolled back toward the ball-room, "who is this Klono, by whom you were swearing a while ago? Another spaceman's god, like Noshabkeming, of the Valerians?"

"Something like him, only more so," he laughed. "A combination of Noshabkeming, some of the gods of the ancient Greeks and Romans, all three of the Fates, and quite a few other things as well. I think, originally, from Corvina, but fairly wide-spread through certain sections of the galaxy now. He's got so much stuff—teeth and horns, claws and whiskers, tail and everything—that he's much more satisfactory to swear by than any other space-god I know of."

"But why do men have to swear at all, Kim?" she queried, curiously. "It's so silly."

"For the same reason that women cry," he countered. "A man swears to keep from crying, a woman cries to keep from swearing. Both are sound psychology. Safety valves—means of blowing off excess pressure that would otherwise blow fuses or burn out tubes."

CHAPTER

3

Dei Ex Machina

IN THE LIBRARY OF THE PORT Admiral's richly comfortable home, a room as heavily guarded against all forms of intrusion as was his private office, two old but active Gray Lensmen sat and grinned at each other like the two conspirators which in fact they were. One took a squat, red bottle of fayalin* from a cabinet and filled two small glasses. The glasses clinked, rim to rim.

"Here's to love!" Haynes gave the toast.

"Ain't it grand!" Surgeon-Marshal Lacy responded.

"Down the hatch!" they chanted in unison, and action followed word.

"You aren't asking if everything stayed on the beam." This from Lacy.

"No need—I had a spy-ray on the whole performance."

"You would—you're the type. However, I would have, too, if I had a panel full of them in *my* office. . . . Well, say it, you old space-hellion!" Lacy grinned again, albeit a trifle wryly.

"Nothing to say, saw-bones. You did a grand job, and you've got nothing to blow a jet about."

---

* A stimulating, although non-intoxicating beverage prepared from the fruit of a Crevenian shrub, *Fayaloclastus Augustifolius Barnstead;* much in favor as a ceremonial drink among those who can afford it. E.E.S.

"No? How would you like to have a red-headed spitfire who's scarcely dry behind the ears yet tell you to your teeth that you've got softening of the brain? That you had the mental capacity of a gnat, the intellect of a Zabriskan fontema? And to have to take it, without even heaving the insubordinate young jade into the can for about twenty-five well-earned black spots?"

"Oh, come, now, you're just blasting. It wasn't that bad!"

"Perhaps not—quite—but it was bad enough."

"She'll grow up, some day, and realize that you were foxing her six ways from the origin."

"Probably. . . . In the meantime, it's all part of the bigger job. . . . Thank God I'm not young any more. They suffer so."

"Check. *How* they suffer!"

"But you saw the ending and I didn't. How did it turn out?" Lacy asked.

"Partly good, partly bad." Haynes slowly poured two more drinks and thoughtfully swirled the crimson, pungently aromatic liquid around and around in his glass before he spoke again. "Hooked—but she knows it, and I'm afraid she'll do something about it."

"She's a smart operator—I told you she was. She doesn't fox herself about anything. Hmm. . . . A bit of separation is indicated, it would seem."

"Check. Can you send out a hospital ship somewhere, so as to get rid of her for two or three weeks?"

"Can do. Three weeks be enough? We can't send him anywhere, you know."

"Plenty—he'll be gone in two." Then, as Lacy glanced at him questioningly, Haynes continued: "Ready for a shock? He's going to Lundmark's Nebula."

"But he *can't!* That would take years! Nobody has ever got back from there yet, and there's this new job of his. Besides, this separation is only supposed to last until you can spare him for a while!"

"If it takes very long he's coming back. The idea has

always been, you know, that intergalactic matter may be so thin—one atom per liter or so—that such a flit won't take one-tenth the time supposed. We recognize the danger—he's going well heeled."

"How well?"

"The very best."

"I hate to clog their jets this way, but it's got to be done. We'll give her a raise when I send her out—make her sector chief. Huh?"

"Did I hear any such words lately as spitfire, hussy, and jade, or did I dream them?" Haynes asked, quizzically.

"She's all of them, and more—but she's one of the best nurses and one of the finest women that ever lived, too!"

"QX, Lacy, give her her raise. Of course she's good. If she wasn't, she wouldn't be in on this deal at all. In fact, they're about as fine a couple of youngsters as old Tellus ever produced."

"They are that. Man, *what* a pair of skeletons!"

*   *   *

And in the Nurses' Quarters a young woman with a wealth of red-bronze-auburn hair and tawny eyes was staring at her own reflection in a mirror.

"You half-wit, you ninny, you lug!" she stormed, bitterly if almost inaudibly, at that reflection. "You lame-brained moron, you red-headed, idiotic imbecile, you micro-cephalic dumb-bell, you *clunker!* Of all the men in this whole cockeyed galaxy, you *would* have to make a dive at Kimball Kinnison, the one man who thinks you're just part of the furniture. At a Gray Lensman. . . ." Her expression changed and she whispered softly, "A . . . Gray . . . Lensman. He *can't* love anybody as long as he's carrying that load. They can't let themselves be human . . . quite . . . perhaps loving *him* will be enough. . . ."

She straightened up, shrugged, and smiled; but even that pitiful travesty of a smile could not long endure.

Shortly it was buried in waves of pain and the girl threw herself down upon her bed.

"Oh Kim, Kim!" she sobbed. "I wish . . . why can't you . . . Oh, why did I ever have to be born!"

*   *   *

Three weeks later, far out in space, Kimball Kinnison was thinking thoughts entirely foreign to his usual pattern. He was in his bunk, smoking dreamily, staring unseeing at the metallic ceiling. He was not thinking of Boskone.

When he had thought at Mac, back there at that dance, he had, for the first time in his life, failed to narrow down his beam to the exact thought being sent. Why? The explanation he had given the girl was totally inadequate. For that matter, why had he been so glad to see her there? And why, at every odd moment, did visions of her keep coming into his mind—her form and features, her eyes, her lips, her startling hair? . . . She was beautiful, of course, but not nearly such a seven-sector callout as that thionite dream he had met on Aldebaran II—and his only thought of *her* was an occasional faint regret that he hadn't half-wrung her lovely neck . . . why, she wasn't really as good-looking as, and didn't have half the *je ne sais quoi* of, that blonde heiress—what was her name?—oh, yes, Forrester. . . .

There was only one answer, and it jarred him to the core—he would not admit it, even to himself. He *couldn't* love anybody—it just simply was not in the cards. He had a job to do. The Patrol had spent a million credits making a Lensman out of him, and it was up to him to give them some kind of a run for their money. No Lensman had any business with a wife, especially a Gray Lensman. He couldn't sit down anywhere, and she couldn't flit with him. Besides, nine out of every ten Gray Lensmen got killed before they finished their jobs, and the one that did happen to live long enough to retire to a desk was almost always half machinery and artificial parts. . . .

No, not in seven thousand years. No woman deserved

to have her life made into such a hell on earth as that would be—years of agony, of heart-breaking suspense, climaxed by untimely widowhood; or, at best, the wasting of the richest part of her life upon a husband who was half steel, rubber, and phenoline plastic. Red in particular was much too splendid a person to be let in for anything like that. . . .

But hold on—jet back! What made him think he rated any such girl? That there was even a possibility—especially in view of the way he had behaved while under her care in Base Hospital—that she would ever feel like being anything more to him than a strictly impersonal nurse? Probably not—he had Klono's own gadolinium guts to think that she would marry *him*, under any conditions, even if he made a full-power dive at her. . . .

Just the same, she might. Look at what women did fall in love with, sometimes. So he'd never make any kind of a dive at her; no, not even a pass. She was too sweet, too fine, too vital a woman to be tied to any space-louse; she deserved happiness, not heartbreak. She deserved the best there was in life, not the worst; the whole love of a whole man for a whole lifetime, not the fractions which were all that he could offer any woman. As long as he could think a straight thought he wouldn't make any motions toward spoiling her life. In fact, he hadn't better see Reddy again. He wouldn't go near any planet she was on, and if he saw her out in space he'd go somewhere else at a hundred parsecs an hour.

With a bitter imprecation Kinnison sprang out of his bunk, hurled his half-smoked cigarette at an ash-tray, and strode toward the control-room.

*   *   *

The ship he rode was of the Patrol's best. Superbly powered, for flight, defense, and offense, she was withal a complete space-laboratory and observatory; and her personnel, over and above her regular crew, was as varied as her equipment. She carried ten Lensmen, a circumstance unique in the annals of space, even for such trouble-shooting battle-wagon as the *Dauntless* was; and a scientific staff which was practically a cross-section of the Tree of Knowledge. She carried Lieutenant Peter vanBuskirk and his company of Valerian wildcats; Worsel of Velantia and three score of his reptilian kinsmen; Tregonsee, the blocky Rigellian Lensman, and a dozen or so of his fellows; Master Technician LaVerne Thordyke and his crew. She carried three Master Pilots, Prime Base's best—Henderson, Schermerhorn and Watson.

The *Dauntless* was an immense vessel. She had to be, in order to carry, in addition to the men and the things requisitioned by Kinnison, the personnel and the equipment which Port Admiral Haynes had insisted upon sending with him.

"But great Klono, Chief, think of what a hole you're making in Prime Base if we don't get back!" Kinnison had protested.

"You're coming back, Kinnison," the Port Admiral had replied, gravely. "That is why I am sending these men and this stuff along—to be as sure as I possibly can that you *do* come back."

Now they were out in inter-galactic space, and the Gray Lensman, closing his eyes, sent his sense of perception out beyond the confining iron walls and let it roam the void. This was better than a visiplate; with no material barriers or limitations he was feasting upon a spectacle scarcely to be pictured in the most untrammeled imaginings of man.

There were no planets, no suns, no stars; no meteorites, no particles of cosmic debris. All nearby space was empty, with an indescribable perfection of emptiness at the very thought of which the mind quailed in incomprehending horror. And, accentuating that emptiness, at such mind-searing distances as to be dwarfed into buttons, and yet, because of their intrinsic massiveness, starkly apparent in their three-dimensional relationships, there hung poised and motionlessly stately the component galaxies of a Universe.

Behind the flying vessel the First Galaxy was a tiny, brightly-shining lens, so far away that such minutiæ as individual solar systems were invisible; so distant that even the gigantic masses of its accompanying globular star-clusters were merged indistinguishably into its sharply lenticular shape. In front of her, to right and to left of her, above and beneath her were other galaxies, never explored by man or by any other beings subscribing to the code of Galactic Civilization. Some, edge on, were thin, wafer-like. Others appeared as full disks, showing faintly or boldly the prodigious, mathematically inexplicable spiral arms by virtue of whose obscure functioning they had come into being. Between these two extremes there was every possible variant in angular dispacement.

Utterly incomprehensible although the speed of the spaceflyer was, yet those galaxies remained relatively motionless, hour after hour. What distances! What magnificence! What grandeur! What awful, what poignantly solemn calm!

Despite the fact that Kinnison had gone out there expecting to behold that very scene, he felt awed to insignificance by the overwhelming, the cosmic immensity of the spectacle. What business had he, a sub-electronic midge from an ultra-microscopic planet, venturing out into macro-cosmic space, a demesne comprehensible only to the omniscient and omnipotent Creator?

He got up, shaking off the futile mood. This wouldn't get him to the first check-station, and he had a job to do. And after all, wasn't man as big as space? Could he have come out here, otherwise? He was. Yes, man was bigger even than space. Man, by his very envisionment of macro-cosmic space, had already mastered it.

Besides, the Boskonians, whoever they might be, had certainly mastered it; he was now certain that they were operating upon an inter-galactic scale. Even after leaving Tellus he had hoped and had really expected that his line would lead to a stronghold in some star-cluster belonging to his own galaxy, so distant from it or perhaps so small as to have escaped the notice of the chart-makers; but such was not the case. No possible error in either the determination or the following of that line placed it anywhere near any such cluster. It led straight to and only to Lundmark's

Nebula; and that galaxy was, therefore, his present destination.

Man was certainly as good as the pirates; probably better, on the basis of past performance. Of all the races of the galaxy, man had always taken the initiative, had always been the leader and commander. And, with the exception of the Arisians, man had the best brain in the galaxy.

The thought of that eminently philosophical race gave Kinnison pause. His Arisian sponsor had told him that by virtue of the Lens the Patrol should be able to make Civilization secure throughout the galaxy. Just what did that mean—that it could not go outside? Or did even the Arisians suspect that Boskonia was in fact inter-galactic? Probably. Mentor had said that, given any one definite fact, a really competent mind could envisage the entire Universe; even though had added carefully that his own mind was not a really competent one.

But this, too, was idle speculation, and it was time to receive and to correlate some more reports. Therefore, one by one, he got in touch with scientists and observers.

The density of matter in space, which had been lessening steadily, was now approximately constant at one atom per four hundred cubic centimeters. Their speed was therefore about a hundred thousand parsecs per hour; and, even allowing for the slowing up at both ends due to the density of the medium, the trip should not take over ten days.

The power situation, which had been his gravest care, since it was almost the only factor not amenable to theoretical solution, was even better than anyone had dared hope; the cosmic energy available in space had actually been increasing as the matter content decreased—a fact which seemed to bear out the contention that energy was continually being converted into matter in such regions. It was taking much less excitation of the intake screens to produce a given flow of power than any figure ever observed in the denser media within the galaxy.

Thus, the atomic motors which served as exciters had a maximum power of four hundred pounds an hour; that is, each exciter could transform that amount of matter into pure energy and employ the output usefully in energizing the intake screen to which it was connected. Each screen, operating normally on a hundred thousand to one ratio, would then furnish its receptor on the ship with energy equivalent to the annihilation of four million pounds per hour of material substance. Out there, however, it was being observed that the intake-exciter ratio, instead of being less than a hundred thousand to one, was actually almost a million to one.

It would serve no useful purpose here to go further into the details of any more of the reports, or to dwell at any great length upon the remainder of the journey to the Second Galaxy. Suffice it to say that Kinnison and his highly-trained crew observed, classified, recorded, and conferred; and that they approached their destination with every possible precaution. Detectors were full out, observers were at every plate, the ship itself was as immune to detection as Hotchkiss' nullifiers could make it.

Up to the Second Galaxy the *Dauntless* flashed, and into it. Was this Island Universe essentially like the First Galaxy as to planets and peoples? If so, had they been won over or wiped out by the horrid culture of Boskonia or was the struggle still going on?

"If we assume, as we must, that the line we followed was the trace of Boskone's beam," argued the sagacious Worsel, "the probability is very great that the enemy is in virtual control of this entire galaxy. Otherwise—if they were in a minority or were struggling seriously for dominion —they could neither have spared the forces which invaded our galaxy, nor would they have been in condition to rebuild their vessels as they did to match the new armaments developed by the Patrol."

"Very probably true," agreed Kinnison, and that was the concensus of opinion. "Therefore we want to do our scouting very quietly. But in some ways that makes it all the better. If they're in control, they won't be unduly suspicious."

And thus it proved. A planet-bearing sun was soon located, and while the *Dauntless* was still light-years distant from it, several ships were detected. At least, the Boskonians were not using nullifiers!

Spy-rays were sent out. Tregonsee the Rigellian Lensman exerted to the full his powers of perception, and Kinnison hurled downward to the planet's surface a mental viewpoint and communications center. That the planet was Boskonian was soon learned, but that was all. It was scarcely fortified: no trace could he find of a beam communicating with Boskone.

Solar system after solar system was found and studied, with like result. But finally, out in space, one of the screens showed activity; a beam was in operation between a vessel then upon the plates and some other station. Kinnison tapped it quickly; and, while observers were determining its direction, hardness, and power, a thought flowed smoothly into the Lensman's brain.

". . . proceed at once to relieve vessel P4K730. Eichlan, speaking for Boskone, ending message."

"Follow that ship, Hen!" Kinnison directed, crisply. "Not too close, but don't lose him!" He then relayed to the others the orders which had been intercepted.

"The same formula, huh?" VanBuskirk roared, and "Just another lieutenant, that sounds like, not Boskone himself." Thorndyke added.

"Perhaps so, perhaps not." The Gray Lensman was merely thoughtful. "It doesn't prove a thing except that Helmuth was not Boskone, which was already fairly certain. If we can prove that there is such a being as Boskone, and that he isn't in this galaxy . . . well, in that case, we'll go somewhere else," he concluded, with grim finality.

The chase was comparatively short, leading toward a yellowish star around which swung eight average-sized planets. Toward one of these flew the unsuspecting pirate, followed by the Patrol vessel, and it soon became apparent that there was a battle going on. One spot upon the planet's surface, either a city or a tremendous military base, was domed over by a screen which was one blinding glare of radiance. And for miles in every direction ships of space were waging spectacularly devastating warfare.

Kinnison shot a thought down into the fortress, and with the least possible introduction or preamble, got into touch with one of its high officers. He was not surprised to learn that those people were more or less human in appearance, since the planet was quite similar to Tellus in age, climate, atmosphere, and mass.

"Yes, we are fighting Boskonia," the answering thought came coldly clear. "We need help, and badly. Can you . . .?"

"We're detected!" Kinnison's attention was seized by a yell from the board. "They're all coming at us at once!"

Whether the scientists of Boskone developed the detector-nullifier before or after Helmuth's failure to deduce the Lensman's use of such an instrument is a nice question, and one upon which a great deal has been said. While interesting, the point is really immaterial here; the facts remaining the same—that the pirates not only had it at the time of the Patrol's first visit to the Second Galaxy, but had used it to such good advantage that the denizens of that recalcitrant planet had been forced, in sheer desperation of self-preservation, to work out a scrambler for that nullification and to surround their world with its radiations. They could not restore perfect detection, but the condition for complete nullification was so critical that it was a comparatively simple matter to upset it sufficiently so that an image of a sort was revealed. And, at that close range, any sort of an image was enough.

The *Dauntless,* approaching the planet, entered the zone of scrambling and stood revealed plainly enough upon the plates of the enemy vessels. They attacked instantly and viciously; within a second after the lookout had shouted his warning the outer screens of the Patrol ship were blazing incandescent under the furious assaults of a dozen Boskonian beams.

F OR A MOMENT ALL EYES WERE fixed apprehensively upon meters and recorders, but there was no immediate cause for alarm. The builders of the *Dauntless* had builded well; her outer screen, the lightest of her series of four, was carrying the attackers' load with no sign of distress.

"Strap down, everybody," the expedition's commander ordered then. "Inert her, Hen. Match velocity with that base," and as Master Pilot Henry Henderson cut his Bergenholm the vessel lurched wildly aside as its intrinsic velocity was restored.

Henderson's fingers swept over his board as rapidly and as surely as those of an organist over the banked keys of his console; producing, not chords and arpeggios of harmony, but roaring blasts of precisely-controlled power. Each key-like switch controlled one jet. Lightly and fleetingly touched, it produced a gentle urge; at sharp, full contact it yielded a mighty, solid shove; depressed still farther, so as to lock into any one of a dozen notches, it brought into being a torrent of propulsive force of any desired magnitude, which ceased only when its key-release was touched.

And Henderson was a virtuoso. Smoothly, effortlessly, but in a space of seconds the great vessel rolled over, spiralled, and swung until her landing jets were in line and exerting five gravities of thrust. Then, equally smoothly, almost imperceptibly, the line of force was varied until the flame-enshrouded dome was stationary below them. Nobody, not even the two other Master Pilots, and least of all Henderson himself, paid any attention to the polished perfection, the consummate artistry, of the performance. That was his job. He was a Master Pilot, and one of the hallmarks of his rating was the habit of making difficult maneuvers look easy.

"Take 'em now, Chief? Can't we, huh?" Chatway, the Chief Firing Officer, did not say those words. He did not need to. The attitude and posture of the C.F.O. and his subordinates made the thought tensely plain.

"Not yet, Chatty," the Lensman answered the unsent thought. "We'll have to wait until they englobe us, so we can get 'em all. It's got to be all or none—if even one of of them gets away or even has time to analyze and report on the stuff we're going to use it'll be just too bad."

He then got in touch with the officer within the beleagured base and renewed the conversation at the point at which it had been broken off.

"We can help you, I think; but to do so effectively we must have clear ether. Will you please order your ships away, out of even extreme range?"

"For how long? They can do us irreparable damage in one rotation of the planet."

"One-twentieth of that time, at most—if we can't do it in that time we can't do it at all. Nor will they direct many beams at you, if any. They'll be working on us."

Then, as the defending ships darted away, Kinnison turned to his C.F.O.

"QX, Chatty. Open up with your secondaries. Fire at will!"

Then from projectors of a power theretofore carried only by maulers there raved out against the nearest Boskonian vessels beams of a vehemence compared to which the enemies' own seemed weak, futile. And those were the secondaries!

As has been intimated, the *Dauntless* was an unusual ship. She was enormous. She was bigger even than a mauler in actual bulk and mass; and from needle-beaked prow to jet-studded stern she was literally packed with power— power for any emergency conceivable to the fertile minds of Port Admiral Haynes and his staff of designers and engineers. Instead of two, or at most three intake-screen exciters, she had two hundred. Her bus-bars, instead of being the conventional rectangular coppers, of a few square inches cross-sectional area, were laminated members built up of co-axial tubing of pure silver to a diameter of over a yard —multiple and parallel conductors, each of whose current-carrying capacity was to be measured only in millions of amperes. And everything else aboard that mighty engine of destruction was upon the same Gargantuan scale.

Titanic though those thrusts were, not a pirate ship was seriously hurt. Outer screans went down, and more than a few of the second lines of defense also failed. But that was the Patrolmen's strategy; to let the enemy know that they had weapons of offense somewhat superior to their own, but not quite powerful enough to be a real menace.

In minutes, therefore, the Boskonians rushed up and proceeded to englobe the newcomer; supposing, of course, that she was a product of the world below, that she was manned by the race who had so long and so successfully fought off Boskonian encroachment.

They attacked, and under the concentrated fury of their beams the outer screen of the Patrol ship began to fail. Higher and higher into the spectrum it radiated, blinding white . . . blue . . . an intolerable violet glare; then, patchily, through the invisible ultra-violet and into the black of extinction. The second screen resisted longer and more subbornly, but finally it also went down; the third automatically taking up the burden of defense. Simultaneously the power of the *Dauntless'* projectors weakened, as though she were shifting her power from offense to defense in order to stiffen her third, and supposedly her last, shielding screen.

"Pretty soon, now, Chatway," Kinnison observed. "Just as soon as they can report that they've got us in a bad way; that it's just a matter of time until they blow us out of the ether. Better report now—I'll put you on the spool."

"We are equipped to energize simultaneously eight of the new, replaceable-unit primary projectors," the C.F.O. stated, crisply. "There are twenty-one vessels englobing us, and no others within detection. With a discharge period of point six zero and a switching interval of point zero nine, the entire action should occupy one point nine eight seconds."

"Chief Communications Officer Nelson on the spool. Can the last surviving ship of the enemy report enough in two seconds to do us material harm?"

"In my opinion it can not, sir," Nelson reported, formally. "The Communications Officer is neither an observer nor a technician; he merely transmits whatever material is given him by other officers for transmission. If he is already working a beam to his base at the moment of our first blast he might be able to report the destruction of vessels, but he could not be specific as to the nature of the agent used. Such a report could do no harm, as the fact of the destruction of the vessels will in any event become apparent shortly. Since we are apparently being overcome easily, however, and this is a routine action, the probability is that this detachment is not in direct communication with Base at any given moment. If not, he could not establish working control in two seconds."

"Kinnison now reporting. Having determined to the best of my ability that engaging the enemy at this time will not enable them to send Boskone any information regarding our primary armament, I now give the word to . . . FIRE!"

The underlying principle of the destructive beam produced by overloading a regulation projector had, it is true, been discovered by a Boskonian technician. Insofar as Boskonia was concerned, however, the secret had died with its inventor; since the pirates had at that time no headquarters in the First Galaxy. And the Patrol had had months of time in which to perfect it, for that work was begun before the last of Helmuth's guardian fortresses had been destroyed.

The projector was not now fatal to its crew, since they were protected from the lethal back-radiation, not only by shields of force, but also by foot after impenetrable foot of lead, osmium, carbon, cadmium, and paraffin. The re-fractories were of neo-carballoy, backed and permeated by M K R fields; the radiators were constructed of the most ultimately resistant materials known to the science of the age. But even so the unit had a useful life of but little over half a second, so frightful was the overload at which it was used. Like a rifle cartridge, it was good for only one shot. Then it was thrown away, to be replaced by a new unit.

Those problems were relatively simple of solution. Switching those enormous energies was the great stumbling block. The old Kimmerling block-dispersion circuit-breaker was prone to arc-over under loads much in excess of a hundred billion KVA, hence could not even be considered in this new application. However, the Patrol force finally suc-ceeded in working out a combination of the immersed-antenna and the semipermeable-condenser types, which they called the Thorndyke heavy-duty switch. It was cumbersome, of course—any device to interrupt voltages and amperages of the really astronomical magnitudes in question could not at that time be small—but it was positive, fast-acting, and reliable.

At Kinnison's word of command eight of those inde-scribable primary beams lashed out; stilettoes of irresistibly pentrant energy which not even a Q-type helix could with-stand. Through screens, through wall-shields, and through metal they hurtled in a space of time almost too brief to be measured. Then, before each beam expired, it was swung a a little, so that the victim was literally split apart or carved into sections. Performance exceeded by far that of the hastily-improvised weapon which had so easily destroyed the heavy cruisers of the Patrol; in fact, it checked almost exactly with the theoretical figure of the designers.

As the first eight beams winked out eight more came into being, then five more; and meanwhile the mighty secondaries were sweeping the heavens with full-aperture cones of destruction. Metal meant no more to those rays than did organic material; everything solid or liquid whiffed into vapor and disappeared. The *Dauntless* lay alone in the sky of that new world.

"Marvelous—wonderful!" the thought beat into Kinnison's brain as soon as he re-established rapport with the being so far below. "We have recalled our ships. Will you please come down to our space-port at once, so that we can put into execution a plan which has been long in preparation?"

"As soon as your ships are down," the Tellurian acquiesced. "Not sooner, as your landing conventions are doubtless very unlike our own and we do not wish to cause disaster. Give me the word when your field is entirely clear."

That word came soon and Kinnison nodded to the pilots. Once more inertialess the *Dauntless* shot downward, deep into atmosphere, before her inertia was restored. Rematching velocity this time was a simple matter, and upon the towering, powerfully resilient pillars of her landing-jets the inconceivable mass of the Tellurian ship of war settled toward the ground, as lightly seeming as a wafted thistledown.

"Their cradles wouldn't fit us, of course, even if they were big enough—which they aren't, by half," Schermerhorn commented, "Where do they want us to put her?"

" 'Anywhere,' they say," the Lensman answered, "but we don't want to take that too literally—without a solid dock she'll make an awful hole, wherever we set her down. Won't hurt her any. She's designed for it—we couldn't expect to find cradles to fit her anywhere except on Tellus. I'd say to lay her down on her belly over there in that corner, out of the way; as close to that big hangar as you can work without blasting it out with your jets."

As Kinnison had intimated, the lightness of the vessel was indeed only seeming. Superbly and effortlessly the big boat seeped downward into the designated corner; but when she touched the pavement she did not stop. Still easily and without jar or jolt she settled—a full twenty feet into the concrete, re-enforcing steel, and hard-packed earth of the field before she came to a halt.

"What a monster! Who are they? Where could they have come from? . . ." Kinnison caught a confusion of startled thoughts as the real size and mass of the visitor became apparent to the natives. Then again came the clear thought of the officer.

"We would like very much to have you and as many as possible of your companions come to confer with us as soon as you have tested our atmosphere. Come in space-suits if you must."

The air was tested and found suitable. True, it did not match exactly that of Tellus, or Rigel IV, or Velantia; but then, neither did that of the *Dauntless,* since that gaseous mixture was a compromise one, and mostly artificial to boot.

"Worsel, Tregonsee, and I will go to this conference," Kinnison decided. "The rest of you sit tight. I don't need to tell you to keep on your toes, that anything is apt to happen, anywhere, without warning. Keep your detectors full out and keep your noses clean—be ready, like the good little Endeavorers you are, 'to do with your might what your hands find to do.' Come on, fellows," and the three Lensmen strode, wriggled, and waddled across the field, to and into a spacious room of the Administration Building.

"Strangers, or, I should say friends, I introduce you to Wise, our President," Kinnison's acquaintance said, clearly enough, although it was plain to all three Lensmen that he was shocked at the sight of the Earthman's companions.

"I am informed that you understand our language . . ." the President began, doubtfully.

He too was staring at Tregonsee and Worsel. He had been told that Kinnison, and therefore, supposedly the rest of the visitors, were beings fashioned more or less after his own pattern. But these two creatures!

For they were not even remotely human in form. Tregonsee, the Rigellian, with his leathery, multi-appendaged, oildrum-like body, his immobile dome of a head and his four blocky pillars of legs must at first sight have appeared fantastic indeed. And Worsel, the Velantian, was infinitely worse. He was repulsive, a thing materialized from sheerest nightmare—a leather-winged, crocodile-headed, crooked-armed, thirty-foot-long, pythonish, reptilian monstrosity!

But the President of Medon saw at once that which the three outlanders had in common. The Lenses, each glowingly aflame with its own innate pseudo-vitality—Kinnison's clamped to his brawny wrist by a bad of metallic alloy; Tregonsee's embedded in the glossy black flesh of one mighty, sinuous arm; Worsel's apparently driven deep and with cruel force into the horny, scaly hide squarely in the middle of his forehead, between two of his weirdly stalked, repulsively extensible eyes.

"It is not your language we understand, but your thoughts, by virtue of these our Lenses which you have already noticed." The President gasped as Kinnison bulleted the information into his mind. "Go ahead . . . Just a minute!" as an unmistakeable sensation swept through his being. "We've gone *free;* the whole planet, I perceive. In that respect, at least, you are in advance of us. As far as I know, no scientist of any of our races has even thought of a Bergenholm big enough to free a world."

"It was long in the designing; many years in the building of its units," Wise replied. "We are leaving this sun in an attempt to escape from our enemy and yours, Boskone. It is our only chance of survival. The means have long been ready, but the opportunity which you have just made for us is the first that we have had. This is the first time in many, many years that not a single Boskonian vessel is in position to observe our flight."

"Where are you going? Surely the Boskonians will be able to find you if they wish."

"That is possible, but we must run that risk. We must have a respite or perish; after a long lifetime of continuous warfare our resources are at the point of exhaustion. There is a part of this galaxy in which there are very few planets, and of those few none are inhabited or habitable. Since nothing is to be gained, ships seldom or never go there. If we can reach that region undetected, the probability is that we shall be unmolested long enough to recuperate."

Kinnison exchanged flashing thoughts with his two fellow Lensmen, then turned again to Wise.

"We come from a neighboring galaxy," he informed him, and pointed out to his mind just which galaxy he meant. "You are fairly close to the edge of this one. Why not move over to ours? You have no friends here, since you think that yours may be the only remaining independent planet. We can assure you of friendship. We can also give you some hope of peace—or at least semi-peace—in the near future, for we are driving Boskonia out of our galaxy."

"What you think of as 'semi-peace' would be tranquility incarnate to us," the old man replied with feeling. "We have in fact considered long that very move. We decided against it for two reasons: first, because we knew nothing about conditions there, and hence might be going from bad to worse; and second and more important, because of lack of reliable data upon the density of matter in inter-galactic space. Lacking that, we could not estimate the time necessary for the journey, and we could have no assurance that our sources of power, great as they are, would be sufficient to make up the heat lost by radiation."

"We have already given you an idea of conditions and we can give you the data you lack."

They did so, and for a matter of minutes the Medonians conferred. Meanwhile Kinnison went on a mental expedition to one of the power-plants. He expected to see super-colossal engines; bus-bars ten feet thick, perhaps cooled in liquid helium; and other things in proportion. But what he actually saw made him gasp for breath and call Tregonsee's attention. The Rigellian sent out his sense of perception with Kinnison's, and he also was almost stunned.

"What's the answer, Trig?" the Earthman asked, finally. "This is more down your alley than mine. That motor's about the size of my foot, and if it isn't eating a thousand pounds an hour I'm Klono's maiden aunt. And the whole output is going out on two wires no bigger than number four, jacketed together like ordinary parallel pair. Perfect insulator? If so, how about switching?"

"That must be it, a substance of practically infinite resistance," the Rigellian replied, absently, studying intently the peculiar mechanisms. "Must have a better conductor than silver, too, unless they can handle voltages of ten to the fifteenth or so, and don't see how they could break such potentials . . . Guess they don't use switches—don't see any —must shut down, the prime sources . . . No, there it is— so small that I overlooked it completely. In that little box there. Sort of a jam-plate type; a thin sheet of insulation with a knife on the leading edge, working in a slot to cut the two conductors apart—kills the arc by jamming into the tight slot at the end of the box. The conductors must fuse together at each make and burn away a little at each break, that's why they have renewable tips. Kim, they've really got something! I certainly am going to stay here and do some studying."

"Yes, and we'll have to rebuild the *Dauntless* . . ."

The two Lensmen were called away from their study by Worsel—the Medonians had decided to accept the invitation to move to the First Galaxy. Orders were given, the course was changed and the planet, now a veritable spaceship, shot away in the new direction.

"Not as many legs as a speedster, of course, but at that, she's no slouch—we're making plenty of lights," Kinnison commented, then turned to the president. "It seems rather presumptive for us to call you simply 'Wise,' especially as I gather that that is not your name . . ."

"That is what I am called, and that is what you are to call me," the oldster replied. "We of Medon do not have names. Each has a number; or, rather, a symbol composed of numbers and letters of our alphabet—a symbol which gives his full classification. Since these things are too clumsy for regular use, however, each of us is given a nickname, usually an adjective, which is supposed to be more less descriptive. You of Earth we could not give a complete symbol; your two companions we could not give any at all. However, you may be interested in knowing that you three have already been named?"

"Very much so."

"You are to be called 'Keen.' He of Rigel IV is 'Strong,' and he of Velantia is 'Agile'."

"Quite complimentary to me, but . . ."

"Not bad at all, I'd say," Tregonsee broke in. "But hadn't we better be getting on with more serious business?"

"We should indeed," Wise agreed. "We have much to discuss with you; particularly the weapon you used."

"Could you get an analysis of it?" Kinnison asked, sharply.

"No. No one beam was in operation long enough. However, a study of the recorded data, particularly the figures for intensity—figures so high as to be almost unbelievable—lead us to believe that the beam is the result of an enormous overload upon a projector otherwise of more or less conventional type. Some of us have wondered why we did not think of the idea ourselves . . ."

"So did we, when it was used on us," Kinnison grinned and went on to explain the origin of the primary. "We will give you the formulæ and also the working hook-up—including the protective devices, because they're mighty dangerous without plenty of force-backing—of the primaries, in exchange for some lessons in power-plant design."

"Such an exchange of knowledge would be helpful indeed," Wise agreed.

"The Boskonians know nothing whatever of this beam, and we do not want them to learn of it," Kinnison cautioned. "Therefore I have two suggestions to make.

"First, that you try everything else before you use this primary beam. Second, that you don't use it even then unless you can wipe out, as nearly simultaneously as we did out there, every Boskonian who may be able to report back to his base as to what really happened. Fair enough?"

"Eminently so. We agree without reservation—it is to our interest as much as yours that such a secret be kept from Boskone."

"QX. Fellows, let's go back to the ship for a couple of minutes." Then, aboard the *Dauntless:* "Tregonsee, you and your crew want to stay with the planet, to show the Medonians what to do and to help them along generally, as well as to learn about their power system. Thordyke, you and your gang, and probably Lensman Hotchkiss, had better study these things too—you'll know what you want as soon as they show you the hook-up. Worsel, I'd like to have you stay with the ship. You're in command of her until further orders. Keep her here for say a week or ten days, until the planet is well out of the galaxy. Then, if Hotchkiss and Thorndyke haven't got all the dope they want, leave them here to ride back with Tregonsee on the planet and drill the *Dauntless* for Tellus. Keep yourself more or less disengaged for a while, and sort of keep tuned to me. I may not need an ultra-long-range communicator, but you never can tell."

"Why such comprehensive orders, Kim?" asked Hotchkiss. "Who ever heard of a commander abandoning his expedition? Aren't you sticking around?"

"Nope—got to do a flit. Think maybe I'm getting an idea. Break out my speedster, will you, Allerdyce?" and the Gray Lensman was gone.

Dessa Desplaines, Zwilnik

KINNISON'S SPEEDSTER SHOT
away and made an undetectable, uneventful voyage back to
Prime Base.

"Why the foliage?" the Port Admiral asked, almost at
sight, for the Gray Lensman was wearing a more-than-half-
grown beard.

"I may need to be Chester Q. Fordyce for a while. If
I don't, I can shave it off quick. If I do, a real beard is a
lot better than an imitation," and he plunged into his subject.

"Very fine work, son, very fine indeed," Haynes con-
gratulated the younger man at the conclusion of his report.
"We shall begin at once, and be ready to rush things through
when the technicians bring back the necessary data from
Medon. But there's one more thing I want to ask you. How
come you placed those spotting-screens so exactly? The beam
practically dead-centered them. You claimed it was surmise
and suspicion before it happened, but you must have had a
much firmer foundation than any kind of a mere hunch.
What was it?"

"Deduction, based upon an unproved, but logical, cos-
mogonic theory—but you probably know more about that
stuff than I do."

"Highly improbable. I read just a smattering now and

then of the doings of the astronomers and astrophysicists. I didn't know that that was one of your specialties, either."

"It isn't, but I had to do a little cramming. We'll have to go back quite a while to make it clear. You know, of course, that a long time ago, before even inter-planetary ships were developed, the belief was general that not more than about four planetary solar systems could be in existence at any one time in the whole galaxy?"

"Yes, in my youth I was exposed to Wellington's Theory. The theory itself is still good, isn't it?"

"Eminently so—every other theory was wrecked by the hard facts of angular momentum and filament energies. But you know already what I'm going to say."

"No, just let's say that a bit of light is beginning to dawn. Go ahead."

"QX. Well, when it was discovered that there were millions of times as many planets in the galaxy as could be accounted for by a Wellington Incident occurring once in two times ten to the tenth years or so, some way had to be figured out to increase, millionfold, the number of such occurrences. Manifestly, the random motion of the stars within the galaxy could not account for it. Neither could the vibration or oscillation of the globular clusters through the galaxy. The meeting of two galaxies—the passage of them completely through each other, edgewise—would account for it very nicely. It would also account for the fact that the solar systems on one side of the galaxy tend to be somewhat older than the ones on the opposite side. Question, find the galaxy. It was van der Schleiss, I believe, who found it. Lundmark's Nebula. It is edge on to us, with a receding velocity of thirty one hundred and sixteen kilometers per second—the exact velocity which, corrected for gravitational decrement, will put Lundmark's Nebula right here at the time when, according to our best geophysicists and geochemists, old Earth was being born. If that theory was correct, Lundmark's Nebula should also be full of planets. Four expeditions went out to check the theory, and none of them came back. We know why, now—Boskone got them. We got back, because of you, and only you."

"Holy Klono!" the old man breathed, paying no attention to the tribute. "It checks—*how* it checks!

"To nineteen decimals."

"But still it doesn't explain why you set your traps on that line."

"Sure it does. How many galaxies are there in the Universe, do you suppose, that are full of planets?"

"Why, all of them, I suppose—or no, not so many perhaps . . . I don't know—I don't remember having read anything on that question."

"No, and you probably won't. Only loose-screwed space detectives, like me, and crackpot science-fiction writers, like Wacky Williamson, have noodles vacuous enough to harbor such thin ideas. But, according to our admittedly highly tenuous reasoning, there are only two such galaxies —Lundmark's nebula and ours."

"Huh? Why?" demanded Haynes.

"Because galactic coalescences don't occur much, if any, oftener than Wellingtons within a galaxy do," Kinnison asserted. "True, they are closer together in space, relative to their actual linear dimensions, than are stars; but on the other hand their relative motions are slower—that is, a star will traverse the average interstellar distance much quicker than a galaxy will the inter-galactic one—so that the whole thing evens up. As nearly as Wacky and I could figure it, two galaxies will collide deeply enough to produce a significant number of planetary solar systems on an average of once in just about one point eight times ten to the tenth years. Pick up your slide rule and check me on it, if you like."

"I'll take your word for it," the old Lensman murmured, absently. "But any galaxy probably has at least a couple of solar systems all the time—but I see your point. The probability is overwhelmingly great that Boskone would be in a galaxy having hundreds of millions of planets rather than in one having only a dozen or less inhabitable worlds.

But at that, they *could* all have lots of planets. Suppose that our wilder thinkers are right, that galaxies are grouped into Universes, which are spaced, roughly, about the same as the galaxies are. Two of them *could* collide, couldn't they?"

"They could, but you're getting 'way out of my range now. At this point the detective withdraws, leaving a clear field for you and the science-fiction imaginationeer."

"Well, finish the thought—that I'm wackier even than he is!" Both men laughed, and the Port Admiral went on: "It's a fascinating speculation . . . it does no harm to let the fancy roam at times . . . but at that, there are things of much greater importance. You think, then, that the thionite ring enters into this matrix?"

"Bound to. Everything ties in. Most of the intelligent races of this galaxy are oxygen-breathers, with warm, red blood: the only kind of physiques which thionite affects. The more of us who get the thionite habit the better for Boskone. It explains why we have never got to the first check-station in getting any of the real higher-ups in the thionite game; instead of being an ordinary criminal ring they've got all the brains and all the resources of Boskonia back of them. But if they're that big . . . and as good as we know they are . . . I wonder why . . ." Kinnison's voice trailed off into silence; his brain raced.

"I want to ask you a question that's none of my business," the young Lensman went on almost immediately, in a voice strangely altered. "Just how long ago was it that you started losing fifth-year men just before graduation? I mean, that boys sent to Arisia to be measured for their Lenses supposedly never got there? Or at least, they never came back and no Lenses were ever received for them?"

"About ten years. Twelve, I think, to be ex . . .," Haynes broke off in the middle of the word and his eyes bored into those of the younger man. "What makes you think there were any such?"

"Deduction again, but this time I know I'm right. At least one every year. Usually two or three."

"Right, but there have always been space accidents . . .

or they were caught by the pirates . . . you think, then, that
. . . ?"

"I don't think. I *know!*" Kinnison declared "They got
to Arisia, and they died there. All I can say is, thank God
for the Arisians. We can still trust our Lenses; they are
seeing to that."

"But why didn't they tell us?" Haynes asked, per-
plexed.

"They wouldn't—that isn't their way," Kinnison stated,
flatly and with conviction. "They have given us an instru-
mentality, the Lens, by virtue of which we should be able
to do the job, and they are seeing to it that that instru-
mentality remains untarnished. We've got to learn how to
handle it, though, ourselves. We've got to fight our own
battles and bury our own dead. Now that we've smeared up
the enemy's military organization in this galaxy by wiping
out Helmuth and his headquarters, the drug syndicate seems
to be my best chance of getting a line on the real Boskone.
While you are mopping up and keeping them from establishing another war base here, I think I'd better be getting
at it, don't you?"

"Probably so—you know your own oysters best. Mind
if I ask where you're going to start in?" Haynes looked at
Kinnison quizzically as he spoke. "Have you deduced that,
too?"

The Gray Lensman returned the look in kind. "No.
Deduction couldn't take me quite that far," he replied in
the same tone. "You're going to tell me that, when you get
around to it."

"Me? Where do I come in?" the Port Admiral feigned
surprise.

"As follows. Helmuth probably had nothing to do with
the dope running, so its organization must still be intact. If
so, they would take over as much of the other branch as they
could get hold of, and hit us harder than ever. I haven't
heard of any unusual activity around here, so it must be
somewhere else. Wherever it is, you would know about it,
since you are a member of the Galactic Council; and Coun-

cillor Ellington, in charge of Narcotics, would hardly take
any very important step without conferring with you. How
near right am I?"

"On the center of the beam, all the way—your deducer
is blasting at maximum," Haynes said, in admiration. "Radelix is the worst—they're hitting it mighty hard. We sent a
full unit over there last week. Shall we recall them, or do
you want to work independently?"

"Let them go on; I'll be of more use working on my
own, I think. I did the boys over there a favor a while back
—they would cooperate anyway, of course, but it's a little
nicer to have them sort of owe it to me. We'll all be able to
play together very nicely, if the opportunity arises."

"I'm mighty glad you're taking this on. The Radeligians
are stuck, and we had no real reason for thinking that our
men could do any better. With this new angle of approach,
however, and with you working behind the scenes, the picture looks entirely different."

"I'm afraid that's unjustifiably high . . ."

"Not a bit of it, lad. Just a minute—I'll break out a
couple of beakers of fayalin . . . Luck!"

"Thanks, chief!"

"Down the hatch!" and again the Gray Lensman was
gone. To the spaceport, into his speedster, and away—
hurtling through the void at the maximum blast of the
fastest space-flyer then boasted by the Galactic Patrol.

During the long trip Kinnison exercised, thought, and
studied spool after spool of tape—the Radeligian language.
Thoughts of the red-headed nurse obtruded themselves
strongly at times, but he put them aside resolutely. He was,
he assured himself, off of women forever—all women. He
cultivated his new beard; trimming it, with the aid of a
triple mirror and four stereoscopic photographs, into something which, although neat and spruce enough, was too full
and bushy by half to be a Van Dyke. Also, he moved his Lens-
bracelet up his arm and rayed the white skin thus exposed
until his whole wrist was the same even shade of tan.

He did not drive his speedster to Radelix, for that racy

little fabrication would have been recognized anywhere for what she was; and private citizens simply did not drive ships of that type. Therefore, with every possible precaution of secrecy, he landed her in a Patrol base four solar systems away. In that base Kimball Kinnison disappeared; but the tall, shock-haired, bushy-bearded Chester Q. Fordyce —cosmopolite, man of leisure, and dilettante in science—who took the next space-liner for Radelix was not precisely the same individual who had come to that planet a few days before with that name and those unmistakeable characteristics.

Mr. Chester Q. Fordyce, then, and not Gray Lensman Kimball Kinnison, disembarked at Ardith, the world-capital of Radelix. He took up his abode at the Hotel Ardith-Splendide and proceeded, with neither too much nor too little fanfare, to be his cosmopolitan self in those circles of society in which, wherever he might find himself, he was wont to move.

As a matter of course he entertained, and was entertained by, the Tellurian Ambassador. Equally as a matter of course he attended divers and sundry functions, at which he made the acquaintance of hundreds of persons, many of them personages. That one of these should have been Lieutenant-Admiral Gerrond, Lensman in charge of the Patrol's Radeligian base, was inevitable.

It was, then, a purely routine and logical development that at a reception one evening Lensman Gerrond stopped to chat for a moment with Mr. Fordyce; and it was purely accidental that the nearest bystander was a few yards distant. Hence, Mr. Fordyce's conduct was strange enough.

"Gerrond!" he said without moving his lips and in a tone almost inaudible, the while he was proffering an Alsakanite cigarette. "Don't look at me particularly right now, and don't show surprise. Study me for the next few minutes, then put your Lens on me and tell me whether you have ever seen me before or not." Then, glancing at the watch upon his left wrist—a timepiece just about as large and as ornate as a wrist-watch could be and still remain in impeccable taste—he murmured something conventional and strolled away.

Ten minutes passed and he felt Gerrond's thought. A peculiar sensation, this, being on the receiving end of a single beam, instead of using his own Lens.

"As far as I can tell, I have never seen you before. You are certainly not one of our agents, and if you are one of Haynes' whom I have ever worked with you have done a wonderful job of disguising. I must have met you somewhere, sometime, else there would be no point to your question; but beyond the evident—and admitted—fact that you are a white Tellurian, I can't seem to place you."

"Does this help?" This question was shot through Kinnison's own Lens.

"Since I have known so few Tellurian Lensmen it tells me that you must be Kinnison, but I do not recognize you at all readily. You seem changed—older—besides, who ever heard of an Unattached Lensman doing the work of an ordinary agent?"

"I am both older and changed—partly natural and partly artificial. As for the work, it's a job that no ordinary agent can handle—it takes a lot of special equipment . . ."

"You've got *that*, indubitably! I get goose-flesh yet every time I think of that trial."

"You think I'm proof against recognition, then, as long as I don't use my Lens?" Kinnison stuck to the issue.

"Absolutely so . . . You're here, then, on thionite?" No other issue, Gerrond knew, could be grave enough to account for this man's presence. "But your wrist? I studied it. You can't have worn your Lens there for months—those Tellurian bracelets leave white streaks an inch wide."

"I tanned it with a pencil-beam. Nice job, eh? But what I want to ask you about is a little cooperation—as you supposed, I'm here to work on this drug ring."

"Surely—anything we can do. But Narcotics is handling that, not us—but you know that, as well as I do . . ." the officer broke off, puzzled.

"I know. That's why I want you—that and because

you handle the secret service. Frankly, I'm scared to death of leaks. For that reason I'm not saying anything to anyone except Lensmen, and I'm having no dealings with anyone connected with Narcotics. I have as unimpeachable an identity as Haynes could furnish. . . ."

"There's no question as to its adequacy, then," the Radeligian interposed.

"I'd like to have you pass the word around among your boys and girls that you know who I am and that I'm safe to play with. That way, if Boskone's agents spot me, it will be for an agent of Haynes's, and not for what I really am. That's the first thing. Can do?"

"Easily and gladly. Consider it done. Second?"

"To have a boat-load of good, tough marines on hand if I should call you. There are some Valerians coming over later but I may need help in the meantime. I may want to start a fight—quite possibly even a riot."

"They'll be ready, and they'll be big, tough, and hard. Anything else?"

"Not just now, except for one question. You know Countess Avondrin, the woman I was dancing with a while ago. Got any dope on her?"

"Certainly not—what do you mean?"

"Huh? Don't you know even that she's a Boskonian agent of some kind?"

"Man, you're crazy! She isn't an agent, she can't be. Why, she's the daughter of a Planetary Councillor, the wife of one of our most loyal officers."

"She would be—that's the type they like to get hold of."

"Prove it!" the Admiral snapped. "Prove it or retract it!" He almost lost his poise, almost looked toward the distant corner in which the bewhiskered gentleman was sitting so idly.

"QX. If she isn't an agent, why is she wearing a thought-screen? You haven't tested her, of course."

Of course not. The amenities, as has been said, demanded that certain reserves of privacy remain inviolate. The Tellurian went on:

"You didn't, but I did. On this job I can recognize nothing of good taste, of courtesy, of chivalry, or even of ordinary common decency. I suspect *everyone* who does not wear a Lens."

"A thought-screen!" exclaimed Gerrond. "How could she, without armor?"

"It's a late model—brand new. Just as good and just as powerful as the one I myself am wearing," Kinnison explained. "The mere fact that she's wearing it gives me a lot of highly useful information."

"What do you want me to do about her?" the Admiral asked. He was mentally a-squirm, but he was a Lensman.

"Nothing whatever—except possibly, for our own information, to find out how many of her friends have become thionite-sniffers lately. If you do anything you may warn them, although I know nothing definite about which to caution you. I'll handle her. Don't worry too much, though; I don't think she's anybody we really want. Afraid she's small fry—no such luck as that I'd get hold of a big one so soon."

"I hope she's small fry," Gerrond's thought was a grimace of distaste. "I hate Boskonia as much as anybody does, but I don't relish the idea of having to put that girl into the Chamber."

"If my picture is half right she can't amount to much," Kinnison replied. "A good lead is the best I can expect . . . I'll see what I can do."

For days, then, the searching Lensman pried into minds: so insidiously that he left no trace of his invasions. He examined men and women, of high and low estate. Waitresses and ambassadors, flunkeys and bankers, ermined prelates and truck-drivers. He went from city to city. Always, but with only a fraction of his brain, he played the part of Chester Q. Fordyce; ninety-nine percent of his stupendous mind was probing, searching, and analyzing. Into what charnel pits of filth and corruption he delved, into what fastnesses of truth and loyalty and high courage and ideals, must be left entirely to the imagination; for the

Lensman never has spoken and never will speak of these things.

He went back to Ardith and, late at night, approached the dwelling of Count Avondrin. A servant arose and admitted the visitor, not knowing then or ever that he did so. The bedroom door was locked from the inside, but what of that? What resistance can any mechanism offer to a master craftsman, plentifully supplied with tools, who can perceive every component part, however deeply buried?

The door opened. The Countess was a light sleeper, but before she could utter a single scream one powerful hand clamped her mouth, another snapped the switch of her supposedly carefully concealed thought-screen generator. What followed was done very quickly.

Mr. Fordyce strolled back to his hotel and Lensman Kinnison directed a thought at Lensman Gerrond.

"Better fake up some kind of an excuse for having a couple of guards or policemen in front of Count Avondrin's town house at eight twenty five this morning. The Countess is going to have a brainstorm."

"What *have* . . . er, what will she do?"

"Nothing much. Scream a bit, rush out-of-doors half dressed, and fight anything and everybody that touches her. Warn the officers that she'll kick, scratch, and bite. There will be plenty of signs of a prowler having been in her room, but if they can find him they're good—*very* good. She'll have all the signs and symptoms, even to the puncture, of having been given a shot in the arm of something the doctors won't be able to find or to identify. But there will be no question raised of insanity or of any other permanent damage—she'll be right as rain in a couple of months."

"Oh, that mind-ray machine of your again, eh? And that's all you're going to do to her?"

"That's all. I can let her off easy and still be just, I think. She's helped me a lot. She'll be a good girl from now on, too; I've thrown a scare into her that will last her the rest of her life."

"Fine business, Gray Lensman! What else?"

"I'd like to have you at the Tellurian Ambassador's Ball day after tomorrow, if it's convenient."

"I've been planning on it, since it's on the 'must' list. Shall I bring anything or anyone special?"

"No. I just want you on hand to give me any information you can on a person who will probably be there to investigate what happened to the Countess."

"I'll be there," and he was.

It was a gay and colorful throng, but neither of the two Lensmen was in any mood for gayety. They acted, of course. They neither sought nor avoided each other; but, somehow, they were never alone together.

"Man or woman?" asked Gerrond.

"I don't know. All I've got is the recognition."

The Radeligian did not ask what that signal was to be. Not that he was not curious; but if the Gray Lensman wanted him to know it he would tell him—if not, he wouldn't tell him even if he asked.

Suddenly the Radeligian's attention was wrenched toward the doorway, to see the most marvelously, the most flawlessly beautiful woman he had ever seen. But not long did he contemplate that beauty, for the Tellurian Lensman's thoughts were fairly seething, despite his iron control.

"Do you mean . . . you can't mean . . ." Gerrond faltered.

"She's the one!" Kinnison rasped. "She looks like an angel, but take it from me, she isn't. She's one of the slimiest snakes that ever crawled—she's so low she could put on a tall silk hat and walk under a duck. I know she's beautiful. She's a riot, a seven-section callout, a thionite dream. So what? She is also Dessa Desplaines, formerly of Aldebaran II. Does that mean anything to you?"

"Not a thing, Kinnison."

"She's in it, clear to her neck. I had a chance to wring her neck once, too, damn it all, and didn't. She's got a carballoy crust, coming here now, with all our Narcotics on the job . . . wonder if they think they've got Enforcement so badly whipped that they can get away with stuff as rough as this . . . sure you don't know her, or know of her?"

"I never saw her before, or heard of her."

"Perhaps she isn't known, out this way. Or maybe they think they're ready for a show-down . . . or don't care. But her being here ties me up in hard knots—*she'll* recognize me, for all the tea in China. You know the Narcotics' Lensmen, don't you?"

"Certainly."

"Call one of them, right now. Tell him that Dessa Desplaines, the zwilnik* houri, is right here on the floor . . . What? He doesn't know her, either? And none of our boys are Lensmen! Make it a three-way. Lensman Winstead? Kinnison of Sol III, Unattached. Sure that none of you recognize this picture?" and he transmitted a perfect image of the ravishing creature then moving regally across the floor. "Nobody does? Maybe that's why she's here, then—they thought she could get away with it. She's your meat—come and get her."

"You'll appear against her, of course?"

"If necessary—but it won't be. As soon as she sees the game's up, all hell will be out for noon."

As soon as the connection had been broken, Kinnison realized that the thing could not be done that way; that he could not stay out of it. No man alive save himself could prevent her from flashing a warning—badly as he hated to, he had to do it. Gerrond glanced at him curiously: he had received a few of those racing thoughts.

"Tune in on this." Kinnison grinned wryly. "If the last meeting I had with her is any criterion, it ought to be good. S'pose anybody around here understands Aldebaranian?"

"Never heard it mentioned if they do."

The Tellurian walked blithely up to the radiant visitor, held out his hand in Earthly—and Aldebaranian—greeting, and spoke:

---

* Any entity connected with the illicit drug traffic. E.E.S.

"Madame Desplaines would not remember Chester Q. Fordyce, of course. It is of the piteousness that I should be so accursedly of the ordinariness; for to see Madame but the one time, as I did at the New Year's Ball in High Altamont, is to remember her forever."

"Such a flatterer!" the woman laughed. "I trust that you will forgive me, Mr. Fordyce, but one meets so many interesting . . ." her eyes widened in surprise, an expression which changed rapidly to one of flaming hatred, not unmixed with fear.

"So you *do* know me, you bedroom-eyed Aldebaranian hell-cat," he remarked, evenly. "I thought you would."

"Yes, you sweet, uncontaminated sissy, you overgrown superboy-scout, I do!" she hissed, malevolently, and made a quick motion toward her corsage. These two, as has been intimated, were friends of old.

Quick though she was, the man was quicker. His left hand darted out to seize her left wrist; his right, flashing around her body, grasped her right and held it rigidly in the small of her back. Thus they walked away.

"Stop!" she flared. "You're making a spectacle of me!"

"Now isn't that just too bad?" His lips smiled, for the benefit of the observers, but his eyes held no glint of mirth. "These folks will think that this is the way all Aldebaranian friends walk together. If you think for a second you've got any chance at all of touching that sounder—think again. Stop wiggling! Even if you can shimmy enough to work it I'll smash your brain to a pulp before it contacts once!"

Outside, in the grounds: "Oh, Lensman, let's sit down and talk this over!" and the girl brought into play everything she had. It was a distressing scene, but it left the Lensman cold.

"Save your breath," he advised her finally, wearily. "To me you're just another zwilnik, no more and no less. A female louse is still a louse; and calling a zwilnik a louse is insulting the whole louse family."

He said that; and, saying it, knew it to be the exact and crystal truth: but not even that knowledge could mitigate in any iota the recoiling of his every fiber from the deed which he was about to do. He could not even pray, with immortal Merritt's *Dwayanu:*

"Luka—turn your wheel so I need not slay this woman!"

It had to be. Why in all the nine hells of Valeria did he have to be a Lensman? Why did he have to be the one to do it? But it had to be done, and soon; they'd be here shortly.

"There's just one thing you can do to make me believe you're even partially innocent," he ground out, "that you have even one decent thought or one decent instinct anywhere in you."

"What is that, Lensman? I'll do it, whatever it is!"

"Release your thought-screen and send out a call to the Big Shot."

The girl stiffened. This big cop wasn't so dumb—he really *knew* something. He must die, and at once. How could she get word to . . .?

Simultaneously Kinnison perceived that for which he had been waiting; the Narcotics men were coming.

He tore open the woman's gown, flipped the switch of her thought-screen, and invaded her mind. But, fast as he was, he was late—almost too late altogether. He could get neither direction line nor location; but only and faintly a picture of a space-dock saloon, of a repulsively obese man in a luxuriously-furnished back room. Then her mind went completely blank and her body slumped down, bonelessly.

Thus Narcotics found them; the woman inert and flaccid upon the bench, the man staring down at her in black abstraction.

Rough-House

SUICIDE? OR DID YOU . . ." GER-rond paused, delicately. Winstead, the Lensman of Narcotics, said nothing, but looked on intently.

"Neither," Kinnison replied, still studying. "I would have had to, but she beat me to it."

"What d'you mean, 'neither'? She's dead, isn't she? How did it happen?"

"Not yet, and unless I'm more cockeyed even than usual, she won't be. She isn't the type to rub herself out. Ever, under any conditions. As to 'how', that was easy. A hollow false tooth. Simple, but new . . . and clever. But why? WHY?" Kinnison was thinking to himself more than addressing his companions. "If they had killed her, yes. As it it, it doesn't make any kind of sense—any of it."

"But the girl's dying!" protested Gerrond. "What're you going to *do?*". .

"I wish to Klono I knew." The Tellurian was puzzled, groping. "No hurry doing anything about her—what was done to her nobody can undo . . . BUT WHY? . . . unless I can fit these pieces together into some kind of a pattern I'll never know what it's all about . . . none of it makes sense . . ." He shook himself and went on : "One thing is plain. She won't die. If they had intended to kill her, she would've died right then. They figure she's worth saving; in which I agree with them. At the same time, they certainly aren't planning on letting me tap her knowledge, and they may be figuring on taking her away from us. Therefore, as long as she stays alive—or even not dead, the way she is now—guard her so heavily that an army can't get her. If she should happen to die, don't leave her body unguarded for a second until she's been autopsied and you know she'll stay dead. The minute she recovers, day or night, call me. Might as well take her to the hospital now, I guess."

The call came soon that the patient had indeed recovered.

"She's talking, but I haven't answered her," Gerrond reported. "There's something strange here, Kinnison."

"There would be—bound to be. Hold everything until I get there," and he hurried to the hospital.

"Good morning, Dessa," he greeted her in Aldebaranian. "You are feeling better, I hope?"

Her reaction was surprising. "You really know me?" she almost shrieked, and flung herself into the Lensman's arms. Not deliberately; not with her wonted, highly effective technique of bringing into play the equipment with which she was overpoweringly armed. No; this was the uttery innocent, the wholly unselfconscious abandon of a very badly frightened young girl. "What happened?" she sobbed, frantically, "Where am I? Why are all these strangers here?"

Her wide, child-like, tear-filled eyes sought his; and as he probed them, deeper and deeper into the brain behind them, his face grew set and hard. Mentally, she now *was* a young and innocent girl! Nowhere in her mind, not even in the deepest recesses of her subconscious, was there the slightest inkling that she had even existed since her fifteenth year. It was staggering; it was unheard of; but it was indubitably a fact. For her, now, the intervening time had lapsed instantaneously—had disappeared so utterly as never to have been!

"You have been very ill, Dessa," he told her gravely, "and you are no longer a child." He led her into another room and up to a triple mirror. "See for yourself."

"But that isn't I!" she protested. "It can't be! Why, she's beautiful!"

"You're all of that," the Lensman agreed casually. "You've had a bad shock. Your memory will return shortly, I think. Now you must go back to bed."

She did so, but not to sleep. Instead, she went into a trance; and so, almost, did Kinnison. For over an hour he lay intensely a-sprawl in an easy chair, the while he engraved, day by day, a memory of missing years into that bare storehouse of knowledge. And finally the task was done.

"Sleep, Dessa," he told her then. "Sleep. Waken in eight hours; whole."

"Lensman, you're a *man!*" Gerrond realized vaguely what had been done. "You didn't give her the truth, of course?"

"Far from it. Only that she was married and is a widow. The rest of it is highly fictitious—just enough like the real thing so she can square herself with herself if she meets old acquaintances. Plenty of lapses, of course, but they're covered by shock."

"But the husband?" queried the inquisitive Radeligian.

"That's her business," Kinnison countered, callously. "She'll tell you sometime, maybe, if she ever feels like it. One thing I did do, though—they'll never use her again. The next man that tries to hypnotize her will be lucky if he gets away alive."

The advent of Dessa Desplaines, however, and his curious adventure with her, had altered markedly the Lensman's situation. No one else in the throng had worn a screen, but there might have been agents . . . anyway, the observed facts would enable the higher-ups to link Fordyce up with what had happened . . . they would know, of course, that the real Fordyce hadn't done it . . . he could be Fordyce no longer . . .

Wherefore the real Chester Q. Fordyce took over and a stranger appeared. A Posenian, supposedly, since against the air of Radelix he wore that planet's unmistakeable armor. No other race of even approximately human shape could "see" through a helmet of solid, opaque metal.

And in this guise Kinnison continued his investigations. That place and that man must be on this planet somewhere; the sending outfit worn by the Desplaines woman could not possibly reach any other. He had a good picture of the room and a fair picture—several pictures, in fact—of the man. The room was an actuality; all he had to do was to fill in the details which definitely, by unmistakable internal evidence, belonged there. The man was different. How much of the original picture was real, and how much of it was bias?

She was, he knew, physically fastidious in the extreme. He knew that no possible hypnotism could nullify completely the basic, the fundamental characteristics of the subconscious. The intrinsic ego could not be changed. Was the man really such a monster, or was the picture in the girl's mind partially or largely the product of her physical revulsion?

For hours he sat at a recording machine, covering yard after yard of tape with every possible picture of the man he wanted. Pictures ranging from a man almost of normal build up to a thing embodying every repulsive detail of the woman's mental image. The two extremes, he concluded, were highly improbable. Somewhere in between . . . the man *was* fat, he guessed. Fat, and had a mean pair of eyes. And, no matter how Kinnison had changed the man's physical shape he had found it impossible to eradicate a personality that was defiinitely bad.

"The guy's a louse," Kinnison decided, finally. "Needs killing. Glad of that—if I have to keep on fighting women much longer I'll go completely nuts. Got enough dope to identify the ape now, I think."

And again the Tellurian Lensman set out to comb the planet, city by city. Since he was not now dealing with

Lensmen, every move he made had to be carefully planned and as carefully concealed. It was heartbreaking; but at long last he found a bartender who knew his quarry. He *was* fat, Kinnison discovered, and he was a bad egg. From that point on, progress was rapid. He went to the indicated city, which was, ironically enough, the very Ardith from which he had set out; and, from a bit of information here and a bit there, he tracked down his man.

Now what to do? The technique he had used so successfully upon Boysia II and in other bases could not succeed here; there were thousands of people instead of dozens, and someone would certainly catch him at it. Nor could he work at a distance. He was no Arisian, he had to be right beside his job. He would have to turn dock-walloper.

Therefore a dock-walloper he became. Not like one, but actually one. He labored prodigiously, his fine hands and his entire being becoming coarse and hardened. He ate prodigiously, and drank likewise. But, wherever he drank, his liquor was poured from the bartender's own bottle or from one of similarly innocuous contents; for then as now bartenders did not themselves imbibe the corrosively potent distillates in which they dealt. Nevertheless, Kinnison became intoxicated—boisterously, flagrantly, and pugnaciously so, as did his fellows.

He lived scrupulously within his dock-walloper's wages. Eight credits per week went to the company, in advance, for room and board; the rest he spent over the fat man's bar or gambled away at the fat man's crooked games—for Bominger, although engaged in vaster commerce far, nevertheless allowed no scruple to interfere with his esurient rapacity. Money was money, whatever its amount or source or however despicable its means of acquirement.

The Lensman knew that the games were crooked, certainly. He could see, however they were concealed, the crooked mechanisms of the wheels. He could see the crooked workings of the dealers' minds as they manipulated their crooked decks. He could read as plainly as his own the cards his crooked opponents held. But to win or to protest would have set him apart, hence he was always destitute before pay-day. Then, like his fellows, he spent his spare time loafing in the same saloon, vaguely hoping for a free drink or for a stake at cards, until one of the bouncers threw him out.

But in his every waking hour, working, gambling, or loafing, he studied Bominger and Bominger's various enterprises. The Lensman could not pierce the fat man's thought-screen, and he could never catch him without it. However, he could and did learn much. He read volume after volume of locked account books, page by page. He read secret documents, hidden in the deepest recesses of massive vaults. He listened in on conference after conference; for a thought-screen of course does not interfere with either sight or sound. The Big Shot did not own—legally—the saloon, nor the ornate, almost palatial back room which was his office. Nor did he own the dance-hall and boudoirs upstairs, nor the narrow, cell-like rooms in which addicts of twice a score of different noxious drugs gave themselves over libidinously to their addictions. Nevertheless, they were his; and they were only a part of that which was his.

Kinnison detected, traced, and identified agent after agent. With his sense of perception he followed passages, leading to other scenes, utterly indescribable here. One comparatively short gallery, however, terminated in a different setting altogether; for there, as here and perhaps everywhere, ostentation and squalor lie almost back to back. Nalizok's Cafe, the highlife hot-spot of Radelix! Downstairs innocuous enough; nothing rough—that is, too rough—was ever pulled there. Most of the robbery there was open and aboveboard, plainly written upon the checks. But there were upstairs rooms, and cellar rooms, and back rooms. And there were addicts, differing only from those others in wearing finer raiment and being of a self-styled higher stratum. Basically they were the same.

Men, women, girls even were there, in the rigid muscle-lock of thionite. Teeth hard-set, every muscle tense and straining, eyes jammed closed, fists clenched, faces white as though carved from marble, immobile in the frenzied emotion which characterizes the ultimately passionate fulfilment of every suppressed desire; in the release of their every inhibition crowding perilously close to the dividing line beyond which lay death from sheer ecstasy. That is the technique of the thionite-sniffer—to take every microgram that he can stand, to come to, shaken and too weak even to walk; to swear that he will never so degrade himself again; to come back after more as soon as he has recovered strength to do so; and finally, with an irresistible craving for stronger and ever stronger thrills, to take a larger dose than his rapidly-weakening body can endure and so to cross the fatal line.

There also were the idiotically smiling faces of the hadive smokers, the twitching members of those who preferred the Centralian nitrolabe-needle, the helplessly stupefied eaters of bentlam—but why go on? Suffice it to say that in that one city block could be found every vice and every drug enjoyed by Radeligians and the usual run of visitors; and if perchance you were an unusual visitor, desiring something unusual, Bominger could get it for you— at a price.

Kinnison studied, perceived, and analyzed. Also, he reported, via Lens, daily and copiously, to Narcotics, under Lensman's Seal.

"But Kinnison!" Winstead protested one day. "How much longer are you going to make us wait?"

"Until I get what I came after or until they get onto me," Kinnison replied, flatly. For weeks his Lens had been hidden in the side of his shoe, in a flat sheath of highly charged metal, proof against any except the most minutely searching spy-ray inspection; but this new location did not in any way interfere with its functioning.

"Any danger of that?" the Narcotics head asked, anxiously.

"Plenty—and getting worse every day. More actors in the drama. Some day I'll make a slip—I can't keep this up forever."

"Turn us loose, then," Winstead urged. "We've got enough now to blow this ring out of existence, all over the planet."

"Not yet. You're making good progress, aren't you?"

"Yes, but considering . . ."

"Don't consider it yet. Your present progress is normal for your increased force. Any more would touch off an alarm. You could take this planet's drug personnel, yes, but that isn't what I'm after. I want big game, not small fry. So sit tight until I give you the go ahead. QX?"

"Got to be QX if you say so, Kinnison. Be careful!"

"I am. Won't be long now, I'm sure. Bound to break very shortly, one way or the other. If possible, I'll give you and Gerrond warning."

Kinnison had everything lined up except the one thing he had come after—the real boss of the zwilniks. He knew where the stuff came in, and when, and how. He knew who received it, and the principal distributors of it. He knew almost all of the secret agents of the ring, and not a few even of the small-fry peddlers. He knew where the remittances went, and how much, and what for. But every lead had stopped at Bominger. Apparently the fat man was the absolute head of the drug syndicate; and that appearance didn't make sense—it *had* to be false. Bominger and the other planetary lieutenants—themselves only small fry if the Lensman's ideas were only half right—*must* get orders from, and send reports and, in all probability, payments to some Boskonian authority; of that Kinnison felt certain, but he had not been able to get even the slightest trace of that higher up.

That the communication would be established upon a thought-beam the Tellurian was equally certain. The Boskonian would not trust any ordinary, tappable communicator beam, and he certainly would not be such a fool as to send any written or taped or otherwise permanently recorded message, however coded. No, that message, when it came, would come as thought, and to receive it the fat man would have to release his screen. Then, and not until then, could

Kinnison act. Action at that time might not prove simple—judging from the precautions Bominger was taking already, he would not release his screen without taking plenty more —but until then the Lensman could do nothing.

That screen had not yet been released, Kinnison could swear to that. True, he had had to sleep at times, but he had slept on a very hair-trigger, with his subconscious and his Lens set to guard that screen and to give the alarm at its first sign of weakening.

As the Lensman had foretold, the break came soon. Not in the middle of the night, as he had half-thought that it would come; nor yet in the quiet of the daylight hours. Instead, it came well before midnight, while revelry was at its height. It did not come suddenly, but was heralded by a long period of gradually increasing tension, of a mental stress very apparent to the mind of the watcher.

Agents of the drug baron came in, singly and in groups, to an altogether unprecedented number. Some of them were their usual viciously self-contained selves, others were slightly but definitely ill at ease. Kinnison, seated alone at a small table, playing a game of Radeligian solitaire, divided his attention between the big room as a whole and the office of Bominger; in neither of which was anything definite happening.

Then a wave of excitement swept over the agents as five men wearing thought-screen entered the room and, sitting down at a reserved table, called for cards and drinks; and Kinnison thought it time to send his warning.

"Gerrond! Winstead! Three-way! It's going to break soon, now, I think—tonight. Agents all over the place— five men with thought-screens here on the floor. Nervous tension high. Lots more agents outside, for blocks. General precaution, I think, not specific. Not suspicious of me, at least not exactly. Afraid of spies with a sense of perception —Rigellians or Posenians or such. Just killed an Ordovik on general principles, over on the next block. Get your gangs ready, but don't come too close—just close enough so you can be here in thirty seconds after I call you."

"What do you mean 'not exactly suspicious'? What have you done?"

"Nothing I know of—any one of a million possible small slips I may have made. Nothing serious, though, or they wouldn't have let me hang around this long."

"You're in danger. No armor, no DeLamater, no anything. Better come out of it while you can."

"And miss what I've spent all this time building up? Not a chance! I'll be able to take care of myself, I think . . . Here comes one of the boys in a screen, to talk to me. I'll leave my Lens open, so you can sort of look on."

Just then Bominger's screen went down and Kinnison invaded his mind; taking complete possession of it. Under his domination the fat man reported to the Boskonian, reported truly and fully. In turn he received orders and instructions. Had any inquisitive stranger been around, or anyone on the planet using any kind of a mind-ray machine since that quadruply-accursed Lensman had held that trial? (Oh, that was what had touched them off! Kinnison was glad to know it.) No, nothing unusual at all . . .

And just at that critical moment, when the Lensman's mind was so busy with its task, the stranger came up to his table and stared down at him dubiously, questioningly.

"Well, what's on *your* mind?" Kinnison growled. He could not spare much of his mind just then, but it did not take much of it to play his part as a dock-walloper. "You another of them slime-lizard house-numbers, snooping around to see if I'm trying to run a blazer? By Klono and all his cubs, if I hadn't lost so much money here already I'd tear up this deck and go over to Croleo's and *never* come near this crummy joint again—his rot-gut can't be any worse than yours is."

"Don't burn out a jet, pal." The agent, apparently reassured, adopted a conciliatory tone.

"Who in hell ever said you was a pal of mine, you Radelig-gig-gigian pimp?" The supposedly three-quarters-drunken, certainly three-quarters-naked Lensman got up, wobbled a little, and sat down again, heavily. "Don't 'pal' me, ape—I'm partic-hic-hicular about who I pal with."

"That's all right, big fellow; no offense intended," soothed the other. "Come on, I'll buy you a drink."

"Don't want no drink 'til I've finished this game," Kinnison grumbled, and took an instant to flash a thought via Lens. "All set, boys? Things're moving fast. If I have to take this drink—it's doped, of course—I'll bust this bird wide open. When I yell, shake the lead out of your pants!"

"Of course you want a drink!" the pirate urged. "Come and get it—it's on me, you know."

"And who are you to be buying me, a Tellurian gentleman, a drink?" the Lensman roared, flaring into one of the sudden, senseless rages of the character he had cultivated so assiduously. "Did I ask you for a drink? I'm educated, I am, and I've got money, I have. I'll buy myself a drink when I want one." His rage mounted higher and higher, visibly. "Did I *ever* ask you for a drink, you (unprintable here, even in a modern and realistic novel, for the space of two long breaths) . . .?"

This was the blow-off. If the fellow was even half level, there would be a fight, which Kinnison could make last as long as necessary. If he did not start slugging after what Kinnison had just called him he was not what he seemed and the Lensman was surely suspect; for the Earthman had dredged the foulest vocabularies of space.

"If you weren't drunk I'd break every bone in your laxlo-soaked carcass." The other man's anger was sternly suppressed, but he looked at the dock-walloper with no friendship in his eyes. "I don't ask lousy space-port bums to drink with me every day, and when I do, they do—or else. Do you want to take that drink now or do you want a couple of the boys to work you over first? Barkeep! Bring two glasses of laxlo over here!"

Now the time was short indeed, but Kinnison would not—could not—act yet. Bominger's conference was still on; the Lensman didn't know enough yet. The fellow wasn't very suspicious, certainly, or he would have made a pass at him before this. Bloodshed meant less than nothing to these gentry; the stranger did not want to incur Bominger's wrath by killing a steady customer. The fellow probably thought the whole mind-ray story was hocuspocus, anyway —not a chance in a million of it being true. Besides he needed a machine, and Kinnison couldn't hide a thing, let alone anything as big as that "mind-ray machine" had been, because he didn't have clothes enough on to flag a hand-car with. But that free drink was certainly doped . . . Oh, they wanted to question him. It would be a truth-dope in the laxlo, then—he certainly couldn't take *that* drink!

Then came the all-important second; just as the bartender set the glasses down Bominger's interview ended. At the signing off, Kinnison got additional data, just as he had expected; and in that instant, before the drugmaster could restore his screen, the fat man died—his brain literally blasted. And in that same instant Kinnison's Lens fairly throbbed with the power of the call he sent out to his allies.

But not even Kinnison could hurl such a mental bolt without some outward sign. His face stiffened, perhaps, or his eyes may have lost their drunken, vacant stare, to take on momentarily the keen, cold ruthlessness that was for the moment his. At any rate, the enemy agent was now definitely suspicious.

"Drink that, bum, and drink it quick—or burn!" he snapped, DeLameter out and poised.

The Tellurian's hand reached for the glass, but his mind also reached out, and faster by a second, to the brains of two nearby agents. Those worthies drew their own weapons and, with wild yells, began firing. Seemingly indiscriminately, yet in those blasts two of the thought-screened minions died. For a fraction of a second even the hard-schooled mind of Kinnison's opponent was distracted, and that fraction was time enough.

A quick flick of the wrist sent the potent liquor into the Boskonian's eyes; a lightning thrust of the knee sent the little table hurtling against his gun-hand, flinging the weapon afar. Simultaneously the Lensman's ham-like fist, urged by all the strength and all the speed of his two hun-

dred and sixteen pounds of rawhide and whalebone, drove
forward. Not for the jaw. Not for the head or the face.
Lensmen know better than to mash bare hands, break fingers
and knuckles, against bone. For the solar plexus. The big
Patrolman's fist sank forearm-deep. The stricken zwilnik
uttered one shrieking grunt, doubled up, and collapsed;
never to rise again. Kinnison leaped for the fellow's De-
Lameter—too late, he was already hemmed in.

One—two—three—four of the nearest men died without having received a physical blow; again and again Kinnison's heavy fists and far heavier feet crashed deep into
vital spots. One thought-screened enemy dived at him
bodily in a Tomingan donganeur, to fall with a broken
neck as the Lensman opposed instantly the only possible
parry—a savage chop, edge-handed, just below the base of
the skull; the while he disarmed the surviving thought-
screened stranger with an accurately-hurled chair. The latter, feinting a swing, launched a vicious French kick. The
Lensman, expecting anything, perceived the foot coming.
His big hands shot out like striking snakes, closing and
twisting savagely in the one fleeting instant, then jerking
upward and backward. A hard and heavy dock-walloper's
boot crashed thuddingly to a mark. A shriek rent the air
and that foeman too was done.

Not fair fighting, no; nor clubby. Lensmen did not and
do not fight according to the tenets of the square ring. They
use the weapons provided by Mother Nature only when they
must; but they can and do use them with telling effect indeed when body-to-body brawling becomes necessary. For
they are skilled in the art—every Lensman has a completely
detailed knowledge of all the lethal tricks of foul combat
known to all the dirty fighters of ten thousand planets for
twice ten thousand years.

And then the doors and windows crashed in, admitting
those whom no other bifurcate race has ever faced willingly
in hand-to-hand combat—full-armed Valerians, swinging
their space-axes!

The gangsters broke, then, and fled in panic disorder;

but escape from Narcotics' fine-meshed net was impossible. They were cut down to a man.

"QX, Kinnison?" came two hard, sharp thoughts. The Lensmen did not see the Tellurian, but Lieutenant Peter vanBuskirk did. That is, he saw him, but did not look at him.

"Hi, Kim, you little Tellurian wart!" That worthy's thought was a yell. "Ain't we got fun?"

"QX, fellows—thanks," to Gerrond and to Winstead, and "Ho, Bus! Thanks, you big, Valerian ape!" to the gigantic Dutch-Valerian with whom he had shared so many experiences in the past. "A good clean-up, fellows?"

"One hundred percent, thanks to you. We'll put you . . ."

"Don't, please. You'll clog my jets if you do. I don't appear in this anywhere—it's just one of your good, routine jobs of mopping up. Clear ether, fellows, I've got to do a flit."

"Where?" all three wanted to ask, but they didn't— the Gray Lensman was gone.

KINNISON DID START HIS FLIT, but he did not get far. In fact, he did not even reach his squalid room before cold reason told him that the job was only half done—yes, less than half. He had to give Boskone credit for having brains, and it was not at all likely that even such a comparatively small unit as a planetary headquarters would have only one string to its bow. They certainly would have been forced to install duplicate controls of some sort or other by the trouble they had had after Helmuth's supposedly impregnable Grand Base had been destroyed.

There were other straws pointing the same way. Where had those five strange thought-screened men come from? Bominger hadn't known of them apparently. If that idea was sound, the other headquarters would have had a spy-ray on the whole thing. Both sides used spy-rays freely, of course, and to block them was, ordinarily, worse than to let them come. The enemies' use of the thought-screen was different. They realized that it made it easy for the unknown Lensman to discover their agents, but they were forced to use it because of the deadliness of the supposed mind-ray. Why hadn't he thought of this sooner, and had the whole area blocked off? Too late to cry about it now, though.

Assume the idea correct. They certainly knew now that he was a Lensman; probably were morally certain that he was *the* Lensman. His instantaneous change from a drunken dock-walloper to a cold-sober, deadly-skilled rough-and-tumble brawler . . . and the unexplained deaths of half-a-dozen agents, as well as that of Bominger himself . . . this was bad. Very, *very* bad . . . a flare-lit tip-off, if there ever was one. Their spy-rays would have combed him, millimeter by plotted cubic millimeter: they knew exactly where his Lens was, as well as he did himself. He had put his tail right into the wringer . . . wrecked the whole job right at the start . . . unless he could get that other headquarters outfit, too, and get them before they reported in detail to Boskone.

In his room, then, he sat and thought, harder and more intensely than he had ever thought before. No ordinary method of tracing would do. It might be anywhere on the planet, and it certainly would have no connection whatever with the thionite gang. It would be a small outfit; just a few men, but under smart direction. Their purpose would be to watch the business end of the organization, but not to touch it save in an emergency. All that the two groups would have in common would be recognition signals, so that the reserves could take over in case anything happened to Bominger—as it already had. They had him, Kinnison, cold . . . What to do? WHAT TO DO?

The Lens. That must be the answer—it *had* to be. The Lens—what was it, really, anyway? Simply an aggregation of crystalloids. Not really alive; just a pseudo-life, a sort of reflection of his own life . . . he wondered . . . Great Klono's tungsten teeth, could *that* be it? An idea had struck him, an idea so stupendous in its connotations and ramifications that he gasped, shuddered, and almost went faint at the shock. He started to reach for his Lens, then forced himself to relax and shot a thought to Base.

"Gerrond! Send me a portable spy-ray block, quick!"

"But that would give everything away—that's why we haven't been using them."

"Are you telling me?" the Lensman demanded. "Shoot it along—I'll explain while it's on the way." He went on to tell the Radeligian everything he thought it well for him to know, concluding: "I'm as wide open as inter-galactic space —nothing but fast and sure moves will do us a bit of good."

The block arrived, and as soon as the messenger had departed Kinnison set it going. He was now the center of a sphere into which no spy-ray beam could penetrate. He was also an object of suspicion to anyone using a spy-ray, but that fact made no difference, then. Snatching off his shoe, he took out his Lens, wrapped it in a handkerchief, and placed it on the floor. Then, just as though he still wore it, he directed a thought at Winstead.

"All serene, Lensman?" he asked, quietly.

"Everything's on the beam," came instant reply. "Why?"

"Just checking, is all." Kinnison did not specify exactly what he was checking!

He then did something which, so far as he knew, no Lensman had ever before even thought of doing. Although he felt stark naked without his Lens, he hurled a thought three-quarters of the way across the galaxy to that dread planet Arisia; a thought narrowed down to the exact pattern of Mentor himself—the gigantic, fearsome Brain who had been his teacher and his sponsor.

"Ah, 'tis Kimball Kinnison, of Earth," that entity responded, in precisely the same modulation it had employed once before. "You have perceived, then, youth, that the Lens is not the supremely important thing you have supposed it to be?"

"I . . . you . . . I mean . . ." the flustered Lensman, taken completely aback, was cut off by a sharp rebuke.

"Stop! You are thinking muddily—conduct ordinarily inexcusable! Now, youth, to redeem yourself, you will explain the phenomenon to me, instead of asking me to explain it to you. I realize that you have just discovered another facet of the Cosmic Truth; I know what a shock it has been to your immature mind; hence for this once it may be permissible for me to overlook your crime. But strive not to repeat the offense, for I tell you again in all possible seriousness—I cannot urge upon you too strongly the fact—that in clear and precise thinking lies your only safeguard through that which you are attempting. Confused, wandering thought will assuredly bring disaster inevitable and irreparable."

"Yes, sir," Kinnison replied meekly; a small boy reprimanded by his teacher. "It must be this way. In the first stage of training the Lens is a necessity; just as is the crystal ball or some other hypnotic object in a seance. In the more advanced stage the mind is able to work without aid. The Lens, however, may be—in fact, it must be—endowed with uses other than that of a symbol of identification; uses about which I as yet know nothing. Therefore, while I can work without it, I should not do so except when it is absolutely necessary, as its help will be imperative if I am to advance to any higher stage. It is also clear that you were expecting my call. May I ask if I am on time?"

"You are—your progress has been highly satisfactory. Also, I note with approval that you are not asking for help in your admittedly difficult present problem."

"I know it wouldn't do me any good—and why." Kinnison grinned wryly. "But I'll bet that Worsel, when he comes up for his second treatment, will know on the spot what it has taken me all this time to find out."

"You deduce truly. He did."

"What? He has been back there already? And you told me . . ."

"What I told you was true and is. His mind is more fully developed and more responsive than yours; yours is of vastly greater latent capacity, capability, and force," and the line of communication snapped.

Calling a conveyance, Kinnison was whisked to Base, the spy-ray block full on all the way. There, in a private room, he put his heavily-insulated Lens and a full spool of tape into a ray-proof container, sealed it, and called in the base commander.

"Gerrond, here is a package of vital importance," he informed him. "Among other things, it contains a record of everything I have done to date. If I don't come back to claim it myself, please send it to Prime Base for personal delivery to Port Admiral Haynes. Speed will be no object, but safety very decidedly of the essence."

"QX—we'll send it in by special messenger."

"Thanks a lot. Now I wonder if I could use your visiphone a minute? I want to talk to the zoo."

"Certainly."

"Zoological Gardens?" and the image of an elderly, white-bearded man appeared upon the plate. "Lensman Kinnison of Tellus—Unattached. Have you as many as three oglons, caged together?"

"Yes. In fact, we have four of them in one cage."

"Better yet. Will you please send them over here to base at once? Lieutenant-Admiral Gerrond, here, will confirm."

"It is most unusual, sir," the graybeard began, but broke off at a curt word from Gerrond. "Very well, sir," he agreed, and disconnected.

"Oglons?" the surprised commander demanded. "OGLONS!"

For the oglon, or Radeligian cateagle, is one of the fiercest, most intractable beasts of prey in existence; it assays more concentrated villainy and more sheerly vicious ferocity to the gram than any other creature known to science. It is not a bird, but a winged mammal; and is armed not only with the gripping, tearing talons of the eagle, but also with the heavy, cruel, needle-sharp fangs of the wildcat. And its mental attitude toward all other forms of life is anti-social to the nth degree.

"Oglons." Kinnison confirmed, shortly. "I can handle them."

"You can, of course. But . . ." Gerrond stopped. This

Gray Lensman was forever doing amazing, unprecedented, incomprehensible things. But, so far, he had produced eminently satisfactory results, and he could not be expected to spend all his time in explanations.

"But you think I'm screwy, huh?"

"Oh, no, Kinnison, I wouldn't say that. I only . . . well . . . after all, there isn't much real evidence that we didn't mop up one hundred per cent."

"Much? Real evidence? There isn't any," the Tellurian assented, cheerfully enough. "But you've got the wrong slant entirely on these people. You are still thinking of them as gangsters, desperadoes, renegade scum of our own civilization. They're not. They are just as smart as we are; some of them are smarter. Perhaps I'm taking unnecessary precautions; but, if so, there's no harm done. On the other hand, there are two things at stake which, to me at least, are extremely important; this whole job of mine and my life: and remember this—the minute I leave this base both of those things are in your hands."

To that, of course, there could be no answer.

While the two men had been talking and while the oglons were being brought out, two trickling streams of men had been passing, one into and one out of the spy-ray-shielded confines of the base. Some of these men were heavily bearded, some were shaven clean, but all had two things in common. Each one was human in type and each one in some respect or other resembled Kimball Kinnison.

"Now remember, Gerrond," the Gray Lensman said impressively as he was about to leave, "They're probably right here in Ardith, but they may be anywhere on the planet. Keep a spy-ray on me wherever I go, and trace theirs if you can. That will take some doing, as he's bound to be an expert. Keep those oglons at least a mile—thirty seconds flying time—away from me; get all the Lensmen you can on the job; keep a cruiser and a speedster hot, but not too close. I may need any of them, or all, or none of them, I can't tell; but I do know this—if I need anything at all, I'll need it fast. Above all, Gerrond, by the Lens you wear, do

nothing whatever, no matter what happens around me or to
me, until I give you the word. QX?"

"QX, Gray Lensman. Clear ether!"

Kinnison took a ground-cab to the mouth of the narrow street upon which was situated his dock-walloper's mean
lodging. This was a desperate, a foolhardy trick—but in its
very boldness, in its insolubly paradoxical aspects, lay its
strength. Probably Boskone could solve its puzzles, but—
he hoped—this ape, not being Boskone, couldn't. And,
paying off the cabman, he thrust his hands into his tattered
pockets and, whistling blithely if a bit raucously through
his stained teeth, he strode off down the narrow way as
though he did not have a care in the world. But he was doing the finest job of acting of his short career; even though,
for all he really knew, he might not have any audience at
all. For inwardly, he was strung to highest tension. His
sense of perception, sharply alert, was covering the full
hemisphere around and above him; his mind was triggered
to jerk any muscle of his body into instantaneous action.

*   *   *

Meanwhile, in a heavily guarded room, there sat a
manlike being, humanoid to eight places. For two hours
he had been sitting at his spy-ray plate, studying with ever-
growing uneasiness the human beings so suddenly and so
surprisingly numerously having business at the Patrol's
base. For minutes he had been studying minutely a man
in a ground-cab, and his uneasiness reached panic heights.

"It *is* the Lensman!" he burst out. "It's *got* to be,
Lens or no Lens. Who else would have the cold nerve to go
back there when he knows he's let the cat completely out
of the bag?"

"Well, get him, then," advised his companion. "All
set, ain't you?"

"But it *can't* be!" the chief went on, reversing himself
in mid-flight. "A Lensman has *got* to have a Lens, and a
Lens *can't* be invisible! And this fellow has not now, and
never has had, a mind-ray machine. He hasn't got *anything!*

And besides, the Lensman we're after wouldn't be sticking around—he disappears."

"Well, drop him and chase somebody else, then," the lieutenant advised, unfeelingly.

"But there's nobody nearly enough like him!" snarled the chief, in desperation. He was torn by doubt and indecision. This whole situation was a mess—it didn't add up right, from any possible angle. "It's got to be him—it can't be anybody else. I've checked and rechecked him. It *is* him, and not a double. He thinks he's safe enough; he can't know about us—can't even suspect. Besides, his only good double, Fordyce—and *he's* not good enough to stand the inspection I just gave him—hasn't appeared anywhere."

"Probably inside base yet. Maybe this is a better double. Perhaps this *is* the real Lensman pretending he isn't, or maybe the real Lensman is slipping out while you're watching the man in the cab." the junior suggested, helpfully.

"Shut up!" the superior yelled. He started to reach for a switch, but paused, hand in air.

"Go ahead. That's it, call District and toss it into their laps, if it's too hot for you to handle. I think myself whoever did this job is a warm number—plenty warm."

"And get my ears burned off with that 'your report is neither complete nor conclusive' of his?" the chief sneered. "And get reduced for incompetence besides? No, we've got to do it ourselves, and do it right . . . but that man there isn't the Lensman—he can't be!"

"Well, you'd better make up your mind—you haven't got all day. And nix on that 'we' stuff. It's *you* that's got to do it—you're the boss, not me," the underling countered, callously. For once, he was really glad that he was not the one in command. "And you'd better get busy and do it, too."

"I'll do it," the chief declared, grimly. "There's a way."

There was a way. One only. He must be brought in alive and compelled to divulge the truth. There was no other way.

The Boskonian touched a stud and spoke. "Don't kill

him—bring him in alive. If you kill him even accidentally I'll kill both of you, myself."

The Gray Lensman made his carefree way down the alley-like thoroughfare, whistling inharmoniously and very evidently at peace with the Universe.

It takes something, friends, to walk knowingly into a trap; without betraying emotion or stress even while a black-jack, wielded by a strong arm, is descending toward the back of your head. Something of quality, something of fiber, something of *je ne sais quoi*. But whatever it took Kinnison in ample measure had.

He did not wink, flinch, or turn an eye as the billy came down. Only as it touched his hair did he act, exerting all his marvelous muscular control to jerk forward and downward, with the weapon and ahead of it, to spare himself as much as possible of the terrific blow.

The black-jack crunched against the base of the Lensman's skull in a shower of coruscating constellations. He fell. He lay there, twitching feebly.

Cateagles

A S HAS BEEN SAID, KINNISON
rode the blow of the blackjack forward and downward, thus
robbing it of some of its power. It struck him hard enough
so that the thug did not suspect the truth; he thought that
he had all but taken the Lensman's life. And, for all the
speed with which the Tellurian had yielded before the
blow, he was hurt; but he was not stunned. Therefore,
although he made no resistance when the two bullies rolled
him over, lashed his feet together, tied his hands behind
him, and lifted him into a car, he was fully conscious
throughout the proceedings.

When the cab was perhaps half an hour upon its way
the Lensman struggled back, quite realistically, to consciousness.

"Take it easy, pal," the larger of his thought-screened
captors advised, dandling the black-jack suggestively before
his eyes. "One yelp out of you, or a signal, if you've got
one of them Lenses, and I bop you another one."

"What the blinding blue hell's coming off here?" demanded the dock-walloper, furiously. "Wha'd'ya think you're
doing, you lop-eared . . ." and he cursed the two, viciously
and comprehensively.

"Shut up or he'll knock you kicking," the smaller thug

advised from the driver's seat, and Kinnison subsided. "Not that it bothers me any, but you're making too damn much noise."

"But what's the matter?" Kinnison asked, more quietly. "What'd you slug me for and drag me off? I ain't done nothing and I ain't got nothing."

"I don't know nothing," the big agent replied. "The boss will tell you all you need to know when we get to where we're going. All I know is the boss says to bop you easy-like and bring you in alive if you don't act up. He says to tell you not to yell and not to use no Lens. If you yell we burn you out. If you use any Lens, the boss he's got his eyes on all the bases and spaceports and everything, and if any help starts to come this way he'll tell us and we fry you and buzz off. We can kill you and flit before any help can get near you, he says."

"Your boss ain't got the brains of a fontema," Kinnison growled. He knew that the boss, wherever he was, could hear every word. "Hell's hinges, if I was a Lensman you think I'd be walloping junk on a dock? Use your head, cully, if you got one."

"I wouldn't know nothing about that," the other returned, stolidly.

"But I ain't got no Lens!" the dock-walloper stormed, in exasperation. "Look at me—frisk me! You'll see I ain't!"

"All that ain't none of my dish." The thug was entirely unmoved. "I don't know nothing and I don't do nothing except what the boss tells me, see? Now take it easy, all nice and quiet-like. If you don't," and he flicked the blackjack lightly against the Lensman's knee, "I'll put out your landing-lights. I'll lay you like a mat, and I don't mean maybe. See?"

Kinnison saw, and relapsed into silence. The automobile rolled along. And, flitting industriously about upon its delivery duties, but never much more or less than one measured mile distant, a panel job pursued its devious way. Oddly enough, its chauffeur was a Lensman. Here and there, high in the heavens, were a few airplanes, gyros, and copters; but they were going peacefully and steadily about their business—even though most of them happened to have Lensmen as pilots.

And, not at the base at all, but high in the stratosphere and so throughly screened that a spy-ray observer could not even tell that his gaze was being blocked, a battle-cruiser, Lensman-commanded, rode poised upon flare-baffled, softly hissing under-jets. And, equally high and as adequately protected against observation, a keen-eyed Lensman sat at the controls of a speedster, jazzing her muffled jets and peering eagerly through a telescopic sight. As far as the Patrol was concerned, everything was on the trips.

The car approached the gates of a suburban estate and stopped. It waited. Kinnison knew that the Boskonian within was working his every beam, alert for any sign of Patrol activity; knew that if there were any such sign the car would be off in an instant. But there was no activity. Kinnison sent a thought to Gerrond, who relayed micrometric readings of the objective to various Lensmen. Still everyone waited. Then the gate opened of itself, the two thugs jerked their captive out of the car to the ground, and Kinnison sent out his signal.

Base remained quiet, but everything else erupted at once. The airplanes wheeled, cruiser and speedster plummeted downward at maximum blast. The panel job literally fell open, as did the cage within it, and four ravening cateagles, with the silent ferocity of their kind, rocketed toward their goal.

Although the oglons were not as fast as the flying ships they did not have nearly as far to go, wherefore they got there first. The thugs had no warning whatever. One instant everything was under control; in the next the noiselessly arrowing destroyers struck their prey with the mad fury that only a striking cateagle can exhibit. Barbed talons dug viciously into eyes, faces, mouths, tearing, rending, wrenching; fierce-driven fangs tore deeply, savagely into defenseless throats.

Once each the thugs screamed in mad, lethal terror,

but no warning was given; for by that time every building upon that pretentious estate had disappeared in the pyrotechnic flare of detonating duodec. The pellets were small, of course—the gunners did not wish either to destroy the nearby residences or to injure Kinnison—but they were powerful enough for the purpose intended. Mansion and outbuildings disappeared, and not even the most thoroughgoing spy-ray search revealed the presence of anything animate or structural where those buildings had been.

The panel job drove up and Kinnison, perceiving that the cateagles had done their work, sent them back into their cage. The Lensman driver, after securely locking cage and truck, cut the Earthman's bonds.

"QX, Kinnison?" he asked.

"QX, Barknett—thanks," and the two Lensmen, one in the panel truck and the other in the gangsters' car, drove back to headquarters. There Kinnison recovered his package.

"This has got me all of a soapy dither, but you have called the turn on every play yet," Winstead told the Tellurian, later. "Is this all of the big shots, do you think, or are there some more of them around here?"

"Not around here, I'm pretty sure," Kinnison replied. "No, two main lines is all they would have had, I think . . . this time. Next time . . ."

"There won't be any next time," Winstead declared.

"Not on this planet, no. Knowing what to expect, you fellows can handle anything that comes up. I was thinking then of my next step."

"Oh. But you'll get 'em, Gray Lensman!"

"I hope so," soberly.

"Luck, Kinnison!"

"Clear ether, Winstead!" and this time the Tellurian really did flit.

As his speedster ripped through the void Kinnison did more thinking, but he was afraid that Menter would have considered the product muddy indeed. He couldn't seem to get to the first check-station. One thing was limpidly clear; this line of attack or any very close variation of it would never work again. He'd have to think up something new. So far, he had got away with his stuff because he had kept one lap ahead of them, but how much longer could he manage to keep up the pace?

Bominger had been no mental giant, of course; but this other lad was nobody's fool and this next higher-up, with whom he had had the interview via Bominger, would certainly prove to be a really shrewd number.

" 'The higher the fewer,' " he repeated to himself the old saying, adding, "and in this case, the smarter." He had to put out some jets, but where he was going to get the fuel he simply didn't know.

Again the trip to Tellus was uneventful, and the Gray Lensman, the symbol of his rank again flashing upon his wrist, sought interview with Haynes.

"Send him in, certainly—send him in!" Kinnison heard the communicator crackle, and the receptionist passed him along. He paused in surprise, however, at the doorway of the office, for Surgeon-Marshal Lacy and a Posenian were in conference with the Port Admiral.

"Come in, Kinnison," Haynes invited. "Lacy wants to see you a minute, too. Doctor Phillips—Lensman Kinnison, Unattached. His name isn't Phillips, of course; we gave him that in self-defense, to keep from trying to pronounce his real one."

Phillips, the Posenian, was as tall as Kinnison, and heavier. His figure was somewhat human in shape, but not in detail. He had four arms instead of two, each arm had two opposed hands, and each hand had two thumbs, one situated about where a little finger would be expected. He had no eyes, not even vestigial ones. He had two broad, flat noses and two toothful mouths; one of each in what would ordinarily be called the front of his round, shining, hairless head; the other in the back. Upon the sides of his head were large, volute, highly dirigible ears. And, like most races having the faculty of perception instead of that of sight, his head was relatively immobile, his neck being short, massive, and tremendously strong.

"You look well, very well." Lacy reported, after feeling and prodding vigorously the members which had been in his splints and casts so long. "Have to take a picture, of course, before saying anything definite. No, we won't either, now. Phillips, look at his . . ." an interlude of technical jargon . . . "and see what kind of a recovery he has made." Then, while the Posenian was examining Kinnison's interior mechanisms, the Surgeon-Marshal went on:

"Wonderful diagnosticians and surgeons, these Posenians—can see into the patient without taking him apart. In another few centuries every doctor will have to have the sense of perception. Phillips is doing a research in neurology—more particularly a study of the neural synapse and the proliferation of neural dendrites . . ."

"La—cy-y-y!" Haynes drawled the word in reproof. "I've told you a thousand times to talk English when you're talking to me. How about it, Kinnison?"

"Afraid I can't quite check you, chief," Kinnison grinned. "Specialists—precisionists—can't talk in Basic."

"Right, my boy—surprisingly and pleasingly right!" Lacy exclaimed. "Why can't you adopt that attitude, Haynes, and learn enough words so you can understand what a man's talking about? But to reduce it to monosyllabic simplicity, Phillips is studying a thing that has baffled us for thousands of years. The lower forms of cells are able to regenerate themselves; wounds heal, bones knit. Higher types, such as nerve cells, regenerate imperfectly, if at all; and the highest type, the brain cells, do not do so under any conditions." He turned a reproachful gaze upon Haynes. "This is terrible. Those statements are pitiful—inadequate —false. Worse than that—practically meaningless. What I wanted to say, and what I'm going to say, is that . . ."

"Oh no you aren't, not in this office," his old friend interrupted. "We got the idea perfectly. The question is, why can't human beings repair nerves or spinal cords, or grow new ones? If such a worthless beastie as a starfish can grow a whole new body to one leg, including a brain, if any, why can't a really intelligent victim of simple infantile paralysis—or a ray—recover the use of a leg that is otherwise in perfect shape?"

"Well, that's something like it, but I hope you can aim closer than that at a battleship," Lacy grunted. "We'll buzz off now, Phillips, and leave these two war-horses alone."

"Here is my report in detail." Kinnison placed the package upon the Port Admiral's desk as soon as the room was sealed behind the visitors. "I talked to you direct about most of it—this is for the record."

"Of course. Mighty glad you found Medon, for our sake as well as theirs. They have things that we need, badly."

"Where did they put them? I suggested a sun near Sol, so as to have them handy to Prime Base."

"Right next door—Alpha Centauri. Didn't get to do much scouting, did you?"

"I'll say we didn't. Boskonia owns that galaxy; lock, stock, and barrel. May be some other independent planets —bound to be, of course; probably a lot of them—but it's too dangerous, hunting them at this stage of the game. But at that, we did enough, for the time being. We proved our point. Boskone, if there is any such being, is certainly in the Second Galaxy. However, it will be a long time before we're ready to carry the war there to him, and in the meantime we've got a lot to do. Check?"

"To nineteen decimals."

"It seems to me, then, that while you are rebuilding our first-line ships, super-powering them with Medonian insulation and conductors, I had better keep on tracing Boskone along the line of drugs. I'm just about sure that they're back of the whole drug business."

"And in some ways their drugs are more dangerous to Civilization than their battleships. More insidious and, ultimately, more fatal."

"Check. And since I am perhaps as well equipped as any of the other Lensmen to cope with that particular problem . . .?" Kinnison paused, questioningly.

"That certainly is no overstatement," the Port Admiral

replied, dryly. "You're the *only* one equipped to cope with it."

"None of the other boys except Worsel, then? . . . I heard that a couple . . ."

"They thought they had a call, but they didn't. All they had was a wish. They came back."

"Too bad . . . but I can see how it would be. It's a rough course, and if a man's mind isn't completely ready for it, it burns out. It almost does, anyway . . . mind is a funny thing. But that isn't getting us anywhere. Can you take time to let me talk at you a few minutes?"

"I certainly can. You've got the most important assignment in the galaxy, and I'd like to know more about it, if it's anything you can pass on."

"Nothing that need be sealed from any Lensman. The main object of all of us, as you know, is to push Boskonia out of this galaxy. From a military standpoint they practically *are* out. Their drug syndicate, however, is very decidedly in, and getting in deeper all the time. Therefore we next push the zwilniks out. They have peddlers and such small fry, who deal with distributors and so on. These fellows form the bottom layer. Above them are the secret agents, the observers, and the wholesale handlers; runners and importers. All these folks are directed and controlled by one man, the boss of each planetary organization. Thus, Bominger was the boss of all zwilnick activities on the whole planet of Radelix.

"In turn the planetary bosses report to, and are synchronized and controlled by a Regional Director, who supervises the activities of a couple of hundred or so planetary outfits. I got a line on the one over Bominger, you know—Prellin, the Kalonian. By the way, you knew, didn't you, that Helmuth was a Kalonian, too?"

"I got it from the tape. Smart people, they must be, but not my idea of good neighbors."

"I'll say not. Well, that's all I really *know* of their organization. It seems logical to suppose, though, that the structure is coherent all the way up. If so, the Regional

Directors would be under some higher-up, possibly a Galactic Director, who in turn might be under Boskone himself— or one of his cabinet officers, at least. Perhaps the Galactic Director might even be a cabinet officer in their government, whatever it is?"

"An ambitious program you've got mapped out for yourself. How are you figuring on swinging it?"

"That's the rub—I don't know," Kinnison confessed, ruefully. "But if it's done at all, that's the way I've got to go about it. Any other way would take a thousand years and more men than we'll ever have. This way works fine, when it works at all."

"I can see that—lop off the head and the body dies," Haynes agreed.

"That's the way it works—especially when the head keeps detailed records and books covering the activities of all the members of his body. With Bominger and the others gone, and with full transcripts of his accounts, the boys mopped up Radelix in a hurry. From now on it will be simple to keep it clean, except of course for the usual bootleg trickle, and that can be reduced to a minimum. Similarly, if we can put this Prellin away and take a good look at his ledgers, it will be easy to clear up his two hundred planets. And so on."

"Very clear, and quite simple . . . in theory." The older man was thoughtful and frankly dubious. "In practice, difficult in the extreme."

"But necessary," the younger insisted.

"I suppose so," Haynes assented finally. "Useless to tell you not to take chances—you'll have to—but for all our sakes, if not for your own, be as careful as you can."

"I'll do that, chief. I think a lot of me. As much as anybody—maybe more—and 'Careful' is my middle name."

"Ummmh," Haynes grunted, skeptically. "We've noticed that. Anything special you want done?"

"Yes, very special," Kinnison surprised him by answering in the affirmative. "You know that the Medonians developed a scrambler for a detector nullifier. Hotchkiss and the boys developed a new line of attack on that—against long-range stuff we're probably safe—but they haven't been able to do a thing on electromagnetics. Well, the Boskonians, beginning with Prellin, are going to start wondering what has been happening. Then, if I succeed in getting Prellin, they're bound to start doing things. One thing they'll do will be to fix up their headquarters so that they'll have about five hundred percent overlap on their electros. Perhaps they'll have outposts, too, close enough together to have the same thing there—possibly two or three hundred even on visuals."

"In that case you stay out."

"Not necessarily. What do electros work on?"

"Iron, I suppose—they did when I went to school last."

"The answer, then, is to build me a speedster that is inherently indetectable—absolutely non-ferrous. Berylumin and so on for all the structural parts . . ."

"But you've got to have silicon-steel cores for your electrical equipment!"

"I was coming to that. Have you? I was reading in the 'Transactions' the other day that force-fields had been used in big units, and were more efficient. Some of the smaller units, instruments and so on, might have to have some iron, but wouldn't it be possible to so saturate those small pieces with a dense field of detector frequencies that they wouldn't react?"

"I don't know. Never thought of it. Would it?"

"I don't know, either—I'm not telling you, I'm just making suggestions. I do know one thing, though. We've got to keep ahead of them—think of things first and oftenest, and be ready to abandon them for something else as soon as we've used them once."

"Except for those primary projectors." Haynes grinned wryly. "They can't be abandoned—even with Medonian power we haven't been able to develop a screen that will stop them. We've got to keep them secret from Boskone—and in that connection I want to compliment you on the suggestion of having Velantian Lensmen as mind-readers wherever those projectors are even being thought of."

"You caught spies, then? How many?"

"Not many—three or four in each base—but enough to have done the damage. Now, I believe, for the first time in history, we can be *sure* of our entire personnel."

"I think so. Mentor says the Lens is enough, if we use it properly. That's up to us."

"But how about visuals?" Haynes was still worrying, and to good purpose.

"Well, we have a black coating now that's ninety nine percent absorptive, and I don't need ports or windows. At that, though, one percent reflection would be enough to give me away at a critical time. How'd it be to put a couple of the boys on that job? Have them put a decimal point after the ninety nine and see how many nines they can tack on behind it?"

"That's a thought, Kinnison. They'll have lots of time to work on it while the engineers are trying to fill your specifications as to a speedster. But you're right, dead right. We—or rather, you—have got to out-think them; and it certainly is up to us to do everything we can to build the apparatus to put your thoughts into practice. And it isn't at some vague time in the future that Boskone is going to start doing something about you and what you've done. It's right now; or even, more probably, a week or so ago. But you haven't said a word yet about the really big job you have in mind."

"I've been putting that off until the last," the Gray Lensman's voice held obscure puzzlement. "The fact is that I simply can't get a tooth into it—can't get a grip on it anywhere. I don't know enough about math or physics. Everything comes out negative for me; not only inertia, but also force, velocity, and even mass itself. Final results always contain an 'i', too, the square root of minus one. I can't get rid of it, and I don't see how it can be built into any kind of apparatus. It may not be workable at all, but before I give up the idea I'd like to call a conference, if it's QX with you and the Council."

"Certainly it is QX with us. You're forgetting again, aren't you, that you're a Gray Lensman?" Haynes' voice held no reproof, he was positively beaming with a super-fatherly pride.

"Not exactly." Kinnison blushed, almost squirmed. "I'm just too much of a cub to be sticking my neck out so far, is all. The idea may be—probably is—wilder than a Radeligian cateagle. The only kind of a conference that could even begin to handle it would cost a young fortune, and I don't want to spend that much money on my own responsibility."

"To date your ideas have worked out well enough so that the Council is backing you one hundred percent," the older man said, dryly. "Expense is no object." Then, his voice changing markedly, "Kim, have you any idea at all of the financial resources of the Patrol?"

"Very little, sir, if any, I'm afraid," Kinnison confessed.

"Here on Tellus alone we have an expendible reserve of over ten thousand million credits. With the restriction of government to its proper sphere and its concentration into our organization, resulting in the liberation of man-power into wealth-producing enterprise, and especially with the enormous growth of inter-world commerce, world-income increased to such a point that taxation could be reduced to a minimum; and the lower the taxes the more flourishing business became and the greater the income.

"Now the tax rate is the lowest in history. The total income tax, for instance, in the highest bracket, is only three point five nine two percent. At that, however, if it had not been for the recent slump, due to Boskonian interference with inter-systemic commerce, we would have had to reduce the tax rate again to avoid serious financial difficulty due to the fact that too much of the galactic total of circulating credit would have been concentrated in the expendible funds of the Galactic Patrol. So don't even think of money. Whether you want to spend a thousand credits, a million, or a thousand million; go ahead."

"Thanks, Chief; glad you explained. I'll feel better now about spending money that doesn't belong to me. Now if you'll give me, for about a week, the use of the librarian in charge of science files and a galactic beam, I'll quit bothering you."

"I'll do that." The Port Admiral touched a button and in a few minutes a trimly attractive blonde entered the room. "Miss Hostetter, this is Lensman Kinnison, Unattached. Please turn over your regular duties to an assistant and work with him until he releases you. Whatever he says, goes; the sky's the limit."

In the Library of Science Kinnison outlined his problem briefly to his new aide, concluding:

"I want only about fifty, as a larger group could not cooperate efficiently. Are your lists arranged so that you can skim off the top fifty?"

"Such a group can be selected, I think." The girl stood for a moment, lower lip held lightly between white teeth. "That is not a standard index, but each scientist has a rating. I can set the acceptor . . . no, the rejector would be better—to throw out all the cards above any given rating. If we take out all ratings over seven hundred we will have only the highest of the geniuses."

"How many, do you suppose?"

"I have only a vague idea—a couple of hundred, perhaps. If too many, we can run them again at a higher level, say seven ten. But there won't be very many, since there are only two galactic ratings higher than seven fifty. There will be duplications, too—such people as Sir Austin Cardynge will have two or three cards in the final rejects."

"QX—we'll want to hand-pick the fifty, anyway. Let's go!"

Then for hours bale after bale of cards went through the machine; thousands of records per minute. Occasionally one card would flip out into a rack, rejected. Finally:

"That's all, I think. Mathematicians, physicists," the librarian ticked off upon pink fingers. "Astronomers, philosophers, and this new classification, which hasn't been named yet."

"The H.T.T.'s." Kinnison glanced at the label, lightly lettered in pencil, fronting the slim packet of cards. "Aren't you going to run them through, too?"

"No. These are the two I mentioned a minute ago—the only ones higher than seven hundred fifty."

"A choice pair, eh? Sort of a *creme de la creme?* Let's look 'em over," and he extended his hand. "What do the initials stand for?"

"I'm awfully sorry, sir, really," the girl flushed in embarrassment as she relinquished the cards in high reluctance. "If I'd had any idea we wouldn't have dared—we call you, among ourselves, the 'High-Tension Thinkers.' "

"Us!" It was the Lensman's turn to flush. Nevertheless, he took the packet and read sketchily the facer: "Class XIX —Unclassifiable at present . . . lack of adequate methods . . . minds of range and scope far beyond any available indices . . . Ratings above high genuis (750) . . . yet no instability . . . power beyond any heretofore known . . . assigned ratings tentative and definitely minimum."

He then read the cards.

"Worsel, Velantia, eight hundred."

And:

"Kimball Kinnison, Tellus, eight hundred seventy-five."

THE PORT ADMIRAL WAS EMInently correct in supposing that Boskone, whoever or whatever he or it might be, was already taking action upon what the Tellurian Lensman had done. For, even as Kinnison was at work in the Library of Science, a meeting which was indirectly to affect him no little was being called to order.

In the immensely distant Second Galaxy was that meeting being held; upon the then planet Jarnevon of the Eich; within that sullen fortress already mentioned briefly. Presiding over it was the indescribable entity known to history as Eichlan; or, more properly, Lan of the Eich.

"Boskone is now in session," that entity announced to the eight other similar monstrosities who in some fashion indescribable to man were stationed at the long, low, wide bench of stone-like material which served as a table of state. "Nine days ago each of us began to search for whatever new facts might bear upon the activities of the as yet entirely hypothetical Lensman who, Helmuth believed, was the real force back of our recent intolerable reverses in the Tellurian Galaxy.

"As First of Boskone I will report as to the military situation. As you know, our positions there became untenable with the fall of our Grand Base and all our mobile forces were withdrawn. In order to facilitate reorganization, coordinating ships were sent out. Some of these ships went to planets held in toto by us. Not one of these vessels has been able to report any pertinent facts whatever. Ships approaching bases of the Patrol, or encountering Patrol ships of war in space, simply ceased communicating. Even their automatic recorders ceased to function without transmitting any intelligible data, indicating complete destruction of those ships. A cascade system, in which one ship followed another at long range and with analytical instruments set to determine the nature of any beam or weapon employed, was attempted. The enemy, however, threw out blanketing zones of tremendous power; and we lost six more vessels without obtaining the desired data. These are the facts, all negative. Theorizing, deduction, summation, and integration will as usual come later. Eichmil, Second of Boskone, will now report."

"My facts are also entirely negative," the Second began. "Soon after our operations upon the planet Radelix became productive of results a contingent of Tellurian narcotic agents arrived; which may or may not have included the Lensman . . ."

"Stick to facts for the time being." Eichlan ordered, curtly.

"Shortly thereafter a minor agent, a female instructed to wear a thought-screen at all times, lost her usefulness by suffering a mental disorder which incapacitated her quite seriously. Then another agent, also a female, this time one of the third order and who had been very useful up to that time, ceased reporting. A few days later Bominger, the Planetary Director, failed to report, as did the Planetary Observer; who, as you know, was entirely unknown to, and had no connection with, the operating staff. Reports from other sources, such as importers and shippers—these, I believe, are here admissible as facts—indicate that all our personnel upon Radelix have been liquidated. No unusual developments have occurred upon any other planet, nor has any significant fact, however small, been discovered."

"Eichnor, Third of Boskone."

"Also negative. Our every source of information from within the bases of the Patrol has been shut off. Every one of our representatives, some of whom have been reporting regularly for many years, has been silent, and every effort to reach any of them has failed."

"Eichsnap, Fourth of Boskone."

"Utterly negative. We have been able to find no trace whatever of the planet Medon, or of any one of the twenty one warships investing it at the time of its disappearance."

And so on, through nine reports, while the tentacles of the mighty First of Boskone played intermittently over the keys of a complex instrument or machine before him.

"We will now reason, theorize, and draw conclusions," the First announced, and each of the organisms fed his ideas and deductions into the machine. It whirred briefly, then ejected a tape, which Eichlan took up and scanned narrowly.

"Rejecting all conclusions having a probability of less than ninety five percent," he announced, "we have: First, a set of three probabilities of a value of ninety nine and ninety nine one-hundredths—virtual certainties—that some one Tellurian Lensman is the prime mover behind what has happened; that he has acquired a mental power heretofore unknown to his race; and that he has been in large part responsible for the development of the Patrol's new and formidable weapons. Second, a probability of ninety nine percent that he and his organization are no longer on the defensive, but have assumed the offensive. Third, one of ninety seven percent that it is not primarily Tellus which is an obstacle, even though the Galactic Patrol and Civilization did originate upon that planet, but Arisia; that Helmuth's report was at least partially true. Fourth, one of ninety five and one half percent that the Lens is also concerned in the disappearance of the planet Medon. There is a lesser probability, but still of some ninety four percent, that that same Lensman is involved here.

"I will interpolate here that the vanishment of that planet is a much more serious matter than it might appear, on the surface, to be. *In situ,* it was a thing of no concern —gone, it becomes an affair of almost vital import. To issue orders impossible of fulfillment, as Helmuth did when he said 'Comb Trenco, inch by inch,' is easy. To comb this galaxy star by star for Medon would be an even more difficult and longer task; but what can be done is being done.

"To return to the conclusions, they point out a state of things which I do not have to tell you is really grave. This is the first major set-back which the culture of the Boskone has encountered since it began its rise. You are familiar with that rise; how we of the Eich took over in turn a city, a race, a planet, a solar system, a region, a galaxy. How we extended our sway into the Tellurian Galaxy, as a preliminary to the extension of our authority throughout all the populated galaxies of the macro-cosmic Universe.

"You know our creed; to the victor the power. He who is strongest and fittest shall survive and shall rule. This so-called Civilization which is opposing us, which began upon Tellus but whose driving force is that which dwells upon Arisia, is a soft, weak, puny-spirited thing indeed to resist the mental and material power of our culture. Myriads of beings upon each planet, each one striving for power and, so striving, giving of that power to him above. Myriads of planets, each, in return for our benevolently despotic control, delegating and contributing power to the Eich. All this power, delegated to the thousands of millions of the Eich of this planet, culminates in and is wielded by the nine of us, who comprise Boskone.

"Power! Our forefathers thought that control of one planet was enough. Later it was declared that mastery of a galaxy, if realized, would sate ambition. We of Boskone, however, now know that our power shall be limited only by the bounds of the Material Cosmic All—every world that exists throughout space shall and must pay homage and tribute to Boskone! What, gentlemen, is the sense of this meeting?"

"Arisia must be visited!" There was no need of integrating this thought; it was dominant and unanimous.

"I would advise caution, however," the Eighth of Boskone amended his ballot. "We are an old race, it is true, and able. I cannot help but believe, however, that in Arisia there exists an unknown quality, an 'x' which we as yet are unable to evaluate. It must be borne in mind that Helmuth, while not of the Eich, was nevertheless an able being; yet he was handled so mercilessly there that he could not render a complete or conclusive report of his expedition, then or ever. With these thoughts in mind I suggest that no actual landing be made, but that the torpedo be launched from a distance."

"The suggestion is eminently sound," the First approved. "As to Helmuth, he was, for an oxygen-breather, fairly able. He was, however, mentally soft, as are all such. Do you, our foremost psychologist, believe that any existent or conceivable mind—even that of a Plooran—could break yours with no application of physical force or device, as Helmuth's reports seemed to indicate that his was broken? I use the word 'seemed' advisedly, for I do not believe that Helmuth reported the actual truth. In fact, I was about to replace him with an Eich, however unpleasant such an assignment would be to any of our race, because of that weakness."

"No," agreed the Eighth. "I do not believe that there exists in the Universe a mind of sufficient power to break mine. It is a truism that no mental influence, however powerful, can affect a strong, definitely and positively opposed will. For that reason I voted against the use of thought-screens by our agents. Such screens expose them to detection and can be of no real benefit. Physical means were—must have been—used first, and, after physical subjugation, the screens were of course useless."

"I am not sure that I agree with you entirely," the Ninth put in. "We have here cogent evidence that there have been employed mental forces of a type or pattern with which we are entirely unfamiliar. While it is the consensus of opinion that the importance of Helmuth's report should be minimized, it seems to me that we have enough corroborative evidence to indicate that this mentality may be able to operate without material aid. If so, rigid screening should be retained, as offering the only possible safeguard from such force."

"Sound in theory, but in practice dubious," the psychologist countered. "If there were any evidence whatever that the screens had done any good I would agree with you. But have they? Screening failed to save Helmuth or his base; and there is nothing to indicate that the screens impeded, even momentarily, the progress of the suppositious Lensman upon Radelix. You speak of 'rigid' screening. The term is meaningless. Perfectly effective screening is impossible. If, as we seem to be doing, we postulate the ability of one mind to control another without physical, bodily contact—nor is the idea at all far-fetched, considering what I myself have done to the minds of many of our agents—the Lensman can work through any unshielded mentality whatever to attain his ends. As you know, Helmuth deduced, too late, that it must have been through the mind of a dog that the Lensman invaded Grand Base."

"Poppycock!" snorted the Seventh. "Or, if not, we can kill the dogs—or screen their minds, too," he sneered.

"Admitted," the psychologist returned, unmoved. "You might conceivably kill all the animals that run and all the birds that fly. You cannot, however, destroy all life in any locality at all extended, clear down to the worms in their burrows and the termites in their hidden retreats; and the mind does not exist which can draw a line of demarcation and say 'here begins intelligent life.'"

"This discussion is interesting, but futile," put in Eichlan, forestalling a scornful reply. "It is more to the point, I think, to discuss that which must be done; or, rather, who is to do it, since the thing itself admits of only one solution—an atomic bomb of sufficient power to destroy every trace of life upon that accursed planet. Shall we send someone, or shall some of us ourselves go? To overestimate a foe is at worst only an unnecessary precaution; to underestimate this one may well prove fatal. Therefore it seems to me that the decision in this matter should lie with our psychologist. I will, however, if you prefer, integrate our various conclusions."

Recourse to the machine was unnecessary; it was agreed by all that Eichamp, the Eighth of Boskone, should decide.

"My decision will be evident," that worthy said, measuredly, "when I say that I myself, for one, am going. The situation is admittedly a serious one. Moreover, I believe, to a greater extent than do the rest of you, that there is a certain amount of truth in Helmuth's version of his experiences. My mind is the only one in existence of whose power I am absolutely certain; the only one which I definitely *know* will not give way before any conceivable mental force, whatever its amount or whatever its method of application. I want none with me save of the Eich, and even those I will examine carefully before permitting them aboard ship with me."

"You decide as I thought," said the First. "I also shall go. My mind will hold, I think."

"It will hold—in your case examination is unnecessary," agreed the psychologist.

"And I! And I!" arose what amounted to a chorus.

"No," came curt denial from the First. "Two are enough to operate all machinery and weapons. To take any more of the Boskone would weaken us here injudiciously; well you know how many are working, and in what fashions, for seats at this table. To take any weaker mind, even of the Eich, might conceivably be to court disaster. We two should be safe; I because I have proven repeatedly my right to hold the title of First of this Council, the rulers and masters of the dominant race of the Universe; Eichamp because of his unparalleled knowledge of all intelligence. Our vessel is ready. We go."

As has been indicated, none of the Eich were, or ever

had been, cowards. Tyrants they were, it is true, and
dictators of the harshest, sternest, and most soulless kind;
callous and merciless they were; cold as the rocks of their
frigid world and as utterly ruthless and remorseless as the
fabled Juggernaut: but they were as logical as they were
hard. He who of them all was best fitted to do any thing
did it unquestioningly and as a matter of course; did it
with the calmly emotionless efficiency of the machine which
in actual fact he was. Therefore it was the First and the
Eighth of Boskone who went.

Through the star-studded purlieus of the Second
Galaxy the black, airless, lightless vessel sped; through
the reaches, vaster and more tenuous far, of inter-galactic
space; into the Tellurian Galaxy; up to a solar system
shunned then as now by all uninvited intelligences—dread
and dreaded Arisia.

Not close to the planet did even the two of Boskone venture; but stopped at the greatest distance at which a torpedo could be directed surely against the target. But even
so the vessel of the Eich had punctured a screen of mental
force; and as Eichlan extended a tentacle toward the firing mechanism of the missiles, watched in as much suspense
as they were capable of feeling by the planet-bound seven
of Boskone, a thought as penetrant as a needle and yet as
binding as a cable of tempered steel drove into his brain.

"Hold!" that thought commanded, and Eichlan held,
as did also his fellow Boskonian.

Both remained rigid, unable to move any single volun-
tary muscle; while the other seven of the Council looked
on in uncomprehending amazement. Their instruments remained dead—since those mechanisms were not sensitive
to thought, to them nothing at all was occurring. Those
seven leaders of the Eich knew that something was happening; something dreadful, something untoward, something
very decidedly not upon the program they had helped to
plan. They, however, could do nothing about it; they could
only watch and wait.

"Ah, 'tis Lan and Amp of the Eich," the thought resounded within the minds of the helpless twain. "Truly, the Elders are correct. My mind is not yet competent, for, although I have had many facts instead of but a single one upon which to cogitate, and no dearth of time in which to do so, I now perceive that I have erred grievously in my visualization of the Cosmic All. You do, however, fit nicely into the now enlarged Scheme, and I am really grateful to you for furnishing new material with which, for many cycles of time to come, I shall continue to build.

"Indeed, I believe that I shall permit you to return unharmed to your own planet. You know the warning we gave Helmuth, your minion, hence your lives are forfeit for violating knowingly the privacy of Arisia; but wanton or unnecessary destruction is not conducive to mental growth. You are, therefore, at liberty to depart. I repeat to you the instructions given your underling; do not return, either in person or by any form whatever of proxy."

The Arisian had as yet exerted scarcely a fraction of his power; although the bodies of the two invaders were practically paralyzed, their minds had not been punished. Therefore the psychologist said, coldly:

"You are not now dealing with Helmuth, nor with any other weak, mindless oxygen-breather, but with the *Eich,*" and, by sheer effort of will, he moved toward the controls.

"What boots it?" The Arisian compressed upon the Eighth's brain a searing force which sent shrieking waves of pain throughout all nearby space. Then, taking over the psychologist's mind, he forced him to move to the communicator panel, upon whose plate could be seen the other seven of Boskone, gazing in wonder.

"Set up planetary coverage," he directed, through Eichamp's organs of speech, "so that each individual member of the entire race of the Eich can understand what I am about to transmit." There was a brief pause, then the deep, measured voice rolled on;

"I am Eukonidor of Arisia, speaking to you through this mass of undead flesh which was once your Chief Psychologist, Eichamp, the Eighth of that high council

which you call Boskone. I had intended to spare the lives
of these two simple creatures, but I perceive that such action
would be useless. Their minds and the minds of all you
who listen to me are warped, perverted, incapable of reason.
They and you would have misinterpreted the gesture completely; would have believed that I did not slay them only
because I could not do so. Some of you would have offended
again and again, until you were so slain; you can be convinced of such a fact only by an unmistakable demonstration of superior force. Force is the only thing you are able
to understand. Your one aim in life is to gain material
power; greed, corruption, and crime are your chosen implements.

"You consider yourselves hard and merciless. In a
sense and according to your abilities you are, although your
minds are too callow to realize that there are depths of
cruelty and of depravity which you cannot even faintly
envision.

"You love and worship power. Why? To any think-
ing mind it should be clear that such a lust intrinsically is,
and forever must by its very nature be, futile. For, even
if any one of you could command the entire material Universe, what good would it do him? None. What would
he have? Nothing. Not even the satisfaction of accomplishment, for that lust is in fact insatiable—it would then turn
upon itself and feed upon itself. I tell you as a fact that
there is only one power which is at one and the same time
illimitable and yet finite; insatiable yet satisfying; one
which, while eternal, yet invariably returns to its possessor
the true satisfaction of real accomplishment in exact ratio
to the effort expended upon it. That power is the power of
the mind. You, being so backward and so wrong of development, cannot understand how this can be, but if any one of
you will concentrate upon one single fact, or small object,
such as a pebble or the seed of a plant or other creature, for
as short a period of time as one hundred of your years, you
will begin to perceive its truth.

"You boast that your planet is old. What of that? We

of Arisia dwelt in turn upon many planets, from planetary youth to cosmic old age, before we became independent of the chance formation of such celestial bodies.

"You prate that you are an ancient race. Compared to us you are sheerly infantile. We of Arisia did not originate upon a planet formed during the recent inter-passage of these two galaxies, but upon one which came into being in an antiquity so distant that the figure in years would be entirely meaningless to your minds. We were of an age to your mentalities starkly incomprehensible when your most remote ancestors began to wriggle about in the slime of your parent world.

" 'Do the men of the Patrol know . . .?' I perceive the question in your minds. They do not. None save a few of the most powerful of their minds has the slightest inkling of the truth. To reveal any portion if it to Civilization as a whole would blight that Civilization irreparably. Though Seekers after Truth in the best sense, they are essentially juvenile and their life-spans are ephemeral indeed. The mere realization that there is in existence such a race as ours would place upon them such an inferiority complex as would make further advancement impossible. In your case such a course of events is not to be expected. You will close your minds to all that has happened, declaring to yourselves that it was impossible and that therefore it could not have taken place and did not. Nevertheless, you will stay away from Arisia henceforth.

"But to resume. You consider yourselves long-lived. Know then, insects, that your life span of a thousand of your years is but a moment. I, myself, have already lived many such periods, and I am but a youth—a mere watchman, not yet to be entrusted with really serious thinking.

"I have spoken over long; the reason for my prolixity being that I do not like to see the energy of a race so misused, so corrupted to material conquest for its own sake. I would like to set your minds upon the Way of Truth, if perchance such a thing should be possible. I have pointed out that Way; whether or not you follow it is for you to decide.

Indeed, I fear that most of you, in your short-sighted pride, have already cast my message aside; refusing point-blank to change your habits of thought. It is, however, in the hope that some few of you will perceive the Way and will follow it that I have discoursed at such length.

"Whether or not you change your habits of thought, I advise you to heed this, my warning. Arisia does not want and will not tolerate intrusion. As a lesson, watch these two violators of our privacy destroy themselves."

The giant voice ceased. Eichlan's tentacles moved toward the controls. The vast torpedo launched itself.

But instead of hurtling toward distant Arisia it swept around in a circle and struck, in direct central impact, the great cruiser of the Eich. There was an appalling crash, a space-wracking detonation, a flare of incandescence incredible and indescribable as the energy calculated to disrupt—almost to volatilize—a world expended itself upon the insignificant mass of one Boskonian battleship and upon the unresisting texture of the void.

ONSIDERABLY MORE THAN THE stipulated week passed before Kinnison was done with the librarian and with the long-range communicator beam, but eventually he succeeded in enlisting the aid of the fifty three most eminent scientists and thinkers of all the planets of Galactic Civilization. From all over the galaxy were they selected; from Vandemar and Centralia and Alsakan; from Chickladoria and Radelix; from the solar systems of Rigel and Sirius and Antares. Millions of planets were not represented at all; and of the few which were, Tellus alone had more than one delegate.

This was necessary, Kinnison explained carefully to each of the chosen. Sir Austin Cardynge, the man whose phenomenal brain had developed a new mathematics to handle the positron and the negative energy levels, was the one who would do the work; he himself was present merely as a coordinator and observer. The meeting-place, even, was not upon Tellus, but upon Medon, the newly acquired and hence entirely neutral planet. For the Gray Lensman knew well the minds with which he would have to deal.

They were all geniuses of the highest rank, but in all too many cases their stupendous mentalities verged altogether too closely upon insanity for any degree of comfort.

Even before the conclave assembled it became evident that jealousy was to be rife and rampant; and after the initial meeting, at which the problem itself was propounded, it required all of Kinnison's ability, authority, and drive: and all of Worsel's vast diplomacy and tact, to keep those mighty brains at work.

Time after time some essential entity, his dignity outraged and his touchy ego infuriated by some real or fancied insult, stalked off in high dudgeon to return to his own planet; only to be coaxed or bullied, or even mentally man-handled by Kinnison or Worsel, or both, into returning to his task.

Nor were those insults all, or even mostly, imaginary. Quarreling and bickering were incessant, violent flare-ups and passionate scenes of denunciation and vituperation were of almost hourly occurrence. Each of those minds had been accustomed to world-wide adulation, to the unquestioned acceptance as gospel of his every idea or pronouncement, and to have to submit his work to the scrutiny and to the unworshipful criticisms of lesser minds—actually to have to give way, at times, to those inferior mentalities—was a situation quite definitely intolerable.

But at length most of them began to work together, as they appreciated the fact that the problem before them was one which none of them singly had been able even partially to solve; and Kinnison let the others, the most fanatically non-cooperative, go home. Then progress began—and none too soon. The Gray Lensman had lost twenty five pounds in weight, and even the iron-thewed Worsel was a wreck. He could not fly, he declared, because his wings buckled in the middle; he could not crawl, because his belly-plates clashed against his back-bone!

And finally the thing was done; reduced to a set of equations which could be written upon a single sheet of paper. It is true that those equations would have been meaningless to almost anyone then alive, since they were based upon a system of mathematics which had been brought into existence at that very meeting, but Kinnison had taken care of that.

No Medonian had been allowed in the Conference—the admittance of one to membership would have caused a massed exodus of the high-strung, temperamental maniacs working so furiously there—but the Tellurian Lensman had had recorded every act, almost every thought, of every one of those geniuses. Those records had been studied for weeks, not only by Wise of Medon and his staff, but also by a corps of the less brilliant, but infinitely better balanced scientists of the Patrol proper.

"Now you fellows can really get to work." Kinnison heaved a sigh of profound relief as the last member of the Conference figuratively shook the dust of Medon off his robe as he departed homeward. "I'm going to sleep for a week. Call me, will you, when you get the model done?"

This was sheerest exaggeration, of course, for nothing could have kept the Lensman from watching the construction of that first apparatus. He watched the erection of a spherical shell of loosely latticed truss-work some twenty feet in diameter. He watched the installation, at its six cardinal points, of atomic exciters, each capable of transforming ten thousand pounds per hour of substance into pure energy. He knew that those exciters were driving their intake screens at a ratio of at least twenty thousand to one; that energy equivalent to the annihilation of at least six hundred thousand tons per hour of material was being hurled into the center of that web from the six small mechanisms which were in fact super-Bergenholms. Nor is that word adequate to describe them; their fabrication would have been utterly impossible without Medonian conductors and insulation.

He watched the construction of a conveyor and a chute, and looked on intently while a hundred thousand tons of refuse—rocks, sand, concrete, scrap iron, loose metal, debris of all kinds—were dropped into that innocuous-appearing sphere, only to vanish as though they had never existed.

"But we ought to be able to see it by this time, I should think!" Kinnison protested once.

"Not yet, Kim," Master Technician LaVerne Thorndyke informed him. "Just forming the vortex—microscopic yet. I haven't the faintest idea of what is going in there; but, man, dear man, *am* I glad I'm here to help make it go on!"

"But *when?*" demanded the Lensman. "How soon will you know whether it's going to work or not? I've got to do a flit."

"You can flit any time—now, if you like," the technician told him, brutally. "We don't need *you* any more—you've done your bit. It's working now. If it wasn't, do you think we could pack all that stuff into that little space? We'll have it done long before you'll need it."

"But I want to see it work, you big lug!" Kinnison retorted, only half playfully.

"Come back in three-four days—maybe a week; but don't expect to see anything but a hole."

"That's exactly what I want to see, a hole in space," and that was precisely what, a few days later, the Lensman did see.

The spherical framework was unchanged, the machines were still carrying easily their incredible working load. Material—any and all kinds of stuff—was still disappearing; instantaneously, invisibly, quietly, with no flash or fury to mark its passing.

But at the center of that massive sphere there now hung poised a . . . a *something*. Or was it a nothing? Mathematically, it was a sphere, or rather a negasphere, about the the size of a baseball; but the eye, while it could see something, could not perceive it analytically. Nor could the mind envision it in three dimensions, for it was not essentially three-dimensional in nature. Light sank into the thing, whatever it was, and vanished. The peering eye could see nothing whatever of shape or of texture; the mind behind the eye reeled away before infinite vistas of nothingness.

Kinnison hurled his extra-sensory perception into it and jerked back, almost stunned. It was neither darkness nor blackness, he decided, after he recovered enough poise to think coherently. It was worse than that—worse than anything imaginable—an infinitely vast and yet non-existent realm of the total absence of everything whatever . . . AB-SOLUTE NEGATION!

"That's it, I guess," the Lensman said then. "Might as well stop feeding it now."

"We would have to stop soon, in any case," Wise replied, "for our available waste material is becoming scarce. It will take the substance of a fairly large planet to produce that which you require. You have, perhaps, a planet in mind which is to be used for the purpose?"

"Better than that. I have in mind the material of just such a planet, but already broken up into sizes convenient for handling."

"Oh, the asteroid belt!" Thorndyke exclaimed. "Fine! Kill two birds with one stone, huh? Build this thing and at the same time clear out the menaces to inert interplanetary navigation? But how about the miners?"

"All covered. The ones actually in development will be let alone. They're not menaces, anyway, as they all have broadcasters. The tramp miners we send—at Patrol expense and grubstake—to some other system to do their mining. But there's one more point before we flit. Are you sure you can shift to the second stage without an accident?"

"Positive. Build another one around it, mount new Bergs, exciters, and screens on it, and let this one, machines and all, go in to feed the kitty—whatever it is."

"QX. Let's go, fellows!"

Two huge Tellurian freighters were at hand; and, holding the small framework between them in a net of tractors and pressors, they set off blithely toward Sol. They took a couple of hours for the journey—there was no hurry, and in the handling of this particular freight caution was decidedly of the essence.

Arrived at destination, the crews tackled with zest and zeal this new game. Tractors lashed out, seizing chunks of iron . . .

"Pick out the little ones, men," cautioned Kinnison. "Nothing over about ten feet in section-dimension will go into this frame. Better wait for the second frame before you try to handle the big ones."

"We can cut 'em up," Thorndyke suggested. "What've we got these shear-planes for?"

"QX if you like. Just so you keep the kitty fed."

"We'll feed her!" and the game went on.

Chunks of debris—some rock, but mostly solid meteoric nickel-iron—shot toward the vessels and the ravening sphere, becoming inertialess as they entered a wide-flung zone. Pressors seized them avidly, pushing them through the interstices of the framework, holding them against the voracious screen. As they touched the screen they disappeared; no matter how fast they were driven the screen ate them away, silently and unspectacularly, as fast as they could be thrown against it. A weird spectacle indeed, to see a jagged fragment of solid iron, having a mass of thousands of tons, drive against that screen and disappear! For it vanished, utterly, along a geometrically perfect spherical surface. From the opposite side the eye could see the mirror sheen of the metal at the surface of disintegration; it was as though the material were being shoved out of our familiar three-dimensional space into another universe— which, as a matter of cold fact, may have been the case.

For not even the men who were doing the work made any pretense of understanding what was happening to that iron. Indeed, the only entities who did have any comprehension of the phenomenon—the forty-odd geniuses whose matematical wizardry had made it possible—thought of it and discussed it, not in the limited, three-dimensional symbols of every-day existence, but only in the language of high mathematics; a language in which few indeed are able really and readily to think.

And while the crews became more and more expert at the new technique, so that metal came in faster and faster —huge, hot-sliced bars of iron ten feet square and a quarter of a mile long were being driven into that enigmatic sphere of extinction—an outer framework a hundred and fifty miles in diameter was being built. Nor, contrary to what might be supposed, was a prohibitive amount of metal or of labor necessary to fabricate that mammoth structure. Instead of six there were six cubed—two hundred sixteen—working stations, complete with generators and super-Bergenholms and screen generators, each mounted upon a massive platform; but, instead of being connected and supported by stupendous beams and trusses of metal, those platforms were linked by infinitely stronger bonds of pure force. It took a lot of ships to do the job, but the technicians of the Patrol had at call enough floating machine shops and to spare.

When the sphere of negation grew to be about a foot in apparent diameter it had been found necessary to surround it with a screen opaque to all visible light, for to look into it long or steadily then meant insanity. Now the opaque screen was sixteen feet in diameter, nearing dangerously the sustaining framework, and the outer frame was ready. It was time to change.

The Lensman held his breath, but the Medonians and the Tellurian technicians did not turn a hair as they mounted their new stations and tested their apparatus.

"Ready," "Ready," "Ready." Station after station reported; then, as Thorndyke threw in the master switch, the primary sphere—invisible now, through distance, to the eye, but plain upon the visiplates—disappeared; a mere morsel to those new gigantic forces.

"Swing into it, boys!" Thorndyke yelled into his transmitter. "We don't have to feed her with a teaspoon any more. Let her have it!"

And "let her have it" they did. No more cutting up of the larger meteorites; asteroids ten, fifteen, twenty miles in diameter, along with hosts of smaller stuff, were literally hurled through the black screen into the even lusher blackness of that which was inside it, without complaint from the quietly humming motors.

"Satisfied, Kim?" Thorndyke asked.

"Uh-*huh!*" the Lensman assented, vigorously. "Nice! . . . Slick, in fact," he commended. "I'll buzz off now, I guess."

"Might as well—everything's on the green. Clear ether, spacehound!"

"Same to you, big fella. I'll be seeing you, or sending you a thought. There's Tellus, right over there. Funny, isn't it, doing a flit to a place you can actually see before you start?"

The trip to Earth was scarcely a hop, even in a supply-boat. To Prime Base the Gray Lensman went, where he found that his new non-ferrous speedster was done; and during the next few days he tested it out thoroughly. It did not register at all, neither upon the regular, long-range utra-instruments nor upon the short-range emergency electros. Nor could it be seen in space, even in a telescope at point-blank range. True, it occulted an occasional star; but since even the direct rays of a search-light failed to reveal its shape to the keenest eye—the Lensmen-chemists who had worked out that ninety nine point nine nine percent absolute black coating had done a wonderful job—the chance of discovery through that occurrence was very slight.

"QX, Kim?" the Port Admiral asked. He was accompanying the Gray Lensman on a last tour of inspection.

"Fine, chief. Couldn't be better—thanks a lot."

"Sure you're non-ferrous yourself?"

"Absolutely. Not even an iron nail in my shoes."

"What is it, then? You look worried. Want something expensive?"

"You hit the thumb, Admiral, right on the nail. But it's not only expensive—we may never have any use for it."

"Better build it, anyway. Then if you want it you'll have it, and if you don't want it we can always use it for something. What is it?"

"A nut-cracker. There are a lot of cold planets around, aren't there, that aren't good for anything?"

"Thousands of them—millions."

"The Medonians put Bergenholms on their planet and flew it from Lundmark's Nebula to here in a few weeks. Why wouldn't it be a sound idea to have the planetographers pick out a couple of useless worlds which, at some points in their orbits, have diametrically opposite velocities, to within a degree or two?"

"You've got something there, my boy. Will do. Very much worth having, just for its own sake, even if we never have any use for it. Anything else?"

"Not a thing in the universe. Clear ether, chief!"

"Light landings, Kinnison!" and gracefully, effortlessly, the dead-black sliver of semi-precious metal lifted herself away from Earth.

*   *   *

Through Bominger, the Radeligian Big Shot, Kinnison had had a long and eminently satisfactory interview with Prellin, the regional director of all surviving Boskonian activities. Thus he knew where he was, even to the street address, and knew the name of the firm which was his alias—Ethan D. Wembleson and Sons, Inc., 4627 Boulevard Dezalies, Cominoche, Quadrant Eight, Bronseca. That name had been his first shock, for that firm was one of the largest and most conservative houses in galactic trade; one having an unquestioned AA-A1 rating in every mercantile index.

However, that was the way they worked, Kinnison reflected, as his speedster reeled off the parsecs. It wasn't far to Bronseca—easy Lens distance—he'd better call somebody there and start making arrangements. He had heard about the planet, although he'd never been there. Somewhat warmer than Tellus, but otherwise very Earthlike. Millions of Tellurians lived there and liked it.

His approach to the planet Bronseca was characterized by all possible caution, as was his visit to Cominoche, the capital city. He found that 4627 Boulevard Dezalies was a structure covering an entire city block and some eighty stories high, owned and occupied exclusively by Wembleson's. No visitors were allowed except by appointment. His first stroll past it showed him that an immense cylinder, comprising almost the whole interior of the building, was shielded by thought screens. He rode up and down in the elevators of nearby buildings—no penetration. He visited a dozen offices in the neighborhood upon various errands, choosing his time with care so that he would have to wait in each an hour or so in order to see his man.

These leisurely scrutinies of his objective failed to reveal a single fact of value. Ethan D. Wembleson and Sons, Inc., did a tremendous business, but every ounce of it was legitimate! That is, the files in the outer offices covered only legitimate transactions, and the men and women busily at work there were all legitimately employed. And the inner offices—vastly more extensive than the outer, to judge by the number of employees entering in the morning and leaving at the close of business—were sealed against his prying, every second of every day.

He tapped in turn the minds of dozens of those clerks, but drew only blanks. As far as they were concerned, there was nothing "queer" going on anywhere in the organization. The "Old Man"—Howard Wembleson, a grand-nephew or something of Ethan—had developed a complex lately that his life was in danger. Scarcely ever left the building—not that he had any need to, as he had always had palatial quarters there—and then only under heavy guard.

A good many thought-screened persons came and went, but a careful study of them and their movements convinced the Gray Lensman that he was wasting his time.

"No soap," he reported to a Lensman at Bronseca's Base. "Might as well try to stick a pin quietly into a cat-eagle. He's been told that he's the next link in the chain, and he's got the jitters right. I'll bet he's got a dozen loose observers, instead of only one. I'll save time, I think, by tracing another line. I have thought before that my best bet is in the asteroid dens instead of on the planets. I let them talk me out of it—it's a dirty job and I've got to establish an identity of my own, which will be even dirtier —but it looks as though I'll have to go back to it."

"But the others are warned, too," suggested the Bronsecan. "They'll probably be just as bad. Let's blast it open and take a chance on finding the data you want."

"No," Kinnison said, emphatically. "Not a chance—

that's not the way to get anything I'm looking for. The others are probably warned, yes, but since they aren't on my direct line to the throne, they probably aren't taking it as seriously as this Prellin—or Wembleson—is. Or if they are, they won't keep it up as long. They can't, and get any joy out of life at all.

"And you can't say a word to Prellin about his screens, either," the Tellurian went on in reply to a thought. "They're legal enough; just as much so as spy-ray blocks. Every man has a right to privacy. Just one question here, or just one suspicious move, is apt to blow everything into a cocked hat. You fellows keep on working along the lines we laid out and I'll try another line. If it works I'll come back and we'll open this can the way you want to. That way, we may be able to get the low-down on about four hundred planetary organizations at one haul."

Thus it came about that Kinnison took his scarcely-used indetectable speedster back to Prime Base; and that, in a solar system prodigiously far removed from both Tellus and Bronseca there appeared another tramp meteor-miner.

Peculiar people, these toilers in the inter-planetary voids; flotsam and jetsam; for the most part the very scum of space. Some solar systems contain more asteroidal and meteoric debris than did ours of Sol, others less, but few if any have none at all. In the main this material is either nickel-iron or rock, but some of these fragments carry prodigious values in platinum, osmium, and other noble metals, and occasionally there are discovered diamonds and other gems of tremendous size and value. Hence, in the asteroid belts of every solar system there are to be found those universally despised, but nevertheless bold and hardy souls who, risking life and limb from moment to moment though they are, yet live in hope that the next lump of cosmic detritus will prove to be Bonanza.

Some of these men are the sheer misfits of life. Some are petty criminals, fugitives from the justice of their own planets, but not of sufficient importance to be upon the "wanted" lists of the Patrol. Some are of those who for some reason or other—addiction to drugs, perhaps, or the overwhelming urge occasionally to go on a spree—are unable or unwilling to hold down the steady jobs of their more orthodox brethren. Still others, and these are many, live that horridly adventurous life because it is in their blood; like the lumberjacks who in ancient times dwelt upon Tellus, they labor tremendously and unremittingly for weeks, only and deliberately to "blow in" the fruits of their toil in a few wild days and still wilder nights of hectic, sanguine, and lustful debauchery in one or another of the spacemen's hells of which every inhabited solar system has its quota.

But, whatever their class, they have much in common. They all live for the moment only, from hand to mouth. They all are intrepid space-men. They have to be—no others last long. They all live hardly, dangerously, violently. They are men of red and gusty passions, and they have, if not an actual contempt, at least a loud-voiced scorn of the law in its every phase and manifestation. "Law ends with atmosphere" is the galaxy-wide creed of the clan, and it is a fact that no law save that of the ray-gun is even yet really enforced in the badlands of the asteroid belts.

Indeed, the meteor miners as a matter of course take their innate lawlessness with them into their revels in the crimson-lit resorts already referred to. In general the nearby Planetary Police adopt a *laissez-faire* attitude, particularly since the asteroids are not within their jurisdictions, but are independent worlds, each with its own world-government. If they kill a dozen or so of each other and of the bloodsuckers who batten upon them, what of it? If everybody in those hells could be 'killed at once, the universe would be that much better off!—and if the Galactic Patrol is compelled, by some unusually outrageous performance, to intervene in the revelry, it comes in, not as single policemen, but in platoons or in companies of armed, full-armored infantry going to war!

Such, then, were those among whom Kinnison chose to cast his lot, in a new effort to get in touch with the Galactic Director of the drug ring.

LTHOUGH KINNISON LEFT Bronseca, abandoning that line of attack completely—thereby, it might be thought, forfeiting all the work he had theretofore done upon it—the Patrol was not idle, nor was Prellin-Wembleson of Cominoche, the Boskonian Regional Director, neglected. Lensman after Lensman came and went, unobstrusively, but grimly determined. There came Tellurians, Venerians, Manarkans, Borovans; Lensmen of every human breed, any of whom might have been, as far as the minions of Boskone knew, the one foe whom they had such good cause to fear.

Rigellian Lensmen came also, and Posenians, and Ordoviks; representatives, in fact, of almost every available race possessing any type or kind of extra-sensory perception, came to test out their skill and cunning. Even Worsel of Velantia came, hurled for days his mighty mind against those screens, and departed.

Whether or not business went on as usual no one could say, but the Patrol was certain of three things. First, that while the Boskonians might be destroying some of their records, they were moving none away, by air, land, or tunnel; second, that there was no doubt in any zwilick mind that the Lensmen were there to stay until they won, in one

way or another; and third, that Prellin's life was not a
happy one!

And while his brothers of the Lens were so efficiently
pinch-hitting for him—even though they were at the same
time trying to show him up and thereby win kudos for
themselves—in mentally investing the Regional stronghold
of Boskone, Kinnison was establishing an identity as a
wandering hellion of the asteroid belts.

There would be no slips this time. He would *be* a
meteor miner in every particular, down to the last, least
detail. To this end he selected his equipment with the most
exacting care. It must be thoroughly adequate and depend-
able, but neither new nor of such outstanding quality or
amount as to cause comment.

His ship, a stubby, powerful space-tug with an over-
sized air-lock, was a used job—hard-used, too—some ten
years old. She was battered, pitted, and scarred; but it
should be noted here, perhaps parenthetically, that when the
Patrol technicians finished their rebuilding she was actually
as staunch as a battleship. His space-armor, Spalding drills,
DeLameters, tractors and pressors, and "spee-gee" (torsion
specific-gravity apparatus) were of the same grade. All bore
unmistakable evidence of years of hard use, but all were
in perfect working order. In short, his outfit was exactly
that which a successful meteor-miner—even such a one as
he was going to become—would be expected to own.

He cut his own hair, and his whiskers too, with ordinary
shears, as was good technique. He learned the polyglot of
the trade; the language which, made up of words from
each of hundreds of planetary tongues, was and is the every-
day speech of human or near-human meteor miners, where-
ever found. By "near-human" is meant a six-place classification of AAAAAA—meaning oxygen-breathing, warm-
blooded, erect, and having more or less humanoid heads,
arms, and legs. For, even in meteor-mining, like runs with
like. Warm-blooded oxygen-breathers find neither welcome
nor enjoyment in a pleasure-resort operated by and for
such a race, say, as the Trocanthers, who are cold-blooded,

quasi-reptilian beings who abhor light of all kinds and who breathe a gaseous mixture not only paralyzingly cold but also chemically fatal to man.

Above all he had to learn how to drink strong liquors and how to take drugs, for he knew that no drink that had ever been distilled, and no drug, with the possible exception of thionite, could enslave the mind he then had. Thionite was out, anyway. It was too scarce and too expensive for meteor miners; they simply didn't go for it. Hadive, heroin, opium, nitrolabe, bentlam—that was it, bentlam. He could get it anywhere, all over the galaxy, and it was very much in character. Easy to take, potent in results, and not as damaging—if you didn't become a real addict—to the system as most of the others. He would become a bentlam-eater.

Bentlam, known also to the trade by such nicknames as "benny," "benweed," "happy-sleep," and others, is a shredded, moistly fibrous material of about the same consistency and texture as fine-cut chewing tobacco. Through his friends of Narcotics the Gray Lensman obtained a supply of "the clear quill, first chop, in the original tins" from a prominent bootlegger, and had it assayed for potency.

The drinking problem required no thought; he would learn to drink, and apparently to like, anything and everything that would pour. Meteor miners did.

Therefore, coldly, deliberately, dispassionately, and with as complete a detachment as though he were calibrating a burette or analyzing an unknown solution, he set about the task. He determined his capacity as impersonally as though his physical body were a volumetric flask; he noted the effect of each measured increment of high-proof beverage and of habit-forming drug as precisely as though he were studying a chemical reaction in which he himself was not concerned save as a purely scientific observer.

He detested the stuff. Every fiber of his being rebelled at the sensations evoked—the loss of coordination and control, the inflation, the aggrandizement, the falsity of values, the sheer hallucinations—nevertheless he went through with the whole program, even to the ex⁺ent of complete physical helplessness for periods of widely varying duration. And when he had completed his researches he was thoroughly well informed.

He knew to a nicety, by feel, how much active principle he had taken, no matter how strong, how weak, or how adulterated the liquor or the drug had been. He knew to a fraction how much more he could take; or, having taken too much, almost exactly how long he would be incapacitated. He learned for himself what was already widely known, that it was better to get at least moderately illuminated before taking the drug; that bentlam rides better on top of liquor than vice versa. He even determined roughly the rate of increase with practice of his tolerances. Then, and only then, did he begin working as a meteor miner.

Working in an asteroid belt of one solar system might have been enough, but the Gray Lensman took no chances at all of having his new identity traced back to its source. Therefore he worked, and caroused, in five; approaching stepwise to the solar system of Borova which was his goal.

Arrived at last, he gave his chunky space-boat the average velocity of an asteroid belt just outside the orbit of the fourth planet, shoved her down into it, turned on his Bergenholm, and went to work. His first job was to "set up"; to install in the extra-large air-lock, already equipped with duplicate controls, his tools and equipment. He donned space-armor, made sure that his DeLameters were sitting pretty—all meteor miners go armed as routine, and the Lensman had altogether too much at stake in any case to forego his accustomed weapons—pumped the air of the lock back into the body of the ship, and opened the outer port. For meteor miners do not work inside their ships. It takes too much time to bring the metal in through the air-locks. It also wastes air, and air is precious; not only in money, although that is no minor item, but also because no small ship, stocked for a six-weeks run, can carry any more air than is really needed.

Set up, he studied his electros and flicked his tractor

beams out to a passing fragment of metal, which flashed up to him, almost instantaneously. Or, rather, the inertialess tugboat flashed across space to the comparatively tiny, but inert, bit of metal which he was about to investigate. With expert ease Kinnison clamped the meteorite down and rammed into it his Spalding drill, the tool which in one operation cuts out and polishes a cylindrical sample exactly one inch in diameter and exactly one inch long. Kinnison took the sample, placed it in the jaw of his spee-gee, and cut his Berg. Going inert in an asteroid belt is dangerous business, but it is only one of a meteor miner's hazards and it is necessary; for the torsiometer is the quickest and simplest means of determining the specific gravity of metal out in space, and no torsion instrument will work upon inertialess matter.

He read the scale even as he turned on the Berg. Seven point nine. Iron. Worthless. Big operators could use it— the asteroid belts had long since supplanted the mines of the worlds as sources of iron—but it wouldn't do him a bit of good. Therefore, tossing it aside, he speared another. Another, and another. Hour after hour, day after day; the back-breaking, lonely labor of the meteor miner. But very few of the bona-fide miners had the Gray Lensman's physique or his stamina, and not one of them all had even a noteworthy fraction of his brain. And brain counts, even in meteor-mining. Hence Kinnison found pay-metal; quite a few really good, although not phenomenally dense, pieces.

Then one day there happened a thing which, if it was not in actual fact premeditated, was as mathematically improbable, almost, as the formation of a planetary solar system; an occurrence that was to exemplify in startling and hideous fashion the doctrine of tooth and fang which is the only law of the asteroid belts. Two tractor beams seized, at almost the same instant, the same meteor! Two ships, flashing up to zone contact in the twinkling of an eye, the inoffensive meteor squarely between them! And in the air lock of the other tug there were two men, not one; two men already going for their guns with the practiced ease of space-hardened veterans to whom the killing of a man was the veriest bagatelle!

They must have been hi-jackers, killing and robbing as a business, Kinnison concluded, afterward. Bona-fide miners almost never work two to a boat, and the fact that they actually beat him to the draw, and yet were so slow in shooting, argued that they had not been taken by surprise, as had he. Indeed, the meteor itself, the bone of contention, might very well have been a bait.

He could not follow his natural inclination to let go, to let them have it. The tale would have spread far and wide, branding him as a coward and a weakling. He would have had to kill, or have been killed by, any number of lesser bullies who would have attacked him on sight. Nor could he have taken over their minds quickly enough to have averted death. One, perhaps, but not two; he was no Arisian. These thoughts, as has been intimated, occurred to him long afterward. During the actual event there was no time to think at all. Instead, he acted; automatically and instantaneously.

Kinnison's hands flashed to the worn grips of his DeLamaters, sliding them from the leather and bringing them to bear at the hip with one smoothly flowing motion that was a marvel of grace and speed. But, fast as he was, he was almost too late. Four bolts of lightning blasted, almost as one. The two desperadoes dropped, cold; the Lensman felt a stab of agony sear through his shoulder and the breath whistled out of his mouth and nose as his space-suit collapsed. Gasping terribly for air that was no longer there, holding onto his senses doggedly and grimly, he made shift to close the outer door of the lock and to turn a valve. He did not lose consciousness—quite—and as soon as he recovered the use of his muscles he stripped off his suit and examined himself narrowly in a mirror.

Eyes, plenty bloodshot. Nose, bleeding copiously. Ears, bleeding, but not too badly; drums not ruptured, fortunately —he had been able to keep the pressure fairly well equalized. Felt like some internal bleeding, but he could see nothing really serious. He hadn't breathed space long enough to do any permanent damage, he guessed.

Then, baring his shoulder, he treated the wound with Zinsmaster burn-dressing. This was no trifle, but at that, it wasn't so bad. No bone gone—it'd heal in two or three weeks. Lastly, he looked over his suit. If he'd only had his G-P armor on—but that, of course, was out of the question. He had a spare suit, but he'd rather . . . Fine, he could replace the burned section easily enough. QX.

He donned his other suit, re-entered the air lock, neutralized the screens, and crossed over; where he did exactly what any other meteor miner would have done. He divested the bloated corpses of their space-suits and shoved them off into space. He then ransacked the ship, transferring from it to his own, as well as four heavy meteors, every other item of value which he could move and which his vessel could hold. Then, inerting her, he gave her a couple of notches of drive and cut her loose, for so a real miner would have done. It was not compunction or scruple that would have prevented any miner from taking the ship, as well as the supplies. Ships were registered, and otherwise were too hot to be handled except by organized criminal rings.

As a matter of routine he tested the meteor which had been the innocent cause of all this strife—or had it been a bait?—and found it worthless iron. Also as routine he kept on working. He had almost enough metal now, even at Miners' Rest prices, for a royal binge, but he couldn't go in until his shoulder was well. And a couple of weeks later he got the shock of his life.

He had brought in a meteor; a mighty big one, over four feet in its smallest dimension. He sampled it, and as soon as he cut the Berg and flicked the sample experimentally from hand to hand, his skilled muscles told him that that metal was astoundingly dense. Heart racing, he locked the test-piece into the spee-gee; and that vital organ almost stopped beating entirely as the indicator needle went up and up and up—stopping at a full twenty two, and the scale went only to twenty four!

"Klono's brazen hoofs and diamond-tipped horns!" he ejaculated. He whistled stridently through his teeth, then measured his find as accurately as he could. Then, speaking aloud "Just about thirty thousand kilograms of something noticeably denser than pure platinum—thirty million credits or I'm a Zabriskan fontema's maiden aunt. What to do?"

This find, as well it might, gave the Gray Lensman pause. It upset all his calculations. It was unthinkable to take that meteor to such a fence's hideout as Miners' Rest. Men had been murdered, and would be again,. for a thousandth of its value. No matter where he took it, there would be publicity galore, and that wouldn't do. If he called a Patrol ship to take the white elephant off his hands he might be seen; and he had put in too much work on this identity to jeopardize it. He'd have to bury it, he guessed— he had maps of the system, and the fourth planet was close by.

He cut off a chunk of a few pounds' weight and made a nugget—a tiny meteor—of it, then headed for the planet, a plainly visible disk some fifteen degrees from the sun. He had a fairly large-scale chart of the system, with notes. Borova IV was uninhabited, except by low forms of life, and by outposts. Cold. Atmosphere thin—good, that meant no clouds. No oceans. No volcanic activity. Very good! He'd look it over, and the first striking landmark he saw, from one diameter out, would be his cache.

He circled the planet once at the equator, observing a formation of five mighty peaks arranged in a semi-circle, cupped toward the world's north pole. He circled it again, seeing nothing as prominent, and nothing else resembling it at all closely. Scanning his plate narrowly, to be sure nothing was following him, he drove downward in a screaming dive toward the middle mountain.

It was an extinct volcano, he discovered, with a level-floored crater more than a hundred miles in diameter. Practically level, that is, except for a smaller cone which reared up in the center of that vast, desolate plain of craggy, tortured lava. Straight down into the cold vent of the inner cone the Lensman steered his ship; and in its exact center he dug a hole and buried his treasure. He then lifted his tug-boat fifty feet and held her there, poised on her raving under-jets, until the lava in the little crater again began sluggishly to flow, and thus to destroy all evidence of his visit. This detail attended to, he shot out into space and called Haynes, to whom he reported in full.

"I'll bring the meteor in when I come—or do you want to send somebody out here after it? It belongs to the Patrol, of course."

"No, it doesn't, Kim—it belongs to you."

"Huh? Isn't there a law that any discoveries made by any employes of the Patrol belong to the Patrol?"

"Nothing as broad as that. Certain scientific discoveries, by scientists assigned to an exact research, yes. But you're forgetting again that you're an Unattached Lensman, and as such are accountable to no one in the Universe. Even the ten-per-cent treasure-trove law couldn't touch you. Besides, your meteor is not in that category, as you are its first owner, as far as we know. If you insist I'll mention it to the Council, but I know in advance what the answer will be."

"QX, Chief—thanks," and the connection was broken.

There, that was that. He had got rid of the white elephant, yet it wouldn't be wasted. If the zwilniks got him, the Patrol would dig it up; if he lived long enough to retire to a desk job he wouldn't have to take any more of the Patrol's money as long as he lived. Financially, he was all set.

And physically, he was all set for his first real binge as a meteor-miner. His shoulder and arm were as good as new. He had a lot of metal; enough so that its proceeds would finance, not only his next venture into space, but also a really royal celebration in the spaceman's resort he had already picked out.

For the Lensman had devoted a great deal of thought to that item. For his purpose, the bigger the resort—within limits—the better. The man he was after would not be a small operator, nor would he deal directly with such. Also, the big king-pins did not murder drugged miners for their ships and outfits, as the smaller ones sometimes did. The big ones realized that there was more long-pull profit in repeat business.

Therefore Kinnison set his course toward the great asteroid Euphrosyne and its festering hell-hole, Miners' Rest. Miners' Rest, to all highly moral citizens the disgrace not only of a solar system but of a sector; the very name of which was (and is) a by-word and a hissing to the blue-noses of twice a hundred inhabited and civilized worlds.

**Wild Bill Williams,
Meteor Miner**

A S HAS BEEN IMPLIED, MINERS'
Rest was the biggest, widest-open, least restrained joint in
that entire sector of the galaxy. And through the underground activities of his fellows of the Patrol, Kinnison knew
that of all the king-snipes of that lawless asteroid, the man
called Strongheart was the Big Shot.

Therefore the Lensman landed his battered craft at
Strongheart's Dock, loaded the equipment of the hi-jacker's
boat into a hand truck, and went into to talk to Strongheart himself. "Supplies—Equipment—Metal—Bought and
Sold" the sign read; but to any experienced eye it was evident that the sign was conservative indeed; that it did not
cover Strongheart's business, by half. There were dance-
halls, there were long and ornate bars, there were rooms in
plenty devoted to various games of so-called chance, and
most significant, there were scores of those unmistakable
cubicles.

"Welcome, stranger! Glad to see you—have a good
trip?" The dive-keeper always greeted new customers ef-
fusively. "Have a drink on the house!"

"Business before pleasure," Kinnison replied, tersely.
"Pretty good, yes. Here's some stuff I don't need any more
that I aim to sell. What'll you gimme for it?"

The dealer inspected the suits and instruments, then bored a keen stare into the miner's eyes; a scrutiny under which Kinnison neither flushed nor wavered.

"Two hundred and fifty credits for the lot," Strongheart decided.

"Best you can do?"

"Tops. Take it or leave it."

"QX, they're yours. Gimme it."

"Why, this just starts our business, don't it? Ain't you got cores? Sure you have."

"Yeah, but not for no"—doubly and unprintably qualified—"damn robber. I like a louse, but you suit me altogether too damn well. Them suits alone, just as they lay, are worth a thousand."

"So what? For why go to insult me, a business man? Sure I can't give what that stuff is worth—who could? You ought to know how I got to get rid of hot goods. You killed, ain't it, the guys what owned it, so how could I treat it except like it's hot? Now be your age—don't burn out no jets," as the Lensman turned with a blistering, sizzling deep-space oath. "I know they shot first, they always do, but how does that change things? But keep your shirt on yet, I don't tell nobody nothing. For why should I? How could I make any money on hot stuff if I talk too much with my mouth, huh? But on cores, that's something else again. Meteors is legitimate merchandise, and I pay you as much as anybody, maybe more."

"QX," and Kinnison tossed over his cores. He had sold the bandits' space-suits and equipment deliberately, in order to minimize further killing.

This was his first visit to Miners' Rest, but he intended to become an habitue of the place; and before he would be accepted as a "regular" he knew that he would have to prove his quality. Buckos and bullies would be sure to try him out. This way was much better. The tale would spread; and any gunman who had drilled two hi-jackers, dead-center through the face-plates, was not one to be challenged lightly. He might have to kill one or two, but not many, nor frequently.

And the fellow was honest enough in his buying of the metal. His Spaldings cut honest cores—Kinnison put micrometers on them to be sure of that fact. He did not underread his torsiometer, and he weighed the meteors upon certified balances. He used Galactic Standard average-value-density tables, and offered exactly half of the calculated average value; which, Kinnison knew, was fair enough. By taking his metal to a mint or a rare-metals station of the Patrol, any miner could get the precise value of any meteor, as shown by detailed analysis. However, instead of making the long trip and waiting—and paying—for the exact analyses, the miners usually preferred to take the "fifty-percent-of-average-density-value" which was the customary offer of the outside dealers.

Then, the meteors unloaded and hauled away, Kinnison dickered with Strongheart concerning the supplies he would need during his next trip; the hundred-and-one items which are necessary to make a tiny space-ship a self-contained, self-sufficient, warm and inhabitable worldlet in the immense and unfriendly vacuity of space. Here, too, the Lensman was overcharged shamelessly; but that, too, was routine. No one would, or could be expected to, do business in any such place as Miners' Rest at any sane or ordinary percentage of profit.

When Strongheart counted out to him the net proceeds of the voyage, Kinnison scratched reflectively at his whiskery chin.

"That ain't hardly enough, I don't think, for the real, old-fashioned, stem-winding bender I was figuring on," he ruminated. "I been out a long time and I was figuring on doing the thing up brown. Have to let go of my nugget, too, I guess. Kinda hate to—been packing it round quite a while—but here she is." He reached into his kit-bag and tossed over the lump of really precious metal. "Let you have it for fifteen hundred credits."

"Fifteen hundred! An idiot you must be, or you should

think I'm one, I don't know!" Strongheart yelped, as he juggled the mass lightly from hand to hand. "Two hundred, you mean . . . well two fifty, then, but that's a nawful high bid, mister, believe me . . . I tell you, I couldn't give my own mother over three hundred—I'd lose money on the goods. You ain't tested it, what makes you think it's such a much?"

"No, and I notice you ain't testing it, neither," Kinnison countered. "Me and you both know metal well enough so we don't need to test no such nugget as that. Fifteen hundred or I flit to a mint and get full value for it. I don't have to stay here, you know, by all the nine hells of Valeria. They's millions of other places where I can get just as drunk and have just as good a time as I can here."

There ensued howls of protest, but Strongheart finally yielded, as the Lensman had known that he would. He could have forced him higher, but fifteen hundred was enough.

"Now, sir, just the guarantee and you're all set for a lot of fun," Strongheart's anguish had departed miraculously upon the instant of the deal's closing. "We take your keys, and when your money's gone and you come back to get 'em, to sell your supplies or your ship or whatever, we takes you, without hurting you a bit more than we have to, and sober you up, quick as scat. A room here, whenever you want it, included. Padded, sir, very nice and comfortable —you can't hurt yourself, possibly. We been in business here for years, with perfect satisfaction. Not one of our customers, and we got hundreds who never go nowhere else, have we ever let sell any of the stuff he had laid in for his next trip, and we never steal none of his supplies, neither. Only two hundred credits for the whole service, sir. Cheap, sir—very, *very* cheap at the price."

"Um . . . m . . . m." Kinnison again scratched meditatively, this time at the nape of his neck.

"I'll take your guarantee, I guess, because sometimes, when I get to going real good, I don't know just exactly when to stop. But I won't need no padded cell. Me, I don't never get violent—I always taper off on twenty four units of benny. That gives me twenty four hours on the shelf, and then I'm all set for another stretch out in the ether. You couldn't get me no benny, I don't suppose, and if you could it wouldn't be no damn good."

This was the critical instant, the moment the Lensman had been approaching so long and so circuitously. Mind was already reading mind; Kinnison did not need the speech which followed.

"Twenty four units!" Strongheart exclaimed. That was a heroic jolt—but the man before him was of heroic mold. "Sure of that?"

"Sure I'm sure; and if I get cut weight or cut quality I cut the guy's throat that peddles it to me. But I ain't out. I got a couple of belts left—guess I'll use my own, and when it gets gone go buy me some from a fella I know that's about half honest."

"Don't handle it myself," this, the Lensman knew, was at least partially true, "but I know a man who has a friend who can get it. Good stuff, too, in the original tins; special import from Corvina II. That'll be four hundred altogether. Gimme it and you can start your helling around."

"Whatja mean, four hundred?" Kinnison snorted. "Think I'm just blasting off about having some left, huh? Here's two hundred for your guarantee, and that's all I want out of you."

"Wait a minute—jet back, brother!" Strongheart had thought that the newcomer was entirely out of his drug, and could therefore be charged eight prices for it. "How much do you get it for, mostly, the clear quill?"

"One credit per unit—twenty four for the belt," Kinnison replied, tersely and truly. That was the prevailing price charged by retail peddlers. "I'll pay you that, and I don't mean twenty five, neither."

"QX, gimme it. You don't need to be afraid of being bumped off or rolled here, neither. We got a reputation, we have."

"Yeah, I been told you run a high-class joint," Kinnison agreed, amiably. "That's why I'm here. But you wanna

be mighty sure the ape don't gyp me on the heft of the belt
—looky here!"

As the Lensman spoke he shrugged his shoulders and
the dive-keeper leaped backward with a shriek; for faster
than sight two ugly DeLameters had sprung into being in
the miner's huge, dirty paws and were pointing squarely at
his midriff!

"Put 'em away!" Strongheart yelled.

"Look 'em over first," and Kinnison handed them over,
butts first. "These ain't like them buzzards' cap-pistols what
I sold you. These is my own, and they're hot and tight. You
know guns, don't you? Look 'em over, pal—real close."

The renegade did know weapons, and he studied these
two with care, from the worn, rough-checkered grips and
full-charged magazines to the burned, scarred, deeply-pitted
orifices. Definitely and unmistakably they were weapons of
terrific power; weapons, withal, which had seen hard and
frequent service; and Strongheart personally could bear
witness to the blinding speed of this miner's draw.

"And remember this," the Lensman went on. "I never
yet got so drunk that anybody could take my guns away from
me, and if I don't get a full belt of benny I get mighty
peevish."

The publican knew that—it was a characteristic of the
drug—and he certainly did not want that miner running
amok with those two weapons in his highly capable hands.
He would, he assured him, get his full dose.

And, for his part, Kinnison knew that he was reasonably
safe, even in this hell of hells. As long as he was active he
could take care of himself, in any kind of company; and
he was fairly certain that he would not be slain, during his
drug-induced physical helplessness, for the value of his
ship and supplies. This one visit had yielded Strongheart
a profit at least equal to everything he had left, and each
subsequent visit should yield a similar amount.

"The first drink's on the house, always," Strongheart
derailed his guest's train of thought. "What'll it be? Tellurian, ain't you—whiskey?"

"Uh-uh. Close, though—Aldebaran II. Got any good old Aldebaranian bolega?"

"No, but we got some good old Tellurian whiskey, about the same thing."

"QX—gimme a shot." He poured a stiff three fingers, downed it at a gulp, shuddered ecstatically, and emitted a wild yell. "Yip-yip-yippee! I'm Wild Bill Williams, the ripping, roaring, ritoodolorum from Aldebaran II, and this is my night to howl. Whee . . . yow . . . owrie-e-e!" Then, quieting down, "This rot-gut wasn't never within a million parsecs of Tellus, but it ain't bad—not bad at all. Got the teeth and claws of holy old Klono himself—goes down your throat just like swallowing a cateagle. Clear ether, pal, I'll be back shortly."

For his first care was to tour the entire Rest, buying scrupulously one good stiff drink, of whatever first came to hand, at each hot spot as he came to it.

"A good-will tour," he explained joyously to Strongheart upon his return. "Got to do it, pal, to keep 'em from calling down the curse of Klono on me, but I'm going to do all my serious drinking right here."

And he did. He drank various and sundry beverages, mixing them with a sublime disregard for consequences which surprised even the hard-boiled booze-fighters assembled there. "Anything that'll pour," he declared, loud and often, and acted accordingly. Potent or mild; brewed, fermented, or distilled; loaded, cut, or straight, all one. "Down the hatch!" and down it went. Here was a two-fisted drinker whose like had not been seen for many a day, and his fame spread throughout the Rest.

Being a "happy jag," the more he drank the merrier he became. He bestowed largess hither and yon, in joyous abandon. He danced blithely with the "hostesses" and tipped them extravagantly. He did not gamble, explaining frequently and painstakingly that that wasn't none of his dish; he wanted to have fun with his money.

He fought, even, without anger or rancor; but gayly, laughing with Homeric gusto the while. He missed with terrific swings that would have felled a horse had they landed; only occasionally getting in, as though by chance, a paralyzing punch. Thus he accumulated an entirely unnecessary mouse under each eye and a sadly bruised nose.

However, his good humor was, as is generally the case in such instances, quite close to the surface, and was prone to turn into passionate anger with less real cause even than the trivialities which started the friendly fist-fights. During various of these outbursts of wrath he smashed four chairs, two tables, and assorted glassware.

But only once did he have to draw a deadly weapon—the news, as he had known it would, had spread abroad that with a DeLameter he was nobody to monkey with—and even then he didn't have to kill the guy. Just winging him—a little bit of a burn through his gun-arm—had been enough.

So it went for days. And finally, it was in immense relief that the hilariously drunken Lensman, his money gone to the last millo, went roistering up the street with a two-quart bottle in each hand; swigging now from one, then from the other; inviting bibulously the while any and all chance comers to join him in one last, fond drink. The sidewalk was not wide enough for him, by half; indeed, he took up most of the street. He staggered and reeled, retaining any semblance of balance only by a miracle and by his rigorous spaceman's training.

He threw away one empty bottle, then the other. Then, as he strode along, so purposefully and yet so futilely, he sang. His voice was not particularly musical, but what it lacked in quality of tone it more than made up in volume. Kinnison had a really remarkable voice, a bass of tremendous power, timbre, and resonance; and, pulling out all the stops, in tones audible for two thousand yards against the wind, he poured out his zestfully lusty reveler's soul. His song was a deep-space chanty that would have blistered the ears of any of the gentler spirits who had known him as Kimball Kinnison, of Earth; but which, in Miners' Rest, was merely a humorous and sprightly ballad.

Up the full length of the street he went. Then back,

as he put it, to "Base." Even if this final bust did make him sicker at the stomach than a ground-gripper going free for the first time, the Lensman reflected, he had done a mighty good job. He had put Wild Bill Williams, meteor-miner, of Aldebaran II, on the map in a big way. It wasn't a faked and therefore fragile identity, either; it was solidly, definitely his own.

Staggering up to his friend Strongheart he steadied himself with two big hands upon the latter's shoulders and breathed a forty-thousand-horsepower breath into his face.

"I'm boiled like a Tellurian hoot-owl," he announced, still happily. "When I'm this stewed I can't say 'partic-hic-hicular-ly' without hic-hicking, but I would partic-hic-hicularly like just one more quart. How about me borrowing a hundred on what I'm going to bring in next time, or selling you . . ."

"You've had plenty, Bill. You've had lots of fun. How about a good chew of sleepy-happy, huh?"

"That's a thought!" the miner exclaimed eagerly. "Lead me to it!"

A stranger came up unobstrusively and took him by one elbow. Strongheart took the other, and between them they walked him down a narrow hall and into a cubicle. And while he walked flabbily along Kinnison studied intently the brain of the newcomer. *This* was what he was after!

The ape had had a screen; but it was such a nuisance he took it off for a rest whenever he came here. No Lensmen on Euphrosyne! They had combed everybody, even this drunken bum here. This was one place that no Lensman would ever come to; or, if he did, he wouldn't last long. Kinnison had been pretty sure that Strongheart would be in cahoots with somebody bigger than a peddler, and so it had proved. This guy knew plenty, and the Lensman was taking the information—all of it. Six weeks from now, eh? Just right—time to find enough metal for another royal binge here . . . And during that binge he would really do things . . .

Six weeks. Quite a while . . . but . . . QX. It would

take some time yet, anyway, probably, before the Regional Directors would, like this fellow, get over their scares enough to relax a few of their most irksome precautions. And, as has been intimated, Kinnison, while impatient enough at times, could hold himself in check like a cat watching a mousehole whenever it was really necessary.

Therefore, in the cell, he seated himself upon the bunk and seized the packet from the hand of the stranger. Tearing it open, he stuffed the contents into his mouth; and, eyes rolling and muscles twitching, he chewed vigorously; expertly allowing the potent juice to trickle down his gullet just fast enough to keep his head humming like a swarm of angry bees. Then, the cud sucked dry, he slumped down upon the mattress, physically dead to the world for the ensuing twenty four G-P hours.

He awakened; weak, flimsy, and supremely wretched. He made heavy going to the office, where Strongheart returned to him the keys of his boat.

"Feeling low, sir." It was a statement, not a question.

"I'll say so," the Lensman groaned. He was holding his spinning head, trying to steady the gyrating universe. "I'd have to look up—'way, 'way up, with a number nine visiplate—to see a snake's belly in a swamp. Make that damn cat quit stomping his feet, can't you?"

"Too bad, but it won't last long." The voice was unctuous enough, but totally devoid of feeling. "Here's a pick-up—you need it."

The Lensman tossed off the potion, without thanks, as was good technique in those parts. His head cleared miraculously, although the stabbing ache remained.

"Come in again next time. Everything's been on the green here, ain't it, sir?"

"Uh-huh, very nice," the Lensman admitted. "Couldn't ask for better. I'll be back in five or six weeks, if I have any luck at all."

As the battered but staunch and powerful meteor-boat floated slowly upward a desultory conversation was taking place in the dive he had left. At that early hour business was slack to the point of non-existence, and Strongheart was chatting idly with a bartender and one of the hostesses.

"If more of the boys was like him we wouldn't have no trouble at all," Strongheart stated with conviction. "Nice, quiet, easy-going—a right guy, I say."

"Yeah, but at that maybe it's a good gag nobody riled him up too much," the barkeep opined. "He could be rough if he wanted to, I bet a quart. Drunk or sober, he's chain lightning with them DeLameters."

"He's so refined, such a perfect gentleman," sighed the woman. "He's nice." To her, he had been. She had had plenty of credits from the big miner, without having given anything save smiles and dances in return. "Them two guys he drilled must have needed killing, or he wouldn't have burned 'em."

And that was that. As the Lensman had intended, Wild Bill Williams was an old, known, and highly respected resident of Miners' Rest!

Out among the asteroids again; more muscle-tearing, back-breaking, lonesome labor. Kinnison did not find any more fabulously rich meteors—such things happen only once in a hundred lifetimes—but he was getting his share of heavy stuff. Then one day when he had about half a load there came screaming in upon the emergency wave a call for help; a call so loud that the ship broadcasting it must be very close indeed. Yes, there she was, right in his lap; startlingly large even upon the low-power plates of his space-tramp.

"Help! Space-ship 'Kahlotus', position . . ." a rattling string of numbers. "Bergenholm dead, meteorite screens practically disabled, intrinsic velocity throwing us into the asteroids. Any space-tugs, any vessels with tractors—help! And hurry!"

At the first word Kinnison had shoved his blast-lever full over. A few seconds of free flight, a minute of inert maneuvering that taxed to the utmost his Lensman's skill and powerful frame, and he was within the liner's air-lock.

"I know something about Bergs!" he snapped. "Take

this boat of mine and pull! Are you evacuating passengers?"
he shot at the mate as they ran toward the engine room.

"Yes, but afraid we haven't boats enough—overloaded,"
was the gasped reply.

"Use mine—fill 'er up!" If the mate was surprised at
such an offer from a despised space-rat he did not show it.
There were many more surprises in store.

In the engine room Kinnison brushed aside a crew of
helplessly futile gropers and threw in switch after switch.
He looked. He listened. Above all, he pried into that sealed
monster of power with all his sense of perception. How glad
he was now that he and Thorndyke had struggled so long
and so furiously with a balky Bergenholm on that trip to
tempestuous Trenco! For as a result of that trip he *did* know
Bergs, with a sure knowledge possessed by few other men
in space.

"Number four lead is shot somewhere," he reported.
"Must be burned off where it clears the pilaster. Careless
overhaul last time—got to take off the lower port third
cover. No time for wrenches—get me a cutting beam, and
get the lead out of your pants!"

The beam was brought on the double and the Lensman
himself blasted away the designated cover. Then, throwing
an insulated plate over the red-hot casing he lay on his
back—"Hand me a light!"—and peered briefly upward into
the bowels of the gargantuan mechanism.

"Thought so," he grunted. "Piece of four-oh stranded,
eighteen inches long. Ditmars number six clip ends, twenty
inches on centers. Myerbeer insulation on center section,
doubled. Snap it up! One of you other fellows, bring me
a short, heavy screw-driver and a pair of Ditmars six
wrenches!"

The technicians worked fast and in a matter of seconds
the stuff was there. The Lensman labored briefly but hugely;
and much more surely than if he were dependent upon the
rays of the hand-lamp to penetrate the smoky, steamy,
greasy murk in which he toiled. Then:

"QX—give her the juice!" he snapped.

They gave it, and to the stunned surprise of all, she took it. The liner again was free!

"Kind of a jury rigging I gave it, but it'll hold long enough to get you into port, sir," he reported to the captain in his sanctum, saluting crisply. He was in for it now, he knew, as the officer stared at him. But he *couldn't* have let that shipload of passengers get ground up into hamburger. Anyway, there was a way out.

In apparent reaction he turned pale and trembled, and the officer hastily took from his medicinal stores a bottle of choice old brandy.

"Here, drink this," he directed, proferring the glass.

Kinnison did so. More, he seized the bottle and drank that, too—all of it—a draft which would have literally turned him inside out a few months since. Then, to the captain's horrified disgust, he took from his filthy dungarees a packet of bentlam and began to chew it, idiotically blissful. Thence, and shortly, into oblivion.

"Poor devil . . . you poor, poor devil," the commander murmured, and had him put into a bunk.

When he had come to and had had his pickup, the captain came and regarded him soberly.

"You were a man once. An engineer—a top-bracket engineer—or I'm an oiler's pimp," he said levelly.

"Maybe," Kinnison replied, white and weak. "I'm all right yet, except once in a while . . ."

"I know," the captain frowned. "No cure?"

"Not a chance. Tried dozens. So . . ." and the Lensman spread out his hands in a hopeless gesture.

"Better tell me your name, anyway—your real name. That'll let your planet know you aren't . . ."

"Better not," the sufferer shook his aching head. "Folks think I'm dead. Let them keep on thinking so. Williams is the name, sir; William Williams, of Aldabaran II."

"As you say."

"How far are we from where I boarded you?"

"Close. Less than half a billion miles. This, the second,

is our home planet; your asteroid belt is just outside the orbit of the fourth."

"I'll do a flit, then."

"As you say," the officer agreed, again. "But we'd like to . . ." and he extended a sheaf of currency.

"Rather not, sir, thanks. You see, the longer it takes me to earn another stake, the longer it'll be before . . ."

"I see. Thanks, anyway, for us all," and captain and mate helped the derelict embark. They scarcely looked at him, scarcely dared look at each other . . . but . . .

Kinnison, for his part, was content. This story, too, would get around. It would be in Miners' Rest before he got back there, and it would help . . . help a lot.

He could not possibly let those officers know the truth, even though he realized full well that at that very moment they were thinking, pityingly:

"The poor devil . . . the poor, brave devil!"

THE GRAY LENSMAN WENT BACK
to his mining with a will and with unimpaired vigor, for his
distress aboard the ship had been sheerest acting. One small
bottle of good brandy was scarcely a cocktail to the physique
that had stood up under quart after quart of the crudest,
wickedest, fieriest beverages known to space; that tiny
morsel of bentlam—scarcely half a unit—affected him no
more than a lozenge of licorice.

Three weeks. Twenty one days, each of twenty four
G-P hours. At the end of that time, he had learned from
the mind of the zwilnik, the Boskonian director of this,
the Borovan solar system, would visit Miners' Rest, to
attend some kind of meeting. His informant did not know
what the meeting was to be about, and he was not unduly
curious about it. Kinnison, however, did and was.

The Lensman knew, or at least very shrewdly suspected,
that that meeting was to be a regional conference of big-
shot zwilniks; he was intensely curious to know all about
everything that was to take place; and he was determined
to be present.

Three weeks was lots of time. In fact, he should be able
to complete his quota of heavy metal in two, or less. It was
there, there was no question of that. Right out there were

the meteors, uncountable thousands of millions of them, and a certain proportion of them carried values. The more and the harder he worked, the more of these worth-while wanderers of the void he would find. Wherefore he labored long, hard, and rapidly, and his store of high-test meteors grew apace.

To such good purpose did he use beam and Spalding drill that he was ready more than a week ahead of time. That was QX—he'd much rather be early than late. Something might have happened to hold him up—things did happen, too often—and he *had* to be at that meeting!

Thus it came about that, a few days before the all-important date, Kinnison's battered treasure-hunter blasted herself down to her second landing at Strongheart's Dock. This time the miner was welcomed, not as a stranger, but as a friend of long standing.

"Hi, Wild Bill!" Strongheart yelled at sight of the big space-hound. "Right on time, I see—glad to see you! Luck, too, I hope—lots of luck, and all good, I bet me—ain't it?"

"Ho, Strongheart!" the Lensman roared in return, pummeling the divekeeper affectionately. "Had a good trip, yeah—a fine trip. Struck a rich sector—twice as much as I got last time. Told you I'd be back in five or six weeks, and made it in five weeks and four days."

"Keeping tabs on the days, huh?"

"I'll say I do. With a thirst like mine a guy can't do nothing else—I tell you all my guts're dryer than any desert on the whole of Rhylce. Well, what're we waiting for? Check this plunder of mine in and let me get to going places and doing things!"

The business end of the visit was settled with neatness and dispatch. Dealer and miner understood each other thoroughly; each knew what could and what could not be done to the other. The meteors were tested and weighed. Supplies for the ensuing trip were bought. The guarantee and twenty four units of benny—QX. No argument. No hysterics. No bickering or quarreling or swearing. Everything on the green, all the way. Gentlemen and friends. Kinnison turned over his keys, accepted a thick sheaf of currency, and, after the first formal drink with his host, set out upon the self-imposed, superstitious tour of the other hot spots which would bring him the favor—or at least would avert the active disfavor—of Klono, his spaceman's deity.

This time, however, that tour took longer. Upon his first ceremonial round he had entered each saloon in turn, had bought one drink of whatever was nearest, had tossed it down, and had gone on to the next place; unobserved and inconspicuous. Now, how different it all was! Wherever the went he was the center of attention.

Men who had met him before flung themselves upon him with whoops of welcome; men who had never seen him clamored to drink with him; women, whether or not they knew him, fawned upon him and brought into play their every lure and wile. For not only was this man a hero and a celebrity of sorts; he was a lucky—or a skillful—miner whose every trip resulted in wads of money big enough to clog the under-jets of a freighter! Moreover, when he was lit up he threw it round regardless, and he was getting stewed as fast as he could swallow. Let's keep him here— or, if we can't do that, let's go along, wherever he goes!

This, too, was strictly according to the Lensman's expectations. Everybody knew that he did not do any serious drinking glass by glass at the bar, but bottle by bottle; that he did not buy individual drinks for his friends, but let them drink as deeply as they would from whatever container chanced then to be in hand; and his vast popularity gave him a sound excuse to begin his bottle-buying at the start instead of waiting until he got back to Strongheart's. He bought, then, several or many bottles and tins in each place, instead of a single drink. And, since everybody knew for a fact that he was a practically bottomless drinker, who was even to suspect that he barely moistened his gullet while the hangers-on were really emptying the bottles, cans, and flagons?

And during his real celebration at Strongheart's, while

he drank enough, he did not drink too much. He waxed exceedingly happy and frolicsome, as before. He was as profligate, as extravagant in tips. He had the same sudden flashes of hot anger. He fought enthusiastically and awkwardly, as Wild Bill Williams did, although only once or twice, that time; and he did not have to draw his DeLameter at all— he was so well known and so beloved! He sang as loudly and as raucously, and with the same fine taste in madrigals.

Therefore, when the infiltration of thought-screened men warned him that the meeting was about to be called Kinnison was ready. He was in fact cold sober when he began his tuneful, last-two-bottles trip up the street, and he was almost as sober when he returned to "Base," empty of bottles and pockets, to make the usual attempt to obtain more money from Strongheart and to compromise by taking his farewell chew of bentlam instead.

Nor was he unduly put out by the fact that both Strongheart and the zwilnik were now wearing screens. He had taken it for granted that they might be, and had planned accordingly. He seized the packet as avidly as before, chewed its contents as ecstatically, and slumped down as helplessly and as idiotically. That much of the show, at least, was real. Twenty four units of that drug will paralyze *any* human body, make it assume the unmistakable pose and stupefied mien of the bentlam eater. But Kinnison's mind was not an ordinary one; the dose which would have rendered any bona-fide miner's brain as helpless as his body did not affect the Lensman's new equipment at all. Alcohol and bentlam together were bad, but the Lensman was sober. Therefore, if anything, the drugging of his body only made it easier to dissociate his new mind from it. Furthermore, he need not waste any thought in making it act. There was only one way it could act, now, and Kinnison let his new senses roam abroad without even thinking of the body he was leaving behind him.

In view of the rigorous orders from higher up the conference room was heavily guarded by screened men; no one except old and trusted employees were allowed to enter it, and they were also protected. Nevertheless, Kinnison got in, by proxy.

A clever pick-pocket brushed against a screened waiter who was about to enter the sacred precincts, lightning fingers flicking a switch. The waiter began to protest—then forgot what he was going to say, even as the pick-pocket forgot completely the deed he had just done. The waiter in turn was a trifle clumsy in serving a certain Big Shot, but earned no rebuke thereby; for the latter forgot the offense almost instantly. Under Kinnison's control the director fumbled at his screen-generator for a moment, loosening slightly a small but important resistor. That done, the Lensman withdrew delicately and the meeting was an open book.

"Before we do anything," the director began, "Show me that all your screens are on." He bared his own—it would have taken an expert service man an hour to find that it was not functioning perfectly.

"Poppycock!" snorted the zwilnik. "Who in all the hells of space thinks that a Lensman would—or *could*—come to Euphrosyne?"

"Nobody can tell what this particular Lensman can or can't do, and nobody knows what he's doing until just before he dies. Hence the strictness. You've searched everybody here, of course?"

"Everybody," Strongheart averred, "even the drunks and the dopes. The whole building is screened, besides the screens we're wearing."

"The dopes don't count, of course, provided they're really doped." No one except the Gray Lensman himself could possibly conceive of a Lensman being—not seeming to be, but actually *being*—a drunken sot, to say nothing of being a confirmed addict of any drug. "By the way, who is this Wild Bill Williams we've been hearing about?"

Strongheart and his friend looked at each other and laughed.

"I checked up on him early," the zwilnik chuckled. "He isn't the Lensman, of course, but I thought at first he might be an agent. We frisked him and his ship thoroughly—no dice—and checked back on him as a miner, four solar systems back. He's clean, anyway; this is his second bender here. He's been guzzling everything in stock for a week, getting more pie-eyed every day, and Strongheart and I just put him to bed with twenty four units of benny. You know what *that* means, don't you?"

"Your own benny or his?" the director asked.

"My own. That's why I know he's clean. All the other dopes are too. The drunks we gave the bum's rush, like you told us to."

"QX. I don't think there's any danger, myself—I think the hot-shot Lensman they're afraid of is still working Bronseca—but these orders not to take any chances at all come from 'way, 'way up."

"How about this new system they're working on, that nobody knows his boss any more? Hooey, I call it."

"Not ready yet. They haven't been able to invent an absolutely safe one that'll handle the work. In the meantime, we're using these books. Cumbersome, but absolutely safe, they say, unless and until the enemy gets onto the idea. Then one group will go into the lethal chambers of the Patrol and the rest of us will use something else. Some say this code can't be cracked; others say any code can be read in time. Anyway here's your orders. Pass them along. Give me your stuff and we'll have supper and a few drinks."

They ate. They drank. They enjoyed an evening and a night of high revelry and low dissipation, each to his taste; each secure in the knowledge that his thought-screen was one hundred percent effective against the one enemy he really feared. Indeed, the screens were that effective—then— since the Lensman, having learned from the director all he knew, had restored the generator to full efficiency in the instant of his relinquishment of control.

Although the heads of the zwilniks, and therefore their minds, were secure against Kinnison's prying, the books of record were not. And, though his body was lying helpless, inert upon a drug-fiend's cot, his sense of perception read those books; if not as readily as though they were in his hands and open, yet readily enough. And, far off in space, a power-brained Lensman yclept Worsel recorded upon imperishable metal a detailed account, including names, dates, facts, and figures, of all the doings of all the zwilniks of a solar system!

The information was coded, it is true; but, since Kinnison knew the key, it might just as well have been printed in English. To the later consternation of Narcotics, however, that tape was sent in under Lensman's Seal—it could not be read until the Gray Lensman gave the word.

In twenty four hours Kinnison recovered from the effects of his debauch. He got his keys from Strongheart. He left the asteroid. He knew the mighty intellect with whom he had next to deal, he knew where that entity was to be found; but, sad to say, he had positively no idea at all as to what he was going to do or how he was going to do it.

Wherefore it was that a sense of relief tempered the natural apprehension he felt upon receiving, a few days later, an insistent call from Haynes. Truly this must be something really extraordinary, for while during the long months of his service Kinnison had called the Port Admiral several times, Haynes had never before Lensed him.

"Kinnison! Haynes calling!" the message beat into his consciousness.

"Kinnison acknowledging, sir!" the Gray Lensman thought back.

"Am I interrupting anything important?"

"Not at all. I'm just doing a little flit."

"A situation has come up which we feel you should study, not only in person, but also without advance information or pre-conceived ideas. Can you come in to Prime Base immediately?"

"Yes, sir. In fact, a little time right now might do me good in two ways—let me mull a job over, and let a nut mellow down to a point where maybe I can crack it. At your orders, sir!"

"Not orders, Kinnison!" the old man reprimanded him sharply. "No one gives Unattached Lensmen orders. We request or suggest, but you are the sole judge as to where your greatest usefulness lies."

"Please believe, sir, that your requests are orders, to me," Kinnison replied in all seriousness. Then, more lightly, "Your calling me in suggests an emergency, and travelling in this miner's scow of mine is just a trifle faster than going afoot. How about sending out something with some legs to pick me up?"

"The *Dauntless,* for instance?"

"Oh—you've got her rebuilt already?"

"Yes."

"I'll bet she's a sweet clipper! She was a mighty slick stepper before; now she must have more legs than a centipede!"

And so it came about that in a region of space entirely empty of all other vessels as far as ultra-powerful detectors could reach, the *Dauntless* met Kinnison's tugboat. The two went inert and maneuvered briefly, then the immense warship engulfed her tiny companion and flashed away.

"Hi, Kim, you old son-of-a-space-flea!" A general yell arose at sight of him, and irrepressible youth rioted, regardless of Regs, in this reunion of old comrades in arms who were yet scarcely more than boys in years.

"His Nibs says for you to call him, Kim, when we're about an hour out from Prime Base," Maitland informed his class-mate irreverently, as the *Dauntless* neared the Solarian system.

"Plate or Lens?"

"Didn't say—as you like, I suppose."

"Plate then, I guess—don't want to butt in," and in moments Port Admiral and Gray Lensman were in image face to face.

"How are you making out, Kinnison?" Haynes studied the young man's face intently, gravely, line by line. Then, via Lens, "We heard about the shows you put on, clear over here on Tellus. A man can't drink and dope the way you did without suffering consequences. I've been wondering if even you can fight it off. How about it? How do you feel now?"

"Some craving, of course," Kinnison replied, shrugging his shoulders. "That can't be helped—you can't make an omelette without breaking eggs. However, it's nothing I can't lick. I've got it pretty well boiled out of my system already."

"Mighty glad to hear that, son. Only Ellison and I know who Wild Bill Williams really is. You had us scared stiff for a while." Then, speaking aloud:

"I would like to have you come to my office as soon as possible."

"I'll be there, chief, two minutes after we hit the bumpers," and he was.

"The admiral busy, Ruby?" he asked, waving an airy salute at the attractive young woman in Haynes' outer office.

"Go right in, Lensman Kinnison, he's waiting for you," and opening the door for him, she stood aside as he strode into the sanctum.

The Port Admiral returned the younger man's punctilious salute, then the two shook hands warmly before Haynes referred to the third man in the room.

"Navigator Xylpic, this is Lensman Kinnison, Unattached. Sit down, please; this may take some time. Now, Kinnison, I want to tell you that ships have been disappearing, right and left, disappearing without sending out an alarm or leaving a trace. Convoying makes no difference, as the escorts also disappear . . ."

"Any with the new projectors?" Kinnison flashed the question via Lens—this was nothing to talk about aloud.

"No," came the reassuring thought in reply. "Every one bottled up tight until we find out what it's all about. Sending out the *Dauntless* after you was the only exception."

"Fine. You shouldn't have taken even that much chance." This interplay of thought took but an instant; Haynes went on with scarcely a break in his voice:

". . . with no more warning or report than the freighters and liners they are supposed to be protecting. Automatic reporting also fails—the instruments simply stop sending. The first and only sign of light—if it *is* such a sign; which frankly, I doubt—came shortly before I called you in, when Xylpic here came to me with a tall story."

Kinnison looked then at the stranger. Pink. Unmistakably a Chickladorian—pink all over. Bushy hair, triangular eyes, teeth, skin; all that same peculiar color. Not the flush of red blood showing through translucent skin, but opaque pigment; the brick-reddish pink so characteristic of the near-humanity of that planet.

"We have investigated this Xylpic thoroughly," Haynes went on, discussing the Chickladorian as impersonally as though he were upon his home planet instead of there in the room, listening. "The worst of it is that the man is absolutely honest—or at least, he thinks he is—in telling this yarn. Also, except for this one thing—this obsession, fixed idea, hallucination, call it what you like; it seems incredible that it *can* be a fact—he not only seems to be, but actually *is*, sane. Now, Xylpic, tell Kinnison what you told the rest of us. And Kinnison, I hope you can make sense of it— none of the rest of us can."

"QX. Go ahead, I'm listening." But Kinnison did far more than listen. As the fellow began to talk the Gray Lensman insinuated his mind into that of the Chickladorian. He groped for moments, seeking the wave-length; then he, Kimball Kinnison, was actually re-living with the pink man an experience which harrowed his very soul.

"The second navigator of a Radeligian vessel died in space, and when it landed on Chickladoria I took the berth. About a week out, the whole crew went crazy, all at once. The first I knew of it was when the pilot on duty beside me left his board, picked up a stool, and smashed the automatic recorder. Then he went inert and neutralized all the controls.

"I yelled at him, but he didn't answer me, and all the men in the control room acted funny. They just milled around like men in a trance. I buzzed the captain, but he didn't acknowledge either. Then the men around me left the control room and went down the companionway toward the main lock. I was scared—my skin prickled and the hair on the back of my neck stood straight up—but I followed along, quite a ways behind, to see what they were going to do. The captain, all the rest of the officers, and the whole crew joined them in the lock. Everybody was in an awful hurry to get somewhere.

"I didn't go any nearer—I wasn't going to go out into space without a suit on. I went back into the control room to get at a spy-ray, then changed my mind. That was the first place they would come to if they boarded us, as they probably would—other ships had disappeared in space, plenty of them. Instead, I went over to a life-boat and used its spy. And I tell you, sirs, there was nothing there—nothing at all!" The stranger's voice rose almost to a shriek, his mind quivered in an ecstasy of horror.

"Steady, Xylpic, steady," the Gray Lensman said, quietingly. "Everything you've said so far makes sense. It all fits right into the matrix. Nothing to go off the beam about, at all."

"What! You believe me!" the Chickladorian stared at Kinnison in amazement, an emotion very evidently shared by the Port Admiral.

"Yes," the man in gray leather asserted. "Not only that, but I have a very fair idea of what's coming next. Shoot!"

"The men walked out into space." The pink man offered this information diffidently, although positively—an oft-repeated but starkly incredible statement. "They did not float outward, sirs, they *walked;* and they acted as if they were breathing air, not space. And as they walked they sort of faded out; became thin, misty-like. This sounds crazy, sir," to Kinnison alone, "I thought then maybe I was cuckoo, and everybody around here thinks I am now, too. Maybe I *am* nuts, sir—I don't know."

"I do. You aren't." Kinnison said calmly.

"Well, and here comes the worst of it, they walked around just as though they were in a ship, growing fainter all the time. Then some of them lay down and something began to *skin* one of them—skin him alive, sir—but there was nothing there at all. I ran, then. I got into the fastest lifeboat on the far side and gave her all the oof she'd take. That's all, sir."

"Not quite all, Xylpic, unless I'm badly mistaken. Why didn't you tell the rest of it while you were at it?"

"I didn't dare to, sir. If I'd told any more they would have *known* I was crazy instead of just thinking so . . ." He broke off sharply, his voice altering strangely as he went on: "What makes you think there was anything more, sir? Do you . . . ?" The question trailed off into silence.

"I do. If what I think happened really did happen there was more—quite a lot more—and worse. Wasn't there?"

"I'll say there was!" The navigator almost exploded in relief. "Or rather, I think now that there was. But I can't describe any of it very well—everything was getting fainter all the time, and I thought I must be imagining most of it."

"You weren't imagining a thing . . ." the Lensman began, only to be interrupted by Haynes.

"Hell's jingling bells!" that worthy shouted. "If you know what it was, spill it!"

"Think I know, but not quite sure yet—got to check it. Can't get it from him—he's told everything he really knows. He didn't really see anything, it was practically invisible. Even if he had tried to describe the whole performance you wouldn't have recognized it. Nobody could have except Worsel and I, and possibly vanBuskirk. I'll tell you the rest of what actually happened and Xylpic can tell us if it checks." His features grew taut, his voice became hard and chill. "I saw it done, once. Worse, I heard it. Saw it and heard it, clear and plain. Also, I knew what it was all about, so I can describe it a lot better than Xylpic possibly can.

"Every man of that crew was killed by torture. Some were flayed alive, as Xylpic said; then they were carved up, slowly and piecemeal. Some were stretched, pulled apart by chains and hooks, on racks. Others twisted on frames. Boiled, little by little. Picked apart, bit by bit. Gassed. Eaten away by corrosives, one molecule at a time. Pressed out flat, as though between two plates of glass. Whipped. Scourged. Beaten gradually to a pulp. Other methods, lots of them—indescribable. All slow, though, and extremely painful. Greenish-yellow light, showing the aura of each man as he died. Beams from somewhere—possibly invisible—consuming the auras. Check, Xylpic?"

"Yes, sir, it checks!" The Chickladorian exclaimed in profound relief; then added, carefully: "That is, that's the way the torture was, exactly, sir, but there was something funny, a difference, about their fading away. I can't describe what was funny about it, but it didn't seem so much that they became invisible as that they went away, sir, even though they didn't go any place."

"That's the way their system of invisibility works. Got to be—nothing else will fit into . . ."

"The Overlords of Delgon!" Haynes rasped, sharply. "But if that's a true picture how in all the hells of space did this Xylpic, alone of all the ship's personnel, get away clean? Tell me that!"

"Simple!" the Gray Lensman snapped back sharply. "The rest were all Radeligians—he was the only Chickladorian aboard. The Overlords simply didn't know he was there—didn't feel him at all. Chickladorians think on a wave nobody else in the galaxy uses—you must have noticed that when you felt of him with your Lens. It took me half a minute to synchronize with him.

"As for his escape, that makes sense, too. The Overlords are slow workers and when they're playing that game they really concentrate on it—they don't pay any attention to anything else. By the time they got done and were ready to take over the ship, he could be almost anywhere."

"But he says that there was no ship there—nothing at all!" Haynes protested.

"Invisibility isn't hard to understand." Kinnison countered. "We've almost got it ourselves—we undoubtedly could have it as good as that, with a little more work on it. There was a ship there, beyond question. Close. Hooked on with magnets, and with a space-tube, lock to lock.

"The only peculiar part of it, and the bad part, is something you haven't mentioned yet. What would the Overlords—if, as we must assume, some of them got away from Worsel and his crew—be doing with a ship? They never had any space-ships that I ever knew anything about, nor any other mechanical devices requiring any advanced engineering skill. Also, and most important, they never did and never could invent or develop such an invisibility apparatus as that."

Kinnison fell silent; and while he frowned in thought Haynes dismissed the Chickladorian, with orders that his every want be supplied.

"What do you deduce from those facts?" the Port Admiral presently asked.

"Plenty," the Gray Lensman said, darkly. "I smell a rat. In fact, it stinks to high Heaven. Boskone."

"You may be right," Haynes conceded. It was hopeless, he knew, for him to try to keep up with this man's mental processes. "But why, and above all, how?"

"'Why' is easy. They both owe us a lot, and want to pay us in full. Both hate us to hell and back. 'How' is immaterial. One found the other, some way. They're together, just as sure as hell's a man-trap, and that's what matters. It's bad. Very, *very* bad, believe me."

"Orders?" asked Haynes. He was a big man; big enough to ask instructions from anyone who knew more than he did—big enough to make no bones of such asking.

"One does not give orders to the Port Admiral," Kinnison mimicked him lightly, but meaningly. "One may request, perhaps, or suggest, but . . ."

"Skip it! I'll take a club to you yet, you young hellion! You said you'd take orders from me. QX—I'll take 'em from you. What are they?"

"No orders yet, I don't think . . ." Kinnison ruminated.

"No . . . not until after we investigate. I'll have to have Worsel and vanBuskirk; we're the only three who have had experience. We'll take the *Dauntless*, I think—it'll be safe enough. Thought-screens will stop the Overlords cold, and a scrambler will take care of the invisibility business."

"Safe enough, then, you think, to let traffic resume, if they're all protected with screens?"

"I wouldn't say so. They've got Boskonian super-dreadnoughts now to use if they want to, and that's something else to think about. Another week or so won't hurt much—better wait until we see what we can see. I've been wrong once or twice before, too, and I may be again."

He was. Although his words were conservative enough, he was certain in his own mind that he knew all the answers. But how wrong he was—how terribly, now tragically wrong! For even his mentality had not as yet envisaged the incredible actuality; his deductions and perceptions fell far, far short of the appalling truth!

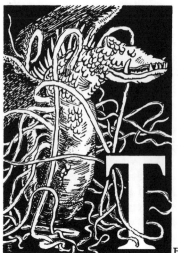

THE FASHION IN WHICH THE
Overlords of Delgon had come under the ægis of Boskone,
while obscure for a time, was in reality quite simple and
logical; for upon distant Jarnevon the Eich had profited
signally from Eichlan's disastrous raid upon Arisia. Not
exactly in the sense suggested by Eukonidor the Arisian
Watchman, it is true, but profited nevertheless. They had
learned that thought, hitherto considered only a valuable
adjunct to achievement, was actually an achievement in itself; that it could be used as a weapon of surpassing power.

Eukonidor's homily, as he more than suspected at the
time, might as well never have been uttered, for all the
effect it had upon the life or upon the purpose in life of
any single member of the race of the Eich. Eichmil, who had
been Second of Boskone, was now First; the others were
advanced correspondingly; and a new Eighth and Ninth
had been chosen to complete the roster of the Council which
was Boskone.

"The late Eichlan," Eichmil stated harshly after calling
the new Boskone to order—which event took place within
a day after it became apparent that the two bold spirits had
departed to a bourne from which there was to be no returning—"erred seriously, in fact fatally, in underestimating an

opponent, even though he himself was prone to harp upon the danger of that very thing.

"We are agreed that our objectives remain unchanged; and also that greater circumspection must be used until we have succeeded in discovering the hitherto unsuspected potentialities of pure thought. We will now hear from one of our new members, the Ninth, also a psychologist, who most fortunately had been studying this situation even before the inception of the expedition which yesterday came to such a catastrophic end."

"It is clear," the Ninth of Boskone began, "that Arisia is at present out of the question. Perceiving the possibility of some such dénouement—an idea to which I repeatedly called the attention of my predecessor psychologist, the late Eighth—I have been long at work upon certain alternative measures.

"Consider, please, the matter of the thought-screens. Who developed them first is immaterial—whether Arisia stole them from Ploor, or vice versa, or whether each developed them independently. The pertinent facts are two:

"First, that the Arisians can break such screens by the application of mental force, either of greater magnitude than they can withstand or of some new and as yet unknown composition or pattern.

"Second, that such screens were and probably still are used largely and commonly upon the planet Velantia. Therefore they must have been both necessary and adequate. The deduction is, I believe, defensible that they were used as a protection against entities who were, and who still may be, employing against the Velantians the weapons of pure thought which we wish to investigate and to acquire.

"I propose, therefore, that I and a few others of my selection continue this research, not upon Arisia, but upon Velantia and perhaps elsewhere."

To this suggestion there was no demur and a vessel set out forthwith. The visit to Velantia was simple and created no disturbance whatever. In this connection it must be remembered that the natives of Velantia, then in the early ecstasies of discovery by the Galactic Patrol and the consequent acquisition of inertialess flight, were fairly reveling in visits to and from the widely-variant peoples of the planets of hundreds of other suns. It must be borne in mind that, since the Eich were physically more like the Velantians than were the men of Tellus, the presence of a group of such entities upon the planet would create less comment than that of a group of human beings. Therefore that fateful visit went unnoticed at the time, and it was only by long and arduous research, after Kinnison had deduced that some such visit must have been made, that it was shown to have been an actuality.

Space forbids any detailed account of what the Ninth of Boskone and his fellows did, although that story of itself would be no mean epic. Suffice it to say, then, that they became well acquainted with the friendly Velantians; they studied and they learned. Particularly did they seek information concerning the noisome Overlords of Delgon, although the natives did not care to dwell at any length upon the subject.

"Their power is broken," they were wont to inform the questioners, with airy flirtings of tail and wing. "Every known cavern of them, and not a few hitherto unknown caverns, have been blasted out of existence. Whenever one of them dares to obtrude his mentality upon any one of us he is at once hunted down and slain. Even if they are not all dead, as we think, they certainly are no longer a menace to our peace and security."

Having secured all the information available upon Velantia, the Eich went to Delgon, where they devoted all the power of their admittedly first-grade minds and all the not inconsiderable resources of their ship to the task of finding and uniting the remnants of what had once been a flourishing race, the Overlords of Delgon.

The Overlords! That monstrous, repulsive, amoral race which, not excepting even the Eich themselves, achieved the most universal condemnation ever to have been given in the long history of the Galactic Union. The Eich, admittedly deserving of the fate which was theirs, had and have their apologists. The Eich were wrong-minded, all admit. They were anti-social, blood-mad, obsessed with an insatiable lust for power and conquest which nothing except complete extinction could extirpate. Their evil attributes were legion. They were, however, brave. They were organizers par excellence. They were, in their own fashion, creators and doers. They had the courage of their convictions and followed them to the bitter end.

Of the Overlords, however, nothing good has ever been said. They were debased, cruel, perverted to a degree starkly unthinkable to any normal intelligence, however housed. In their native habitat they had no weapons, nor need of any. Through sheer power of mind they reached out to their victims, even upon other planets, and forced them to come to the gloomy caverns in which they had their being. There the victims were tortured to death in numberless unspeakable fashions, and while they died the captors *fed,* ghoulishly, upon the departing life-principle of the sufferers.

The mechanism of that absorption is entirely unknown; nor is there any adequate evidence as to what end was served by it in the economy of that horrid race. That these orgies were not essential to their physical well-being is certain, since many of the creatures survived for a long time after the frightful rites were rendered impossible.

Be that is it may, the Eich sought out and found many surviving Overlords. The latter tried to enslave the visitors and to bend them to their hideously sadistic purposes, but to no avail. Not only were the Eich protected by thought-screens; they had minds stronger even than the Overlord's own. And, after the first overtures had been made and channels of communication established, the alliance was a natural.

Much has been said and written of the binding power of love. That, and other noble emotions, have indeed performed wonders. It seems to this historian, however, that all too little has been said of the effectiveness of pure hate as a cementing material. Probably for good and sufficient moral reasons; perhaps because—and for the best—its application has been of comparatively infrequent occurrence. Here, in the case in hand, we have history's best example of two entirely dissimilar peoples working efficiently together under the urge, not of love or of any other lofty sentiment, but of sheer, stark, unalloyed and corrosive, but common, hate.

Both hated Civilization and everything pertaining to it. Both wanted revenge; wanted it with a searing, furious need almost tangible: a gnawing, burning lust which neither countenanced palliation nor brooked denial. And above all, both hated vengefully, furiously, esuriently—every way except blindly—an as yet unknown and unidentified wearer of the million-times-accursed Lens of the Galactic Patrol!

The Eich were hard, ruthless, cold; not even having such words in their language as "conscience," "mercy," or "scruple." Their hatred of the Lensman was then a thing of an intensity unknowable to any human mind. Even that emotion however, grim as it was and fearsome, paled beside the passionately vitriolic hatred of the Overlords of Delgon for the being who had been the Nemesis of their race.

And when the sheer mental power of the Overlords, unthinkably great as it was and operative withal in a fashion utterly incomprehensible to us of Civilization, was combined with the ingenuity, resourcefulness, and drive, as well as with the scientific ability of the Eich, the results would in any case have been portentous indeed.

In this case they were more than portentous, and worse. Those prodigious intellects, fanned into fierce activity by fiery blasts of hatred, produced a thing incredible.

Overlords of Delgon

BEFORE HIS SHIP WAS SERVICED for the flight into the unknown Kinnison changed his mind. He was vaguely troubled about the trip. It was nothing as definite as a "hunch"; hunches are, the Gray Lensman knew, the results of the operation of an extrasensory perception possessed by all of us in greater or lesser degree. It was probably not an obscure warning to his super-sense from an other, more pervasive dimension. It was, he thought, a repercussion of the doubt in Xylpic's mind that the fading out of the men's bodies had been due to simple invisibility.

"I think I'd better go alone, chief," he informed the Port Admiral one day. "I'm not quite as sure as I was as to just what they've got."

"What difference does that make?" Haynes demanded.

"Lives," was the terse reply.

"*Your* life is what I'm thinking about. You'll be safer with the big ship, you can't deny that."

"We-ll, perhaps. But I don't want . . ."

"What you want is immaterial."

"How about a compromise? I'll take Worsel and van-Buskirk. When the Overlords hypnotized him that time it made Bus so mad that he's been taking treatments from

Worsel. Nobody can hypnotize him now, Worsel says, not even an Overlord."

"No compromise. I can't order you to take the *Dauntless,* since your authority is transcendent. You can take anything you like. I can, however, and shall, order the *Dauntless* to ride your tail wherever you go."

"QX, I'll have to take her then." Kinnison's voice grew somber. "But suppose half the crew don't get back . . . and that I do?"

"Isn't that what happened on the *Brittania?*"

"No," came flat answer. "We were all taking the same chance then—it was the luck of the draw. This is different."

"How different?"

"I've got better equipment than they have . . . I'd be a murderer, cold."

"Not at all, no more than then. You had better equipment then, too, you know, although not as much of it. Every commander of men has that same feeling when he sends men to death. But put yourself in my place. Would you send one of your best men, or let him go, alone on a highly dangerous mission when more men or ships would improve his chances? Answer that, honestly."

"Probably I wouldn't," Kinnison admitted, reluctantly.

"QX. Take all the precautions you can—but I don't have to tell you that. I know you will."

Therefore it was the *Dauntless* in which Kinnison set out a day or two later. With him were Worsel and van-Buskirk, as well as the vessel's full operating crew of Tellurians. As they approached the region of space in which Xylpic's vessel had been attacked every man in the crew got his armor in readiness for instant use, checked his sidearms, and took his emergency battle-station. Kinnison turned then to Worsel.

"How d'you feel, fellow old snake?" he asked.

"Scared," the Velantian replied, sending a rippling surge of power the full length of the thirty-foot-long cable of supple, leather-hard flesh that was his body. "Scared to the tip of my tail. Not that they can treat me as they did before—we three, at least, are safe from their minds—but at what they will *do*. Whatever it is to be, it will not be what we expect. They certainly will not do the obvious."

"That's what's clogging my jets," the Lensman agreed. "As a girl told me once, I'm getting the screaming meamies."

"That's what you mugs get for being so brainy," van-Buskirk put in. With a flick of his massive wrist he brought his thirty-pound space-axe to the "ready" as lightly as though it were a Tellurian dress saber. "Bring on your Overlords—squish! Just like that!" and a whistling sweep of his atrocious weapon was illustration enough.

"May be something in that, too, Bus," he laughed. Then, to the Velantian, "About time to tune in on 'em, I guess."

He was in no doubt whatever as to Worsel's ability to reach them. He knew that that incredibly powerful mind, without Lens or advanced Arisian instruction, had been able to cover eleven solar systems: he knew that, with his present ability, Worsel could cover half of space!

Although every fiber of his being shrieked protest against contact with the hereditary foe of his race, the Velantian put his mind en rapport with the Overlords and sent out his thought. He listened for seconds, motionless, then glided across the room to the thought-screened pilot and hissed directions. The pilot altered his course sharply and gave her the gun.

"I'll take her over now," Worsel said, presently. It'll look better that way—more as though they had us all under control."

He cut the Bergenholm, then set everything on zero—the ship hung, inert and practically motionless, in space. Simultaneously twenty unscreened men—volunteers—dashed toward the main airlock, overcome by some intense emotion.

"Now! Screens on! Scramblers!" Kinnison yelled; and at his words a thought-screen enclosed the ship; high-powered scramblers, within whose fields no invisibility apparatus could hold, burst into action. There the vessel was, right beside the *Dauntless,* a Boskonian in every line and member! "Fire!"

But even as she appeared, before a firing-stud could be pressed, the enemy craft almost disappeared again; or rather, she did not really appear at all, except as the veriest wraith of what a good, solid ship of space-alloy ought to be. She was a ghost-ship, as unsubstantial as fog. Misty, tenuous, immaterial; the shadow of a shadow. A dream-ship, built of the gossamer of dreams, manned by figments of horror recruited from sheerest nightmare. Not invisibility this time, Kinnison knew with a profound shock. Something else—something entirely different—something utterly incomprehensible. Xylpic had said it as nearly as it could be put into understandable words—the Boskonian ship was *leaving,* although it was standing still! It was monstrous—it *couldn't be done!*

Then, at a range of only feet instead of the usual "pointblank" range of hundreds of miles, the tremendous secondaries of the *Dauntless* cut loose. At such a ridiculous range as that—why, the screens themselves kept anything further away from them than that ship was—they *couldn't* miss. Nor did they; but neither did they hit. Those ravening beams went through and through the tenuous fabrication which should have been a vessel, but they struck nothing whatever. They went *past*—entirely harmlessly past—both the ship itself and the wraithlike but unforgettable figures which Kinnison recognized at a glance as Overlords of Delgon. His heart sank with a thud. He knew when he had had enough; and this was altogether too much.

"Go free!" he rasped. "Give 'er the oof!"

Energy poured into and through the great Bergenholm, but nothing happened; ship and contents remained inert. Not exactly inert, either, for the men were beginning to feel a new and unique sensation.

Energy raved from the driving jets, but still nothing happened. There was none of the thrust, none of the reaction of an inert start; there was none of the lashing, quivering awareness of speed which affects every mind, however hardened to free flight, in the instant of change from rest to a motion many times faster than that of light.

"Armor! Thought-screen! Emergency stations all!" Since they could not run away from whatever it was that was coming, they would face it.

And something was happening now, there was no doubt of that. Kinnison had been seasick and airsick and spacesick. Also, since cadets must learn to be able to do without artificial gravity, pseudo-inertia, and those other refinements which make space-liners so comfortable, he had known the nausea and the queasily terrifying endless-fall sensations of weightlessness, as well as the even worse outrages to the sensibilities incident to inertialessness in its crudest, most basic applications. He thought that he was familiar with all the untoward sensations of every mode of travel known to science. This, however, was something entirely new.

He felt as though he were being compressed; not as a whole, but atom by atom. He was being twisted—corkscrewed in a monstrously obscure fashion which permitted him neither to move from his place nor to remain where he was. He hung there, poised, for hours—or was it for a thousandth of a second? At the same time he felt a painless, but revolting transformation progress in a series of waves throughout his entire body; a rearrangement, a writhing, crawling distortion, an incomprehensibly impossible extrusion of each ultimate corpuscle of his substance in an unknowable and non-existent direction!

As slowly—or as rapidly?—as the transformation had waxed, it waned. He was again free to move. As far as he could tell, everything was almost as before. The *Dauntless* was about the same; so was the almost-invisible ship attached to her so closely. There was, however, a difference. The air seemed thick . . . familiar objects were seen blurrily, dimly . . . distorted . . . outside the ship there was nothing except a vague blur of grayness . . . no stars, no constellations . . .

A wave of thought came beating into his brain. He

had to leave the *Dauntless*. It was most vitally important to get into that dimly-seen companion vessel without an instant's delay! And even as his mind instinctively reared a barrier, blocking out the intruding thought, he recognized it for what it was—the summons of the Overlords!

But how about the thought screens, he thought in a semi-daze, then reason resumed accustomed sway. He was no longer in space—at least, not in the space he knew. That new, indescribable sensation had been one of *acceleration*—when they attained constant velocity it stopped. Acceleration—velocity—in what? To what? He did not know. Out of space as he knew it, certainly. Time was distorted, unrecognizable. Matter did not necessarily obey the familiar laws. Thought? QX—thought, lying in the sub-ether, probably was unaffected. Thought-screen generators, however, being material might not—in fact, did not—work. Worsel, vanBuskirk, and he did not need them, but those other poor devils . . .

He looked at them. The men—all of them, officers and all—had thrown off their armor, thrown away their weapons, and were again rushing toward the lock. With a smothered curse Kinnison followed them, as did the Velantian and the giant Dutch-Valerian. Into the lock. Through it, into the almost invisible space-tube, which, he noticed, was floored with a solider-appearing substance. The air felt heavy; dense, like water, or even more like metallic mercury. It breathed, however, QX. Into the Boskonian ship, along corridors, into a room which was precisely such a torture-chamber as Kinnison had described. There they were, ten of them; ten of the dragon-like, reptilian Overlords of Delgon!

They moved slowly, sluggishly, as did the Tellurians, in that thick, dense medium which was not, could not be, air. Ten chains were thrown, like pictures in slow motion, about ten human necks; ten entranced men were led unresistingly to anguished doom. This time the Gray Lensman's curse was not smothered—with a blistering deep-space oath he pulled his DeLameter and fired—once, twice, three times. No soap—he knew it, but he had to try. Furious, he launched himself. His taloned fingers, ravening to tear, went past, not around, the Overlord's throat; and the scimitared tail of the reptile, fierce-driven, apparently went through the Lensman, screens, armor, and brisket, but touched none of them in passing. He hurled a thought, a more disastrous bolt by far than he had sent against any mind since he had learned the art. In vain—the Overlords, themselves masters of mentality, could not be slain or even swerved by any forces at his command.

Kinnison reared back then in thought. There must be some ground, some substance common to the planes or dimensions involved, else they could not be here. The deck, for instance, was as solid to his feet as it was to the enemy. He thrust out a hand at the wall beside him—it was not there. The chains, however, held his suffering men, and the Overlords held the chains. The knives, also, and the clubs, and the other implements of torture being wielded with such peculiarly horrible slowness.

To think was to act. He leaped forward, seized a maul and made as though to swing it in terrific blow; only to stop, shocked. The maul did not move! Or rather, it moved, but *so* slowly, as though he were hauling it through putty! He dropped the handle, shoving it back, and received another shock, for it kept on coming under the urge of his first mighty heave—kept coming, knocking him aside as it came!

Mass! Inertia! The stuff must be a hundred times as dense as platinum!

"Bus!" he flashed a thought to the staring Valerian. "Grab one of these clubs here—a little one, even *you* can't swing a big one—and get to work!"

As he thought, he leaped again; this time for a small, slender knife, almost a scalpel, but with a long, keenly thin blade. Even though it was massive as a dozen broadswords he could swing it and he did so; plunging lethally as he swung. A full-arm sweep—razor edge shearing, crunching through plated, corded throat—grisly head floating one way, horrid body the other!

Then an attack in waves of his own men! The Overlords knew what was toward. They commanded their slaves
to abate the nuisance, and the Gray Lensman was buried
under an avalanche of furious, although unarmed, humanity.

"Chase 'em off me, will you, Worsel?" Kinnison pleaded.
"You're husky enough to handle 'em all—I'm not. Hold 'em
off while Bus and I polish off this crowd, huh?" And
Worsel did so.

VanBuskirk, scorning Kinnison's advice, had seized
the biggest thing in sight, only to relinquish it sheepishly—
he might as well have attempted to wield a bridge-girder!
He finally selected a tiny bar, only half an inch in diameter
and scarcely six feet long; but he found that even this sliver
was more of a bludgeon than any space-axe he had ever
swung.

Then the armed pair went joyously to war, the Tellurian with his knife, the Valerian with his magic wand. When
the Overlords saw that a fight to the finish was inevitable
they also seized weapons and fought with the desperation
of the cornered rats they were. This, however, freed Worsel
from guard duty, since the monsters were fully occupied in
defending themselves. He seized a length of chain, wrapped
six feet of tail in an unbreakable anchorage around a torture rack, and set viciously to work.

Thus again the intrepid three, the only minions of
Civilization theretofore to have escaped alive from the
clutches of the Overlords of Delgon, fought side by side.
VanBuskirk particularly was in his element. He was used
to a gravity almost three times Earth's, he was accustomed
to enormously heavy, almost viscous air. This stuff, thick
as it was, tasted infinitely better than the vacuum that Tellurians liked to breathe. It let a man *use* his strength; and
the gigantic Dutchman waded in happily, swinging his
frightfully massive weapon with devastating effect. Crunch!
Splash! THWUCK! When that bar struck it did not stop.
It went through; blood, brains, smashed heads and dismembered limbs flying in all directions. And Worsel's lethal
chain, driven irresistibly at the end of the twenty-five-foot

lever of his free length of body, clanked, hummed, and snarled its way through reptilian flesh. And, while Kinnison was puny indeed in comparison with his two brothers-in-arms, he had selected a weapon which would make his skill count; and his wicked knife stabbed, sheared, and trenchantly bit.

And thus, instead of dealing out death, the Overlords died.

HE CARNAGE OVER, KINNISON made his way to the control board, which was more or less standard in type. There were, however, some instruments new to him; and these he examined with care, tracing their leads throughout their lengths with his sense of perception before he touched a switch. Then he pulled out three plungers, one after the other.

There was a jarring "thunk"! and a reversal of the inexplicable, sickening sensations he had experienced previously. They ceased; the ships, solid now and still locked side by side, lay again in open, familiar space.

"Back to the *Dauntless*," Kinnison directed, tersely, and they went; taking with them the bodies of the slain Patrolmen. The ten who had been tortured were dead; twelve more had perished under the mental forces or the physical blows of the Overlords. Nothing could be done for any of them save to take their remains back to Tellus.

"What do we do with this ship—let's burn her out, huh?" asked vanBuskirk.

"Not on Tuesdays—the College of Science would fry me to a crisp in my own lard if I did," Kinnison retorted. "We take her in, as is. Where are we, Worsel? Have you and the navigator found out yet?"

" 'Way, 'way out—almost out of the galaxy," Worsel replied, and one of the computers recited a string of numbers, then added, "I don't see how we could have come so far in that short a time."

"How much time was it—got any idea?" Kinnison asked, pointedly.

"Why, by the chronometers . . . Oh . . ." the man's voice trailed off.

"You're getting the idea. Wouldn't have surprised me much if we'd been clear out of the known Universe. Hyperspace is funny that way, they say. Don't know a thing about it myself, except that we were in it for a while, but that's enough for me."

Back to Tellus they drove at the highest practicable speed, and at Prime Base scientists swarmed over and throughout the Boskonian vessel. They tore down, rebuilt, measured, analyzed, tested, and conferred.

"They got some of it, but they say you missed a lot," Thorndyke reported to his friend Kinnison one day. "Old Cardynge is mad as a cateagle about your report on that vortex or tunnel or whatever it was. He says your lack of appreciation of the simplest fundamentals is something pitiful, or words to that effect. He's going to blast you to a cinder as soon as he can get hold of you."

"Vell, ve can't all be first violiners in der orchestra, some of us got to push vind t'rough der trombone," Kinnison quoted, philosophically. "I done my damndest—how's a guy going to report accurately on something he can't hear, see, feel, taste, smell, or sense? But I heard that they've solved that thing of the interpenetrability of the two kinds of matter. What's the low-down on that?"

"Cardynge says it's simple. Maybe it is, but I'm a technician myself, not a mathematician. As near as I can get it, the Overlords and their stuff were treated or conditioned with an oscillatory of some kind, so that under the combined action of the fields generated by the ship and the shore station all their substance was rotated almost out of space. Not out of space, exactly, either, more like, say, very

nearly one hundred eighty degrees out of phase; so that
two bodies—one untreated, our stuff—could occupy the
same place at the same time without perceptible interference.
The failure of either force, such as your cutting the ship's
generators, would relieve the strain."

"It did more than that—it destroyed the vortex . . .
but it might, at that," the Lensman went on, thoughtfully.
"It could very well be that only that one special force,
exerted in the right place relative to the home-station generator, could bring the vortex into being. But how about that
heavy stuff, common to both planes, or phases, of matter?"

"Synthetic, they say. They're working on it now."

"Thanks for the dope. I've got to flit—got a date with
Haynes. I'll see Cardynge later and let him get it off his
chest," and the Lensman strode away toward the Port
Admiral's office.

Haynes greeted him cordially; then, at sight of the
storm signals flying in the younger man's eyes, he sobered.

"QX," he said, wearily. "If we have to go over this
again, unload it, Kim."

"Twenty two good men," Kinnison said, harshly. "I
murdered them. Just as surely, if not quite as directly, as
though I brained them with a space-axe."

"In one way, if you look at it fanatically enough, yes,"
the older man admitted, much to Kinnison's surprise. "I'm
not asking you to look at it in a broader sense, because you
probably can't—yet. Some things you can do alone; some
things you can do even better alone than with help. I have
never objected, nor shall I ever object to your going alone
on such missions, however dangerous they may be. That is,
and will be, your job. What you are forgetting in the luxury
of giving way to your emotions is that the Patrol comes
first. The Patrol is of vastly greater importance than the
lives of any man or group of men in it."

"But I know that, sir," protested Kinnison. "I . . ."

"You have a peculiar way of showing it, then," the
admiral broke in. "You say that you killed twenty two men.
Admitting it for the moment, which would you say was

better for the Patrol—to lose those twenty two good men in a successful and productive operation, or to lose the life of one Unattached Lensman without gaining any information or any other benefit whatever thereby?"

"Why . . . I . . . If you look at it that way, sir . . ." Kinnison still knew that he was right, but in that form the question answered itself.

"That is the only way it can be looked at," the old man returned, flatly. "No heroics on your part, no maudlin sentimentality. Now, as a Lensman, is it your considered judgment that it is best for the Patrol that you traverse that hyperspatial vortex alone, or with all the resources of the *Dauntless* at your command?"

Kinnison's face was white and strained. He could not lie to the Port Admiral. Nor could he tell the truth, for the dying agonies of those fiendishly tortured boys still racked him to the core.

"But I *can't* order men into any such death as that," he broke out, finally.

"You must," Haynes replied, inexorably. "Either you take the ship as she is or else you call for volunteers—and you know what that would mean."

Kinnison did, too well. The surviving personnel of the two *Brittanias,* the full present complement of the *Dauntless,* the crews of every other ship in Base, practically everybody on the Reservation—Haynes himself certainly, even Lacy and old von Hohendorff, everybody, even or especially if they had no business on such a trip as that—would volunteer; and every man jack of them would yell his head off at being left out. Each would have a thousand reasons for going.

"QX, I suppose. You win." Kinnison submitted, although with ill grace, rebelliously. "But I don't like it, nor any part of it. It clogs my jets."

"I know it, Kim," Haynes put a hand upon the boy's shoulder, tightening his fingers. "We all have it to do; it's part of the job. But remember always, Lensman, that the Patrol is not an army of mercenaries or conscripts. Any one of them, just as would you yourself, would go out there, *knowing* that it meant death in the torture-chambers of the Overlords, if in so doing he knew that he could help to end the torture and the slaughter of non-combatant men, women, and children that is now going on."

Kinnison walked slowly back to the field; silenced, but not convinced. There was something screwy somewhere, but he couldn't . . ."

"Just a moment, young man!" came a sharp, irritated voice. "I have been looking for you. At what time do you propose to set out for that which is being so loosely called the 'hyperspatial vortex'?"

He pulled himself out of his abstraction to see Sir Austin Cardynge. Testy, irascible, impatient, and vitriolic of tongue, he had always reminded Kinnison of a frantic hen attempting to mother a brood of ducklings.

"Hi, Sir Austin! Tomorrow—hour fifteen. Why?" The Lensman had too much on his mind to be ceremonious with this mathematical nuisance.

"Because I find that I must accompany you, and it is most damnably inconvenient, sir. The Society meets Tuesday week, and that ass Weingarde will . . ."

"Huh?" Kinnison ejaculated. "Who told you that you had to go along, or that you even *could,* for that matter?"

"Don't be a fool, young man!" the peppery scientist advised. "It should be apparent even to your feeble intelligence that after your fiasco, your inexcusable negligence in not reporting even the most elementary vectorial-tensorial analysis of that extremely important phenomenon, someone with a brain should . . ."

"Hold on, Sir Austin!" Kinnison interrupted the harangue, "You want to come along just to study the *mathematics* of that damn . . . ?"

"Just to study it!" shrieked the old man, almost tearing his hair. "You dolt—you blockhead! My God, why should anything with such a brain be permitted to live? Don't you even know, Kinnison, that in that vortex lies the solution of one of the greatest problems in all science?"

"Never occurred to me," the Lensman replied, un-ruffled by the old man's acid fury. He had had weeks of it, at the Conference.

"It is imperative that I go," Sir Austin was still acerbic, but the intensity of his passion was abating. "I must analyze those fields, their patterns, interactions and reactions, myself. Unskilled observations are useless, as you learned to your sorrow, and this opportunity is priceless—possibly it is unique. Since the data must be not only complete but also entirely authoritative, I myself must go. That is clear, is it not, even to you?"

"No. Hasn't anybody told you that everybody aboard is simply flirting with the undertaker?"

"Nonsense! I have subjected the affair, every phase of it, to a rigid statistical analysis. The probability is signifi-cantly greater than zero—oh, ever so much greater, almost point one nine, in fact—that the ship will return, with my notes."

"But listen, Sir Austin," Kinnison explained patiently. "You won't have time to study the generators at the other end, even if the folks there felt inclined to give us the chance. Our object is to blow the whole thing clear out of space."

"Of course, of course—certainly! The mere generating mechanisms are immaterial. Analyses of the forces them-selves are the sole desiderata. Vectors—tensors—perform-ance of mechanisms in reception—ethereal and sub-ethereal phenomena—propagation—extinction—phase angles—com-plete and accurate data upon hundreds of such items—slighting even one would be calamitous. Having this ma-terial, however, the mechanism of energization becomes a mere detail—complete solution and design inevitable, abso-lute—childishly simple."

"Oh." The Lensman was slightly groggy under the barrage. "The ship may get back, but how about you, per-sonally?"

"What difference does that make?" Cardynge snapped fretfully. "Even if, as is theoretically probable, we find that communication is impossible, my notes have a very good chance—very good indeed—of getting back. You do not seem to realize, young man, that to science that data is *necessary*. I *must* accompany you."

Kinnison looked down at the wispy little man in surprise. Here was something he had never suspected. Cardynge was a scientific wizard, he knew. That he had a phenomenal mind there was no shadow of doubt, but the Lensman had never thought of him as being physically brave. It was not merely courage, he decided. It was something bigger—better. Transcendent. An utter selflessness, a devotion to science so complete that neither physical welfare nor even life itself could be given any consideration whatever.

"You think, then, that this data is worth sacrificing the lives of four hundred men, including yours and mine, to get?" Kinnison asked, earnestly.

"Certainly, or a hundred times that many," Cardynge snapped, testily. "You heard me say, did you not, that this opportunity is priceless, and may very well be unique?"

"QX, you can come," and Kinnison went on into the *Dauntless*.

He went to bed wondering. Maybe the chief was right. He woke up, still wondering. Perhaps he was taking himself too seriously. Perhaps he was, as Haynes had more than intimated, indulging in mock heroics.

He prowled about. The two ships of space were still locked together. They would fly together to and along that dread tunnel, and he had to see that everything was on the green.

He went into the wardroom. One young officer was thumping the piano right tunefully and a dozen others were rending the atmosphere with joyous song. In that room any formality or "as you were" signal was unnecessary; the whole bunch fell upon their commander gleefully and with a complete lack of restraint, in a vociferous hilarity very evidently neither forced nor assumed.

Kinnison went on with his tour. "What was it?" he demanded of himself. Haynes didn't feel guilty. Cardynge was worse—he would kill forty thousand men, including the Lensman and himself, without batting an eye. These kids didn't give a damn. Their fellows had been slain by the Overlords, the Overlords had in turn been slain. All square—QX. Their turn next? So what? Kinnison himself did not want to die—he wanted to live—but if his number came up that was part of the game.

What was it, this willingness to give up life itself for an abstraction? Science, the Patrol, Civilization—notoriously ungrateful mistresses. Why? Some inner force—some compensation defying sense, reason, or analysis?

Whatever it was, he had it, too. Why deny it to others? What in all the nine hells of Valeria was he griping about?

"Maybe *I'm* nuts!" he concluded, and gave the word to blast off.

To blast off—to find and to traverse wholly that awful hyper-tube, at whose far terminus there would be lurking no man knew what.

Down the Hyper-Spatial Tube

OUT IN OPEN SPACE KINNISON called the entire crew to a mass meeting, in which he outlined to them as well as he could that which they were about to face.

"The Boskonian ship will undoubtedly return automatically to her dock," he concluded. "That there is probably docking-space for only one ship is immaterial, since the *Dauntless* will remain free. That ship is not manned, as you know, because no one knows what is going to happen when the fields are released in the home dock. Consequences may be disastrous to any foreign, untreated matter within her. Some signal will undoubtedly be given upon landing, although we have no means of knowing what that signal will be and Sir Austin has pointed out that there can be no communication between that ship and her base until her generators have been cut.

"Since we also will be in hyper-space until that time, it is clear that the generator must be cut from within the vessel. Electrical and mechanical relays are out of the question. Therefore two of our personnel will keep alternate watches in her control-room, to pull the necessary switches. I am not going to order any man to such a duty, nor am I going to ask for volunteers. If the man on duty is not killed outright—this is a distinct possibility, although perhaps not a probability—speed in getting back here will be decidedly of the essence. It seems to me that the best interests of the Patrol will be served by having the two fastest members of our force on watch. Time trials from the Boskonian panel to our airlock are, therefore, now in order."

This was Kinnison's device for taking the job himself. He was, he knew, the fastest man aboard, and he proved it. He negotiated the distance in seven seconds flat, over half a second faster than any other member of the crew. Then:

"Well, if you small, slow runts are done playing creepie-mousie, get out of the way and let folks run that really can," vanBuskirk boomed. "Come on, Worsel, I see where you and I are going to get ourselves a job."

"But see here, you can't!" Kinnison protested, aghast. "I said members of the crew."

"No, you didn't," the Valerian contradicted. "You said 'two of our personnel,' and if Worsel and I ain't personnel, what are we? We'll leave it to Sir Austin."

"Indubitably 'personnel,'" the arbiter decided, taking a moment from the apparatus he was setting up. "Your statement that speed is a prime requisite is also binding."

Whereupon the winged Velantian flew and wriggled the distance in two seconds, and the giant Dutch-Valerian ran it in three!

"You big, knot-headed Valerian ape!" Kinnison hissed a malevolent thought; not as the expedition's commander to a subordinate, but as an outraged friend speaking plainly to friend. "You knew I wanted that job myself, you clunker—damn your thick, hard crust!"

"Well, so did I, you poor, spindly little Tellurian wart, and so did Worsel," vanBuskirk shot back in kind. "Besides, it's for the good of the Patrol—you said so yourself! Comb *that* out of your whiskers, half-portion!" he added, with a wide and toothy grin, as he swaggered away, lightly brandishing his ponderous mace.

The run to the point in space where the vortex had been was made on schedule. Switches drove home, most of the fabric of the enemy vessel went out of phase, the voyagers experienced the weirdly uncomfortable acceleration along an impossible vector, and the familiar firmament disappeared into an impalpable but impenetrable murk of featureless, textureless gray.

Sir Austin was in his element. Indeed, he was in a seventh heaven of rapture as he observed, recorded, and calculated. He chuckled over his interferometers, he clucked over his meters, now and again he emitted shrill whoops of triumph as a particularly abstruse bit of knowledge was torn from its lair. He strutted, he gloated, he practically purred as he recorded upon the tape still another momentous conclusion or a gravid equation, each couched in terms of such incomprehensibly formidable mathematics that no one not a member of the Conference of Scientists could even dimly perceive its meaning.

Cardynge finished his work; and, after doing everything that could be done to insure the safe return to Science of his priceless records, he simply preened himself. He wasn't like an old hen, after all, Kinnison decided. More like a lean, gray tomcat. One that has just eaten the canary and, contemplatively smoothing his whiskers, is full of pleasant, if somewhat sanguine visions of what he is going to do to those other felines at that next meeting.

Time wore on. A long time? Or a short? Who could tell? What possible measure of that unknown and intrinsically unknowable concept exists or can exist in that fantastic region of—hyper-space? Inter-space? Pseudo-space? Call it what you like.

Time, as has been said, wore on. The ships arrived at the enemy base, the landing signal was given. Worsel, on duty at the time, recognized it for what it was—with his brain that was a foregone conclusion. He threw the switches, then flew and wriggled as even he had never done before, hurling a thought as he came.

And as the Velantian, himself in the throes of weird

deceleration, tore through the thinning atmosphere, the queasy Gray Lensman watched the development about them of a forbiddingly inimical scene.

They were materializing upon a landing field of sorts, a smooth and level expanse of black igneous rock. Two suns, one hot and close, one pale and distant, cast the impenetrable shadows so characteristic of an airless world. Dwarfed by distance, but still massively, craggily tremendous, there loomed the encircling rampart of the volcanic crater upon whose floor the fortress lay.

And what a fortress; New—raw—crude . . . but fanged with armament of might. There was the typically Boskonian dome of control, there were powerful ships of war in their cradles, there beside the *Dauntless* was very evidently the power-plant in which was generated the cryptic force which made inter-dimensional transit an actuality. But, and here was the saving factor which the Lensman had dared only half hope to find, those ultra-powerful defensive mechanisms were mounted to resist attack from without, not from within. It had not occurred to the foe, even as a possibility, that the Patrol might come upon them in panoply of war through their own hyper-spatial tube!

Kinnison knew that it was useless to assault that dome. He could, perhaps, crack its screens with his primaries, but he did not have enough stuff to reduce the whole establishment and therefore could not use the primaries at all. Since the enemy had been taken completely by surprise, however, he had a lot of time—at least a minute, perhaps a trifle more—and in that time the old *Dauntless* could do a lot of damage. The power-plant came first; that was what they had come out here to get.

"All secondaries fire at will!" Kinnison barked into his microphone. He was already at his conning board; every man of the crew was at his station. "All of you who can reach twenty-seven three-oh-eight, hit it—hard. The rest of you do as you please."

Every beam which could be brought to bear upon the power-house, and there were plenty of them, flamed out

practically as one. The building stood for an instant, starkly
outlined in a raging inferno of incandescence, then slumped
down flabbily; its upper, nearer parts flaring away in clouds
of sparklingly luminous vapor even as its lower members
flowed sluggishly together in streams of molten metal.
Deeper and deeper bore the frightful beams; foundations,
sub-cellars, structural members and gargantuan mechanisms
uniting with the obsidian of the crater's floor to form a
lake of bubbling, frothing lava.

"QX—that's good!" Kinnison snapped. "Scatter your
stuff, fellows—hit 'em!" He then spoke to Henderson, his
chief pilot. "Lift us up a bit, Hen, to give the boys a better
sight. Be ready to flit, fast; all hell's going to be out for
noon any second now!"

The time of the *Dauntless* was short, but she was working fast. Her guns were not being tripped. Instead, every
firing lever was jammed down into its last notch and was
locked there. Into the plates stared hard-faced young firing
officers, keen eyes glued to crossed hair-lines, grimly steady
right and left hands spinning controller-rheostats by touch
alone, tensely crouched as though by sheer driving force of
will they could energize to even higher levels the ravening
beams which were weaving beneath and around the Patrol's
super-dreadnought a writhing, flaming pattern of death
and destruction.

Ships—warships of Boskone's mightiest—caught cold.
Some crewless; some half-manned; none ready for the
stunning surprise attack of the Patrolmen. Through and
through them the ruthless beams tore; leaving, not ships,
but nondescript masses of half-fused metal. Hangars, ma-
chine-shops, supply depots suffered the same fate; a good
third of the establishment became a smoking, smouldering
heap of junk.

Then, one by one, the fixed-mount weapons of the
enemy, by dint of what Herculean efforts can only be surmised, were brought to bear upon the bold invader. Brighter
and brighter flamed her prodigiously powerful defensive
screens. Number One faded out; crushed flat by the hellish

energies of Boskone's projectors. Number Two flared into even more spectacular pyrotechnics, until soon even its tremendous resources of power became inadequate—blotchily, in discrete areas, clinging to existence with all the might of its Medonian generators and transmitters, it, too, began to fail.

"Better we flit, Hen, while we're all in one piece—right now," Kinnison advised the pilot then. "And I don't mean loaf, either—let's see you burn a hole in the ether."

Henderson's fingers swept over his board, depressing to maximum and locking down key after key. From her jets flared blast after blast of energies whose intensity paled the brilliance of the madly warring screens, and to Boskone's observers the immense Patrol raider vanished from all ken.

At that drive, the *Dauntless'* incomprehensible maximum, there was little danger of pursuit: for, as well as being the biggest and the most powerfully armed, she was also the fastest thing in space.

Out in open inter-galactic space—safe—discipline went by the board as though on signal and all hands joined in a release of pent-up emotion. Kinnison threw off his armor and, seizing the scandalized and highly outraged Cardynge, spun him around in dizzying, though effortless circles.

"Didn't lose a man—NOT A MAN!" he yelled, exuberantly.

He plucked the now idle Henderson from his board and wrestled with him, only to drift lightly away, ahead of a tremendous slap aimed at his back by vanBuskirk. Inertialessness takes most of the edge off of rough-housing, but the performance did relieve the tension and soon the ebullient youths quieted down.

The enemy base was located well outside the galaxy. Not, as Kinnison had feared, in the Second Galaxy, but in a star cluster not too far removed from the First. Hence the flight to Prime Base did not take long.

Sir Austin Cardynge was more like a self-satisfied tomcat than ever as he gathered up his records, gave a corps of aides minute instructions regarding the packing of his

equipment, and set out, figuratively but very evidently lick-
ing his chops, rehearsing the scene in which he would confound his allegedly learned fellows, especially that insuf-
ferable puppy, that upstart Weingarde . . .

"And that's that," Kinnison concluded his informal report to Haynes. "They're all washed up, there, at least. Before they can rebuild, you can wipe out the whole nest. If
there should happen to be one or two more such bases, the
boys know now how to handle them. I think I'd better be
getting back onto my own job, don't you?"

"Probably so," Haynes thought for moments, then continued: "Can you use help, or can you work better alone?"

"I've been thinking about that. The higher the tougher,
and it might not be a bad idea at all to have Worsel standing
by in my speedster: close by and ready all the time. He's
pretty much of an army himself, mental and physical. QX?"

"Can do," and thus it came about that the good ship
Dauntless flew again, this time out Borova way; her sole
freight a sleek black speedster and a rusty, battered meteor-
tug, her passengers a sinuous Velantian and a husky
Tellurian.

"Sort of a thin time for you, old man, I'm afraid."
Kinnison leaned unconcernedly against the towering pillar
of his friend's tail, whereupon four or five grotesquely
stalked eyes curled out at him speculatively. To these two,
each other's appearance and shape were neither repulsive
nor strange. They were friends, in the deepest, truest sense.
"He's so hideous that he's positively distinguished-looking,"
each had boasted more than once of the other to friends
of his own race.

"Nothing like that." The Velantian flashed out a leather
wing and flipped his tail aside in a playfully unsuccessful
attempt to catch the Earthman off balance. "Some day, if
you ever learn really to think, you will discover that a few
weeks' solitary, undisturbed and concentrated thought is a
rare treat. To have such an opportunity in the line of duty
makes it a pleasure unalloyed."

"I always did think that you were slightly screwy at

times, and now I know it," Kinnison retorted, unconvinced. "Thought is—or should be—a means to an end, not an end in itself; but if that's your idea of a wonderful time I'm glad to be able to give it to you."

They disembarked carefully in far space, the complete absence of spectators assured by the warship's fullest reach of detectors, and Kinnison again went down to Miners Rest. Not, this time, to carouse. Miners were not carousing there. Instead, the whole asteroid was buzzing with news of the fabulously rich finds which were being made in the distant solar system of Tressilia.

Kinnison had known that the news would be there, for it was at his instructions that those rich meteors had been placed there to be found. Tressilia III was the home of the regional director with whom the Gray Lensman had important business to transact; he had to have a solid reason, not a mere excuse, for Bill Williams to leave Borova for Tressilia.

The lure of wealth, then as ever, was stronger even than that of drink or of drug. Miners came to revel, but instead they outfitted in haste and hied themselves to the new Klondike. Nor was this anything out of the ordinary. Such stampedes occurred every once in a while, and Strongheart and his minions were not unduly concerned. They'd be back, and in the meantime there was the profit on a lot of metal and an excess profit due to the skyrocketing prices of supplies.

"You too, Bill?" Strongheart asked without surprise.

"I'll tell the Universe!" came ready answer. "If they's metal there I'll find it, pal." In making this declaration he was not boasting, he was merely voicing a simple truth. By this time the meteor belts of a hundred solar systems knew for a fact that Wild Bill Williams of Aldebaran II could find metal if metal was there to be found.

"If it's a bloomer, Bill, come back," the dive-keeper urged. "Come back anyway when you've worked it a couple of drunks."

"I'll do that, Strongheart, old pal, I sure will," the Lensman agreed, amiably enough. "You run a nice joint here and I like it."

Thus Kinnison went to the asteroid belts of Tressilia and there Bill Williams found rich metal. Or, more precisely, he dumped out into space and then recovered a very special meteor indeed—one in whose fabrication Kinnison's own treasure-trove had played the leading part. He did not find it the first day, of course, nor during the first week—it would be a trifle smelly to have even Wild Bill strike it rich too soon—but after a decent interval of time.

His Tressilian find had to be very much worth while, far too much so to be left to chance; for Edmund Crowninshield, the Regional Director, inhabited no such rawly obvious dive as Miners' Rest. He catered only to the upper crust; meteor miners and other similar scum were never permitted to enter his door.

When Kinnison repaired the Bergenholm of the Borovan space-liner he had, by sheerest accident, laid the groundwork of a perfect approach, and now he was taking advantage of the circumstance. That incident had been reported widely: it was well known that Wild Bill Williams had been a gentleman once. If he should strike it rich—really rich—what would be more natural than that he should forsake the noisome space-hells he had been wont to frequent in favor of such gilded palaces of sin as the Crown-On-Shield?

In due time, then, Kinnison "found" his special meteor, which was big enough and rich enough so that any miner would have taken it to a Patrol station instead of to a spacerobber. He disposed of his whole load by analysis; then, with more money in the bank than William Williams had ever dreamed of having, he hesitated visibly before embarking upon one of the gorgeous, spectacular sprees from which he had derived his nickname. He hesitated; then, with an effort apparent to all observers, he changed his mind.

He had been a gentleman once, he would be again. He had his hair cut, he had himself shaved every day. Manicurists dug away and scrubbed away the ingrained grime from his hardened, meteor-miner's paws. His nails, even, became pink and glossy. He bought clothes, including the full-dress shorts, barrel-top jacket, and voluminous cloak of the Aldebaranian gentleman, and wore them with easy grace. And in the meantime he was drinking steadily. He drank, however, only the choicest beverages; decorously and —for him—sparingly. Thus, while he was seldom what would be called strictly sober, he was never really drunk. He shunned low resorts, living in the best hotel and frequenting only the finest taverns. The finest, that is, with one exception, the Crown-On-Shield. Not only did he not go there, he never spoke of or would discuss the place. It was as though for him it did not exist.

Occasionally he escorted—oh, so correctly!—a charming companion to supper or to the theater, but ordinarily he was alone. Alone by choice. Aloof, austere, possibly not quite sure of himself. He rebuffed all attempts to inveigle him into any one of the numerous cliques with which the "upper crust" abounded. He waited for what he knew would come.

Underlings of gradually increasing numbers and importance came to him with invitations to the Crown-On-Shield, but he refused them all; curtly, definitely and without giving reason or excuse. In the light of what he was going to do there he could not be seen in the place unless and until it was clear to all that the visit was not of his design. Finally Crowninshield himself met the ex-miner as though by accident.

"Why haven't you been out to our place, Mr. Williams?" he asked, heartily.

"Because I didn't want to, and don't want to." Kinnison replied, flatly and definitely.

"But why?" demanded the Boskonian director, this time in genuine surprise. "It's getting talked about—*everybody* comes to the Crown!—people are wondering why you never even look in on us."

"You know who I am, don't you?" The Lensman's voice was coldly level, uninflected.

"Certainly. William Williams, formerly of Aldebaran II."

"No. Wild Bill Williams, meteor-miner. The Crown-On-Shield boasts that it does not solicit the patronage of men of my profession. If I go there some dim-wit will start blasting off about miners. Then you'll have the job of mopping him up off the floor with a sponge and the Patrol will be after me with a speedster. Thanks just the same, but none of that for me."

"Oh, is *that* all?" Crowinshield smiled in relief. "Perhaps a natural misapprehension, Mr. Williams, but you are entirely mistaken. It is true that practicing miners do not find our society congenial, but you are no longer a miner and we never refer to any man's past. As an Aldebaranian gentleman we would welcome you. And, in the extremely remote contingency to which you refer, I assure you that you would not have to act. Any guest so boorish would be expelled."

"In that case I would really enjoy spending a little time with you. It has been a long time since I associated with persons of breeding," he explained, with engaging candor.

"I'll have a boy see to the transfer of your things," and thus the Gray Lensman allowed the zwilnik to persuade him to visit the one place in the Universe where he most ardently wished to be.

For days in the new environment everything went on with the utmost decorum and circumspection, but Kinnison was not deceived. They would feel him out some way, just as effectively if not as crassly as did the zwilniks of Miners' Rest. They would have to—this was Regional Headquarters. At first he had been suspicious of thionite, but since the high-ups were not wearing anti-thionite plugs in their nostrils, he wouldn't have to either.

Then one evening a girl—young, pretty, vivacious—approached him, a pinch of purple powder between her fingers. As the Gray Lensman he knew that the stuff was not thionite, but as William Williams he did not.

"Do have a tiny smell of thionite, Mr. Williams!" she urged, coquettishly, and made as though to blow it into his face.

Williams reacted strangely, but instantaneously. He ducked with startling speed and the flat of his palm smacked ringingly against the girl's cheek. He did not slap her hard—it looked and sounded much worse than it really was—the only actual force was in the follow-up push that sent her flying across the room.

"Wha'ja mean, you? You can't slap girls around like that here!" and the chief bouncer came at him with a rush.

This time the Lensman did not pull his punch. He struck with everything he had, from heels to finger-tips. Such was the sheer brute power of the blow that the bouncer literally somersaulted half the length of the room, bringing up with a crash against the wall; so accurate was its placement that the victim, while not killed outright, would be unconscious for hours to come.

Others turned then, and paused; for Williams was not running away; he was not even giving ground. Instead, he stood lightly poised upon the balls of his feet, knees bent the veriest trifle, arms hanging at ready, eyes as hard and as cold as the iron meteorites of the space he knew so well.

"Any others of you damn zwilniks want to make a pass at me?" he demanded, and a concerted gasp arose: the word "zwilnik" was in those circles far worse than a mere fighting word. It was absolutely tabu: it was *never,* under any circumstance, uttered.

Nevertheless, no action was taken. At first the cold arrogance, the sheer effrontery of the man's pose held them in check; then they noticed one thing and remembered another, the combination of which gave them most emphatically to pause.

No garment, even by the most deliberate intent, could possibly have been designed as a better hiding-place for DeLameters than the barrel-topped full-dress jacket of Aldebaran II; and—

Mr. William Williams, poised there in steel-spring

readiness for action; so coldly self-confident; so inexplicably, so scornfully derisive of that whole roomful of men not a few of whom he knew must be armed; was also the Wild Bill Williams, meteor miner, who was widely known as the fastest and deadliest performer with twin DeLameters who had ever infested space!

Crown On Shield

EDMUND CROWNINSHIELD SAT in his office and seethed quietly, the all-pervasive blueness of the Kalonian brought out even more prominently than usual by his mood. His plan to find out whether or not the ex-miner was a spy had back-fired, badly. He had had reports from Euphrosyne that the fellow was not—*could* not be—a spy, and now his test had confirmed that conclusion, too thoroughly by far. He would have to do some mighty quick thinking and perhaps some salve-spreading or lose him. He certainly didn't want to lose a client who had over a quarter of a million credits to throw away, and who could not possibly resist his cravings for alcohol and bentlam very much longer! But curse him, what had the fellow meant by having a kit-bag built of indurite, with a lock on it that not even his cleverest artists could pick?

"Come in," he called, unctuously, in answer to a tap. "Oh, it's you! What did you find out?"

"Janice isn't hurt. He didn't make a mark on her—just gave her a shove and scared hell out of her. But Clovis was nudged, believe me. He's still out—will be for an hour, the doctor says. What a sock that guy's got! He looks like he'd been hit with a tube-maul."

"You're sure he was armed?"

"Must have been. Typical gun-fighter's crouch. He was ready, not bluffing, believe me. The man don't live that could bluff a roomful of us like that. He was betting he could whiff us all before we could get a gun out, and I wouldn't wonder if he was right."

"QX. Beat it, and don't let anyone come near here except Williams."

Therefore the ex-miner was the next visitor.

"You wanted to see me, Crowinshield, before I flit." Kinnison was fully dressed, even to his flowing cloak, and he was carrying his own kit. This, in an Aldebaranian, implied the extremest height of dudgeon.

"Yes, Mr. Williams, I wish to apologize for the house. However," somewhat exasperated, "it does seem that you were abrupt, to say the least, in your reaction to a childish prank."

"Prank!" The Aldebaranian's voice was decidedly unfriendly. "Sir, to me thionite is no prank. I don't mind nitrolabe or heroin, and a little bentlam now and then is good for a man, but when anyone comes around me with thionite I object, sir, vigorously, and I don't care who knows it."

"Evidently. But that wasn't really thionite—we would never permit it—and Miss Carter is an exemplary young lady . . ."

"How was I to know it wasn't thionite?" Williams demanded. "And as for your Miss Carter, as long as a woman acts like a lady I treat her like a lady, but if she acts like a zwilnik . . ."

"Please, Mr. Williams . . .!"

"I treat her like a zwilnik, and that's that."

"Mr. Williams, please! Not that word, ever!"

"No? A planetary idiosyncrasy, perhaps?" The ex-miner's towering wrath abated into curiosity. "Now that you mention it, I do not recall having heard it lately, nor hereabouts. For its use please accept my apology."

Oh, this was better. Crowninshield was making headway. The big Aldebaranian didn't even know thionite when he saw it, and he had a rabid fear of it.

"There remains, then, only the very peculiar circumstance of your wearing arms here in a quiet hotel . . ."

"Who says I was armed?" Kinnison demanded.

"Why . . . I . . . it was assumed . . ." The proprietor was flabbergasted.

The visitor threw off his cloak and removed his jacket, revealing a shirt of sheer glamorette through which could be plainly seen his hirsute chest and the smooth, bronzed skin of his brawny shoulders. He strode over to his kit-bag, unlocked it, and took out a double DeLameter harness and his weapons. He donned them, put on jacket and cloak —open, now, this latter—shrugged his shoulders a few times to settle the burden into its wonted position, and turned again to the hotel-keeper.

"This is the first time I have worn this hardware since I came here," he said, quietly. "Having the name, however, you may take it upon the very best of authority that I will be armed during the remaining minutes of my visit here. With your permission, I shall leave now."

"Oh, no, that won't do, sir, really." Crowinshield was almost abject at the prospect. "We should be desolated. Mistakes will happen, sir—planetary prejudices—misunderstandings . . . Give us a little more time to get really acquainted, sir . . ." and thus it went.

Finally Kinnison let himself be mollified into staying on. With true Aldebaranian mulishness, however, he wore his armament, proclaiming to all and sundry his sole reason therefor: "An Aldebaranian gentleman, sir, keeps his word; however lightly or under whatever circumstances given. I said that I would wear these things as long as I stay here; therefore wear them I must and I shall. I will leave here any time, sir, gladly; but while here I remain armed, every minute of every day."

And he did. He never drew them, was always and in every way a gentlemen. Nevertheless, the zwilniks were always uncomfortably conscious of the fact that those grim, formidable portables were there—always there and always ready. The fact that they themselves went armed with weapons deadly enough was all too little reassurance.

Always the quintessence of good behavior, Kinnison began to relax his barriers of reserve. He began to drink— to buy, at least—more and more. He had taken regularly a little bentlam; now, as though his will to moderation had begun to go down, he took larger and larger doses. It was not a significant fact to any one except himself that the nearer drew the time for a certain momentous meeting the more he apparently drank and the larger the doses of bentlam became.

Thus it was a purely unnoticed coincidence that it was upon the afternoon of the day during whose evening the conference was to be held that Williams' quiet and gentlemanly drunkenness degenerated into a noisy and obstreperous carousal. As a climax he demanded—and obtained —the twenty four units of bentlam which, his host knew, comprised the highest-ceiling dose of the old, unregenerate mining days. They gave him the Titanic jolt, undressed him, put him carefully to bed upon a soft mattress covered with silken sheets, and forgot him.

Before the meeting every possible source of interruption or spying was checked, rechecked, and guarded against; but no one even thought of suspecting the free-spending, hard-drinking, drug-soaked Williams. How could they?

And so it came about that the Gray Lensman attended that meeting also; as insidiously and as successfully as he had the one upon Euphrosyne. It took longer, this time, to read the reports, notes, orders, addresses, and so on, for this was a regional meeting, not merely a local one. However, the Lensman had ample time and was a fast reader withal; and in Worsel he had an aide who could tape the stuff as fast as he could send it in. Wherefore when the meeting broke up Kinnison was well content. He had forged another link in his chain—was one link nearer to Boskone, his goal.

As soon as Kinnison could walk without staggering he

sought out his host. He was ashamed, embarrassed, bitterly and painfully humiliated; but he was still—or again—an Aldebaranian gentleman. He had made a resolution, and gentlemen of that planet did not take their gentlemanliness lightly.

"First, Mr. Crowninshield, I wish to apologize, most humbly, most profoundly, sir, for the fashion in which I have outraged your hospitality." He could slap down a girl and half-kill a guard without loss of self-esteem, but no gentleman, however inebriated, should descend to such depths of commonness and vulgarity as he had plumbed here. Such conduct was inexcusable. "I have nothing whatever to say in defense or palliation of my conduct. I can only say that in order to spare you the task of ordering me out, I am leaving."

"Oh, come, Mr. Williams, that is not at all necessary. Anyone is apt to take a drop too much occasionally. Really, my friend, you were not at all offensive: we have not even entertained the thought of your leaving us." Nor had he. The ten thousand credits which the Lensman had thrown away during his spree would have condoned behavior a thousand times worse; but Crowinshield did not refer to that.

"Thank you for your courtesy, sir, but I remember some of my actions, and I blush with shame," the Aldebaranian rejoined, stiffly. He was not to be mollified. "I could never look your other guests in the face again. I think, sir, that I can still be a gentleman; but until I am certain of the fact—until I know I can get drunk as a gentleman should— I am going to change my name and disappear. Until a happier day, sir, goodbye."

Nothing could make the stiff-necked Williams change his mind, and leave he did, scattering five-credit notes abroad as he departed. However, he did not go far. As he had explained so carefully to Crowninshield, William Williams did disappear—forever, Kinnison hoped; he was all done with him—but the Gray Lensman made connections with Worsel.

"Thanks, old man," Kinnison shook one of the Velantian's gnarled, hard hands, even though Worsel never had had much use for that peculiarly human gesture. "Nice work. I won't need you for a while now, but I probably will later. If I succeed in getting the data I'll Lens it to you as usual for record—I'll be even less able than usual, I imagine, to take recording apparatus with me. If I can't get it I'll call you anyway, to help me make other arrangements. Clear ether, big fella!"

"Luck, Kinnison," and the two Lensmen went their separate ways; Worsel to Prime Base, the Tellurian on a long flit indeed. He had not been surprised to learn that the galactic director was not in the galaxy proper, but in a star cluster; nor at the information that the entity he wanted was one Jalte, a Kalonian. Boskone, Kinnison thought, was a highly methodical sort of a chap—he marked out the best way to do anything, and then stuck by it through thick and thin.

Kinnison was almost wrong there, for not long afterward Boskone was called in session and that very question was discussed seriously and at length.

"Granted that the Kalonians are good executives," the new Ninth of Boskone argued. "They are strong of mind and do produce results. It cannot be claimed, however, that they are in any sense comparable to us of the Eich. Eichlan was thinking of replacing Helmuth, but he put off acting until it was too late."

"There are many factors to consider," the First replied, gravely. "The planet is uninhabitable save for warm-blooded oxygen-breathers. The base is built for such, and such is the entire personnel. Years of time went into the construction there. One of us could not work efficiently alone, insulated against its heat and its atmosphere. If the whole dome were conditioned for us, we must needs train an entire new organization to man it. Then, too, the Kalonians have the work well in hand and, with all due respect to you and others of your mind, it is by no means certain that even Eichlan could have saved Helmuth's base had he been there. Eichlan's own doubt upon this point had much to do with his delay in acting. In the end it comes down to efficiency, and some Kalonians are efficient. Jalte is one. And, while it may seem as though I am boasting of my own selection of directors, please note that Prellin, the Kalonian director upon Bronseca, seems to have been able to stop the advance of the Patrol."

" 'Seems to' may be too exactly descriptive for comfort," said another, darkly.

"That is always a possibility," was conceded, "but whenever that Lensman has been able to act, he has acted. Our keenest observers can find no trace of his activities elsewhere, with the possible exception of the misfunctioning of the experimental hyer-spatial tube of our allies of Delgon. Some of us have from the first considered that venture ill-advised, premature; and its seizure by the Patrol smacks more of their able mathematical physicists than of a purely hypothetical, super-human Lensman. Therefore it seems logical to assume that Prellin has stopped him. Our observers report that the Patrol is loath to act illegally without evidence, and no evidence can be obtained. Business was hurt, but Jalte is reorganizing as rapidly as may be."

"I still say that the galactic base should be rebuilt and manned by the Eich," Nine insisted. "It is our sole remaining Grand Headquarters there, and since it is both the brain of the peaceful conquest and the nucleus of our new military organization, it should not be subjected to any unnecessary risk."

"And you will, of course, be glad to take that highly important command, man the dome with your own people, and face the Lensman—if and when he comes—backed by the forces of the Patrol?"

"Why . . . ah . . . no," the Ninth managed. "I am of so much more use here . . ."

"That's what we all think," the First said, cynically. "While I would like very much to welcome that hypothetical Lensman here, I do not care to meet him upon any other planet. I really believe, however, that any change in our organization would weaken it seriously. Jalte is capable, energetic, and is as well informed as is any of us as to the possibilities of invasion by the Lensman or his Patrol. Beyond asking him whether he needs anything, and sending him everything he may wish of supplies and of reenforcements, I do not see how we can improve matters."

They argued pro and con, bringing up dozens of points which cannot be detailed here, then voted. The decision sustained the First: they would send, if desired, munitions and men to Jalte.

But even before the question was put, Kinnison's blackly invisible, indetectable speedster was well within the star cluster. The guardian fortresses were closer spaced by far than Helmuth's had been. Electromagnetics had a three hundred percent overlap; ether and sub-ether alike were suffused with vibratory fields in which nullification of detection was impossible, and the observers were alert and keen. To what avail? The speedster was non-ferrous, intrinsically indetectable; the Lensman slipped through the net with ease.

Sliding down the edge of the world's black shadow he felt for the expected thought-screen, found it, dropped cautiously through it, and poised there; observing during one whole rotation. This had been a fair, green world—once. It had had forests. It had once been peopled by intelligent, urban dwellers, who had had roads, works, and other evidences of advancement. But the cities had been melted down into vast lakes of lava and slag. Cold now for years, cracked, fissured, weathered; yet to Kinnison's probing sense they told tales of horror, revealed all too clearly the incredible ferocity and ruthlessness with which the conquerors had wiped out all the population of a world. What had been roads and works were jagged ravines and craters of destruction. The forests of the planet had been burned, again and again; only a few charred stumps remaining to mark where a few of the mightiest monarchs had stood. Except for the Boskonian base the planet was a scene of desolation and ravishment indescribable.

"They'll pay for that, too," Kinnison gritted, and

directed his attention toward the base. Forbidding indeed it loomed; thrice a hundred square miles of massively banked offensive and defensive armament, with a central dome of such colossal mass as to dwarf even the stupendous fabrications surrounding it. Typical Boskonian layout, Kinnison thought, very much like Helmuth's Grand Base. Fully as large and as strong, or stronger . . . but he had cracked that one and he was pretty sure that he could crack this. Exploringly he sent out his sense of perception; nor was he surprised to find that the whole aggregation of structures was screened. He had not thought that it would be as easy as that!

He did not need to get inside the dome this time, as he was not going to work directly upon the personnel. Inside the screen anywhere would do. But how to get there? The ground all around the thing was flat, as level as molten lava would cool, and every inch of it was bathed in the white glare of flood-lights. They had observers, of course, and photo-cells, which were worse.

Approach then, either through the air or upon the ground, did not look so promising. That left only underground. They got water from somewhere—wells, perhaps—and their sewage went somewhere unless they incinerated it, which was highly improbable. There was a river over there; he'd see if there wasn't a trunk sewer running into it somewhere. There was. There was also a place within easy flying distance to hide his speedster, an overhanging bank of smooth black rock. The risk of his being seen was nil, anyway, for the only intelligent life left upon the planet inhabited the Boskonian fortress and did not leave it.

Donning his space-black, indetectable armor, Kinnison flew down the river to the sewer's mouth. He lowered himself into the placid stream and against the sluggish current of the sewer he made his way. The drivers of his suit were not as efficient in water as they were in air or in space, and in the dense medium his pace was necessarily slow. But he was in no hurry. It was fast enough—in a few hours he was beneath the stronghold.

Here the trunk began to divide into smaller and smaller mains. The tube running toward the dome, however, was amply large to permit the passage of his armor. Close enough to his objective, he found a long-disused manhole and, bracing himself upright, so that he would be under no muscular strain, he prepared to spend as long a time as would prove necessary.

He then began his study of the dome. It was like Helmuth's in some ways, entirely different from it in others. There were fully as many firing stations, each with its operators ready at signal to energize and to direct the most terrifically destructive agencies known to the science of the time. There were fewer visiplates and communicators, fewer catwalks; but there were vastly more individual offices and there were ranks and tiers of filing cabinets. There would have to be; this was headquarters for the organized illicit commerce of an entire galaxy. There was the familiar center, in which Jalte sat at his great desk; and near that desk there sparkled the peculiar globe of force which the Lensman now knew was an intergalactic communicator.

"Ha!" Kinnison exclaimed triumphantly if inaudibly to himself, "the real boss of the outfit—Boskone—*is* in the Second Galaxy!

He would have to wait until that communicator went into action, if it took a month. But in the meantime there was plenty to do. Those cabinets at least were not thought-screened, they held all the really vital secrets of the drug ring, and it would take many days to transmit the information which the Patrol must have if it were to make a one hundred percent clean-up of the whole zwilnik organization.

He called Worsel, and, upon being informed that the recorders were ready, he started in. Characteristically, he began with Prellin of Bronseca, and memorized the data covering that wight as he transmitted it. The next one to go down upon the steel tape was Crowninshield of Tressilia. Having exhausted all the filed information upon the organizations controlled by those two regional directors, he took the rest of them in order.

He had finished his real task and had practically finished a detailed survey of the entire base when the force-ball communicator burst into activity. Knowing approximately the analysis of the beam and exactly its location in space, it took only seconds for Kinnison to tap it; but the longer the interview went on the more disappointed the Lensman grew. Orders, reports, discussions of broad matters of policy—it was simply a conference between two high executives of a vast business firm. It was interesting enough, but in it there was no grist for the Lensman's mill. There was no new information except a name. There was no indication as to who Eichmil was, or where, there was no mention whatever of Boskone. There was nothing even remotely of a personal nature until the very last.

"I assume from lack of mention that the Lensman has made no farther progress." Eichmil concluded.

"Not so far as our best men can discover," Jalte replied, carefully, and Kinnison grinned like the Cheshire cat in his secure, if uncomfortable, retreat. It tickled his vanity immensely to be referred to so matter-of-factly as "the" Lensman, and he felt very smart and cagy indeed to be within a few hundred feet of Jalte as the Boskonian uttered the words. "Lensmen by the score are still working Prellin's base in Cominoche. Some twelve of these—human or approximately so—have been returning again and again. We are checking those with care, because of the possibility that one of them may be the one we want, but as yet I can make no conclusive report."

The connection was broken, and the Lensman's brief thrill of elated self-satisfaction died away.

"No soap," he growled to himself in disgust. "I've *got* to get into that guy's mind, some way or other!"

How could he make the approach? Every man in the base wore a screen, and they were mighty careful. No dogs or other pet animals. There were a few birds, but it would smell very cheesy indeed to have a bird flying around, pecking at screen generators. To anyone with half a brain that would tell the whole story, and these folks were really smart. What, then?

There was a nice spider up there in a corner. Big enough to do light work, but not big enough to attract much, if any, attention. Did spiders have minds? He could soon find out.

The spider had more of a mind than he had supposed, and he got into it easily enough. She could not really think at all, and at the starkly terrible savagery of her tiny ego the Lensman actually winced, but at that she had redeeming features. She was willing to work hard and long for a comparatively small return of food. He could not fuse his mentality with hers smoothly, as he could do in the case of creatures of greater brain power, but he could handle her after a fashion. At least she knew that certain actions would result in nourishment.

Through the insect's compound eyes the room and all its contents were weirdly distorted, but the Lensman could make them out well enough to direct her efforts. She crawled along the ceiling and dropped upon a silken rope to Jalte's belt. She could not pull the plug of the power-pack —it loomed before her eyes, a gigantic metal pillar as immovable as the Rock of Gibraltar—therefore she scampered on and began to explore the mazes of the set itself. She could not see the thing as a whole, it was far too immense a structure for that; so Kinnison, to whom the device was no larger than a hand, directed her to the first grid lead.

A tiny thing, thread-thin in gross; yet to the insect it was an ordinary cable of stranded soft-metal wire. Her powerful mandibles pried loose one of the component strands and with very little effort pulled it away from its fellows beneath the head of a binding screw. The strand bent easily, and as it touched the metal of the chassis the thought-screen vanished.

Instantly Kinnison insinuated his mind into Jalte's and began to dig for knowledge. Eichmil was his chief—Kinnison knew that already. His office was in the Second Galaxy, on the planet Jarnevon. Jalte had been there . . . coordinates

so and so, courses such and such . . . Eichmil reported to
Boskone . . .

The Lensman stiffened. Here was the first positive
evidence he had found that his deductions were correct—
or even that there really *was* such an entity as Boskone!
He bored anew.

Boskone was not a single entity, but a council . . . probably of the Eich, the natives of Jarnevon . . . weird impres-
sions of coldly intellectual reptilian monstrosities, horrific,
indescribable . . . Eichmil must know exactly who and where
Boskone was. Jalte did not. Kinnison finished his research
and abandoned the Kalonian's mind as insidiously as he
had entered it. The spider opened the short, restoring the
screen to usefulness. Then, before he did anything else,
the Lensman directed his small ally to a whole family of
young grubs just under the cover of his manhole. Lensmen paid their debts, even to spiders.

Then, with a profound sigh of relief, he dropped down
into the sewer. The submarine journey to the river was
made without incident, as was the flight to his speedster.
Night fell, and through its blackness there darted the even
blacker shape which was the Lensman's little ship. Out into
inter-galactic space she flashed, and homeward. And as she
flew the Tellurian scowled.

He had gained much, but not enough by far. He had
hoped to get all the data on Boskone, so that the zwilniks'
headquarters could be stormed by Civilization's armada,
invincible in its newly-devised might.

No soap. Before he could do that he would have to
scout Jarnevon . . . in the Second Galaxy . . . alone. Alone?
Better not. Better take the flying snake along. Good old
dragon! That was a mighty long flit to be doing alone, and
one with some mighty high-powered opposition at the other
end of it.

EFORE YOU GO ANYWHERE; OR, rather, whether you go anywhere or not, we want to knock down that Bronsecan base of Prellin's," Haynes declared to Kinnison in no uncertain voice. "It's a galactic scandal, the way we've been letting them thumb their noses at us. Everybody in space thinks that the Patrol has gone soft all of a sudden. When are you going to let us smack them down? Do you know what they've done now?"

"No—what?"

"Gone out of business. We've been watching them so closely that they couldn't do any queer business—goods, letters, messages, or anything—so they closed up the Bronseca branch entirely. 'Unfavorable conditions,' they said. Locked up tight—telephones disconnected, communicators cut, everything."

"Hm . . . m . . . In that case we'd better take 'em, I guess. No harm done, anyway, now—maybe all the better. Let Boskone think that our strategy failed and we had to fall back on brute force."

"You say it easy. You think it'll be a push-over, don't you?"

"Sure—why not?"

"You noticed the shape of their screens?"

"Roughly cylindrical," in surprise. "They're hiding a lot of stuff, of course, but they can't possibly. . . ."

"I'm afraid that they can, and will. I've been checking up on the building. Ten years old. Plans and permits QX except for the fact that nobody knows whether or not the building resembles the plans in any way."

"Klono's whiskers!" Kinnison was aghast, his mind was racing. "How could that be, chief? Inspections—builders—contractors—workmen?"

"The city inspector who had the job came into money later, retired, and nobody has seen him since. Nobody can locate a single builder or workman who saw it constructed. No competent inspector has been in it since. Cominoche is lax—all cities are, for that matter—with an outfit as big as Wembleson's, who carries its own insurance, does its own inspecting, and won't allow outside interference. Wembleson's isn't alone in that attitude—they're not all zwilniks, either."

"You think it's really fortified, then?"

"Sure of it. That's why we ordered a gradual, but complete, evacuation of the city, beginning a couple of months ago."

"How could you?" Kinnison was growing more surprised by the minute. "The businesses—the houses—the expense!"

"Martial law—the Patrol takes over in emergencies, you know. Businesses moved, and mostly carrying on very well. People ditto—very nice temporary camps, lake- and river-cottages, and so on. As for expense, the Patrol pays damages. We'll pay for rebuilding the whole city if we have to—much rather that than leave that Boskonian base there alone."

"What a mess! Never thought of it that way, but you're right, as usual. They wouldn't be there at all unless they thought . . . but they must know, chief, that they can't hold off the stuff you can bring to bear."

"Probably betting that we won't destroy our own city

to get them—if so, they're wrong. Or possibly they hung on a few days too long."

"How about the observers?" Kinnison asked. "They have four auxiliaries there, you know."

"That's strictly up to you." Haynes was unconcerned. "Smearing that base is the only thing I insist on. We'll wipe out the observers or let them observe and report, whichever you say; but that base goes—it has been there far too long already."

"Be nicer to let them alone," Kinnison decided. "We're not supposed to know anything about them. You won't have to use primaries, will you?"

"No. It's a fairly large building, as business blocks go, but it lacks a lot of being big enough to be a first class base. We can burn the ground out from under its deepest possible foundations with our secondaries."

He called an adjutant. "Get me Sector Nineteen." Then, as the seamed, scarred face of an old Lensman appeared upon a plate:

"You can go to work on Cominoche now, Parker. Twelve maulers. Twenty heavy caterpillars and about fifty units of Q-type mobile screen, remote control. Supplies and service. Have them muster all available fire-fighting apparatus. If desirable, import some—we want to save as much of the place as we can. I'll come over in the *Dauntless*."

He glanced at Kinnison, one eyebrow raised quizzically.

"I feel as though I rate a little vacation; I think I'll go and watch this," he commented. "The *Dauntless* can get us there soon enough. Got time to come along?"

"I think so. It's more or less on my way to Lundmark's Nebula."

Upon Bronseca then, as the *Dauntless* ripped her way through protesting space, there converged structures of the void from a dozen nearby systems. There came maulers; huge, ungainly flying fortresses of stupendous might. There came transports, bearing the commissariat and the service units. Vast freighters, under whose unimaginable mass the Gargantuanly braced and latticed and trussed docks yielded visibly and groaningly, crushed to a standstill and disgorged their varied cargoes.

What Haynes had so matter-of-factly referred to as "heavy" caterpillars were all of that, and the mobile screens were even heavier. Clanking and rumbling, but with their weight so evenly distributed over huge, flat treads that they sank only a foot or so into even ordinary ground, they made their ponderous way along Cominoche's deserted streets.

What thoughts seethed within the minds of the Boskonians can only be imagined. They knew that the Patrol had landed in force, but what could they do about it? At first, when the Lensmen began to infest the place, they could have fled in safety; but at that time they were too certain of their immunity to abandon their richly established position. Even now, they would not abandon it until that course became absolutely necessary.

They could have destroyed the city, true; but it was not until after the noncombatant inhabitants had unobstrusively moved out that that course suggested itself as an advisability. Now the destruction of mere property would be a gesture worse than meaningless; it would be a waste of energy which would all too certainly be needed badly and soon.

Hence, as the Patrol's land forces ground clangorously into position the enemy made no demonstration. The mobile screens were in place, surrounding the doomed section with a wall of force to protect the rest of the city from the hellish energies so soon to be unleashed. The heavy caterpillars, mounting projectors quite comparable in size and power with the warships' own—weapons similar in purpose and function to the railway-carriage coast-defense guns of an earlier day—were likewise ready. Far back of the line, but still too close, as they were to discover later, heavily armored men crouched at their remote controls behind their shields; barriers both of hard-driven, immaterial fields of force and of solid, grounded, ultra-refrigerated walls of the most refractory materials possible of fabrication. In the sky hung

the maulers, poised stolidly upon the towering pillars of
flame erupting from their under-jets.

Cominoche, Bronseca's capital city, witnessed then
what no one there present had ever expected to see; the
warfare designed for the illimitable reaches of empty space
being waged in the very heart of its business district!

For Port Admiral Haynes had directed the investment
of this minor stronghold almost as though it were a regulation base, and with reason. He knew that from their
coigns of vantage afar four separate Boskonian observers
were looking on, charged with the responsibility of recording and reporting everything that transpired, and he wanted
that report to be complete and conclusive. He wanted Boskone, whoever and wherever he might be, to know that when
the Galactic Patrol started a thing it finished it; that the
mailed fist of Civilization would not spare an enemy base
simply because it was so located within one of humanity's
cities that its destruction must inevitably result in severe
property damage. Indeed, the Port Admiral had massed
there thrice the force necessary, specifically and purposely
to drive that message home.

At the word of command there flamed out almost as
one a thousand lances of energy intolerable. Masonry, brickwork, steel, glass, and chromium trim disappeared; flaring
away in sparkling, hissing vapor or cascading away in brilliantly mobile streams of fiery, corrosive liquid. Disappeared,
revealing the unbearably incandescent surface of the Boskonian defensive screen.

Full-driven, that barrier held, even against the Titanic
thrusts of the maulers above and of the heavy defense-guns
below. Energy rebounded in scintillating torrents, shot off
in blinding streamers, released itself in bolts of lightning
hurling themselves frantically to ground.

Nor was that superbly-disguised citadel designed for
defense alone. Knowing now that the last faint hope of
continuing in business upon Bronseca was gone, and grimly
determined to take full toll of the hated Patrol, the defenders in turn loosed their beams. Five of them shot out simul-

taneously, and five of the panels of mobile screen flamed instantly into eye-tearing violet. Then black. These were not the comparatively feeble, antiquated beams which Haynes had expected, but were the output of up-to-the-minute, first-line space artillery!

Defenses down, it took but a blink of time to lick up the caterpillars. On, then, the destroying beams tore, each in a direct line for a remote-control station. Through tremendous edifices of masonry and steel they drove, the upper floors collapsing into the cylinder of annihilation only to be consumed almost as fast as they could fall.

"All screen-control stations, back! Fast!" Haynes directed, crisply. "Back, dodging. Put your screens on automatic block until you get back beyond effective range. Spyray men! See if you can locate the enemy observers directing fire!"

Three or four of the crews were caught, but most of the men were able to get away, to move back far enough to save their lives and their equipment. But no matter how far back they went, Boskonian beams still sought them out in grimly persistent attempts to slay. Their shielding fields blazed white, their refractories wavered in the high blue as the over-driven refrigerators strove mightily to cope with the terrific load. The operators, stifling, almost roasting in their armor of proof, shook sweat from the eyes they could not reach as they drove themselves and their mechanisms on to even greater efforts; cursing luridly, fulminantly the while at carrying on a space-war in the hotly reeking, the hellishly reflecting and heat-retaining environment of a metropolis!

And all around the embattled structure, within the Patrol's now partially open wall of screen, spread holocaust supreme, holocaust spreading wider and wider during each fractional split second. In an instant, it seemed, nearby buildings burst into flame. The fact that they were fireproof meant nothing whatever. The air inside them, heated in moments to a point far above the ignition temperature of organic material, fed furiously upon furniture, rugs, drapes, and whatever else had been left in place. Even without such adventitious aids the air itself, expanding tremendously, irresistibly, drove outward before it the glass of windows and the solid brickwork of walls. And as they fell glass and brick ceased to exist as such. Falling, they fused; coalescing and again splashing apart as they descended through the inferno of annihilatory vibrations in an appalling rain which might very well have been sprinkled from the hottest middle of the central core of hell itself. And in this fantastically potent, this incredibly corrosive flood the very ground, the metaled pavement, the sturdily immovable foundations of sky-scrapers, dissolved as do lumps of sugar in boiling coffee. Dissolved, slumped down, flowed away in blindingly turbulent streams. Superstructures toppled into disintegration, each discrete particle contributing as it fell to the utterly indescribable fervency of the whole.

More and more panels of mobile screen went down. They were not designed to stand up under such heavy projectors as "Wembleson's" mounted, and the Boskonians blasted them down in order to get at the remote-control operators back of them. Swath after swath of flaming ruin was cut through the Bronsecan metropolis as the enemy gunners followed the dodging caterpillar tractors.

"Drop down, maulers!" Haynes ordered. "Low enough so that your screens touch ground. Never mind damage— they'll blast the whole city if we don't stop those beams. Surround him!"

Down the maulers came, ringwise; mighty protective envelopes overlapping, down until the screens bit ground. Now the caterpillar and mobile-screen crews were safe; powerful as Prellin's weapons were, they could not break through those maulers' screens.

Now holocaust waxed doubly infernal. The wall was tight, the only avenue of escape of all that fiercely radiant energy was straight upward; adding to the furor were the flaring underjets—themselves destructive agents by no means to be despised!

Inside the screens, then, raged pure frenzy. At the

line raved the maulers' prodigious lifting blasts. Out and away, down every avenue of escape, swept torrents of super-heated air at whose touch anything and everything combustible burst into flame. But there could be no fire-fighting —yet. Outlying fires, along the line of destruction previously cut, yes; but personal armor has never been designed to enable life to exist in such an environment as that near those screens then was.

"Burn out the ground under them!" came the order. "Tip them over—slag them down!"

Sharply downward angled two-score of the beams which had been expending their energies upon Boskone's radiant defenses. Downward into the lake of lava which had once been pavement. That lake had already been seething and bubbling; from moment to moment emitting bursts of lambent flame. Now it leaped into a frenzy of its own, a transcendent fury of volatilization. High-explosive shells by the hundred dropped also into the incandescent mess, hurling the fiery stuff afar; deepening, broadening the sulphurous moat.

"Deep enough," Haynes spoke calmly into his microphone. "Tractors and pressors as assigned—tip him over."

The intensity of the bombardment did not slacken, but from the maulers to the north there reached out pressors, from those upon the south came tractors: each a beam of terrific power, each backed by all the mass and all the driving force of a veritable flying fortress.

Slowly that which had been a building leaned from the perpendicular, its inner defensive screen still intact.

"Chief?" From his post as observer Kinnison flashed a thought to Haynes. "Are you beginning to think any funny thoughts about that ape down there?"

"No. Are you? What?" asked the Port Admiral in surprise.

"Maybe I'm nuts, but it wouldn't surprise me if he'd start doing a flit pretty quick. I've got a CRX tracer on him, just in case, and it might be smart to caution Henderson to be on his toes."

"Your diagnosis—'nuts'—is correct, I think," came the answering thought; but the Port Admiral followed the suggestion, nevertheless.

And none too soon. Deliberately, grandly the Colossus was leaning over, bowing in stately fashion toward the awful lake in which it stood. But only so far. Then there was a flash, visible even in the inferno of energies already there at war, and the already coruscant lava was hurled to all points of the compass as the full-blast drive of a super-dreadnought was cut loose beneath its surface!

To the eye the thing simply and instantly disappeared; but not to the ultra-vision of the observers' plates, and especially not to the CRX tracers solidly attached by Kinnison and by Henderson. They held, and the chief pilot, already warned, was on the trail as fast as he could punch his keys.

Through atmosphere, through stratosphere, into interplanetary space flew pursued and pursuer at ever-increasing speed. The *Dauntless* overtook her proposed victim fairly easily. The Boskonian was fast, but the Patrol's new flyer was the fastest thing in space. But tractors would not hold against the now universal standard equipment of shears, and the heavy secondaries served only to push the fleeing vessel along all the faster. And the dreadful primaries could not be used—yet.

"Not yet," cautioned the admiral. "Don't get too close —wait until there's nothing detectable in space."

Finally an absolutely empty region was entered, the word to close up was given and Prellin drank of the bitter cup which so many commanders of vessels of the Patrol had had to drain—the gallingly fatal necessity of engaging a ship which was both faster and more powerful than his own. The Boskonian tried, of course. His beams raged out at full power against the screens of the larger ship, but without effect. Three primaries lashed out as one. The fleeing vessel, structure and contents, ceased to be. The *Dauntless* returned to the torn and ravaged city.

The maulers had gone. The lumbering caterpillars— what were left of them—were clanking away; reeking, smoking hot in every plate and member. Only the firemen were left, working like Trojans now with explosives, rays, water, carbon-dioxide snow, clinging and smothering chemicals; anything and everything which would isolate, absorb, or dissipate any portion of the almost incalculable heat energy so recently and so profligately released.

Fire apparatus from four planets was at work. There were pumpers, ladder-trucks, hose- and chemical-trucks. There were men in heavily-insulated armor. Vehicles and men alike were screened against the specific wave-lengths of heat; and under the direction of a fire-marshal in his red speedster high in air they fought methodically and efficiently the conflagration which was the aftermath of battle. They fought, and they were winning.

And then it rained. As though the heavens themselves had been outraged by what had been done they opened and rain sluiced down in level sheets. It struck hissingly the nearby structures, but it did not touch the central area at all. Instead it turned to steam in midair, and, rising or being blown aside by the tempestuous wind, it concealed the redly glaring, raw wound beneath a blanket of crimson fog.

"Well, that's that," the Port Admiral said, slowly. His face was grim and stern. "A good job of clean-up . . . expensive, in men and money, but well worth the price . . . so be it to every pirate base and every zwilnik hideout in the galaxy . . . Henderson, land us at Cominoche Space-Port."

And from four other cities of the planet four Boskonian observers, each unknown to all the others, took off in four spaceships for four different destinations. Each had reported fully and accurately to Jalte everything that had transpired until the two flyers faded into the distance. Then, highly elated—and probably, if the truth could be known, no little surprised as well—at the fact that he was still alive, each had left Bronseca at maximum blast.

The galactic director had done all that he could, which was little enough. At the Patrol's first warlike move he had ordered a squadron of Boskone's ablest fighting ships to Prellin's aid. It was almost certainly a useless gesture, he knew as he did it. Gone were the days when pirate bases dotted the Tellurian Galaxy; only by a miracle could those ships reach the Bronsecan's line of flight in time to be of service.

Nor could they. The howl of interfering vibrations which was smothering Prelin's communicator beam snapped off into silence while the would-be rescuers were many hours away. For minutes then Jalte sat immersed in thought, his normally bluish face turning a sickly green, before he called the planet Jarnevon to report to Eichmil, his chief.

"There is, however, a bright side to the affair," he concluded. "Prellin's records were destroyed with him. Also there are two facts—that the Patrol had to use such force as practically to destroy the city of Cominoche, and that our four observers escaped unmolested—which furnish conclusive proof that the vaunted Lensman failed completely to penetrate with his mental powers the defenses we have been using against him."

"Not conclusive proof," Eichmil rebuked him harshly. "Not proof at all, in any sense—scarcely a probability. Indeed, the display of force may very well mean that he has already attained his objective. He may have allowed the observers to escape, purposely, to lull our suspicions. You yourself are probably the next in line. How certain are you that your own base has not already been invaded?"

"Absolutely certain, sir." Jalte's face, however, turned a shade greener at the thought.

"You use the term 'absolutely' very loosely—but I hope that you are right. Use all the men and all the equipment we have sent you to make sure that it remains impenetrable."

N THEIR NON-MAGNETIC,
practically invisible speedster Kinnison and Worsel entered
the terra incognita of the Second Galaxy and approached
the solar system of the Eich, slowing down to a crawl as
they did so. They knew as much concerning dread Jarnevon,
the planet which was their goal, as did Jalte, from whom
the knowledge had been acquired; but that was all too little.

They knew that it was the fifth planet out from the sun
and that it was bitterly cold. It had an atmosphere, but one
containing no oxygen, one poisonous to oxygen-breathers.
It had no rotation—or, rather, its day coincided with its
year—and its people dwelt upon its eternally dark hemisphere. If they had eyes, a point upon which there was
doubt, they did not operate upon the frequencies ordinarily
referred to as "visible" light. In fact, about the Eich as
persons or identities they knew next to nothing. Jalte had
seen them, but either he did not perceive them clearly or
else his mind could not retain their true likeness; his only
picture of the Eichian physique being a confusedly horrible
blue.

"I'm scared, Worsel," Kinnison declared. "Scared
purple, and the closer we come the worse scared I get."

And he was scared. He was afraid as he had never be-

fore been afraid in all his short life. He had been in dangerous situations before, certainly; not only that, he had been
wounded almost fatally. In those instances, however, peril
had come upon him suddenly. He had reacted to it automatically, having had little if any time to think about it
beforehand.

Never before had he gone into a place in which he knew
in advance that the advantage was all upon the other side;
from which his chance of getting out alive was so terrifyingly
small. It was worse, much worse, than going into that vortex. There, while the road was strange, the enemy was known
to be one he had conquered before, and furthermore, he
had had the *Dauntless,* its eager young crew, and the scientific self-abnegation of old Cardynge to back him. Here he
had the speedster and Worsel—and Worsel was just as
scared as he was.

The pit of his stomach felt cold, his bones seemed
bits of rubber tubing. Nevertheless the two Lensman were
going in. That was their job. They had to go in, even though
they knew that the foe was at least their equal mentally,
was overwhelmingly their superior physically and was upon
his own ground.

"So am I," Worsel admitted. "I'm scared to the tip
of my tail. I have one advantage over you, however—I've
been that way before." He was referring to the time when
he had gone to Delgon, abysmally certain that he would
not return. "What is fated, happens. Shall we prepare?"

They had spent many hours in discussion of what could
be done, and in the end had decided that the only possible
preparation was to make sure that if Kinnison failed his
failure would not bring disaster to the Patrol.

"Might as well. Come in, my mind's wide open."

The Velantian insinuated his mind into Kinnison's and
the Earthman slumped down, unconscious. Then for many
minutes Worsel wrought within the plastic brain. Finally:

"Thirty seconds after you leave me these inhibitions
will become operative. When I release them your memory

and your knowledge will be exactly as they were before I began to operate," he thought; slowly, intensely, clearly. "Until that time you know nothing whatever of any of these matters. No mental search, however profound; no truth-drug, however potent; no probing even of the subconscious will or can discover them. They do not exist. They have never existed. They shall not exist until I so allow. These other matters have been, are, and shall be facts until that instant. Kimball Kinnison, awaken!"

The Tellurian came to, not knowing that he had been out. Nothing had occurred, for him no time whatever had elapsed. He could not perceive even that his mind had been touched.

"Sure it's done, Worsel? I can't find a thing!" Kinnison, who had himself operated tracelessly upon so many minds, could scarcely believe his own had been tampered with.

"It is done. If you could detect any trace of the work it would have been poor work, and wasted."

Down dropped the speedster, as nearly as the Lensmen dared toward Jarnevon's tremendous primary base. They did not know whether they were being observed or not. For all they knew these incomprehensible beings might be able to see or to sense them as plainly as though their ship were painted with radium and were landing openly, with search-lights ablaze and with bells a-clang. Muscles tense, ready to hurl their tiny flyer away at the slightest alarm, they wafted downward.

Through the screens they dropped. Power off, even to the gravity-pads; thought, even, blanketed to zero. Nothing happened. They landed. They disembarked. Foot by foot they made their cautious way forward.

In essence the plan was simplicity itself. Worsel would accompany Kinnison until both were within the thought-screens of the dome. Then the Tellurian would get, some way or other, the information which the Patrol had to have, and the Velantian would get it back to Prime Base. If the Gray Lensman could go too, QX. And after all, there was no real reason to think that he couldn't—he was merely playing safe on general principles. But, if worst came to worst . . . well . . .

They arrived.

"Now remember, Worsel, no matter what happens to me, or around me, you stay out. Don't come in after me. Help me all you can with your mind, but not otherwise. Take everything I get, and at the first sign of danger you flit back to the speedster and give her the oof, whether I'm around or not. Check?"

"Check," Worsel agreed, quietly. Kinnison's was the harder part. Not because he was the leader, but because he was the better qualified. They both knew it. The Patrol came first. It was bigger, vastly more important, than any being or any group of beings in it.

The man strode away and in thirty seconds underwent a weird and striking mental transformation. Three-quarters of his knowledge disappeared so completely that he had no inkling that he had ever had it. A new name, a new personality were his, so completely and indisputably his that he had no faint glimmering of a recollection that he had ever been otherwise.

He was wearing his Lens. It could do no possible harm, since it was almost inconceivable that the Eich could be made to believe that any ordinary agent could have penetrated so far, and the fact should not be revealed to the foe that any Lensman could work without his Lens. That would explain far too much of what had already happened. Furthermore, it was a necessity in the only really convincing role which Kinnison could play in the event of capture.

As he neared his objective he slowed down. There were pits beneath the pavement, he observed, big enough to hold a speedster. Traps. He avoided them. There were various mechanisms within the blank walls he skirted. More traps. He avoided them. Photo-cells, trigger-beams, invisible rays, networks. He avoided them all. Close enough.

Delicately he sent out a mental probe, and almost in the instant of its sending cables of steel came whipping from afar. He perceived them as they came, but could not dodge them. His projectors flamed briefly, only to be sheared away. The cables wrapped about his arms, binding him fast. Helpless, he was carried through the atmosphere, into the dome, through an airlock into a chamber containing much grimly unmistakable apparatus. And in the council chamber, where the nine of Boskone and one armored Delgonian Overlord held meeting, a communicator buzzed and snarled.

"Ah!" exclaimed Eichmil. "Our visitor has arrived and is awaiting us in the Delgonian hall of question. Shall we meet again, there?"

They did so; they of the Eich armored against the poisonous oxygen, the Overlord naked. All wore screens.

"Earthling, we are glad indeed to see you here," the First of Boskone welcomed the prisoner. "For a long time we have been anxious indeed . . .

"I don't see how that can be," the Lensman blurted. "I just graduated. My first big assignment, and I have failed," he ended, bitterly.

A start of surprise swept around the circle. Could this be?

"He is lying." Eichmil decided. "You of Delgon, take him out of his armor." The Overlord did so, the Tellurian's struggles meaningless to the reptile's superhuman strength. "Release your screen and see whether or not you can make him tell the truth."

After all, the man might not be lying. The fact that he could understand a strange language meant nothing. All Lensmen could.

"But in case he *should* be the one we seek . . ." the Overlord hesitated.

"We will see to it that no harm comes to you . . ."

"We cannot," the Ninth—the psychologist—broke in. "Before any screen is released I suggest that we question him verbally, under the influence of the drug which renders it impossible for any warm-blooded oxygen-breather to tell anything except the complete truth."

The suggestion, so eminently sensible, was adopted forthwith.

"Are you the Lensman who has made it possible for the Patrol to drive us out of the Tellurian Galaxy?" came the sharp demand.

"No," was the flat and surprising reply.

"Who are you, then?"

"Philip Morgan, Class of . . ."

"Oh, this will take forever!" snapped the Ninth. "Let me question him. Can you control minds at a distance and without previous treatment?"

"If they are not too strong, yes. All of us specialists in psychology can do that."

"Go to work upon him, Overlord!"

The now reassured Delgonian snapped off his screen and a battle of wills ensued which made the sub-ether boil. For Kinnison, although he no longer knew what the truth was, still possessed the greater part of his mental power, and the Delgonian's mind, as has already been made clear, was a capable one indeed.

"Desist!" came the command. "Earthman, what happened?"

"Nothing," Kinnison replied, truthfully. "Each of us could resist the other; neither could penetrate or control."

"Ah!" and nine Boskonian screens snapped off. Since the Lensman could not master one Delgonian, he would not be a menace to the massed minds of the Nine of Boskone and the questioning need not wait upon the slowness of speech. Thoughts beat into Kinnison's brain from all sides.

This power of mind was relatively new, yes. He did not know what it was. He went to Arisia, fell asleep, and woke up with it. A refinement, he thought, of hypnotism. Only advanced students in psychology could do it. He knew nothing except by hearsay of the old *Brittania*—he was a cadet then. He had never heard of Blakeslee, or of anything unusual concerning any one hospital ship. He did not know who had scouted Helmuth's base, or put the thionite into it. He had no idea who it was who had killed Helmuth. As far as he knew, nothing had ever been done about any

Boskonian spies in Patrol bases. He had never happened to hear of the planet Medon, or of anyone named Bominger, or Madame Desplaines, or Prellin. He was entirely ignorant of any unusual weapons of offense—he was a psychologist, not an engineer or a physicist. No, he was not unusually adept with DeLameters . . .

"Hold on!" Eichmil commanded. "Stop questioning him, everybody! Now, Lensman, instead of telling us what you do not know, give us positive information, in your own way. How do you work? I am beginning to suspect that the man we really want is a director, not an operator."

That was a more productive line. Lensmen, hundreds of them, each worked upon definite assignment. None of them had ever seen or ever would see the man who issued orders. He had not even a name, but was a symbol—Star A Star. They received orders through their Lenses, wherever they might be in space. They reported back to him in the same way. Yes, Star A Star knew what was going on there, he was reporting constantly . . .

A knife descended viciously. Blood spurted. The stump was dressed, roughly but efficiently. They did not wish their victim to bleed to death when he died, and he was not to die in any fashion—yet.

And in the instant that Kinnison's Lens went dead Worsel, from his safely distant nook, reached out direct to the mind of his friend, thereby putting his own life in jeopardy. He knew that there was an Overlord in that room, and the grue of a thousand helplessly-sacrificed generations of forebears swept his sinuous length at the thought, despite his inward certainty of the new powers of his mind. He knew that of all the entities in the Universe the Delgonians were most sensitive to the thought-vibrations of Velantians. Nevertheless, he did it.

He narrowed the beam down to the smallest possible coverage, employed a frequency as far as possible from that ordinarily used by the Overlords, and continued to observe. It was risky, but it was necessary. It was beginning to appear as though the Earthman might not be able to escape, and he must not die in vain.

"Can you communicate now?" In the ghastly chamber the relentless questioning went on.

"I can not communicate."

"It is well. In one way I would not be averse to letting your Star A Star know what happens when one of his minions dares to spy upon the Council of Boskone itself, but the information is as yet a trifle premature. Later, he shall learn . . ."

Kinnison did not consciously thrill at that thought. He did not know that the news was going beyond his brain; that he had achieved his goal. Worsel, however, did; and Worsel thrilled for him. The Gray Lensman had finished his job; all that was left to do was to destroy that base and the power of Boskone would be broken. Kinnison could die, now, content.

But no thought of leaving entered Worsel's mind. He would of course stand by as long as there remained the slightest shred of hope, or until some development threatened his ability to leave the planet with his priceless information. And the pitiless inquisition went on.

Star A Star had sent him to investigate their planet, to discover whether or not there was any connection between it and the zwilnik organization. He had come alone, in a speedster. No, he could not tell them even approximately where the speedster was. It was so dark, and he had come such a long distance on foot. In a short time, though, it would start sending out a thought-signal which he could detect . . .

"But you must have some ideas about this Star A Star!" This director was the man they want so desperately to get. They believed implicitly in this figment of a Lensman-Director. Fitting in so perfectly with their own ideas of efficient organization, it was more convincing by far than the actual truth would have been. They knew now that he would be hard to find. They did not now insist upon facts; they wanted every possible crumb of surmise. "You must have wondered who and where Star A Star is? You must have tried to trace him?"

Yes, he had tried, but the problem could not be solved. The Lens was non-directional, and the signals came in at practically the same strength, anywhere in the galaxy. They were, however, very much fainter out here. That might be taken to indicate that Star A Star's office was in a star cluster, well out in either zenith or nadir direction . . .

The victim sucked dry, eight of the Council departed, leaving Eichmil and the Overlord with the Lensman.

"What you have in mind to do, Eichmil, is childish. Your basic idea is excellent, but your technique is pitifully inadequate."

"What could be worse?" Eichmil demanded. "I am going to dig out his eyes, smash his bones, flay him alive, roast him, cut him up into a dozen pieces, and send him back to his Star A Star with a warning that every creature he sends into this galaxy will be treated the same way. What would *you* do?"

"You of the Eich lack finesse," the Delgonian sighed. "You have no subtlety, no conception of the nicer possibilities of torture, either of an individual or of a race. For instance, to punish Star A Star adequately this man must be returned to him alive, not dead."

"Impossible! He dies, *here!*"

"You misunderstand me. Not alive as he is now—but not entirely dead. Bones broken, yes, and eyes removed; but those minor matters are but a beginning. If I were doing it, I should then apply several of these devices here, successively; but none of them to the point of complete incompatibility with life. I should inoculate the extremities of his four limbs with an organism which grows—shall we say unpleasantly? Finally, I should extract his life force and consume it—as you know, that material is a rarely satisfying delicacy with us—taking care to leave just enough to maintain a bare existence. I should then put what is left of him aboard his ship, start it toward the Tellurian Galaxy, and send notice to the Patrol as to its exact course and velocity."

"But they would find him *alive!*" Eichmil stormed.

"Exactly. For the fullest vengeance they must, as I have said. Which is worse, think you? To find a corpse, however dismembered, and to dispose of it with full military honors, or to find and to have to take care of for a full lifetime a something that has not enough intelligence even to swallow food placed in its mouth? Remember also that the organism will be such that they themselves will be obliged to amputate all four of the creature's limbs to save its life."

While thinking thus the Delgonian shot out a slender tentacle which, slithering across the floor, flipped over the tiny switch of a small mechanism in the center of the room. This entirely unexpected action almost stunned Worsel. He had been debating for moments whether or not to release the Gray Lensman's inhibitions. He would have done so instantly if he had had any warning of what the Delgonian was about to do. Now it was too late.

"I have set up a thought-screen about the room. I do not wish to share this tid-bit with any of my fellows, as there is not enough to divide," the monster explained, parenthetically. "Have you any suggestion as to how my plan may be improved?"

"No. You have shown that you understand torture better than we do."

"I should, since we Overlords have practiced it as a fine art since our beginnings as a race. Do you wish the pleasure of breaking his bones now?"

"I do not break bones for pleasure. Since you do, you may carry out the procedure as outlined. All I want is the assurance that he will be an object-lesson and a warning to Star A Star of the Patrol."

"I can assure you definitely that it will be both. More, I will show you the results when I have finished my work. Or, if you like, I would be glad to have you stay and look on—you will find the spectacle interesting, entertaining, and highly instructive."

"No, thanks." Eichmil left the room and the Delgonian turned his attention to the bound and helpless Lensman.

It is best, perhaps, to draw a kindly veil over the events of the next two hours. Kinnison himself refuses positively to discuss it, except to say:

"I knew how to set up a nerve-block then, so I can't say that any of it really hurt me. I wouldn't let myself feel it. But all the time I knew what he was doing to me and it made me sick. Did you ever watch a surgeon while he was taking out your appendix? Like that, only worse. It wasn't funny. I didn't like it a bit. Your readers wouldn't like it, either, so you'd better lay off that stuff entirely."

The mere fact that the Overlord had established coverage was of course sufficient to set up in the Lensman's mind a compulsion to knock it down. He *had* to break that screen! But there were no birds here; no spiders. Was there any life at all? There was. That torture room had been used fully and often; the muck in its drains was rich pasture for the Jarnevonian equivalent of worms.

Selecting a big one, long and thick, Kinnison tuned down to its mental level and probed. This took time—much, much too much time. The creature did not have nearly the intelligence of a spider, but it did have a dim consciousness of being, and therefore an ego of a sort. Also, when Kinnison finally got in touch with that ego, it reacted very favorably to his suggestion of food.

"Hurry, worm! Snap it up!" and the little thing really did hurry. Scrambling, squirming, almost leaping along the floor it hurried, in a very grotesquerie of haste.

The Delgonian's leisurely preliminary work was done. The feast was ready. The worm reached the generator while the Overlord was warming up the tubes of the apparatus which was to rive away that which made the man Kinnison everything that he was.

Curling one end of its sinuous shape around a convenient anchorage, Kinnison's small proxy reached up and looped the other about the handle of the switch. Then, visions of choice viands suffusing its barely existent con- sciousness, it contracted convulsively. There was a snap and the mental barrier went out of existence.

At the tiny sound the Delgonian whirled—and stopped. Worsel's gigantic mentality had been beating ceaselessly against that screen ever since its erection, and in the instant of its fall Kinnison again became the Gray Lensman of old. And in the next instant both those prodigious minds—the two most powerful then known to Civilization—had hurled themselves against that of the Delgonian. Bitter though the ensuing struggle was, it was brief. Nothing short of an Arisian mind could have withstood the venomous fury, the Berserk power, of that concerted and synchronized attack.

Brain half burned out, the Overlord wilted; and, docility itself, he energized the communicator.

"Eichmil? The work is done. Thoroughly done and well. Do you wish to inspect it before I put what is left of the Lensman into his ship?"

"No." Eichmil, as a high executive, was accustomed to delegating far more important matters than that to com- petent underlings. "If you are satisfied, I am."

Weirdly enough to any casual observer, the Overlord's first act was to deposit the worm, carefully and tenderly, in a spot in which the muck was particularly rich and tooth- some. Then, picking up the hideously mangled thing that was Kinnison's body, he encased it in its armor and, donning his own, wriggled boldly away with his burden.

"Clear the way for me, please," he requested of Eichmil. "I go to place this residuum within its ship and to return it to Star A Star."

"You will be able to find the speedster?"

"Certainly. He was to find it. Whatever he could have done I, working through the cells of his brain, can likewise do."

"Can you handle him alone, Kinnison?" Worsel asked presently. "Can you hold out to the speedster?"

"Yes to both. I can handle him—we whittled him down to a nub. I'll last—I'll make myself last long enough."

"I go, then, lest they be observing with spy-rays."

To the black flyer, then, the completely subservient Delgonian carried his physically disabled master, and carefully he put him aboard. Worsel helped openly there, for he had screened the speedster against all forms of intrusion. The vessel took off and the Overlord wriggled blithely back toward the dome. He was full of the consciousness of a good job well done. He even felt the sensation of repletion concomitant with having consumed practically all of Kinnison's life force!

"I hate to let him go!" Worsel's thought was a growl of baffled hatred. "It gripes me to let him think that he did everything he set out to do, even though I know it had to be that way. I wanted—I still want—to tear him apart for what he has done to you, my friend."

"Thanks, old snake." Kinnison's thought came faintly. "Just temporary. He's living on borrowed time. He'll get his. You've got everything under control, haven't you?"

"On the green. Why?"

"Because I can't hold this nerve-block any longer . . . It hurts . . . I'm sick. I think I'm going to . . ."

He fainted. More, he plunged parsecs deep into the blackest depths of oblivion as outraged Nature took the toll she had been so long denied.

Worsel hurled a call to Earth, then turned to his maimed and horribly broken companion. He applied splints to the shattered limbs, he dressed and bandaged the hideous wounds and the raw sockets which had once held eyes, he ministered to the raging, burning thirst. Whenever Kinnison's mind wearied he held for him the nerve-block; the priceless anodyne without which the Gray Lensman must have died from sheerest agony.

"Why not allow me, friend, to relieve you of all consciousness until help arrives?" the Velantian asked, pityingly.

"Can you do it without killing me?"

"If you so allow, yes. If you offer any resistance, I do not believe that any mind in the universe could."

"I won't resist. Come in," and Kinnison's suffering ended.

But kindly Worsel could do nothing about the fantastically atrocious growth which were transforming the Earthman's legs and arms into monstrosities out of nightmare.

He could only wait—wait for the skilled assistance which he knew must be so long in coming.

WHEN WORSEL'S HARD-DRIVEN
call impinged upon the Port Admiral's Lens he dropped everything to take the report himself. Characteristically Worsel
sent first and Haynes first recorded a complete statement of
the successful mission to Jarnevon. Last came personalities,
the tale of Kinnison's ordeal and his present plight.

"Are they following you in force, or can't you tell?"

"Nothing detectable, and at the time of our departure
there had been no suggestion of any such action," Worsel
replied, carefully.

"We'll come in force, anyway, and fast. Keep him alive
until we meet you," Haynes urged, and disconnected.

It was an unheard-of occurrence for the Port Admiral
to turn over his very busy and extremely important desk to
a subordinate without notice and without giving him instructions, but Haynes did it now.

"Take charge of everything, Southworth!" he snapped.
"I'm called away—emergency. Kinnison found Boskone—
got away—hurt—I'm going after him in the *Dauntless*. Taking the new flotilla with me. Indefinite time—probably a few
weeks."

He strode toward the communicator desk. The *Dauntless* was, as always, completely serviced and ready for any

emergency. Where was that fleet of her sister-ships, on its shake-down cruise? He'd shake them down! They had with them the new hospital-ship, too—the only Red Cross ship in space that could leg it, parsec for parsec, with the *Dauntless.*

"Get me Navigations . . . Figure best point of rendez-vous for *Dauntless* and Flotilla ZKD, both at full blast, en route to Lundmark's Nebula. Fifteen minutes departure. Figure approximate time of meeting with speedster, also at full blast, leaving that nebula hour nine fourteen today. Correction! Cancel speedster meeting, we can compute that more accurately later. Advise adjutant. Admiral Southworth will send order, through channels. Get me Base Hospital . . . Lacy, please . . . Kinnison's hurt, sawbones, bad. I'm going out after him. Coming along?"

"Yes. How about . . ."

"On the green. Flotilla ZKD, including your new two-hundred-million-credit hospital, is going along. Slip twelve, *Dauntless,* eleven and one-half minutes from now. Hipe!" and the Surgeon-Marshal "hiped."

Two minutes before the scheduled take-off Base Navi-gations called the chief navigating officer of the *Dauntless.*

"Course to rendezvous with Flotilla ZKD latitude three fifty four dash thirty longitude nineteen dash forty two time approximately twelve dash seven dash twenty six place one dash three dash zero outside arbitrary galactic rim check and repeat" rattled from the speaker without pause or punc-tuation. Nevertheless the chief navigator got it, recorded it, checked and repeated it.

"Figures only approximations because of lack of exact data on variations in density of medium and on distance necessarily lost in detouring stars" the speaker chattered on "suggest instructing your second navigator to communicate with navigating officers Flotilla ZKD at time twelve dash zero to correct courses to compensate unavoidably erroneous assumptions in computation Base Navigations off."

"I'll say he's off! 'Way off!" growled the Second.

"What does he think I am—a complete nitwit? Pretty soon he'll be telling me two plus two equals four point zero."

The fifteen-second warning bell sounded. Every man came to the ready at his post, and precisely upon the designated second the super-dreadnought blasted off. For four or five miles she rose inert upon her under-jets, sirens and flaring lights clearing her way. Then she went free, her needle prow slanted sharply upward, her full battery of main driving projectors burst into action, and to all intents and purposes she vanished.

The Earth fell away from her at an incredible rate, dwindling away into invisibility in less than a minute. In two minutes the sun itself was merely a bright star, in five it had merged indistinguishably into the sharply-defined, brilliantly white belt of the Milky Way.

Hour after hour, day after day the *Dauntless* hurtled through space, swinging almost imperceptibly this way and that to avoid the dense ether in the neighborhood of suns through which the designated course would have led; but never leaving far or for long the direct line, almost exactly in the equatorial plane of the galaxy, between Tellus and the place of meeting. Behind her the Milky Way clotted, condensed, gathered itself together; before her and around her the stars began rapidly to thin out. Finally there were no more stars in front of her. She had reached the "arbitrary rim" of the galaxy, and the second navigator, then on duty, plugged into Communications.

"Please get me Flotilla ZKD, Flagship Navigations," he requested; and, as a clean-cut young face appeared upon his plate, "Hi, Harvey, old spacehound! Fancy meeting you out here! It's a small Universe, ain't it? Say, did that crumb back there at Base tell you, too, to be sure and start checking course before you over-ran the rendezvous? If he was singling me out to make that pass at, I'm going to take steps, and not through channels, either."

"Yeah, he told me the same. I thought it was funny, too—an oiler's pimp would know enough to do that without being told. We figured maybe he was jittery on account of

us meeting the admiral or something. What's burned out
all the jets, Paul, to get the big brass hats 'way out here and
all dithered up, and to pull us offa the cruise this way? Must
be a hell of an important flit! You're computing the Old
Man himself, you must know something. What's this speedster that we're going to escort, and why? Give us the dope!"

"I don't know anything, Harvey, honest, any more than
you do. They didn't put out a thing. Well, we'd better be
getting onto the course—'to compensate unavoidably erroneous assumptions in computation,'" he mimicked, caus-
tically. "What do you read on my lambda? Fourteen—three
—point zero six—decrement . . ."

The conversation became a technical jargon; because
of which, however, the courses of the flying space-ships
changed subtly. The flottila swung around, through a small
arc of a circle of prodigious radius, decreasing by a tenth
its driving force. Up to it the *Dauntless* crept; through it
and into the van. Then again in cone formation, but with
fifty five units instead of fifty four, the flotilla screamed
forward at maximum blast.

Well before the calculated time of meeting the speedster a Velantian Lensman who knew Worsel well put himself en rapport with him and sent a thought out far ahead
of the flying squadron. It found its goal—Lensmen of that
race, as has been brought out, have always been extraor-
dinarily capable communicators—and once more the course
was altered slightly. In due time Worsel reported that he
could detect the fleet, and shortly thereafter:

"Worsel says to cut your drive to zero," the Velantian
transmitted. "He's coming up . . . He's close . . . He's going
to go inert and start driving . . . We're to stay free until we
see what his intrinsic velocity is . . . Watch for his flare."

It was a weird sensation, this of knowing that a speedster—quite a sizable chunk of boat, really—was almost in
their midst, and yet having all their instruments, even the
electros, register empty space . . .

There it was! The flare of the driving blast, a brilliant
streamer of fierce white light, sprang into being and drifted

rapidly away to one side of their course. When it had attained a safe distance:

"All ships of the flotilla except the *Dauntless* go inert," Haynes directed. Then, to his own pilot. "Back us off a bit, Henderson, and do the same," and the new flagship, too, went inert.

"How can I get onto the *Pasteur* the quickest, Haynes?" Lacy demanded.

"Take a gig," the Admiral grunted, "and tell the boys how much you want to take. Three G's is all we can use without warning and preparation."

There followed a curious and fascinating spectacle, for the hospital ship had an intrinsic velocity entirely different from that of either Kinnison's speedster or Lacy's powerful gig. The *Pasteur*, gravity pads cut to zero, was braking down by means of her under-jets at a conservative one point four gravities—hospital ships were not allowed to use the brutal accelerations employed as a matter of course by ships of war.

The gig was on her brakes at five gravities, all that Lacy wanted to take—but the speedster! Worsel had put his patient into a pressure-pack and had hung him on suspension, and was "balancing her down on her tail" at a full eleven gravities!

But even at that, the gig first matched the velocity of the hospital ship. The intrinsics of those two were at least of the same order of magnitude, since both had come from the same galaxy. Therefore Lacy boarded the Red Cross vessel and was escorted to the office of the chief nurse while Worsel was still blasting at eleven G's—fifty thousand miles distant then and getting farther away by the second—to kill the speedster's Lundmarkian intrinsic velocity. Nor could the tractors of the warships be of any assistance—the speedster's own vicious jets were fully capable of supplying more acceleration than even a pressure-packed human body could endure.

"How do you do, Doctor Lacy? Everything is ready." Clarrissa MacDougal met him, hand outstretched. Her saucy

white cap was worn as perkily cocked as ever: perhaps even
more so, now that it was emblazoned with the cross-sur-
mounted wedge which is the insignia of sector chief nurse.
Her flaming hair was as gorgeous, her smile as radiant, her
bearing as confidently—Kinnison has said of her more than
once that she is the only person he has ever known who can
strut sitting down!—as calmly poised. "I'm very glad to
see you, doctor. It's been quite a while . . ." Her voice died
away, for the man was looking at her with an expression
defying analysis.

For Lacy was thunder-struck. If he had ever known it
—and he must have—he had completely forgotten that Mac-
Dougall had this ship. This was awful—terrible!

"Oh, yes . . . yes, of course. How do you do? Mighty
glad to see you again. How's everything going?" He pumped
her hand vigorously, thinking frantically the while what he
would—what he *could* say next. "Oh, by the way, who is
to be in charge of the operating room?"

"Why, I am, of course," she replied in surprise. "Who
else would be?"

"*Anyone* else!" he wanted to say, but did not— then.
"Why, that isn't at all necessary . . . I would suggest . . ."

"You'll suggest nothing of the kind!" She stared at
him intently; then, as she realized what his expression really
meant—she had never before seen such a look of pitying
anguish upon his usually sternly professional face—her own
turned white and both hands flew to her throat.

"Not Kim, Lacy!" she gasped. Gone now was everything of poise, of insouciance, which had so characterized
her a moment before. She who had worked unflinchingly
upon all sorts of dismembered, fragmentary, maimed and
mangled men was now a pleading, stricken, desperately
frightened girl. "Not Kim—please! Oh, merciful God, don't
let it be my Kim!"

"You *can't* be there, Mac." He did not need to tell her.
She knew. He knew that she knew. "Somebody else—*anybody* else."

"No!" came the hot negative, although the blood drained

completely from her face, leaving it as white as the im-
maculate uniform she wore. Her eyes were black, burning
holes. "It's my job, Lacy, in more ways than one. Do you
think I'd let anyone else work on *him?*" she finished
passionately.

"You'll have to," he declared. "I didn't want to tell
you this, but he's a mess." This, from a surgeon of Lacy's
long and wide experience, was an unthinkable statement.
Nevertheless:

"All the more reason why I've got to do it. No matter
what shape he's in I'll let no one else work on my Kim!"

"I say no. That's an order—official!"

"Damn such orders!" she flamed. "There's nothing
back of it—you know that as well as I do!"

"See here, young woman . . . !"

"Do you think you can order me not to perform the
very duties I swore to do?" she stormed. "And even if it
were not my job, I'd come in and work on him if I had to
get a torch and cut my way in to do it. The only way you
can keep me out is to have about ten of your men put me
into a strait-jacket—and if you do that I'll have you kicked
out of the Service bodily!"

"QX, MacDougall, you win." She had him there. This
girl could and would do exactly that. "But if you faint I'll
make you wish. . . ."

"You know me better than that, doctor." She was cold
now as a woman of marble. "If he dies I'll die too, right
then; but if he lives I'll stand by."

"You would, at that," the surgeon admitted. "Probably
you would be able to hold together better than any one else
could. But there'll be after-effects in your case, you know."

"I know." Her voice was bleak. "I'll live through them
. . . if Kim lives." She became all nurse in the course of a
breath. White, cold, inhuman; strung to highest tension and
yet placidly calm, as only a truly loving woman in life's
great crises can be. "You have had reports on him, doctor.
What is your provisional diagnosis?"

"Something like elephantiasis, only worse, affecting both

arms and both legs. Drastic amputations indicated. Eye-sockets. Burns. Multiple and compound fractures. Punctured and incised wounds. Traumatism, ecchymosis, extensive extravasations, œdema. Profound systemic shock. The prognosis, however, seems to be favorable, as far as we can tell."

"Oh, I'm glad of that," she breathed, the woman for a moment showing through the armor of the nurse. She had not dared even to think of prognosis. Then she had a thought. "Is that really true, or are you just giving me a shot in the arm?" she demanded.

"The truth—strictly," he assured her. "Worsel has an excellent sense of perception, and has reported fully and clearly. His brain, mind, and spine are not affected in any way, and we should be able to save his life. That is the one good feature of the whole thing."

The speedster finally matched the intrinsic velocity of the hospital ship. She went free, flashed up to the *Pasteur,* inerted, and maneuvered briefly. The larger vessel engulfed the smaller. The Gray Lensman was carried into the operating room. The anæsthetist approached the table and Lacy was stunned at a thought from Kinnison.

"Never mind the anæsthetic, Doctor Lacy. You can't make me unconscious without killing me. Just go ahead with your work. I held a nerve-block while the Delgonian was doing his stuff and I can hold it while you're doing yours."

"But we can't, man!" Lacy exclaimed. "You've got to be under a general for this job—we can't have you conscious. You're raving, I think. It will work—it always has. Let us try it, anyway, won't you?"

"Sure. It'll save me the trouble of holding the block, even though it won't do anything else. Go ahead."

The attendant doctor did so, with the same cool skill and to the same end-point as in thousands of similar and successful undertakings. At its conclusion, "Gone now, aren't you, Kinnison?" Lacy asked, through his Lens.

"No," came the surprising reply. "Physically, it worked. I can't feel a thing and I can't move a muscle, but mentally I'm still here."

"But you shouldn't be!" Lacy protested. "Perhaps you were right, at that—we can't give you much more without danger of collapse. But you've *got* to be unconscious! Isn't there some way in which you can be made so?"

"Yes, there is. But why do I have to be unconscious?" he asked, curiously.

"To avoid mental shock—seriously damaging," the surgeon explained. "In your case particularly the mental aspect is graver than the purely physical one."

"Maybe you're right, but you can't do it with drugs. Call Worsel; he has done it before. He had me unconscious most of the way over here except when he had to give me a drink or something to eat. He's the only man this side of Arisia who can operate on my mind."

Worsel came. "Sleep, my friend," he commanded, gently but firmly. "Sleep profoundly, body and mind, with no physical or mental sensations, no consciousness, no perception even of the passage of time. Sleep so until someone having authority to do so bids you awaken."

And Kinnison slept; so deeply that even Lacy's probing Lens could elicit no response.

"He will *stay* that way?" Lacy asked in awe.

"Yes."

"For how long?"

"Indefinitely. Until one of you doctors or nurses tells him to wake up, or until he dies for lack of food or water."

"He'll get nourishment. He would make a much better recovery if we could keep him in that state until his injuries are almost healed. Would that hurt him?"

"Not at all."

Then the surgeons and the nurses went to work. Since it has already been made amply plain what had to be done to the Gray Lensman, no good end is to be served by following in revolting detail the stark hideousness of its actual doing. Suffice it to say, then, that Lacy was not guilty of exaggeration when he described Kinnison as being a "mess." He was. The job was long and hard. It was heart-breaking, even for those to whom Kinnison was merely another case, not a beloved personality. What they had to do they did, and the white-marble chief nurse carried on through every soul-wrenching second, through every shocking, searing motion of it. She did her part, stoically, unflinchingly, as efficiently as though the patient upon the table were a total stranger undergoing a simple appendectomy and not the one man in her entire Universe undergoing radical dismemberment. Nor did she faint—then.

"Three or four of the girls fainted dead away, and a couple of the internes turned sort of green around the gills," she explained to your historian in reply to a direct question. She can bring herself to discuss the thing, now that it is so happily past, although she does not like to do so. "But I held on until it was all over. I did more than faint then." She smiled wryly at the memory. "I went into such a succession of hysterical cat-fits that they had to give me hypos and keep me in bed, and they didn't let me see Kim again until we had him back in Base Hospital, on Tellus. But even old Lacy himself was so woozy that he had to have a couple of snifters of brandy, so the show I put on wasn't too much out of order, at that."

Back in Base Hospital, then, time wore on until Lacy decided that the Lensman could be aroused from his trance. Clarrissa woke him up. She had fought for the privilege: first claiming it as a right and then threatening to commit mayhem upon the person of anyone else who dared even to think of doing it.

"Wake up, Kim dear," she whispered. "The worst of it is over now. You are getting well."

The Gray Lensman came to instantly, in full command of every faculty; knowing everything that had happened up to the instant of his hypnosis by Worsel. He stiffened, ready to establish again the nerve-block against the intolerable agony to which he had been subjected so long, but there was no need. His body was, for the first time in untold eons, free from pain; and he relaxed blissfully, reveling in the sheer comfort of it.

"I'm *so* glad that you're awake, Kim," the nurse went

on. "I know that you can't talk to me—we can't unbandage your jaw until next week—and you can't think at me, either, because your new Lens hasn't come yet. But I can talk to you and you can listen. Don't be discouraged, Kim. Don't let it get you down. I love you just as much as I ever did, and as soon as you can talk we're going to get married. I am going to take care of you . . ."

"Don't 'poor dear' me, Mac," he interrupted her with a vigorous thought. "You didn't say it, I know, but you were thinking it. I'm not half as helpless as you think I am. I can still communicate, and I can see as well as I ever could, or better. And if you think I'm going to let you marry me to take care of me, you're crazy."

"You're raving! Delirious! Stark, staring mad!" She started back, then controlled herself by an effort. "Maybe you can think at people without a Lens—of course you can, since you just did, at me—but you *can't* see, Kim, possibly. Believe me, boy, I *know* you can't. I was there . . ."

"I can, though," he insisted. "I got a lot of stuff on my second trip to Arisia that I couldn't let anybody know about then, but I can now. I've got as good a sense of perception as Tregonsee has—maybe better. To prove it, you look thin, worn—whittled down to a nub. You've been working too hard—on me."

"Deduction," she scoffed. "You'd know I would."

"QX. How about those roses over there on the table? White ones, yellow ones, and red ones? With ferns?"

"You can smell them, perhaps," dubiously. Then, with more assurance, "You would know that practically all the flowers known to botany would be here."

"Well, I'll count 'em and point 'em out to you, then— or better, how about that little gold locket, with 'CM' engraved on it, that you're wearing under your uniform? I can't smell that, nor the picture in it . . ." The man's thought faltered in embarrassment. "*My* picture! Klono's whiskers, Mac, where did you get that—and why?"

"It's a reduction that Admiral Haynes let me have made. I am wearing it because I love you—I've said that before."

The girl's entrancing smile was now in full evidence. She knew now that he *could* see, that he would never be the helpless hulk which she had so gallingly thought him doomed to become, and her spirits rose in ecstatic relief. But he would *never* take the initiative now. QX, then—she would; and this was as good an opening as she would ever have with the stubborn brute. Therefore:

"More than that, as I also said before, I am going to marry you, whether you like it or not." She blushed a heavenly (and discordant) magenta, but went on unfalteringly: "And not out of pity, either, Kim, or just to take care of you. It's older than that—much older."

"It can't be done, Mac." His thought was a protest to high Heaven at the injustice of Fate. "I've thought it over out in space a thousand times—thought until I was black in the face—but I get the same result every time. It's just simply no soap. You are much too fine a woman—too splendid, too vital, too much of everything a woman should be —to be tied down for life to a thing that's half steel, rubber, and phenoline. It just simply isn't on the wheel, that's all."

"You're full of pickles, Kim." Gone was all her uncertainty and nervousness. She was calm, poised; glowing with a transcendent inward beauty. "I didn't really *know* until this minute that you love me, too, but I do now. Don't you realize, you big, dumb, wonderful clunker, that as long as there's one single, little bit of a piece of you left alive I'll love that piece more than I ever could any other man's entire being?"

"But I *can't,* I tell you!" He groaned the thought. "I can't and I won't! My job isn't done yet, either, and next time they'll probably get me. I *can't* let you waste yourself, Mac, on a fraction of a man for a fraction of a lifetime!"

"QX, Gray Lensman." Clarissa was serene, radiantly untroubled. She could make things come out right now; everything was on the green. "We'll put this back up on the shelf for a while. I'm afraid that I have been terribly remiss in my duties as nurse. Patients mustn't be excited or quarreled with, you know."

"That's another thing. How come you, a sector chief, to be doing ordinary room duty, and night duty at that?"

"Sector chiefs assign duties, don't they?" she retorted sunnily. "Now I'll give you a rub and change some of these dressings."

CHAPTER

22

Regeneration

H

I, SKELETON-GAZER!"

"Ho, Big Chief Feet-on-the-Desk!"

"I see your red-headed sector chief is still occupying all strategic salients in force." Haynes had paused in the Surgeon-Marshal's office on his way to another of his conferences with the Gray Lensman. "Can't you get rid of her or don't you want to?"

"Don't want to. Couldn't, anyway, probably. The young vixen would tear down the hospital—she might even resign, marry him out of hand, and lug him off somewhere. You want him to recover, don't you?"

"Don't be any more of an idiot than you have to. What a question!"

"Don't work up a temperature about MacDougall, then. As long as she's around him—and that's twenty four hours a day—he'll get everything in the universe that he can get any good out of."

"That's so, too. This other thing's out of our hands now, anyway. Kinnison can't hold his position long against her and himself both—overwhelmingly superior force. Just as well, too—Civilization needs more like those two."

"Check, but the affair isn't out of our hands, by any means—we've got quite a little fine work to do there yet, as you'll see, before it'll be a really good job. But about Kinnison . . ."

"Yes. When are you going to fit arms and legs on him? He should be practising with them at this stage of the game, I should think—I was."

"You *should* think—but unfortunately, you don't," was the surgeon's dry rejoinder. "If you did, you would have paid more attention to what Phillips has been doing. He's making the final test today. Come along and we'll explain it to you again—your conference with Kinnison can wait half an hour."

In the research laboratory which had been assigned to Phillips they found von Hohendorff with the Posenian. Haynes was surprised to see the old Commandant of Cadets, but Lacy quite evidently had known that he was to be there.

"Phillips," the Surgeon-Marshal began, "explain to this warhorse, in words of as few syllables as possible, what you are doing."

"The original problem was to discover what hormone or other agent caused proliferation of neural tissue . . ."

"Wait a minute, I'd better do it," Lacy broke in. "Besides, you wouldn't do yourself justice. The first thing he found out was that the problem of repairing damaged nervous tissue was inextricably involved with several other unknown things, such as the original growth of such tissue, its relationship to growth in general, the regeneration of lost members in lower forms, and so on. You see, Haynes, it's a known fact that nerves do grow, or else they could not exist; and in lower forms of life they regenerate. Those facts were all he had, at first. In higher forms, even during the growth stage, regeneration does not occur spontaneously. Phillips set out to find out why.

"The thyroid controls growth, but does not initiate it, he learned. This fact seemed to indicate that there was an unknown hormone involved—that certain lower types possess an endocrine gland which is either atrophied or non-existent in higher types. If the latter, it was no landing. He reasoned, however, since higher types evolved from lower, that the gland in question might very well exist in a vestigial state. He studied animals, thousands of them, from the germ upward. He exhausted the patience of the Posenian authorities; and when they cut off his appropriation, on the ground that the thing was impossible, he came here. We felt that if he were so convinced of the importance of the work as to be willing to spend his whole life on it, the least we could do would be to support him. We gave him carte blanche.

"The man is a miracle of perseverance, a keen observer, a shrewd reasoner, and a mechanic par excellence—a born researcher. So he finally found out what it must be—the pineal. Then he had to find the stimulant. Drugs, chemicals, the spectrum of radiation; singly and in combination. Years of plugging, with just enough progress to keep him at it. Visits to other planets peopled by races human to two places or more; learning everything that had been done along that line. When you fellows moved Medon over here he visited it as routine, and there he hit the jackpot. Wise himself is a surgeon, and the Medonians have had warfare and grief enough to develop the medical and surgical arts no end.

"They knew how to stimulate the pineal, but their method was dangerous. With Phillips' fresh viewpoint, his wide knowledge, and his mechanical genius, they worked out a new and highly satisfactory technique. He was going to try it out on a pirate slated for the lethal chamber, but von Hohendorff heard about it and insisted on being the guinea pig. Got up on his Unattached Lensman's high horse and won't come down. So here we are."

"Hm . . . m . . . interesting!" The admiral had listened attentively. "You're pretty sure it'll work, then, I gather?"

"As sure as we can be of any technique so new. Ninety percent probability, say—perhaps ninety five."

"Good enough odds." Haynes turned to von Hohendorff. "What do you mean, you old reprobate, by sneaking around behind my back and horning in on my reservation? I rate Unattached too, you know, and it's mine. You're out, Von."

"I saw it first and I refuse to relinquish." Von Hohendorff was adamant.

"You've got to," Haynes insisted. "He isn't your cub any more, he's my Lensman. Besides, I'm a better test than you are—I've got more parts to replace than you have."

"Four or five make just as good a test as a dozen," the commandant declared.

"Gentlemen, think!" the Posenian pleaded. "Please consider that the pineal is actually inside the brain. It is true that I have not been able to discover any brain injury so far, but the process has not yet been applied to a Tellurian brain and I can offer no assurance whatever that some obscure injury will not result."

"What of it?" and the two old Unattached Lensmen resumed their battle, hammer and tongs. Neither would yield a millimeter.

"Operate on them both, then, since they're both above law or reason," Lacy finally ordered in exasperation. "There ought to be a law to reduce Gray Lensmen to the ranks when they begin to suffer from ossification of the intellect."

"Starting with yourself, perhaps?" the admiral shot back, not at all abashed.

Haynes relented enough to let von Hohendorff go first, and both were given the necessary injections. The commandant was then strapped solidly into a chair; his head was immobilized with clamps.

The Posenian swung his needle-rays into place; two of them, each held rigidly upon micrometered racks and each operated by two huge, double, rock-steady hands. The operator *looked* entirely aloof—being eyeless and practically headless, it is impossible to tell from a Posenian's attitude or posture anything about the focal point of his attention—but the watchers knew that he was observing in microscopic detail the tiny gland within the old Lensman's skull.

Then Haynes. "Is this all there is to it, or do we come back for more?" he asked, when he was released from his shackles.

"That's all," Lacy answered. "One stimulation lasts for

life, as far as we know. But if the treatment was successful
you'll come back—about day after tomorrow, I think—to
go to bed here. Your spare equipment won't fit and your
stumps may require surgical attention."

Sure enough, Haynes did come back to the hospital,
but not to go to bed. He was too busy. Instead, he got a
wheel-chair and in it he was taken back to his now boiling
office. And in a few more days he called Lacy in high
exasperation.

"Know what you've done?" he demanded. "Not satisfied with taking my perfectly good parts away from me,
you took my teeth too! They don't fit—I can't eat a thing!
And I'm hungry as a wolf—I don't think I was ever so
hungry in my life! I *can't* live on soup, man; I've got
work to do. What are you going to do about it?"

"*Ho-ho-haw!*" Lacy roared. "Serves you right—von
Hohendorff is taking it easy here, sitting on top of the
world. Easy, now, sailor, don't rupture your aorta. I'll send
a nurse over with a soft-boiled egg and a spoon. *Teething*—
at *your* age—*Haw-ho-haw!*"

But it was no ordinary nurse who came, a few minutes
later, to see the Port Admiral; it was the sector chief herself. She looked at him pityingly as she trundled him into
his private office and shut the door, thereby establishing
complete coverage.

"I had no idea, Admiral Haynes, that you . . . that
there . . ." she paused.

"That I was so much of a rebuild?" complacently.
"Except in the matter of eyes—which he doesn't need anyway—our mutual friend Kinnison has very little on me, my
dear. I got so handy with the replacements that very few people
knew how much of me was artificial. But it's these teeth
that are taking all the joy out of life. I'm hungry, confound
it! Have you got anything really satisfying that I can eat?"

"I'll say I have!" She fed him; then, bending over, she
squeezed him tight and kissed him emphatically. "You and
the commandant are just perfectly wonderful old darlings,
and I *love* you!" she declared. "Lacy was simply poisonous

to laugh at you the way he did. Why, you're two of the world's very best! And he knew perfectly well all the time, the lug, that of course you'd be hungry; that you'd have to eat twice as much as usual while your legs and things are growing. Don't worry, admiral, I'll feed you until you bulge. I want you to hurry up with this, so they'll do it to Kim."

"Thanks, Mac," and as she wheeled him back into the main office he considered her anew. A ravishing creature, but sound. Rash, and a bit stubborn, perhaps; impetuous and headstrong; but clean, solid metal all the way through. She had what it takes—she qualified. She and Kinnison would make a mighty fine couple when the lad got some of that heroic damn nonsense knocked out of his head . . . but there was work to do.

There was. The Galactic Council had considered thoroughly Kinnison's reports; its every member had conferred with him and with Worsel at length. Throughout the First Galaxy the Patrol was at work in all its prodigious might, preparing to wipe out the menace to Civilization which was Boskone. First-line super-dreadnoughts—no others would go upon that mission—were being built and armed, rebuilt and re-armed.

Well it was that the Galactic Patrol had previously amassed an almost inexhaustible supply of wealth, for its "reserves of expendable credit" were running like water.

Weapons, supposedly already of irresistible power, were made even more powerful. Screens already "impenetrable" were stiffened into even greater stubbornness. Primary projectors were made to take even higher loads for longer times. New and heavier Q-type helices were designed and built. Larger and more destructive duodec bombs were hurled against already ruined, torn, and quivering testplanets. Uninhabited worlds were being equipped with super-Bergenholms and with driving projectors. The negasphere, the most incredible menace to navigation which had ever existed in space, was being patrolled by a cordon of guard-ships.

And all this activity centered in one vast building and

culminated in one man—Port Admiral Haynes, Galactic Councillor. And Haynes could not get enough to eat because he was cutting a new set of teeth!

He cut them, all thirty two of them. Arm and leg, foot and hand grew perfectly, even to the nails. Hair grew upon what had for years been a shining expanse of pate. But, much to Lacy's relief, it was old skin, not young, that covered the new limbs. It was white hair, not brown, that was dulling the glossiness of Haynes' bald old head. His tri-focals, unchanged, were still necessary if he were to see anything clearly, near or far.

"Our experimental animals aged and died normally," he explained graciously, "but I was beginning to wonder if we had rejuvenated you two, or perhaps endowed you with eternal life. Glad to see that the new parts have the same physical age as the rest of you—It would be mildly embarrassing to have to kill two Gray Lensmen to get rid of them."

"You're about as funny as a rubber crutch," Haynes grunted. "When are you going to give Kinnison the works? Don't you realize we need him?"

"Pretty quick now. Just as soon as we give you and Von your psychological examinations."

"Bah! That isn't necessary—my brain's QX!"

"That's what you think, but what do you know about brains? Worsel will tell us what shape your mind—if any —is in."

The Velantian put both Haynes and von Hohendorff through a gruelling examination, finding that their minds had not been affected in any way by the stimulants applied to their pineal glands.

Then and only then did Phillips operate upon Kinnison; and in his case, too, the operation was a complete success. Arms and legs and eyes replaced themselves flawlessly. The scars of his terrible wounds disappeared, leaving no sign of ever having been.

He was a little slower, however; somewhat clumsy, and woefully weak. Therefore, instead of discharging him from the hospital as cured, which procedure would have restored to him automatically all the rights and privileges of an Unattached Lensman, the Council decided to transfer him to a physical-culture camp. A few weeks there would restore to him entirely the strength, speed, and agility which had formerly been his, and he would then be allowed to resume active duty.

Just before he left the hospital, Kinnison strolled with Clarrissa out to a bench in the grounds.

". . . and you're making a perfect recovery," the girl was saying. "You'll be exactly as you were. But things between us aren't just as they were, and they never can be again. You know that, Kim. We've got unfinished business to transact—let's take it down off the shelf before you go."

"Better let it lay, Mac." All the new-found joy of existence went out of the man's eyes. "I'm whole, yes, but that angle was really the least important of all. You never yet have faced squarely the fact that my job isn't done and that my chance of living through it is just about one in ten. Even Phillips can't do anything about a corpse."

"I won't face it, either, unless and until I must." Her reply was tranquility itself. "Most of the troubles people worry about in advance never do materialize. And even if it did, you ought to know that I . . . that any woman would rather . . . well, that half a loaf is better than no bread."

"QX. I haven't mentioned the worst thing. I didn't want to—but if you've got to have it, here it is," the man wrenched out. "Look at what I am. A bar-room brawler. A rum-dum. A hard-boiled egg. A cold-blooded, ruthless murderer; even of my own men . . ."

"Not that, Kim, ever, and you know it," she rebuked him.

"What else can you call it?" he grated. "A killer besides—a red-handed butcher if there ever was one; then, now, and forever. I've got to be. I can't get away from it. Do you think that you, or any other decent woman, could stand it to live with me? That you could feel my arms around you, feel my gory paws touching you, without going sick at the stomach?"

"Oh, so *that's* what's been really griping you all this time?" Clarrissa was surprised, but entirely unshaken. "I don't have to think about that, Kim—I *know*. If you were a murderer or had the killer instinct, that would be different, but you aren't and you haven't. You are hard, of course. You have to be . . . but do you think I'd be running a temperature over a softy? You brawl, yes—like the world's champion you are. Anybody you ever killed needed killing, there's no question of that. You don't do these things for fun; and the fact that you can drive yourself to do the things that have to be done shows your real size.

"Nor have you even thought of the obverse; that you lean over backwards in wielding that terrific power of yours. The Desplaines woman, the countess—lots of other instances. I respect and honor you more than any other man I have ever known. Any woman who really knew you would —she *must!*

"Listen, Kim. Read my mind, all of it. You'll really know me then, and understand me better than I can ever explain myself."

"Have you got a picture of me doing that?" he asked, flatly.

"No, you big, unreasonable clunker, I haven't!" she flared, "and that's just what's driving me mad!" Then, voice dropping to a whisper, almost sobbing; "Cancel that, Kim— I didn't mean it. You wouldn't—you *couldn't*, I suppose, and still be you, the man I love. But isn't there something— *anything*—that will make you understand what I really am?"

"I know what you are." Kinnison's voice was uninflected, weary. "As I told you before—the universe's best. It's what I am that's clogging the jets—what I have been and what I've got to keep on being. I simply don't rate up, and you'd better lay off me, Mac, while you can. There's a poem by one of the ancients—Kipling—the 'Ballad of Boh Da Thone'—that describes it exactly. You wouldn't know it . . ."

"You just think I wouldn't," nodding brightly. "The only trouble is, you always think of the wrong verses. Part of it really *is* descriptive of you. You know, where all the soldiers of the Black Tyrone thought so much of their captain?"

She recited:

" 'And worshipped with fluency, fervor, and zeal

" 'The mud on the boot-heels of "Crook" O'Neil.'

"That describes you to a 'T.' "

"You're crazy for the lack of sense," he demurred. "I don't rate like that."

"Sure you do," she assured him. "All the men think of you that way. And not only men. Women, too, darn 'em—and the next time I catch one of them at it I'm going to kick her cursed teeth out, one by one!"

Kinnison laughed, albeit a trifle sourly. "You're raving, Mac. Imagining things. But to get back to that poem, what I was referring to went like this . . ."

"I know how it goes. Listen:

" 'But the captain had quitted the long-drawn strife

" 'And in far Simoorie had taken a wife;

" 'And she was a damsel of delicate mold,

" 'With hair like the sunshine and heart of gold.

" 'And little she knew the arms that embraced

" 'Had cloven a man from the brow to the waist:

" 'And little she knew that the loving lips

" 'Had ordered a quivering life's eclipse,

" 'And the eyes that lit at her lightest breath

" 'Had glared unawed in the Gates of Death.

" '(For these be matters a man would hide,

" 'As a general thing, from an innocent bride.)'

"That's what you mean, isn't it?" she asked, quietly.

"Mac, you know a lot of things you've got no business knowing." Instead of answering her question, he stared at her speculatively. "My sprees and brawls, Dessa Desplaines and the Countess Avondrin, and now this. Would you mind telling me how you get the stuff?"

"I'm closer to you than you suspect, Kim—I've always been. Worsel calls it being 'en rapport.' You don't need to think at me—in fact, you have to put up a conscious block to keep me out. So I know a lot that I shouldn't, but Lensmen aren't the only ones who don't talk. You'd been thinking about that poem a lot—it worried you—so I checked with Archeology on it. I memorized most of it."

"Well, to get the true picture of me you'll have to multiply that by a thousand. Also, don't forget that loose heads might be rolling out onto your breakfast table almost any morning instead of only once."

"So what?" she countered evenly. "Do you think I could sit for Kipling's portrait of Mrs. O'Neil? Nobody ever called my mold delicate, and Kipling, if he had been describing me, would have said:

" 'With hair like a conflagration,
" 'And a heart of solid brass!'

"Captain O'Neil's bride, as well as being innocent and ignorant, strikes me as having been a good deal of a sissy, something of a weeping willow, and no little of a shrinking violet. Tell me, Kim, do you think she would have made good as a sector chief nurse?"

"No, but that's neither . . ."

"It is, too," she interrupted. "You've got to consider that I did, and that it's no job for any girl with a weak stomach. Besides, the Boh's head took the fabled Mrs. O'Neil by surprise. She didn't know that her husband used to be in the wholesale mayhem-and-killing business. I do.

"And lastly, you big lug, do you think I'd be making such bare-faced passes at you unless I knew exactly what the score is—exactly where *you* stand? You're too much of a gentleman to read my mind; but I'm not that sque . . . I *had* to know."

"Huh?" he demanded, blushing fiercely. "You really know, then, that . . ." he would not say it, even then.

"Of course I know!" She nodded; then, as the man spread his hands helplessly, she abandoned her attempt to keep the conversation upon a light level.

"I know, my dear. There's nothing we can do about it yet." Her voice was unsteady, her heart in every word. "You have to do your job, and I honor you for that, even if it does take you away from me. It'll be easier for you, though, I think, and I *know* it will be easier for me, to have it out in the open. Whenever you're ready, Kim, I'll be here—or somewhere—waiting. Clear ether, Gray Lensman!" and, rising to her feet, she turned back toward the hospital.

"Clear ether, Chris!" Unconsciously he used the pet name by which he had thought of her so long. He stared after her for a minute, hungrily. Then, squaring his shoulders, he strode away.

* * *

And upon far Jarnevon Eichmil, the First of Boskone, was conferring with Jalte via communicator. Long since, the Kalonian had delivered through devious channels the message of Boskone to an imaginary director of Lensmen; long since had he received this cryptically direful reply:

"Morgan lives, and so does—Star A Star."

Jalte had not been able to report to his chief any news concerning the fate of that which the speedster bore, since spies no longer existed within the reservations of the Patrol. He had learned of no discovery that any Lensman had made. He could not venture a hypothesis as to how this Star A Star had heard of Jarnevon or had learned of its location. He was sure of only one thing, and that was a grimly disturbing fact indeed. The Patrol was re-arming throughout the galaxy, upon a scale theretofore unknown. Eichmil's thought was cold:

"That means but one thing. A Lensman invaded you

and learned of us here—in no other way could knowledge of Jarnevon have come to them."

"Why me?" Jalte demanded. "If there exists a mind of power sufficient to break my screens and tracelessly to invade my mind, what of yours?"

"It is proven by the outcome." The Boskonian's statement was a calm summation of fact. "The messenger sent against you succeeded; the one against us failed. The Patrol intends and is preparing: certainly to wipe out our remaining forces within the Tellurian Galaxy; probably to attack your stronghold; eventually to invade our own galaxy."

"Let them come!" snarled the Kalonian. "We can and will hold this planet forever against anything they can bring through space!"

"I would not be too sure of that," cautioned the superior. "In fact, if—as I am beginning to regard as a probability—the Patrol does make a concerted drive against any significant number of our planetary organizations, you should abandon your base there and return to Kalonia, after disbanding and so preserving for future use as many as possible of the planetary units."

"Future use? In that case there will be no future."

"There will so," Eichmil replied, coldly vicious. "We are strengthening the defenses of Jarnevon to withstand any conceivable assault. If they do not attack us here of their own free will we shall compel them to do so. Then, after destroying their every mobile force, we shall again take over their galaxy. Arms for the purpose are even now in the building. Is the matter clear?"

"It is clear. We shall warn all our groups that such an order may issue, and we shall prepare to abandon this base should such a step become desirable."

So it was planned; neither Eichmil nor Jalte even suspecting two startling truths:

First, that when the Patrol was ready it would strike hard and without warning, and

Second, that it would strike, not low, but high!

KNNISON PLAYED, WORKED, rested, ate, and slept. He boxed, strenuously and viciously, with masters of the craft. He practised with his DeLameters until he had regained his old-time speed and dead-center accuracy. He swam for hours at a time, he ran in cross-country races. He lolled, practically naked, in hot sunshine. And finally, when his muscles were writhing and rippling as of yore beneath the bronzed satin of his skin, Lacy answered his insistent demands by coming to see him.

The Gray Lensman met the flyer eagerly, but his face fell when he saw that the surgeon-marshal was alone.

"No, MacDougall didn't come—she isn't around any more," he explained, guilefully.

"Huh?" came startled query. "How come?"

"Out in space—out Borova way somewhere. What do you care? After the way you acted you've got the crust of a rhinoceros to . . ."

"You're crazy, Lacy. Why, we . . . she . . . it's all fixed up."

"Funny kind of fixing. Moping around Base, crying her red head off. Finally, though, she decided she had some Scotch pride left, and I let her go aboard again. If she isn't all done with you, she ought to be." This, Lacy figured, would be good for what ailed the big sap-head. "Come on, and I'll see whether you're fit to go back to work or not."

He was fit. "QX, lad—flit!" Lacy discharged him informally with a slap upon the back. "Get dressed and I'll take you back to Haynes—he's been snapping at me like a turtle ever since you've been out here."

At Prime Base Kinnison was welcomed enthusiastically by the admiral.

"Feel those fingers, Kim!" he exclaimed. "Perfect! Just like the originals!"

"Mine, too. They do feel good."

"It's a pity you got your new ones so quick. You'd appreciate 'em much more after a few years without 'em. But to get down to business. The fleets have been taking off for weeks—we're to join up as the line passes. If you haven't anything better to do I'd like to have you aboard the Z9M9Z."

"I don't know of any place I'd rather be, sir—thanks."

"QX. Thanks should be the other way. You can make yourself mighty useful between now and zero time." He eyed the younger man speculatively.

Haynes had a special job for him, Kinnison knew. As a Gray Lensman, he could not be given any military rank or post, and he could not conceive of the admiral of Grand Fleet wanting him around as an aide-de-camp.

"Spill it, chief," he invited. "Not orders, of course— I understand that perfectly. Requests or—ah-hum—suggestions."

"I *will* crown you with something yet, you whelp!" Haynes snorted, and Kinnison grinned. These two were very close, in spite of their disparity in years; and very much of a piece. "As you get older you'll realize that it's good tactics to stick pretty close to Gen Regs. Yes, I *have* got a job for you, and a nasty one. Nobody has been able to handle it, not even two companies of Rigellians. Grand Fleet Operations."

"*Grand Fleet Operations!*" Kinnison was aghast. "Holy

—Klono's—Iridium—Intestines! What makes you think I've got jets enough to swing *that* load?"

"I haven't any idea whether you can or not. If you can't, though, nobody can; and in spite of all the work we've done on the thing we'll have to operate as a mob, the way we did before; not as a fleet. If so, I shudder to think of the results."

"QX. If you'll send for Worsel we'll try it a fling or two. It'd be a shame to build a whole ship around an Operations tank and then not be able to use it. By the way, I haven't seen my head nurse—Miss MacDougall, you know —around any place lately. Have you? I ought to tell her 'thanks' or something—maybe send her a flower."

"Nurse? MacDougall? Oh, yes, the red-head. Let me see—did hear something about her the other day. Married? No . . . took a hospital ship somewhere. Alsakan? Vandemar? Didn't pay any attention. She doesn't need thanks— or flowers, either—getting paid for her work. Much more important, don't you think, to get Operations straightened out?"

"Undoubtedly, sir," Kinnison replied, stiffly; and as he went out Lacy came in.

The two old conspirators greeted each other with knowing grins. *Was* Kinnison taking it big! He was falling, like ten thousand bricks down a well.

"Do him good to undermine his position a bit. Too cocky altogether. But *how* they suffer!"

"Check!"

The Gray Lensman rode toward the flagship in a mood which even he could not have described. He had expected to see her, as a matter of course . . . he wanted to see her . . . confound it, he *had* to see her! Why did she have to do a flit now, of all the times on the calendar? She knew the fleet was shoving off, and that he'd have to go along . . . and nobody knew where she was. When he got back he'd find her if he had to chase her all over the galaxy. He'd put and end to this. Duty was duty, of course . . . but Chris was CHRIS . . . and half a loaf *was* better than no bread!

He jerked back to reality as he entered the gigantic tear-drop which was technically the Z9M9Z, socially the *Directrix,* and ordinarily GFHQ. She had been designed and built specifically to be Grand Fleet Headquarters, and nothing else. She bore no offensive armament, but since she had to protect the presiding geniuses of combat she had every possible defense.

Port Admiral Haynes had learned a bitter lesson during the expedition to Helmuth's base. Long before that relatively small fleet got there he was sick to the core, realizing that fifty thousand vessels simply could not be controlled or maneuvered as a group. If that base had been capable of an offensive or even of a real defense, or if Boskone could have put their fleets into that star-cluster in time, the Patrol would have been defeated ignominiously; and Haynes, wise old tactician that he was, knew it.

Therefore, immediately after the return from that "triumphant" venture, he gave orders to design and to build, at whatever cost, a flagship capable of directing efficiently a million combat units.

The "tank"—the minutely cubed model of the galaxy which is a necessary part of every pilot room—had grown and grown as it became evident that it must be the prime agency in Grand Fleet Operations. Finally, in this last rebuilding, the tank was seven hundred feet in diameter and eighty feet thick in the middle—over seventeen million cubic feet of space in which more than two million tiny lights crawled hither and thither in helpless confusion. For, after the technicians and designers had put that tank into actual service, they had discovered that it was useless. No available mind had been able either to perceive the situation as a whole or to identify with certainty any light or group of lights needing correction; and as for linking up any particular light with its individual, blanket-proof communicator in time to issue orders in space-combat . . . !

Kinnison looked at the tank, then around the full circle of the million-plug board encircling it. He observed the horde of operators, each one trying frantically to do something. Next he shut his eyes, the better to perceive everything at once, and studied the problem for an hour.

"Attention, everybody!" he thought then. "Open all circuits—do nothing at all for a while." He then called Haynes.

"I think we can clean this up if you'll send over some Simplex analyzers and a crew of technicians. Helmuth had a nice set-up on multiplex controls, and Jalte had some ideas, too. If we add them to this we may have something."

And by the time Worsel arrived, they did.

"Red lights are fleets already in motion," Kinnison explained rapidly to the Velantian. "Greens are fleets still at their bases. Ambers are the planets the reds took off from—connected, you see, by Ryerson string-lights. The white star is us, the *Directrix*. That violet cross 'way over there is Jalte's planet, our first objective. The pink comets are our free planets, their tails showing their intrinsic velocities. Being so slow, they had to start long ago. The purple circle is the negasphere. It's on its way, too. You take that side, I'll take this. They were supposed to start from the edge of the twelfth sector. The idea was to make it a smooth, bowl-shaped sweep across the galaxy, converging upon the objective, but each of the system marshals apparently wants to run this war to suit himself. Look at that guy there—he's beating the gun by nine thousand parsecs. Watch me pin his ears back!"

He pointed his Simplex at the red light which had so offendingly sprung into being. There was a whirring click and the number 449276 flashed above a board. An operator flicked a switch.

"Grand Fleet Operations!" Kinnison's thought snapped across space. "Why are you taking off without orders?"

"Why, I . . . I'll give you the marshal, sir . . ."

"No time! Tell your marshal that one more such break will put him in irons. Land at once! GFO—off.

"With around a million fleets to handle we can't spend much time on any one," he thought at Worsel. "But after we get them lined up and get our Rigellians broken in, it won't be so bad."

The breaking in did not take long; definite and meaningful orders flew faster and faster along the tiny, but steel-hard beams of the communicators.

"Take off . . . Increase drive four point five . . . Decrease drive two point eight . . . Change course to . . ." and so it went, hour after hour and day after day.

And with the passage of time came order out of chaos. The red lights formed a gigantically sweeping, curving wall; its almost imperceptible forward crawl representing an actual velocity of almost a hundred parsecs an hour. Behind that wall blazed a sea of amber, threaded throughout with the brilliant filaments which were the Ryerson lights. Ahead of it lay a sparkling, almost solid blaze of green. Closer and closer the wall crept toward the bright white star.

And in the "reducer"—the standard, ten-foot tank in the lower well—the entire spectacle was reproduced in miniature. It was plainer there, clearer and much more readily seen: but it was so crowded that details were indistinguishable.

Haynes stood beside Kinnison's padded chair one day, staring up into the immense lens and shaking his head. He went down the flight of stairs to the reducer, studied that, and again shook his head.

"This is very pretty, but it doesn't mean a thing," he thought at Kinnison. "It begins to look as though I'm going along just for the ride. You—or you and Worsel—will have to do the fighting, too, I'm afraid."

"Uh-uh," Kinnison demurred. "What do we—or anyone else—know about tactics, compared to you? You've got to be the brains. That's why we had the boys rig up the original working model there, for a reducer. On that you can watch the gross developments and tell us in general terms what to do. Knowing that, we'll know who ought to do what, from the big chart here, and pass your orders along."

"Say, that *will* work, at that!" and Haynes brightened

visibly. "Looks as though a couple of those reds are going to knock our star out of the tank, doesn't it?"

"It'll be close in that reducer—they'll probably touch. Close enough in real space—less than three parsecs."

The zero hour came and the Tellurian armada of eighty one sleek space-ships—eighty super-dreadnoughts and the *Directrix*—spurned Earth and took its place in that hurtling wall of crimson. Solar system after solar system was passed: fleet after fleet leaped into the ether and fitted itself into the smoothly geometrical pattern which Grand Fleet Operations was nursing along so carefully.

Through the galaxy the formation swept and out of it, toward a star cluster. It slowed its mad pace, the center hanging back, the edges advancing and folding in.

"Surround the cluster and close in," the admiral directed; and, under the guidance now of two hundred Rigellians, Civilization's vast Grand Fleet closed smoothly in and went inert. Drivers flared white as they fought to match the intrinsic velocity of the cluster.

"Marshals of all system-fleets, attention! Using secondaries only, fire at will upon any enemy object coming within range. Engage outlying structures and such battle craft as may appear. Keep assigned distance from planet and stiffen cosmic screens to maximum. Haynes—off!"

From millions upon millions of projectors there raved out gigantic rods, knives, and needles of force, under the impact of which the defensive screens of Jalte's guardian citadels flamed into terrible refulgence. Duodec bombs were hurled—tight-beam-directed monsters of destruction which, looping around in vast circles to attain the highest possible measure of momentum, flung themselves against Boskone's defenses in Herculean attempts to smash them down. They exploded; each as it burst filling all nearby space with blindingly intense violet light and with flying scraps of metal. Q-type helices, driven with all the frightful kilowattage possible to Medonian conductors and insulation, screwed in; biting, gouging, tearing in wild abandon. Shear-planes, hellish knives of force beside which Tellurian lightning is pale and wan, struck and struck and struck again—fiendishly, crunchingly.

But those grimly stolid fortresses could take it. They had been repowered; their defenses stiffened to such might as to defy, in the opinion of Boskone's experts, any projectors capable of being mounted upon mobile bases. And not only could they take it—those formidably armed and armored planetoids could dish it out as well. The screens of the Patrol ships flared high into the spectrum under the crushing force of sheer enemy power. Not a few of those defenses were battered down, clear to the wall-shields, before the unimaginable ferocity of the Boskonian projectors could be neutralized.

And at this spectacularly frightful deep-space engagement Galactic Director Jalte, and through him Eichmil, First of Boskone itself, stared in stunned surprise.

"It is insane!" Jalte gloated. "The fools judged our strength by that of Helmuth, not considering that we, as well as they, would be both learning and doing during the intervening time. They have a myriad of ships, but mere numbers will never conquer my outposts, to say nothing of my works here."

"They are not fools. I am not so sure . . ." Eichmil cogitated.

He would have been even less sure could he have listened to a conversation which was even then being held.

"QX, Thorndyke?" Kinnison asked.

"On the green," came instant reply. "Intrinsic, placement, releases—everything on the green."

"Cut!" and the lone purple circle disappeared from tank and from reducer. The master technician had cut his controls and every pound of metal and other substance surrounding the negasphere had fallen into that enigmatic realm of nothingness. No connection or contact with it was now possible; and with its carefully established intrinsic velocity it rushed engulfingly toward the doomed planet. One of the mastodonic fortresses, lying in its path, vanished utterly, with nothing save a burst of invisible cosmics to mark its passing. It approached its goal. It was almost upon it before any of the defenders perceived it, and even then they could neither understand nor grasp it. All detectors and other warning devices remained static, but:

"Look! There! Something's *coming!*" an observer jittered, and Jalte swung his plate. He saw—nothing. Eichmil saw the same thing. There was nothing to see. A vast, intangible nothing—yet a nothing tangible enough to occult everything material in a full third of the cone of vision! Jalte's operators hurled into it their mightiest beams. Nothing happened. They struck nothing and disappeared. They loosed their heaviest duodec torpedoes; gigantic missiles whose warheads contained enough of that frightfully violent detonate to disrupt a world. Nothing happened—not even an explosion. Not even the faintest flash of light. Shell and contents alike merely—and Oh! so incredibly peacefully! —ceased to exist. There were important bursts of cosmics, but they were invisible and inaudible; and neither Jalte nor any member of his force was to live long enough to realize how terribly he had already been burned.

Gigantic pressors shoved against it: beams of power sufficient to deflect a satellite; beams whose projectors were braced, in steel-laced concrete down to bedrock, against any conceivable thrust. But this was *negative,* not positive matter —matter negative in every respect of mass, inertia, and force. To it a push was a pull. Pressors to it were tractors —at contact they pulled themselves up off their massive foundations and hurtled into the appalling blackness.

Then the negasphere struck. Or did it? Can nothing strike anything? It would be better, perhaps, to say that the spherical hyper-plane which was the three-dimensional cross-section of the negasphere began to occupy the same volume of space as that in which Jalte's unfortunate world already was. And at the surface of contact of the two the materials of both disappeared. The substance of the planet vanished, the incomprehensible nothingness of the negasphere faded away into the ordinary vacuity of empty space.

Jalte's base, the whole three hundred square miles of it,

was taken at the first gulp. A vast pit opened where it had been, a hole which deepened and widened with horrifying rapidity. And as the yawning abyss enlarged itself the stuff of the planet fell into it, in turn to vanish. Mountains tumbled into it, oceans dumped themselves into it. The hot, frightfully compressed and nascent material of the planet's core sought to erupt—but instead of moving, it, too, vanished. Vast areas of the world's surface crust, tens of thousands of square miles in extent, collapsed into it, splitting off along crevasses of appalling depth, and became nothing. The stricken globe shuddered, trembled, ground itself to bits in paroxysm after ghastly paroxysm of disintegration.

What was happening? Eichmil did not know, since his "eye" was destroyed before any really significant developments could eventuate. He and his scientists could only speculate and deduce—which, with surprising accuracy, they did. The officers of the Patrol ships, however, *knew* what was going on, and they were scanning with tensely narrowed eyes the instruments which were recording instant by instant the performance of the new cosmic super-screens which were being assaulted so brutally.

For, as has been said, the negasphere was composed of negative matter. Instead of electrons its building-blocks were positrons—the "Dirac holes" in an infinity of negative energy. Whenever the field of a positron encountered that of an electron the two neutralized each other, giving rise to two quanta of hard radiation. And, since those encounters were occurring at the rate of countless trillions per second, there was tearing at the Patrol's defenses a flood of cosmics of an intensity which no space-ship had ever before been called upon to withstand. But the new screens had been figured with a factor of safety of five, and they stood up.

The planet dwindled with soul-shaking rapidity to a moon, to a moonlet, and finally to a discretely conglomerate aggregation of meteorites before the mutual neutralization ceased.

"Primaries now," Haynes ordered briskly, as the needles

of the cosmic-ray-screen meters dropped back to the green lines of normal functioning. The probability was that the defenses of the Boskonian citadels would now be automatic only, that no life had endured through that awful flood of lethal radiation; but he was taking no chances. Out flashed the penetrant super-rays and the fortresses, too, ceased to exist save as the impalpable infra-dust of space.

And the massed Grand Fleet of the Galactic Patrol, re-making its formation, hurtled outward through the inter-galactic void.

"THEY ARE NOT FOOLS. I AM NOT so sure . . ." Eichmil had said; and when the last force-ball, his last means of inter-galactic communication, went dead the First of Boskone became very unsure indeed. The Patrol undoubtedly had something new—he himself had had glimpses of it—but what was it?

That Jalte's base was gone was obvious. That Boskone's hold upon the Tellurian Galaxy was gone followed as a corollary. That the Patrol was or soon would be wiping out Boskone's regional and planetary units was a logical inference. Star A Star, that accursed Director of Lensmen, had—must have—succeeded in stealing Jalte's records, to be willing to destroy out of hand the base which housed them.

Nor could Boskone do anything to help the underlings, now that the long-awaited attack upon Jarnevon itself was almost certainly coming. Let the Patrol come—they were ready. Or were they, quite? Jalte's defenses were strong, but they had not withstood that unknown weapon even for seconds.

Eichmil called a joint meeting of Boskone and the Academy of Science. Coldly and precisely he told them everything that he had seen. Discussion followed.

"Negative matter beyond a doubt," a scientist summed up. "It has long been surmised that in some other, perhaps hyper-spatial, universe there must exist negative matter of mass sufficient to balance the positive material of the universe we know. It is conceivable that by hyper-spatial explorations and manipulations the Tellurians have discovered that other universe and have transported some of its substance into ours."

"Can they manufacture it?" Eichmil demanded.

"The probability that such material can be manufactured is exceedingly small," was the studied reply. "An entirely new mathematics would be necessary. In all probability they found it already existent."

"We must find it also, then, and at once."

"We will try. Bear in mind, however, that the field is large, and do not be optimistic of an early success. Note also that that substance is not necessary—perhaps not even desirable—in a defensive action."

"Why not?"

"Because, by directing pressors against such a bomb, Jalte actually pulled it into his base, precisely where the enemy wished it to go. As a surprise attack, against those ignorant of its true nature, such a weapon would be effective indeed; but against us it will prove a boomerang. All that is needful is to mount tractor heads upon pressor bases, and thus drive the bombs back upon those who send them." It did not occur, even to the coldest scientist of them all, that that bomb had been of planetary mass. Not one of the Eich suspected that all that remained of the entire world upon which Jalte's base had stood was a handful of meteorites.

"Let them come, then," said Eichmil, grimly. "Their dependence upon a new and supposedly unknown weapon explains what would otherwise be insane tactics. With that weapon impotent they cannot possibly win a long war waged so far from their bases. We can match them ship for ship, and more; and our supplies and munitions are close at hand. We will wear them down—blast them out—the Tellurian Galaxy shall yet be ours!"

*　　*　　*

Admiral Haynes spent almost every waking hour setting up and knocking down tactical problems in the practice tank, and gradually his expression changed from one of strained anxiety to one of pleased satisfaction. He went over to his sealed-band transmitter, called all communications officers to attention, and thought:

"Each vessel will direct its longest-range detector, at highest possible power, centrally upon the objective galaxy. The first observer to find detectable activity, however faint, will report it instantly to GHQ. We will send out a general C.B., at which every vessel in Grand Fleet will cease blasting at once; remaining motionless in space until further orders." He then called Kinnison.

"Look here," he directed the attention of the younger man into the reducer, which now represented inter-galactic space, with a portion of the Second Galaxy filling one edge. "I have a solution, but its practicability depends upon whether or not it calls for the impossible from you, Worsel, and your Rigellians. You remarked at the start that I knew my tactics. I wish I knew more—or at least could be certain that Boskone and I agree on what constitutes good tactics. I feel quite safe in assuming, however, that we shall meet their Grand Fleet well outside the galaxy . . ."

"Why?" asked the startled Kinnison. "If I were Eichmil I'd pull every ship I had in around Jarnevon and keep it there! They can't force engagement with us!"

"Poor tactics. The very presence of their fleet out in space will force engagement, and a decisive one at that. From his viewpoint, if he defeats us there, that ends it. If he loses, that's only his first line of defense. His observers will have reported fully. He will have invaluable data to work upon, and much time before even his outlying fortresses can be threatened.

"From our viewpoint, we can't refuse battle if his fleet is there. It would be suicidal for us to enter that galaxy, leaving intact outside it a fleet as powerful as that one is bound to be."

"Why? Harrying us from the rear might be bothersome, but I don't see how it could be disastrous."

"Not that. They could, and would, attack Tellus."

"Oh—I never thought of that. But couldn't they anyway—two fleets?"

"No. He knows that Tellus is very strongly held, and that this is no ordinary fleet. He will have to concentrate everything he has upon either one or the other—it is almost inconceivable that he would divide his forces."

"QX. I said that you're the brains of the outfit. You are!"

"Thanks, lad. At the first sign of detection, we stop. They may be able to detect us, but I doubt it, since we're looking for them with special instruments. But that's immaterial. What I want to know is, can you and your crew split Grand Fleet, making two big, hollow hemispheres of it? Let this group of ambers represent the enemy. Since they know we'll have to carry the battle to them, they'll probably be in fairly close formation. Set your two hemispheres—the reds—there, and there. Close them in, thus englobing their whole fleet. Can you do it?"

Kinnison whistled through his teeth, a long, low, unmelodious whistle. "Yes—but Klono's carballoy claws, chief, suppose they catch you at it?"

"How can they? If you were using detectors, instead of double-end, tight-beam binders, how many of our own vessels could you locate?"

"That's right, too—about two percent of them. They couldn't tell that they were being englobed until long after it was done. They could, however, globe up inside us . . ."

"Yes—and that would give them the tactical advantage of position," the admiral admitted. "We probably have, however, enough superiority in fire-power, if not in actual tonnage, to make up the difference. Also, we have speed enough, I think, so that we could retire in good order. But you're assuming that they can maneuver as rapidly and as surely as we can, a condition which I do not consider at all probable. If, as I believe much more likely, they have no better Grand Fleet Operations than we had in Helmuth's star-cluster—if they haven't the equivalent of you and Worsel and this super-tank here—then what?"

"In that case it'd be just too bad. Just like pushing baby chicks into a pond." Kinnison saw the possibilities very clearly after they had been explained to him.

"How long will it take you?"

"With Worsel and me and both full crews of Rigellians I would guess it at about ten hours—eight to compute and assign positions and two to get there."

"Fast enough—faster than I would have thought possible. Oil up your Simplexes and calculating machines and get ready."

In due time the enemy fleet was detected and the "cease blasting" signal was given. Civilization's prodigious fleet stopped dead; hanging motionless in space at the tantalizing limit of detectability from the warships awaiting them. For eight hours two hundred Rigellians stood at whirring calculators, each solving course-and-distance problems at the rate of ten per minute. Two hours or less of free flight and Haynes rejoiced audibly in the perfection of the two red hemispheres shown in his reducer. The two huge bowls flashed together, rim to rim. The sphere began inexorably to contract. Each ship put out a red K6T screen as a combined battle flag and identification, and the greatest naval engagement of the age was on.

It soon became evident that the Boskonians could not maneuver their forces efficiently. The fleet was too huge, too unwieldy for their Operations officers to handle. Against an equally uncontrollable mob of battle craft it would have made a showing, but against the carefully-planned, chronometer-timed attack of the Patrol individual action, however courageous or however desperate, was useless.

Each red-sheathed destroyer hurtled along a definite course at a definite force of drive for a definite length of time. Orders were strict; no ship was to be lured from course, pace, or time. They could, however fight *en passant* with their every weapon if occasion arose; and occasion did arise, some thousands of times. The units of Grand Fleet flashed inward, lashing out with their terrible primaries at everything in space not wearing the crimson robe of Civilization. And whatever those beams struck did not need striking again.

The warships of Boskone fought back. Many of the Patrol's defensive screens blazed hot enough almost to mask the scarlet beacons; some of them went down. A few Patrol ships were englobed by the concerted action of two or three sub-fleet commanders more cooperative or more farsighted than the rest, and were blasted out of existence by an overwhelming concentration of power. But even those vessels took toll with their primaries as they went out: few indeed were the Boskonians who escaped through holes thus made.

At a predetermined instant each dreadnought stopped: to find herself one unit of an immense, red-flaming hollow sphere of ships packed almost screen to screen. And upon signal every primary projector that could be brought to bear hurled bolt after bolt, as fast as the burned-out shells could be replaced, into the ragingly incandescent inferno which that sphere's interior instantly became. For two hundred million discharges such as those will convert a very large volume of space into something utterly impossible to describe.

The raving torrents of energy subsided and keen-eyed observers swept the scene of action. Nothing was there except jumbled and tumbling white-hot wreckage. A few vessels had escaped during the closing in of the sphere, but none inside it had survived this climactic action—not one in five thousand of Boskone's massed fleet made its way back to Jarnevon.

"Maneuver fifty-eight—hipe!" Haynes ordered, and again Grand Fleet shot away. There was no waiting, no hesitation. Every course and time had been calculated and assigned.

Into the Second Galaxy the scarcely diminished armada of the Patrol hurtled—to Jarnevon's solar system—around it. Once again the crimson sheathing of Civilization's messengers almost disappeared in blinding coruscance as the outlying fortresses unleashed their mighty weapons; once again a few ships, subjected to such concentrations of force as to overload their equipment, were lost; but this conflict, though savage in its intensity, was brief. Nothing mobile *could* withstand for long the utterly hellish energies of the primaries, and soon the armored planetoids, too, ceased to be.

"Maneuver fifty-nine—hipe!" and Grand Fleet closed in upon dark Jarnevon.

"Sixty!" It rolled in space, forming an immense cylinder; the doomed planet the mid-point of its axis.

"Sixty-one!" Tractors and pressors leaped out from ship to ship and from ship to shore. The Patrolmen did not know whether or not the scientists of the Eich could render their planet inertialess, and now it made no difference. Planet and fleet were for the time being one rigid system.

"Sixty-two—Blast!" And against the world-girdling battlements of Jarnevon there flamed out in all their appalling might the dreadful beams against which the defensive screens of battleships and of mobile citadels alike had been so pitifully inadequate.

But these which they were attacking now were not the limited installations of a mobile structure. The Eich had at their command all the resources of a galaxy. Their generators and conductors could be of any desired number and size. Hence Eichmil, in view of prior happenings, had strengthened Jarnevon's defenses to a point which certain of his fellows derided as being beyond the bounds of sanity or reason.

Now those unthinkably powerful screens were being tested to the utmost. Bolt after bolt of quasi-solid lightning struck against them, spitting mile-long sparks in baffled fury as they raged to ground. Plain and encased in Q-type helices they came: biting, tearing, gouging. Often and often, under the thrust of half a dozen at once, local failures appeared; but these were only momentary and even the newly devised shells of the Patrol's projectors could not stand the load long enough to penetrate effectively Boskone's indescribably capable defenses. Nor were Jarnevon's offensive weapons less capable.

Rods, cones, planes, and shears of pure force bored, cut, stabbed, and slashed. Bombs and dirigible torpedoes charged to the skin with duodec sought out the red-cloaked ships. Beams, sheathed against atmosphere in Q-type helices, crashed against and through their armoring screens; beams of an intensity almost to rival that of the Patrol's primary weapons and of a hundred times their effective aperture. And not singly did those beams come. Eight, ten, twelve at once they clung to and demolished dreadnought after dreadnought of the Expeditionary Force.

Eichmil was well content. "We can hold them and we are burning them down," he gloated. "Let them loose their negative-matter bombs! Since they are burning out projectors they cannot keep this up indefinitely. We will blast them out of space!"

He was wrong. Grand Fleet did not stay there long enough to suffer serious losses. For even while the cylinder was forming Kinnison was in rapid but careful consultation with Thorndyke, checking intrinsic velocities, directons, and speeds. "QX, Verne, *cut!*" he yelled.

Two planets, one well within each end of the combat cylinder, went inert at the word; resuming instantaneously their diametrically opposed intrinsic velocities of some thirty miles per second. And it was these two very ordinary, but utterly irresistible planets, instead of the negative-matter bombs with which the Eich were prepared to cope, which hurtled then along the axis of the immense tube of warships toward Jarnevon. Whether or not the Eich could make their planet inertialess has never been found out. Free or inert, the end would have been the same.

"Every Y14M officer of every ship of the Patrol, attention!" Haynes ordered. "Don't get all tensed up. Take it easy, there's lots of time. Any time within a second after I give the word will be p-l-e-n-t-y o-f t-i-m-e . . . CUT!"

The two worlds rushed together, doomed Jarnevon

squarely between them. Haynes snapped out his order as
the three were within two seconds of contact; and as he
spoke all the pressors and all the tractors were released. The
ships of the Patrol were already free—none had been inert
since leaving Jalte's ex-planet—and thus could not be harmed
by flying debris.

The planets touched. They coalesced, squishingly at
first, the encircling warships drifting lightly away before a
cosmically violent blast of superheated atmosphere. Jarnevon
burst open, all the way around, and spattered; billions upon
billions of tons of hot core-magma being hurled afar in
gouts and streamers. The two planets, crashing through
what had been a world, met, crunched, crushed together in
all the unimaginable momentum of their masses and velocities. They subsided, crashingly. Not merely mountains, but
entire halves of worlds disrupted and fell, in such Gargantuan paroxysms as the eye of man had never elsewhere
beheld. And every motion generated heat. The kinetic
energy of translation of two worlds became heat. Heat added
to heat, piling up ragingly, frantically, unable to escape!

The masses, still falling upon and through and past
themselves and each other melted—boiled—vaporized in-
candescently. The entire mass, the mass of three fused
worlds, began to equilibrate; growing hotter and hotter
as more and more of its terrific motion was converted into
pure heat. Hotter! *Hotter!* HOTTER!

And as the Grand Fleet of the Galactic Patrol blasted
through inter-galactic space toward the First Galaxy and
home, there glowed behind it a new, small, comparatively
cool, and probably short-lived companion to an old and long-
established star.

THE UPROAR OF THE LANDING
was over; the celebration of victory had not yet begun. Haynes
had, peculiarly enough, set a definite time for a conference
with Kinnison and the two of them were in the admiral's
private office, splitting a bottle of fayalin and discussing—
apparently—nothing at all.

"Narcotics has been yelling for you," Haynes finally
got around to business. "But they don't need you to help
them clean up the zwilnik mess; they just want to work
with you. So I told Ellington, as diplomatically as possible,
to take a swan-dive off of an asteroid. Hicks wants you,
too; and Spencer and Frelinghuysen and thousands of
others. See that basket-full of junk? All requests for you,
to be submitted to you for your consideration. I submit 'em,
thus—into the circular file. You see, there's something really
important . . ."

"Nix, chief, nix—jet back a minute, please!" Kinnison
implored. "Unless it's something that's got to be done right
away, gimme a break, can't you? I've got a couple of things
to do—stuff to attend to. Maybe a little flit somewhere, too,
I don't know yet."

"More important than Patrol business?" dryly.

"Until it's cleaned up, yes." Kinnison's face burned

scarlet and his eyes revealed the mental effort necessary to make that statement. "The most important thing in the universe," he finished, quietly but doggedly.

"Well, of course I can't give you orders . . ." Haynes' frown was instinct with disappointment.

"Don't, chief—that hurts. I'll be back, honest, as soon as I possibly can, and I'll do anything you want me to . . ."

"That's enough, son." Haynes stood up and grasped Kinnison's hands—hard—in both his own. "I know. Forgive me for taking you for this little ride, but you and Mac suffer so! You're so young, so intense, so insistent upon carrying the entire Cosmos on your shoulders—I couldn't help it. You won't have to do much of a flit." He glanced at his chronometer. "You'll find all your unfinished business in Room 7295, Base Hospital."

"Huh? You know, then?"

"Who doesn't? There may be a few members of some backward race somewhere who don't know all about you and your red-headed sector riot, but I don't know . . ." He was addressing empty air.

Kinnison shot out of the building and, exerting his Gray Lensman's authority, he did a thing which he had always longed boyishly to do but which he had never before really considered doing. He whistled, shrill and piercingly, and waved a Lensed arm, even while he was directing a Lensed thought at the driver of the fast ground-car always in readiness in front of Haynes' office.

"Base Hospital—full emergency blast!" he ordered, and the Jehu obeyed. That chauffeur loved emergency stuff and the long, low, wide racer took off with a deafening roar of unmuffled exhaust and a scream of tortured, burning rubber. Two projectors flamed, sending out for miles ahead of the bellowing roadster twin beams of a redness so thick as to be felt, not merely seen. Simultaneously the mighty, four-throated siren began its ululating, raucously overpowering yell, demanding and obtaining right of way over any and all traffic—particularly over police, fire, and other ordinary emergency apparatus—which might think it had some rights upon the street!

"Thanks, Jack—you needn't wait." At the hospital's door Kinnison rendered tribute to fast service and strode along a corridor. An express elevator whisked him up to the seventy-second floor, and there his haste departed completely. This was Nurse's Quarters, he realized suddenly. He had no more business there than . . . yes he did, too. He found Room 7295 and rapped upon its door. Boldly, he intended, but the resultant sound was surprisingly small.

"Come in!" called a clear contralto. Then, after a moment: *"Come in!"* more sharply; but the Lensman did not, could not obey the summons. She might be . . . dammit-all, he *didn't* have any business on this floor! Why hadn't he called her up or sent her a thought or something . . . ? Why didn't he think at her now?

The door opened, revealing the mildly annoyed sector chief. At what she saw her hands flew to her throat and her eyes widened in starkly unbelieving rapture.

"KIM!" She shrieked in ecstasy.

"Chris . . . my Chris!" Kinnison whispered unsteadily, and for minutes those two uniformed minions of the Galactic Patrol stood motionless upon the room's threshold, strong young arms straining; nurse's crisp and spotless white crushed unregarded against Lensman's pliant gray.

"Oh . . . I've missed you so terribly, my darling," she crooned. Her voice, always sweetly rich, was pure music.

"You don't know the half of it. This can't be real—nothing *can* feel this good!"

"You *did* come back to me—you really did!" she lilted. "I didn't dare hope you could come so soon."

"I had to." Kinnison drew a deep breath, "I simply couldn't stand it. It'll be tough, maybe, but you were right—half a loaf *is* better than no bread."

"Of course it is!" She released herself—partially—after the first transports of their first embrace and eyed him shrewdly. "Tell me, Kim, did Lacy have a hand in this surprise?"

"Uh-uh," he denied. "I haven't seen him for ages—but jet back! Haynes told me—say, what'll you bet those two old hard-heads haven't been giving us the works?"

"Who are old hard-heads?" Haynes—in person—demanded. So deeply immersed had Kinnison been in his rapturous delirium that even his sense of perception was in abeyance; and there, not two yards from the entranced couple, stood the two old Lensmen under discussion!

The culprits sprang apart, flushing guiltily, but Haynes went on imperturbably, quite as though nothing out of the ordinary had been either said or done:

"We gave you fifteen minutes, then came up to be sure to catch you before you flitted off to the celebration or somewhere. We have matters to discuss."

"QX. Come in, all of you." As she spoke the nurse stood aside in invitation. "You know, don't you, that it's exceedingly much contra Regs for nurses to entertain visitors of the opposite sex in their rooms? Fifty demerits per offense. Most girls never get a chance at even one Gray Lensman, and here I've got three!" She giggled infectiously. "Wouldn't it be one for the book for me to get a hundred and fifty black spots for this? And to have Surgeon-Marshal Lacy, Port Admiral Haynes, and Unattached Lensman Kimball Kinnison, all heaved into the clink to boot? Boy, oh boy, ain't we got fun?"

"Lacy's too old and I'm too moral to be affected by the wiles even of the likes of you, my dear," Haynes explained equably, as he seated himself upon the davenport—the most comfortable thing in the room.

"Old? Moral? Tommyrot!" Lacy glared an "I'll-see-you-later" look at the admiral, then turned to the nurse. "Don't worry about that, MacDougall. No penalties accrue— Regulations apply only to nurses in the Service . . ."

"And what . . ." she started to blaze, but checked herself and her tone changed instantly. "Go on—you interest me strangely, sir. I'm just going to love this!" Her eyes sparkled, her voice was vibrant with unconcealed eagerness.

"Told you she was quick on the uptake," Lacy gloated. "Didn't fox her for a second!"

"But say—listen—what's this all about, anyway?" Kinnison demanded.

"Never mind, you'll learn soon enough," from Lacy, and:

"Kinnison, you are very urgently invited to attend a meeting of the Galactic Council tomorrow afternoon," from Haynes.

"Huh? What's up now?" Kinnison protested. His arm tightened about the girl's supple waist and she snuggled closer, a trace of foreboding beginning to dim the eagerness in her eyes.

"Promotion. We want to make you something—galactic coordinator, director, something like that—the job hasn't been named yet. In plain language, the Big Shot of the Second Galaxy, formerly known as Lundmark's Nebula."

"But listen, chief! I couldn't handle such a job as that —I simply haven't got the jets!"

"You always yelp about a dynage deficiency whenever a new job is mentioned, but you deliver the goods. Who else could we wish it onto?"

"Worsel," Kinnison declared with hesitation. "He's . . ."

"Balloon-juice!" snorted the older man.

"Well, then . . . ah . . . er . . ." he stopped. Clarrissa opened her mouth, then shut it, ridiculously, without having uttered a word.

"Go ahead, MacDougall. You're an interested party, you know."

"No." She shook her spectacular head. "I'm not saying a word nor thinking a thought to sway his decision one way or the other. Besides, he'd have to flit around then as much as now."

"Some travel involved, of course," Haynes admitted. "All over that galaxy, some in this one, and back and forth between the two. However, the *Dauntless*—or something newer, bigger, and faster—will be his private yacht, and I don't see why it is either necessary or desirable that his flits be solo."

"Say, I never thought of that!" Kinnison blurted; and as thoughts began to race through his mind of what he could do, with Chris beside him all the time, to straighten out the mess in the Second Galaxy:

"Oh, Kim!" Clarrissa squealed in ecstasy, squeezing his arm even tighter against her side.

"Hooked!" Lacy chortled in triumph.

"But I'd have to retire!" That thought was the only thorn in Kinnison's whole wreath of roses. "I wouldn't like that."

"Certainly you wouldn't," Haynes agreed. "But remember that all such assignments are conditional, subject to approval, and with a very definite cancellation agreement in case of what the Lensman regards as an emergency. If a Gray Lensman had to give up his right to serve the Patrol in any way he considered himself most able, they'd have to shoot us all before they could make executives out of us. And finally, I don't see how the job we're talking about can be figured as any sort of a retirement. You'll be as active as you are now—yes, more so, unless I miss my guess."

"QX. I'll be there—I'll try it," Kinnison promised.

"Now for some more news," Lacy announced. "Haynes didn't tell you, but he has been made president of the Galactic Council. You are his first appointment. I hate to say anything good about the old scoundrel, but he has one outstanding ability. He doesn't know much or do much himself, but he certainly can pick the men who have to do the work for him!"

"There's something vastly more important than that." Haynes steered the acclaim away from himself.

"Just a minute," Kinnison interposed. "I haven't got this all straight yet. What was the crack about active nurses awhile ago?"

"Why, Doctor Lacy was just intimating that I had resigned, goose," Clarrissa chuckled. "I didn't know a thing about it myself, but I imagine it must have been just before this conference started. Am I right, doctor?" she asked innocently.

"Or tomorrow, or even yesterday—any convenient time will do," Lacy blandly assented. "You see, young man, MacDougall has been a mighty busy girl, and wedding preparations take time, too. Therefore we have very reluctantly accepted her resignation."

"Especially preparations take time when it's going to be such a wedding as the Patrol is going to throw," Haynes commented. "That was what I was starting to talk about when I was so rudely interrupted."

"Nix! Not in seven thousand years!" Kinnison exploded. "Cancel that, right now—I won't stand for it—I'll not . . ."

"Cancel nothing. Baffle your jets, Kim," the admiral said, firmly. "Bridegrooms are to be seen—just barely visible —but that's all. No voice. Weddings are where the girls really strut their stuff. How about it, you gorgeous young menace to Civilization?"

"I'll say so!" she exclaimed in high animation. "I'd just *love* it, admiral . . ." She broke off, aghast. Her face fell. "No, I'll take that back. Kim's right. Thanks a million, just the same, but . . ."

"But nothing!" Haynes broke in. "I know what's the matter. Don't try to fox an old campaigner, and don't be silly. I said the Patrol was throwing this wedding. All you have to do is participate in the action. Got any money, Kinnison? On you, I mean?"

"No," in surprise. "What would I be doing with money?"

"Here's ten thousand credits—Patrol funds. Take it and . . ."

"He will not!" the nurse stormed. "No! You can't, admiral, really. Why, a bride has *got* to buy her own clothes!"

"She's right, Haynes," Lacy announced. The admiral stared at him in wrathful astonishment and even Clarissa seemed disappointed at her easy victory. "But listen to this.

As surgeon-marshal, et cetera, in recognition of the unselfish services, et cetera, unflinching bravery under fire, et cetera, performances beyond and above requirements or reasonable expectations, et cetera, et cetera; Sector Chief Nurse Clarrissa May MacDougall, upon the occasion of her separation from the Service, is hereby granted a bonus of ten thousand credits. That goes on the record as of hour twelve, today.

"Now, you red-headed young spit-fire, if you refuse to accept that bonus I'll cancel your resignation and put you back to work. What do you say?"

"I say thanks, Doctor Lacy. Th . . . thanks a million . . . both of you . . . you're two of the most wonderful men that ever lived, and I . . . I . . . I just *love* you!" The happy girl kissed them both, then turned to Kinnison.

"Let's go and hike about ten miles, shall we, Kim? I've got to do *something* or I'll explode!"

And the tall Lensman—no longer unattached—and the radiant nurse swung down the hall.

Side by side; in step; heads up; laughing: a beginning symbolical indeed of the life they were to live together.

THE END